· ESSIEN OF ALKEBULAN ·

WIELDERS OF
FLOODS & FLAMES

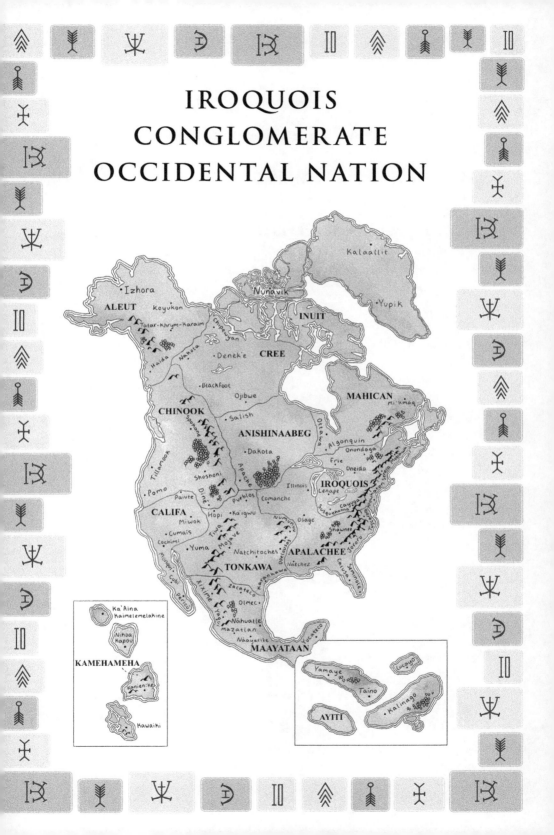

ALSO BY DIDI ANOFIENEM

◆

Descendants of Fire and Water

· ESSIEN OF ALKEBULAN ·

WIELDERS OF FLOODS & FLAMES

· DIDI ANOFIENEM ·

KEYLIGHT BOOKS
AN IMPRINT OF TURNER PUBLISHING

*To the women of the world, who use their magic
to create life and build futures.*

KEYLIGHT BOOKS
AN IMPRINT OF TURNER PUBLISHING COMPANY
Nashville, Tennessee
www.turnerpublishing.com

Wielders of Floods & Flames
Copyright © 2025 by Didi Anofienem. All rights reserved.

This book or any part thereof may not be reproduced or transmitted in any form or by any means, electronic or mechanical, including photocopying, recording, or by any information storage and retrieval system, without permission in writing from the publisher. This is a work of fiction. All the characters and events portrayed in this book are either products of the author's imagination or are used fictitiously.

Cover illustration by Della Rhodes
Cover design by William Ruoto
Book design by William Ruoto

Library of Congress Cataloging-in-Publication Data
Names: Anofienem, Didi, author.
Title: Wielders of flood and flame / by Didi Anofienem.
Description: Nashville, Tennessee : Keylight Books, 2025. | Series: Essien
   of Alkebulan ; book 2 | Audience term: Teenagers
Identifiers: LCCN 2024030501 (print) | LCCN 2024030502 (ebook) | ISBN
   9798887980362 (hardcover) | ISBN 9798887980379 (paperback) | ISBN
   9798887980386 (epub)
Subjects: CYAC: Ability--Fiction. | Magic--Fiction. | Black
   people--Fiction. | Fantasy fiction. | LCGFT: Fantasy fiction. | Novels.
Classification: LCC PZ7.1.A57 Wi 2025 (print) | LCC PZ7.1.A57 (ebook) |
   DDC [Fic]--dc23
LC record available at https://lccn.loc.gov/2024030501
LC ebook record available at https://lccn.loc.gov/2024030502

Printed in the United States of America

In order to rise
From its own ashes,
A phoenix
First
Must
Burn.

—Octavia Butler, *Parable of the Talents*

PART I

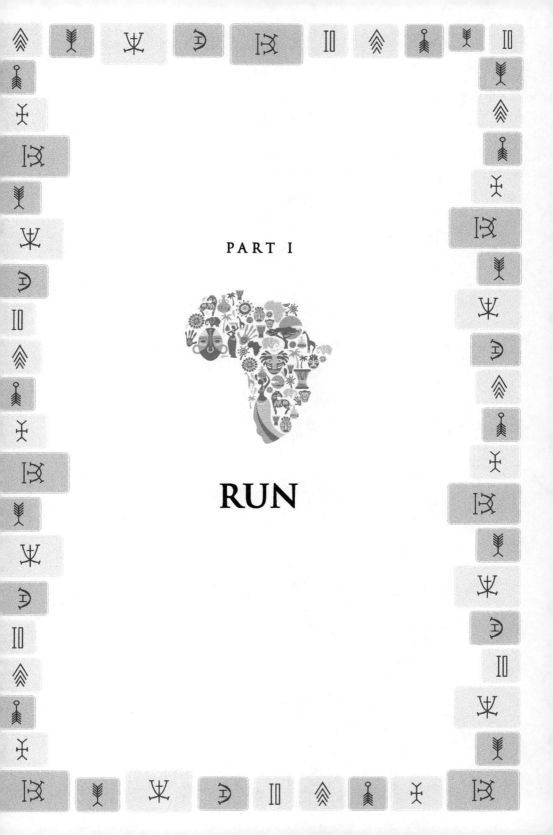

RUN

CHAPTER ONE

◆

ESSIEN COULDN'T STOP FEELING ASHES ALL OVER HER BODY, like walking through cobwebs and brushing and brushing but still experiencing the unsettling creeping-crawling sensations. She was flying in a skycraft through a deep purple dawn of early morning, with the clouds just gray smears across the light of the silver moon.

She'd kept her eyes closed after that glimpse, her hands gripped tightly in Enyemaka's, a grip he hadn't released the entire way. He hadn't told her how long they'd be flying or where they were heading. It was better that way. If she knew, she might release that information and lead them right into their own recapture. She clenched his hands tighter, feeling ashes spreading like fine powder over her fingertips and palms. She tried to breathe deeper than the shallow breaths she'd been taking. She felt trapped and wanted to take her hands back. She started to pull and felt the crumble of loose granules that weren't there at all. Enyemaka tightened his grip, pulling her forward.

Essien opened her eyes and looked at Enyemaka for the first time since she'd boarded the skycraft that had come to rescue her. A rescue from the most powerful man in Alkebulan. She hadn't wanted to see the ground rushing away or the empty sky surrounding her that had quickly turned dark blue and then dark gray before settling into a deep indigo. Now she looked at Enyemaka and tried not to be afraid. She had willingly, if somewhat naively, walked out of that hospital with him, and she hadn't really thought what it would mean.

Enyemaka stared at her with eyes that were the same amber brown as the elixirs Gabriel drank. At the thought of his name, Essien snatched her hands out of Enyemaka's grip milliseconds before orange and red flames flared over her palm, sliding over her fingertips. The fire wasn't hot to her, but she could feel the heat emanating outward. She stared down at her palm, transfixed by the center of pure golden light firing from the place where four palm lines crossed. She bit her lip to hold back the scream.

"Breathe, Essien. You can do this. Breathe."

"I have to go back. You have to set us down, so I can go back."

"There's nothing but forest out here, Essien. We can't set down anywhere for stadia yet. Plus, I can feel him trying to worm his way inside of you. It's like the smell right before it starts to rain."

"I don't want to hurt you or the pilot. You don't understand; you didn't see it."

"I heard about it. We weren't able to recover any footage, but some retained their memories of what happened and were able to tell others. It got out."

"Then you know I could dissolve this metal around us!"

Lightning zapped a jagged streak to their right, followed by the boom of thunder, and then wet droplets hit the sides of the skycraft with splatters that soon covered the glass. The sudden noise startled and extinguished the flames in Essien's hand with a hiss of smoke and singe of her skin.

The pilot began flicking switches and relaying something in a short, clipped code that Essien couldn't hear over the rattle of metal around them and the rumble of the wind just on the other side of that metal.

"I'm still blocking you; he doesn't know where you are. He won't be able to find you. I promise." Enyemaka reached for her hands again. She stared down at the smaller-than-normal hand lying there so supportively. His fingers flexed showing clipped and clean nails. She couldn't stop feeling the aching memory of flames flaring up into an inferno hot enough to blast bodies down into piles of ashes. She didn't want to burn him, too. Essien took a deep breath and gripped Enyemaka's hands again, closing her eyes. His hands were rough and calloused in the same places hers were.

He'd risked his own life coming to rescue her. She hadn't asked him to, but she was grateful. She wouldn't squander the gift he'd given her by forcing him to betray himself—and whatever cause had armed him with a skycraft that could land undetected on top of a hospital in the middle of Lagos, the capital of Igbo State. Eventually the President would tire of using magic to find her, and he'd switch up his tactics. Enyemaka tightened his hands on her.

"Keep your thoughts here, Essien. If you think of him..."

"Then talk to me, help distract me. I'm trying, but it's like he's there right under the surface."

"It'll be weird talking to me with your eyes closed."

"My ears are working perfectly fine. I can hear you."

"What should I tell you?"

"I don't know. I can't... Tell me about your childhood. Tell me about where you grew up."

Enyemaka chuckled, and they were close enough that his breath brushed over her lips, her hands. "I am from Biafra, in southeastern Igbo State, same state as you...my village was called Nok, after our ancestors, and it was just a small village, mostly my ancestral family homes. There was little in the way of careers beyond metalworking but onye ikpi, the goat herders, and lots of carpenters. Joining the military seemed like my only way out."

"You could have taken up your father's profession." Essien heard herself and snorted. Oh, how her own father had begged her not to join the military. She shook her head and tried not to think about anything but the grip of Enyemaka's hands, his first finger that had started rubbing back and forth over her wrist...back and forth, back and forth.

"My father wanted me to remain in Nok and apprentice at his forge as an igwe ola, a metalworker, to spend my life finding uses for his metal contraptions."

"That sounds better than hand-holding an out-of-control onye anwansi who can call fire if I get too scared or threatened." She couldn't get a full breath in, the sides of the skycraft seeming to clench tighter around them.

"You called me Enyi once...that was my father's nickname for me. He'd say, 'Enyi, when you are ready, all of this will be yours. Finish your five years of apprenticeship, and I promise to sign it all over to you.' Back then, I couldn't hear what he was offering me. He wanted to step down, so I could take over. And I? I just wanted a thrill. I wanted something to boast about. Making pipes for plumbing and wires for electricity and statues to decorate an ancestral home wasn't that exciting to me then."

Essien wanted to open her eyes and see what face went with how his voice sounded. Like he regretted his decisions almost as much as she did.

"How did you end up with the rebels after..." She couldn't bring herself to say it.

Enyemaka filled in for her, "After I was booted out of the military by the President?" He sounded like he was smiling, but there was nothing positive in the words. "The engine dropped me off at a transportation center with nothing but the duffel bag I'd arrived with and any remaining Naira in my suddenly closed military financial accounts. It all felt so unreal. I was staring up at the signage and trying to decide where to go when a man walked up to me wearing a uniform that looked formal, but it was dark green instead of black.

"'I was sent to retrieve you by Rebel Leader Mansa Musa the twenty-first.' I couldn't believe my hearing, and I was enticed to join the man just to see if what he was saying might be true."

"Mansa Musa the twenty-first?"

She could hear the smile get bigger. "The last living descendant of Mansa Musa the first."

"The former tribal leader of Soninke, the one who fought so fiercely against the Great Unification that Alkebulan almost didn't exist?"

Enyemaka's voice was a lot tamer when he said, "Yes, that one exactly."

So many questions. "How did he know to find you?"

She felt his shrug through her hands. "To this day, I'm not sure. All I know is that I was just reckless enough to go with this man in his engine to a place that could have been a catastrophic risk for me. It still could."

"So you joined with him almost immediately? You've been with him this whole time since?"

"Mansa let me know everything I was feeling. He validated how betrayed I felt. He showed me what the President was doing, what he planned, what we needed to do to stop him."

Essien thought of that vision Gabriel had shown her, and suddenly she was back inside of it as though it were real. Instead of ashes, she felt cool metal, heavy and solid, resting on her brow. She put her hand up to smooth over the lumpy ridges of precious stones embedded around the center rim of the crown.

She could hear her name being called, but it was muffled and distant, like talking across several rooms with closed doors.

She turned to where she thought the voice was coming from, and there was Gabriel standing tall and dark in front of her with a sneer of cruelty flaring his nostrils and thinning his usually plump, pink lips into an angry, thin scowl above his jawline. She stared into his eyes like sparkling brown jewels that snatched at her and jerked her away.

Essien's hands were ripped out of Enyemaka's as an unseen force slammed her back into the side of the aircraft. The burst of flames roared through her ears.

"Essien!"

She felt a blow like a fist and then blood in her mouth like a hot explosion of salty metal flooding over her tongue and pouring over her lips.

"I'm sorry! I'm so sorry!" she heard seconds before black faded over her vision.

CHAPTER TWO

◆

THERE WERE SILENT SCREAMS IN THE DEEP BLUE DEPTHS. THE angry, foaming waves had appeared out of nowhere after a great shout pierced through the walls of the massive building. Water, water everywhere, flooding the rooms and the hallways of every level of the presidential compound, that majestic earth-colored building on top of Capital Island.

As suddenly as the water had come crashing through the ceiling, cascading down the walls, pouring out through opened windows and doors in the kitchen and the great dining hall, the waters receded and then drained away, dissolving into the floorboards, through the rafters, into the air. Instantly, everyone knew who had done it.

The attendants of the compound and the men who made up the Uzo Nchedo, Alkebulan's elite presidential Guard, coughed up water from their lungs, still prone and sprawled across the floors of almost every room. Those who had been outside on the grounds came running to help pump the chests and beat on the backs of those who hadn't been so fortunate. The rooms were filled with the weary exchange of glances. Eyes surveyed around the room where not even a hint of moisture remained to show what had just happened.

None of them dared to speak. Another round of coughs, a sputter. One man had to be rolled on his side, so that the expulsion of vomit didn't choke him to death. A lone brave guard, just one of the remaining ninety-eight Uzo Nchedo assigned to the President's personal protection squad, used a handheld communicator to call for Antonious, the President's right hand.

The call was answered immediately, a short brief message relayed. There wasn't much good the call would do after the fact.

If they hadn't known before what they were signing up for when they joined the President's personal Guard, they had definitely learned it in their time since. Even the newest member had been with the administration for nearly ten years. Each of them was bound by a signed contract that prevented them ever uttering a word of what they had seen and done to anyone outside those compound walls. It wasn't a bond just of military contracts, but one as tightly wound as the blood surging toward their heart through their veins.

As they helped each other regain their wits, a silence fell over the entire compound. One guard lay prone on his back in the middle of the floor in the mgbati while two others worked on him. His arms and legs flopped bonelessly as two of the guards moved him around, and his eyes stayed closed. More guards stood around, their eyes on their unconscious comrade. The two guards trying to help him were beating on his chest and slapping his cheeks. One of them tried to give him air through puffed cheeks while the other thrust on the ribs to keep the heart pumping. Then they heard the shouting and roaring take up again from a few floors higher in the compound. They cast nervous glances around the room, wondering and hoping and praying against that tide of water that could kill them with a thought from the person who controlled it.

Someone else became brave, or afraid enough of death, to approach the sound of that yelling. The guard had never imagined that becoming a soja and then a part of the Uzo Nchedo would bring his fear of water to life to haunt him. He had spent his entire life in Hausa State, where he was born and raised, and no training of his youth had prepared him to deal with bodies of water suddenly crashing over him from nowhere. He took a deep breath and stepped off the rise onto the President's floor.

The shiny reflection of gold everywhere seemed brighter after the darkness of being underneath those waves. The gold was on the floors, a thick, shiny tile with shimmery gold grout edging straight lines all the way down the hallway to the window at its end. The walls were covered in a shimmery gold wallpaper with a textured pattern. The guard was tempted to touch it every time he came to this floor. He had seen streets of gold on his travels to Maasai and Mbuti States, but that had been a bustling city metropolis where rich people lived. Of course, the President of Alkebulan was a rich man, too.

The President was standing in a circle of military councilmen, their backs to the door. They were all in their everyday clothes, different-colored tunics and agbadas and wraps on each of them. Gabriel was in the center of them in a stiff black tunic and slacks, his face completely transformed by the rage that belted out of his lungs. He was in the middle of ranting something when he saw the guard at the door and stopped mid-word.

"It's Onwu, Ser," the guard said. "Mbiliten Onwu. He's not breathing, Ser."

The President's head snapped up almost as swiftly as he pushed through the circle around him and raced toward the doors then out of them. The guard rushed to follow him to the rise in order to lead him to the floor containing the mgbati, the fitness center where the guard exercised daily. When they arrived, they saw that the floor of gray mats was cleared of everything except for one body, lying on its back. The body was that of a man Gabriel had personally handpicked to join his elite squad of highly trained bodyguards. The man was from Amhara State. Gabriel was certain the man had no children or spouse, as that was a requirement for joining the Uzo Nchedo. He was fit and tone, his muscles stretched taut under reddish brown skin. His face was shaved clean and smooth all the way up to his head.

Gabriel knelt carefully beside the man, noting no evidence of breath or movement from the body. He put his hand on the man's chest, naked and slightly dewy, likely not from his workout. He felt the heart give a mighty thump and then go completely still.

Gabriel could sense the other guards crowding into the space now, moving up behind them. Gabriel didn't take his hands off Mbiliten Onwu's chest or his mind off the heart within it, and the ribs and chest plate covering them. He flexed his fingers, sending sizzles of his power, like electric blue energy, into the man's body. His arms and limbs reacted with a twinge, cringing upward like they were reaching to give a hug. The man's eyes flew open, and he took in a rasping breath that expanded his chest under Gabriel's hand. Then he fell back and onto his side, so he could cough up mouthfuls of clear water.

Gabriel sat back on his heels, watching the man. Another guard stepped up with a medical bag in one hand. He began using his medical instruments to check the man's vitals, peering into his eyes with a light and listening to his chest and back in different places. Gabriel covered his face for a second, the shame and pity hitting him full on. These men were entrusted with his life, and he had almost accidentally claimed one of theirs. It was unacceptable. Gabriel stood without saying a word and returned to the rise. He still had his meeting of advisors to get through. Now something else weighed heavily on his mind besides Essien.

CHAPTER THREE

◆

WHEN ESSIEN OPENED HER EYES AGAIN, THE FIRST THING she saw was trees spread out above her like a living canopy of green waves that stretched out to mountains she could see to the north and the blank space of empty air to the south. Without moving, she could feel that she was lying in a burned-out patch of cleared land next to the small skycraft that had flown her away from the hospital roof.

Around her, she could hear steps approaching from the other side of the skycraft. Accompanying voices rose and fell, but she couldn't understand the language. A group of men she didn't recognize stepped into view and didn't glance her way. They were wearing faded green pants with many of them wearing matching overcoats or walking shirtless with their tops tied at their waists. She counted five of them who climbed onto the skycraft next to her and began helping to unload the crates and bags that Essien had barely even noticed on the trip here.

Essien lay there unmoving until a sixth stepped into view, much shorter than the rest. Enyemaka was thinner than she'd remembered him, more gaunt and hollow about the cheeks. His hair was grown out into a short, dark Afro that made his face look even older. She stared at him as he walked closer.

"Did you have to punch me?" she asked by way of greeting. The movement of her lips and jaw ached, not like open wounds, but feeling more like old injuries. He shook his head and covered his eyes for a second. He was wearing his overcoat open over a dingy white shirt underneath, the neck and armpits stained a faded yellow.

"It was the only way I could stop what was happening. You were about to erupt. And I could feel the President this close to entering your mind again. It was like he was sitting right between us in that skycraft. You couldn't hear me or see me anymore. I had to do something. When we finally landed, I had the holy man, their ndi nso, in the camp come and bless you with a protection spell."

At that point, another of the men she hadn't noticed stepped up to her other side across from Enyemaka. He was medium height, taller than them both, with a shaved head and a black goatee at the end of his squared jaw. He wore a white tunic and white robes belted shut over his waist with a rapid fire that Essien vaguely recognized dangling from one hand. None of the other men were armed as far as she could see.

The man was frowning. "The spell will last as long as you are with us. It should keep you safe for as long as you wish to be kept safe. There are additional protections I can add, if you'd prefer."

Essien just stared up at him from where she still lay on the ground. She hadn't tried to move yet. She could feel her jaw give a sharp pulse.

"I imagine you want to get off the ground. Can we help you up?" The bald man reached down at the same time Enyemaka did, and they got her standing on her feet between them. The world seemed to waver, and then she felt steady enough to take a few steps. Her stomach chose that moment to remind her she was still alive and human.

Enyemaka must have heard it because he said, "We'll lead you to the camp now."

The men had already set off into the trees around the landing patch carrying the boxes and bags and bundles they'd unloaded. Enyemaka followed them, and the holy man who hadn't introduced himself followed behind him. Essien had no choice but to follow. The men at the front continued to chatter, but Enyemaka fell silent.

She was led through green-and-gold-flecked tunnels that led down and down into a buried underground campsite. As they trekked into the gently sloping tunnel, Essien noticed the wooden slats framing out the stairs and girders along the walls and ceiling to keep it from caving in. Filtered sunlight puddled in the large square room the tunnel opened into. At the other end of the room, the dirt walls opened onto the lush green stretch of a grassy field with trees bordering its edges all the way out to the face of a brown stone mountain. The drop on the edge of that cliff was several hundred feet below into a rushing, rocky river. The sun hit the smooth surface of the lake at the end of the river at the bottom of the valley. The bright color sent fireballs of light in every direction as Essien passed silently through the tunnels leading deeper underground.

Below ground, there were mostly men practicing loading and unloading rifles that looked even more familiar to Essien's expert eyes. The magazine batteries she saw being loaded into the weapons looked to hold upwards of ten thousand. The military was limited to five thousand projectile magazines. The country's manufacturers couldn't make anything more than five thousand. Essien didn't know why that rule had been made, probably some obscure rule against foreign investment. The higher magazine rapid fires were made overseas. Essien took note of their features, the color and how it differed from the weapons she was used to. Then she realized for whom she was noting the features and shook her head.

They walked further through what was starting to feel like a crisscrossed maze of hallways and stairs leading up and then down onto the same floors with spaced openings looking out over the sheer drop of the cliff. One of the openings stretched out into another clearing with rows of dark green tents. Past the tents, Essien saw a group of men lined up in rows practicing formations that showed them scrambling in lines from one side of the field to the other. Other men huddled together inside open tent flaps. Essien realized there were women, too, some of them sitting with the men in the tents, others standing next to an open flame stirring bubbling pots on the open grills strung over those wood fires surrounded by stones. At one point as they led Essien past another opening onto a clearing full of trees, she thought she heard the tinkling glee of childish laughter.

A few more twists and turns, and then there was a large tent set off by itself, dark green to match the leafy surroundings. The tent seemed to be supported by a wooden frame. The men ducked inside through the flap of fabric covering the opening, Enyemaka going in with them. Essien followed.

More men in the same uniform Enyemaka and his companions wore. Over a dozen of them, she quickly counted. Some of them were gathered around the square table staring down at something. As they walked closer, Essien saw what looked like a cartograph with symbols and colors representing a guide for something. Essien stared around at the men as their conversations died down, and they turned to her.

The front room seemed rather large and not what she'd expected from outside. There was a large wooden table off to the left side of the room with metal chairs around it. On the other side, long metal boxes were piled up all the way to the top of the tent. Straight ahead, a flap of gray fabric covered a passageway deeper into the tent. The ground consisted of a floor covering that crinkled as she walked over it.

The holy man who had healed her said, "This is the President's bonded. I can feel traces of him all over her. Even with my amoosu, I could only create a protection spell. I couldn't actually break his hold on her."

Hearing those words seemed to crack something open inside Essien that felt like a bottomless pit, an endless abyss where something dark and ancient stared back at her. A jolt of shivers spread through all her limbs, and she visibly reacted.

"What do you mean by 'his bonded'? I was not romantically involved with the President. He and I were nothing more than a commander and his subordinate. I made sure of it. I don't know what information you've gotten, but I can tell you that, at least, is wrong." Essien felt like she had to defend something precious that was at stake. She didn't want to name what it was putting that firmness in her throat. It hit her for the first time that she was alone in a room full of men she didn't know who held her life in their hands.

The man sitting in the central chair on one side of the table raised a hand, waving it around. His countenance seemed ashen, from his skin to his hair in thin, long locks. He looked like he was sickly or recovering from a long illness. Essien got a sense of respect and deference from the men as they all fell silent at just the wave of that wrinkled, nut-brown hand.

"Let us introduce ourselves before we get into serious conversation." He waved his hand, and the men around the room began sharing their names. She didn't recognize any of their faces. Their names meant nothing to her at all. She didn't know which state they were in, but she knew it wasn't Igbo State anymore. They could have been every man from any village. She just stared around the tent as each spoke and nodded. None of them offered to touch palms. They were all wearing what she had figured out was their uniform: dark green slacks and overcoat, brown or black boots. Some wore dark green caps.

Essien's eyes fell on the older man last. "I am Mansa Musa the twenty-first, but you might have thought I'd be younger." His voice sounded old, but his mouth when it smiled gave him the appearance of a much younger man. His eyes were covered with a sheen of wetness that looked like a teardrop about to spill over at any second. She couldn't tell if he was about to cry, had just finished crying, or had severe allergies.

His voice sounded chalky as he said, "There are over two billion people in Alkebulan. If even a fraction of them could be won over to our side, we could bring this country to its knees in a matter of years. I inherited this rebellion from my progenitor. The infamous Mansa Musa the first, the man who stood against the building of a nation and almost toppled it. He was a remarkable man I was always told, if not somewhat barbaric in his dreams.

I have been leading his efforts, which are now mine for over half my life now. I feel I do not have much longer to give to the cause."

Essien's head tilted as the old man's words sank in. "Enyemaka told me about you, but I did not expect to actually meet you. I'd imagine you'd be too busy being a descendant of the most wanted man to ever exist in Alkebulan. Do you have something to say to atone for your ancestor? He wanted to enslave millions of people in order to prevent the Unification of a continent at war with itself. If he had succeeded? I don't think there would have been an Alkebulan to speak of today." A rustle went through the room, wordlessly spreading outward from where Essien stood before the table with her chin up and her shoulders back. It was the old man who dropped his head.

"My elder father may have been a bit uncouth in his methods," he said still looking down. "But his heart was pure. He thought the nation would have been stronger under his rule and the rule of his family's lineage. He thought—"

Essien scoffed, "So how is he any different from what Gabriel has done? Would you have us exchange one authoritarian for another? One dangerously misguided man's thirst for power for another one just like him?"

The men around them rustled in another wave of irritation, and she knew that if there was a line, she had just crossed it. She wanted to look around for Enyemaka, but she didn't want the man in front of her to think the man behind her meant too much.

"I have no plans to continue my ancestor's strategy. I have my own strategy to win this war, and I shall issue any decree you'd like using griots and town criers to spread the word."

The man held her eyes. Essien felt like her own eyes were suctioned onto his, and she couldn't look away. The sides of her vision began to blur and fade out, but still she stared down the tunnel that had become their locked gazes. She noticed his eyes were an aged and faded stone gray with flecks of gold in their depths. The gold began to flash and swirl around his pupil as she watched, and she heard herself asking, "And what is your strategy to win this war?"

"Yes, about that...I want you to burn for me. I want you to use your fire to make this nation feel even a small odachi of what we have felt all these many long centuries. Help me bring Alkebulan down. Help me bring this President to his knees before he says udo and surrenders." The voice stopped, and Essien could suddenly look away. She looked to where

Enyemaka had been just to her right. He met her eyes, but whatever he saw there made him shuffle his feet back and forth and then take a step back from her. The sound of that step was loud in the quiet tent.

"I don't know what you mean by burn and fire. I'm not—"

"Enyi has already told us everything he knows about you. We know what you can do with your flames. We want you to do it for us. No civilians, just cutting away at the power of this government and this illegitimate nation until we can finally reduce it to rubble. This cause needs your help. You were born to support this mission."

Essien stared down at the map. At some point while Mansa was talking, she'd walked closer to the table. The men around it had moved out of her way. She could clearly see the map marked with black dots and triangles and red circles and blue stars and yellow lines connecting them all. She couldn't make out what the symbols meant or tell where they were positioned from just looking at it.

She looked back at Mansa. He'd folded his hands on the table. Essien didn't look into his eyes again as she thought fiercely on the best way to respond.

"Again, what makes you think I can just do something like that at will? Do you think magic is a weapon? Then it's the most ineffective one possible. You might as well put a rapid fire in my hands and tell me where to point it."

A man she couldn't see called out from the back of the room, "I heard it from my cousin, who heard it from his barber, who heard it from his university instructor, who heard it from a night janitor, who heard it from his military son, who was high up enough in the Soja to have access to internal communications. According to him, she lit the festival that was held to honor her, and the President helped hide the bodies and any evidence."

She could have continued denying their knowledge; in fact, she wanted to. The way the man had described her made her sound like a heartless monster, like a cruel barbarian who was just as bad as the President, even if everyone she'd killed at that festival had been trying to kill her. She'd been injured so severely she needed both medical and magical healing. Maybe they didn't know that part. There were no wounds to show them either.

Enyemaka's voice dropped into the room finally. "I shared those details so that you might know who our greatest ally could be. But I never thought you'd want her to actually use her flames to...do what?"

Mansa put one hand flat on the map and pointed at Essien with the other. "Say you'll burn for me, and I will put every force I have behind helping you do that. I have targets picked out, strategic points that will force the President to act, but he won't know what hits him, as by the time he can react, we'll be in a different place with a different target. Once this whole nation is in flames, with our hands pouring on the accelerant, he'll have to come back to the negotiating table."

That fiery core inside of her suddenly wanted out, beating against her lungs and her heart like unerupted magma. It was an excruciating pressure pushing up from her stomach where that bottomless well yawned like a ravenous need for air to breathe. She wanted to let it out, needed to. If she could learn to control the flames, and this was the way, then she would take it.

Something in the back of her mind begged to be noticed, a memory that was there and not. As she tried to reach for it again, a mental force pushed her away, like herding cattle into a pen. Don't look over here, it warned her. Block out the past, block out everything from before. This is now. She found herself staring into Mansa's eyes while she listened to those whispers, straining to hear. She looked around at the other men. They were all watching her with an eager violence spilling out of their eyes and curling their fingers into fists. They were fiending for the violence that only she had seen up close and personal.

Enyemaka hadn't moved any closer to her. He was still silent and stony when she glanced sideways at him. She wanted to ask him why he'd revealed her secret. He wouldn't look at her as she stared at him.

Just as she was about to ask, a man entered through the tent flap behind them, the intrusion of light into the darkened, low-lit room putting a halt to the discussions that had started to brew at her silence. He stepped around all the men, right up to Mansa, and began whispering to him quickly. Essien couldn't hear anything even though she was standing right at the table's edge now.

Mansa's eyes slid over to Enyemaka. "This is my cousin, Sundiata the twenty-second," he introduced the man to Essien. She nodded. "He has another mission for you, Enyi. He'll tell you about it on the way to the skycraft."

Essien's eyes shifted to where Enyemaka stood. A vein in his neck tightened, but he still wouldn't look at her. Whatever she needed to say to him would have to wait. Essien thought about opening her aura but quickly doused the idea. She wasn't good enough yet at any of this to do it with the finesse needed to keep Gabriel out at the same time. Thinking of his name made a fluttering start from the bottom of her heart.

She watched Enyemaka walk out of the tent with Sundiata. He glanced back at her once before disappearing through the tent entrance.

She turned back to the man who had been patiently waiting for her to decide.

She swallowed a shallow breath stuck in her chest and said in a rushed and breathless voice, "If I burn for you—"

CHAPTER FOUR

◆

THE ERUPTION OF CHEERS AND SHOUTS OF MALE TRIUMPH drowned out what she said next, so that Mansa had to raise a hand again to quiet the room.

"I have one condition," she agreed reluctantly. Mansa leaned forward, smiling, already sure of her place in his carefully laid-out plans. The men around her had started to murmur, so sure of her now there was no further need for them to know what she said. They would see her fabled flames used against their enemies; there was a violent glee coming off them in rays.

Staring at Mansa, Essien said, "I want you to train me to master my magic."

Mansa's eyebrows rose to his forehead with surprise. He stared at her silently, his head tilted away from her slightly. The men shifted around her, their conversations growing louder.

"Is it amoosu? Or something else?"

She shook her head. "Something else." He nodded as if confirming what he'd thought.

"Does that something else have anything to do with the man you fled?"

She swallowed, feeling her suddenly dry mouth and not wanting to answer right away.

"If I say yes?"

With the slow and methodical press of his weakening arms on the table, Mansa stood up. His overcoat was unbuttoned over a tunic of the same color. The man was old, but once he was standing, he moved like he still had oil in his joints.

"Then your lesson starts tonight. For now, follow me."

WHEN DARKNESS WOKE UP OVER THE LAND, A LARGE GROUP OF the rebels along with Mansa led her back to the landing patch where the skycraft had been. Even as the twilight of evening settled over everything with gentle hands, Essien could see that the clearing was empty, and the skycraft was gone. They passed through the clearing all the way to the end where a thin line of trees separated this patch from a grassy clearing on the other side. There was a small fleet of rickety engines with gray, black, and tan sides covered in rust and almost bald tires. The rebels loaded the back of the engines with several of those long metal boxes that Essien knew contained rapid fires.

Mansa came into the clearing last, having walked to this spot on the arm of a rebel who had his same gold-flecked gray eyes. As the young man helped Mansa climb into the front of an engine, he waved Essien into the seat behind his.

The sides of the engine were open to the night air that blew past in a dry snatching of the small hairs around her forehead and neck. Her eyes roamed over the light-speckled valley they were riding toward on the winding road that sometimes let them see all the way to the other side. The lights were sparse this far up from a major city, but there was the definite sparkle of an entertainment district with its late-night hours away in the distance. A few other sparks in the dark that could be anything, but most of the land was in the shadow of late evening.

Essien felt hollow where earlier she'd felt claws of heat stretching up out of a bottomless abyss. She reached inside herself gently, with eyes not noticing anything around her now. The engine continued its jarring travel down and down into the valley that opened up before them, but Essien was trying to feel her power. There, just there, behind her heart, confined within the bars of her rib cage, she felt the lion of flames roar up from a dying ember.

In the front of the engine, Mansa turned to her with a smile pushing his cheeks up into his eyes. "I do not think I shall need to give you many lessons at all."

"I wasn't born with this flame, if that's what you think."

"I couldn't tell. Feels ancient...primordial."

"What?"

"Your power."

The engine slowed, pulled over onto softer gravel, and then stopped. The night pushed into the still vehicle. Essien could hear croackers and night creatures waking up to the moon. The luminators of the engine were quickly extinguished, and complete darkness sank around them.

"It's showtime," Mansa said, his voice too soft in the dark.

For a moment, Essien could hear her heart beating loud inside her mouth and a pulsing inside her ears that thrilled down into her fingers and feet. The young man with Mansa's eyes was outside their engine and opening his door, and then all the other doors creaked open. Boots thudded, and metal grated against metal. The young man handed Mansa a wooden stick. Mansa was opening her door then and standing there with a straight face.

"It's your time to shine," he said. "You want me to teach you control. This is it. Light up the field and prove you can do it without burning us alive in the process."

Essien still sat inside the engine. Mansa's face was obscured by the darkness of the late hour. So was the man's standing quietly next to him as just a towering shadow form.

"This is my grandson, Mansa Musa the twenty-third. He fusses over me and insists on being my personal bodyguard. You'd think I wasn't waging a war against one of the most powerful nations on earth. Here, let him help you out."

The young man moved to take Essien's arm, but she was already setting her foot down on rocky dry ground. They had come to a section far away from their buried campsite where there was nothing but those stretching stadia of land on both sides of the road they'd taken to get here. If it were daytime, Essien thought she might be able to see those jagged brown mountains on the other side of the valley from here.

"The time is now, Essien. There is no other time but this one. If you fail us...well, there is no chance that you will fail. This will be easy compared to what you did at the festival."

If his words were meant to motivate Essien, they had the opposite effect. Suddenly, she felt her stomach turning and roiling and threatening to push its contents up into her throat. She swallowed a mouthful of saliva and stepped away from the engine, just to move and get away from the feeling of being sick. She would not lose it here in front of Mansa and his grandson and these rebels whom she did not know.

A field of waving grain was being pushed this way and that by the invisible night wind. She turned away from that peaceful, welcoming sight, not yet ready to accept what cruelty she was about to unleash upon it. Mansa stood right behind her, one of his hands now resting on the polished wooden head of a walking staff.

Around them, the rebels were armed with rapid fires that pointed out into the dark night. They had spread out at intervals in the grass and along the dirt lip of a ditch on the other side of the field. Essien hadn't let herself think about the festival since taking off in that skycraft, and she had not tried again to let her flames come out. She remembered almost losing control in the air, the tang of blood in her mouth before she was knocked unconscious by Enyemaka.

Essien glanced around and wished he was here with her. Then she wondered at her own wishing for him, a foreign and new concept. He had rescued her, but they weren't friends. This was a newborn situation without the trials of having built up enough trust. It had been years since she'd seen him. They were both very different people than those sojas who had clung to each other with desperation—and repulsion, too. She felt like someone she didn't know at all.

"Think of it like a locked door, Essien." Mansa's voice seemed to match the gentleness of the wind. "You can open that door with a key that only you possess and unleash your power. And when you want to put the power away, all you have to do is lock it again."

Taking a deep breath of the dry winds blowing through the tops of the trees, Essien turned back to the field and looked inside of herself again. She tried to imagine a locked door, with a key held tightly in her grasp. Like an intruder ready to pounce the minute an advantage opens, that heat poured up out of her like an angry, rage-filled wave. It came quickly, easily, ready and waiting and willing. She didn't even have to call it as it burst forth from her as first a whisper of smoke drifting up from her palms, then a guttering crackle that produced a gush of flames turning on like a waterspout. The flames leapt out of her hands and flashed into the dark night as red, orange, and yellow flecks danced and jumped to the ground.

The men behind her gave a collective gasp of astonishment, and she heard safeties clicking off weapons and rapid fires being adjusted. Essien turned to look at them over her shoulder, her hands held down near her hips. The flames were still flowing out of her and falling on the ground like a cascade of neon drops of light. Where the flames touched, the dirt sizzled and smoked around her. The rebels weren't pointing their rapid fires at her; she wasn't sure what she would have done if they had been.

She tried to ignore them and stared down at her hands, the flames closest to her skin turning wispy blue and smoky white, spreading up her wrists with gently reaching probes. She was shocked again that the flames didn't hurt her at all. She couldn't even feel the heat that the flames were emanating. It felt like a cold breeze blowing over the center of her hands.

Mansa's voice was like that breeze, blowing around her like she was in the center of a hurricane.

"Your control is astounding. You doubted yourself? You thought you were a danger to others? The way you hold back that flame that could engulf us all makes me want to weep just to behold it. Now burn for me, Essien. Turn that flame into a weapon and burn for me. Don't just use your hands. Become the flame!"

Staring into the sea of grain and hearing his voice like ashes swirling in the wind, Essien directed her hands in front of her, and the flames seemed to pour out like so much gushing water.

"It's not just your hands, Essien!" Mansa's voice had to be louder because all she could hear was the crackling hunger of fire in her ears.

Within seconds, the flames had caught and were beginning to spread, devouring the greenish-brown heads into darkened and shriveled husks as she watched.

It felt unbelievably good to let the flame do what it wanted and consume. Like stretching after a restful night's sleep. Like slipping into warm water lapping gently against one's skin. Like merging one's body so completely with another that each slips into the other's consciousness, experiencing a pure, heart-stopping breath. It felt like coming home. She didn't stop or pull back until that sea of grain had become an ocean of flames. The part of the field closest to her had already disintegrated into ashes that piled up into small hills. She took a step forward, a scrape of boots on hard ground.

She felt the flames wanting to spread around and behind her to sweep across the other field beyond the ditch and those blinking lights scattered here and there down in the valley bowl. She blew out a breath she had been holding and tried to imagine that door and the key.

Mansa's calm, aged voice carried over the roar of fire in her ears. "Now is when you reel it in. Like spooling a thread. Wind the power back into yourself. Don't try to dampen it all at once or too soon because it could explode out of you without even a second's warning. Pull all that power back in slowly. When it's back inside you, lock the door."

Essien could feel the flames fighting against her. Like they had a mind of their own. There was still so much kindling and accelerant. The winds were blowing just right, dry and not a touch of moisture. Essien closed her eyes, so she wouldn't keep seeing the golden shimmers dancing so enticingly in front of her. She clenched her fists, the tips of her nails digging into the skin at the base of her thumbs. Her breathing sped up a bit as she felt like she couldn't catch enough air.

"Essien, now is when you show your power who is dominant. Do not let it get out of your control. Don't let this night become another festival."

Every time Mansa mentioned what she'd done that day that was meant to be a day of celebration for her, a stinging stab of shame crept into her psyche. It didn't matter that she hadn't meant to do it. It didn't matter that it had been the first time her flames manifested, so of course she was inexperienced and hadn't known what to do. She still didn't know what to do. Her breath was an uneven rasp in her ears, and Mansa's voice was still drilling into her, reminding her what was at stake.

"Show me your control, or this deal is off. Stop those flames—now!"

Essien thought it was ironic. Mansa had wanted her to show him her flames, and now that she had, she could hear the fear and revulsion with every word he spoke. No, it wasn't the flames. It was the thought of those flames burning people they didn't intend to burn.

Essien's mouth was dry and parched. She could feel her heartbeat like an anvil in her chest, the rhythmic throbbing echoing in her entire body. She gripped her teeth into her bottom lip, tasting her own blood spreading over her tongue.

The door was burning, the flames eating over it all in one gush of orange and gold. The key was melting out of her hand. There was no door that could shut this power in. There was no lock and key that could calm it where raging, grasping heat wanted out, to stretch out in the cool air that was blowing just right.

An ember floated up on a draft, the current floating it up and up, so small and bright in the darkness. The ember landed on the bottom hem of one of the men's trousers. He'd told her his name only hours ago. That was all it took. Suddenly, the flames were burning up those uniformed legs, and she heard a startled scream. Then the man's rapid fire clattered to the ground, and he was hopping around and batting at his legs with both hands.

Essien turned away from the fields for a second, and again, that was all it took. The flames were roaring across the fields, into territory she hadn't been told to burn. If Mansa was still talking, she couldn't hear him at all now. Essien thought of the one element that could douse her flames.

She had no water magic; the two likely canceled each other out. If Gabriel were here... Just the thought made Essien shudder and squeeze her fists closed. She felt a sudden sweat bead across her upper lip and forehead; the heat of the flames before her seemed to wilt and waver.

Then she felt it, the temperature starting to drop around her. She opened her eyes. The flames across the field were already smoldering down into embers, the majority of that expanse gray and black piles of burnt matter. Slowly, painfully, the flames were being pulled back and in, triggered by her own confusion and anxiety. Finally, finally they turned off. Her palm gave a final hiss, singing her skin with a red welt in the shape of a half moon in the center of her palm.

Breath rushed into her lungs, and the breeze that touched her forehead was cool and gentle. She turned away from what she had done to find that the shadowy figures of all of the rebels had their weapons pointed vaguely in her direction, none of them truly aimed, but wanting to be. She couldn't make out their features now as darkness sank back in, the burning field now banked into coal and ashes. Only one of the men behind her was smiling.

Mansa came forward, the *thump-thump* of his walking staff accenting his approach.

His smile grew whiter the closer he came. "That was your first lesson, and I must say, you met my expectations. Never mind the minor mishap. We'll put a bigger perimeter around you next time. Oh, I am going to make a rebel out of you before this is all said and done."

Essien felt that spell click into place for the first time as she tried to remember a face to go with that name, and she couldn't. It was like there was a space in her brain where the information once had been—had been just seconds ago—but she couldn't access it. She tried to push against that foggy emptiness where she was absolutely sure something had been. She would have kept thinking about it, but Mansa put his other hand on her shoulder and helped her lead him back to their engine. He held her door open and slammed it shut once she was inside.

CHAPTER FIVE

◆

THEY STARTED TREATING HER AS LITTLE MORE THAN A CAP-
tive after that, and it was so subtle that at first, Essien was willing to
let it go. When she stepped out of the tent Mansa had assigned her the
following morning, there were two rebels coming to attention as they'd
been slouching and sitting nearby. They wore their uniforms with casual-
ness, rolled pant legs and unbuttoned overcoats. They held their rapid fires
pointed down at the ground, but their abrupt snapping into stiffness and
tension when she appeared gave her the sense that they were given orders to
watch her and were on edge waiting for her to erupt again.

When she walked toward the bathing tent with a bundle of clothes
she'd been given last night under her arm, the two rebels fell into step a few
paces behind her. Essien scowled over her shoulder at the following of their
steps but kept traveling down several paths that wound deeper into the
rebel camp. She noticed tent flaps held open with tied rope and got a flash
of their interiors as she passed. Cots just like her own, a few with a folding
table and folding chair, others with chests pushed against the walls or a
colorful mat over the waterproof canvas tent floor. Essien smelled a spiced
aroma moments before the path widened out into a clearing that opened
onto the fresh air of a cliffside facing a steep drop into the valley below. The
clearing had stone-constructed grills erected at various places throughout
the space paved with smooth, flat gray stones, and several women were stirring huge cauldrons of boiling contents.

The women stared at Essien, and she stared back. None of them looked
alike, as if they could have come from north, south, or east of here—wherever here was. They all wore uwes made of a stretching fabric wrapped
around and around them and sandals with straps wound up their ankles
and calves. One woman had her hair in braids pulled back into a bun just
like Essien. Another wore her hair in hanging locks that hit her waist and
had golden tips. The last woman had her hair cut short, barely a shadow of
fuzz on her scalp. They were a light brown, a medium brown, and a deep

brown, respectively. Essien nodded at them as she passed in front of where they were preparing meals.

The uniform they gave her matched the one all the men wore. It was dark green, and the pants fit snugly. The undershorts and undershirt were a thin white cotton material, and the overcoat was the same color and material as the pants. She kept the same slippers she'd been wearing since the hospital. When she stepped out of the bathing tent, a third rebel had joined the first two standing across the path. He had a pair of brown boots in his hands.

He silently extended them toward her as she crossed the path to them.

"If you're going to be following me everywhere, at least remind me of your names," she said.

"We haven't met," the one who handed her the boots replied. He backed up to get back in the line that the other two made side by side.

"I guess you weren't at the meeting yesterday when I was introduced then. I'm Essien. You are?"

They all shared glances with each other instead of answering her. Essien noticed that they all looked alike—same hair color, hair style, and height. Their skin was brown, a few shades lighter than hers, the color of dark chocolate. Their hair was cut almost as short as the woman she'd seen—just a sparse covering over their nearly bald heads. They were each at least a foot taller than her, so, being in such close proximity to them, she was definitely looking up. They quickly rattled off their names, but she forgot them as soon as they said them.

Essien shrugged and turned to go back to her tent.

The one who had given her the boots said, "Mansa Musa requested you at the war tent."

She looked back with a smirk. "Then lead the way. I don't quite remember where it is from here."

That got a chuckle out of two of the three, but not the one standing in front of her. He just turned and began walking in the opposite direction from where she had come. She followed, constructing a mental map in her head of the maze of tunnels that connected the massive underground camp. There seemed to be one central path leading from the sloping stair of the front entrance down all the way through to the side she was currently in, with crisscrossing paths extending off into the darkness of more tunnels. She guessed there were probably stadia of underground chambers and walled spaces that likely stretched beneath and along the sides of the entire mountain.

They reached the war tent in a clearing that several tunnels opened on to. The rebel at the front held the tent flap open for her but did not step through. She did, not having to duck at all. The room was packed, and she realized there had to be hundreds of rebels in this camp—far more than their reports and estimates had ever measured.

A wall of eyes turned to her as she entered and began to push her way forward. The men stepped out of her way, parting like automatic doors. Standing next to the table, Enyemaka's face was scarily blank, like he was hiding what he truly felt, and already putting up shields against her. She thought about pushing against the solid wall of space keeping her from knowing if the absence of feelings on his face could translate to fear or wariness. He, alone, of all of them, knew enough about what else she could do without a single atom of fire magic. He, alone, knew that her power came from akukoifo, those ancient spiritual beings that served the Mothers, the Creators of all the multiverses. He, alone, knew the training they had both received before he had been discharged. And Enyemaka, alone, knew that the flames were only one side of the sand dune that could bury them all if they attempted to shift in ways that were untenable.

Mansa Musa the twenty-first was sitting in the same chair where he had been before, but this time he was wearing a dark brown overcoat and pants instead of the dark green of everyone else. His grandson was at his right shoulder, his hands planted on his hips, right near the hilts of two rapid fires, one on each side. His eyes flicked down to Essien when she got close to the table, and then he went back to scanning the faces of the men in the room.

"Thank you for joining us, Essien. We have discussed much, and we are ready to dispatch you on your first real test."

Essien was already shaking her head. "I thought you were going to train me. I could have killed all of you last night, do you understand that?" She felt, more than saw, Enyemaka make a movement, and her eyes jumped to his. But he was looking at Mansa.

"I don't doubt your loyalty, Essien, but many of the rebels do. They worry that you were sent to us as a trap. They don't think we have the time it would take to train you fully, the way you might want."

She gritted her teeth and tried to speak calmly. "You don't have the time to *not* train me! This power? I fear it. What could happen if these flames got out of hand? I won't kill innocent people!" Her voice had risen by the end, and as she looked frantically around at everyone, no one would meet her eyes. Except Mansa.

Mansa was nodding. "While I am willing to give you the time and the trust that I know you will earn, the rest of my men need more proof...more assurances that they won't follow you out into an ambush or betrayal."

Essien's eyes swung to Enyemaka again, standing right there at the table near the front of the crowd seeming to press closer. He lifted his eyes from the ground to finally look at her. *Please*, she tried to beg him. *Help me convince them!* They couldn't let her go out on some rebel mission without more training. It could go so wrong, so quickly. There was someone she wanted to avoid; someone she didn't want to be caught by. If her flames got out of hand, there was no way she'd remain free after that. She wouldn't deserve to.

Mansa said, "Our next targets are the fields belonging to anyone in the Military Council."

Essien frowned. "The Military Council owns fields? How many of them own land that could be burned?"

Mansa Musa's face was grave when he answered, "That's the problem. Too many of them. Much of the land we've tracked to military councilmen came into some of their hands via fraud and theft."

"Explain." She had never heard of any of this, so there was no way she could be to blame. But once she knew, didn't that mean she was obligated to act on the side of justice?

"When a village elder dies, sometimes there are no immediate blood relatives in the area available to take over the lands. Instead of notifying the distant or foreign families, the Councilmen will engineer a fraudulent sale of the lands, sometimes before the dead have had their burial rites. The land would then be signed into their names, or the names of their proxies, and they go in with local enforcement officers and bulldozers to remove anyone from the land. Some of them aren't that corrupted, and they continue to tend the land based on its indigenous routines and practices. A few have even been known to let the families stay on the land. Most of them though? They have greedily turned stadia upon stadia of land into concrete jungles to create entertainment districts and business districts, and now the need for arable land to feed and house our population grows while they sit on piles and piles of it."

Essien looked down at her nails, picking at them, as she realized that not knowing wasn't an excuse. It was her duty to know, but she couldn't remember what that duty came from. It wasn't just being an Alkebulanian, with family all over the country, the world even. She remembered learning and experiencing that the military councilmen were tasked with mediating between the Tribal Council and the President, and the Tribal Council was tasked with acting as representatives between the various tribes under their leadership in each state and the Military Council. So, ultimately, wasn't it the President's fault, then?

"What of the tribal Councilmen? Do they know?"

"As yet, we have found none of their names or their representatives' names on the property registration, but that doesn't mean they aren't willing participants. We first tried to meet with the Tribal Council about the matter, many years ago now, but our efforts were unsuccessful. They refused to meet with us, or scheduled meetings and kept rescheduling them. It would seem they are as involved as the military councilmen we can prove."

Essien wanted to ask them if they had tried any other way. The news reels? The investigative agencies? There had to be some better way to stop corruption in the government, if that's what truly had been happening. There was no way Gabriel didn't know about this.

The name sounded inside of her head like a horn, loud and piercing, making her wince against its echoes vibrating down through the rest of her body. Her legs shivered, but she remained upright.

Mansa kept talking as if he didn't notice. "The council is not supposed to take sides, but when it came to the defense of the nation, its growth and progress, perhaps they had taken a side unknown to the rest of us. Perhaps they do not represent the rest of us at all. If that is so, then we have a duty to dispossess ourselves of them."

"I didn't know any of this," Essien whispered helplessly, trying to get her bearings from the vibrating shock still quaking through her bones. The sound went away, but the feeling of surprise remained. She wondered about what had caused it but was afraid to think too hard about it. With a deep sigh, she said, "What is the first target?"

"Five hundred stadia several hectares away that's been slated for development into a combination business and entertainment complex. Last we heard, reports said they were building a strip for nightclubs and other nightlife offerings, if you understand me. It's been heavily guarded, so we may have to engage before you can work your magic and destroy everything on that site."

Essien shook her head. "There can't be any people there."

Mansa nodded. "All of our reports indicate that all human personnel leave the site at the end of the day, and the guards are posted in two watchtowers at the front and back edge of the property."

"Is there a way to deal with the guards without hurting them?"

Mansa said, "We will handle them before you even arrive on site."

She nodded. "Who hired them? Who's behind the land? Why this land?" Essien felt like she had to be sure. Absolutely sure that she wasn't harming innocents, people who had done no wrong, so they deserved no punishment. She couldn't let her fire be used wantonly, not if she could help it.

"The land was purchased in a quiet sale—no witnesses, no clerks, just exchanging land by word and a palm touch, if they even had the decency to touch palms. The family whose land is being developed came to us directly, with bills of ownership filed with the courts and with witnesses, many decades ago."

"If you have proof, why not go to the Council themselves?" Essien didn't understand how this had become their only avenue for redress. She had thought Alkebulan was a safe and orderly country, a just and righteous nation. Nothing she had seen since joining the military had confirmed that childish belief.

"Should we petition the Council to investigate the Council?"

Essien sighed, defeated. If this was the only way. "When do we move?"

Mansa's smile was genuine and pleased. "This evening, right before sunset. We'll reach the location just after full dark. You'll get to show us what your flames can do on a site this big and against more than just dirt."

"What's on the site?"

"Building materials, equipment, and machines...they moved all their supplies down there. This will make your job so much easier. And oh the message this will send! We'll have to be on our defense afterward, of course, and cover our tracks coming back, but I think you are what will turn the tide of this revolution."

"Let's survive a few of these battles before we call it a revolution."

"What do you think we have been doing all these many generations? Did you think my family carried my ancestor's name down into this era but not his conviction?"

From outside the tent, there was the sound of a three-note whistle.

One of the rebels behind them said, "Dinner is ready. The rush will be fierce today. We had a group of eighty return from a recruiting expedition. Returning is great, but they brought back twenty new recruits who've been testing in the jungle for weeks and are probably starving for a hot meal. Mothers, let's get there quick."

The rebels were already filing out of the tent behind her. Essien felt someone hovering at her elbow and turned to see Enyemaka.

His eyes were for Mansa. "I'll walk her over and make sure she gets back to her tent."

Mansa nodded, still sitting. "Feel free to tell her what to expect." To Essien he said, "Enyemaka was one of our scouts we sent ahead yesterday to set up for our plan tonight. He'll be leading you into the construction site."

"I FEEL LIKE YOU LIED TO GET ME HERE, ENYEMAKA."

"I didn't lie," he said, his voice low as they flowed with the rest of the crowd pouring out of their tents and up the paths toward where dinner would be served to everyone in the camp. "I just didn't tell you all of the reasons we came to rescue you. I knew I would be here to protect you."

"Protect me from being used and abused by these...men who call themselves rebels? Where have I heard those exact words before?" She walked faster to get away from him, suddenly so angry that she couldn't see straight. She had to stay calm, otherwise those flames...they were just waiting to explode out of her at any provocation. She had to be careful. And calm. She heard Enyemaka closing the distance between them and sped up even more. She brushed around the shoulders and high backs of several men as she moved faster. Enyemaka didn't call out to her to wait or to stop.

The women who had cooked the stew and the greens and the white rice inside the steel cauldrons were nowhere to be seen. Essien filed into the line and got her portion of everything all together in a gourd bowl. A ball of warm fufu was handed to her in a corn leaf. Essien sat down on the first spot of ground near a mixed group of men and women. The women were very into the men, sitting close to them, touching them, putting pieces of meat from their own bowls into the men's. Essien guessed they might be wives or girlfriends based on the intimacy. She used pieces torn off the warm ball of fufu to swipe up mouthfuls of the spicy stew with hunks of tender beef and chopped pieces of salty green leaves and chewy bits of rice. Essien cleared the bowl with the last piece of fufu and gave a contented sigh as she realized it was her first meal in several days.

Two scuffed black boots stopped just in front of her outstretched legs. Enyemaka leaned down, took the empty bowl out of her hands, and then pushed a cracked-open coconut into her hand. Clear liquid pooled at the top of the coconut with the creamy white lining of the coconut shell peeking out around the edges of the sliced cut. Essien put her mouth over the hole and tilted the shell up. The water that slid down her throat was cool and fresh and tasted buttery and slightly sweet. After all the coconut water was sipped away, she widened the hole at the tip with a finger and scooped out the white meat. It slid off the sides and into her mouth like slippery jelly that had an even more intense flavor than the water. When she was done, she silently handed the empty coconut to Enyemaka and then stood, stepping around him and the remaining seated rebels. Using just her memory of the walk over, she then took the maze of paths back to the tent where she was to stay for who knew how long.

Essien lay on her back on the cot and knew that she had been brought here to be used for her flames, and she had agreed to it so naively that she had no one to blame but herself. Yes, she needed to learn to control her power, she needed to practice turning those flames on and off, increasing their intensity and holding back. She needed to find out her limits and be sure she stayed away from them. This was a weapon, a dangerous one, and she needed to practice with the same intensity she had learned when using a rapid fire. If this was to be the price, then she needed to seriously weigh if it was a price she was willing to pay.

As she was immersed in her reflections, she heard the sound of someone clearing their throat outside the tent, followed by Enyemaka's voice saying, "Essien, I'm with Osiris...he's here to redo the spell."

Essien stood up from the cot with an abrupt jerk and smacked the tent flap open, stepping outside. Standing with Enyemaka was the holy man she had seen during her first night in the clearing. He stood taller than Enyemaka, as nearly everyone did, and he wore the traditional white tunic over white pants with white loafers stained and dirty from walking the dirt paths. His head was covered with a white cap. In his arms he carried a bundle of incense sticks of different colors and a glass vial of some purplish liquid.

"May we come inside?"

Essien stared at Enyemaka, but she retreated into the tent, and they followed. She sat down on the side of the cot to give them room to stand inside the now crowded space.

Osiris kneeled in front of her, breaking the string that tied the incense together and placing the sticks in a row. He held up the first incense and looked at her with a twinkling in his eye.

"A light please, ara?"

Essien had to smile, but then she quickly frowned. "I don't know if I can—"

"You can. Trust yourself."

She took in a deep breath; the herbal, spicy, pungent scent of the incense sticks was strong. She proceeded to open the door inside herself just a sliver; a crack in the wall holding back the flames. The door, made of azobe, she decided—the strongest Alkebulanian ironwood—held strong this time. She coaxed a small spark out around the doorjamb and then shut the door tightly. She brought the flame up to her surface, while holding herself still. Instead of her palm, this time, the flame sparked as an orangey-red wisp at the tip of her first finger.

A smile spread Osiris's dark brown cheeks wide. Enyemaka took a step back, but his face remained composed. The holy man brought the end of the first incense stick up to Essien's finger. She didn't even have to touch it before her flames ignited the tip of the stick, and its blue smoke sparkled and popped and began wafting up in a swirling line.

Osiris held her eyes as he said, "I shouldn't have to redo the spell this often, but as the hours stretch on, I can feel their strength wearing away— being stripped away, more accurately."

As he talked, his hand swirled the incense over Essien's head. The blue smoke wafted down over her, its smell like fresh herbs that stung her nose.

"What do you mean stripped away?" Essien asked, her voice barely above a whisper. The smell of the incense was pleasant now, cleansing and bringing much-welcomed fresh air into the stuffy, cramped tent.

"It is as if some force—an unbearable energy—is hammering against the other side of the shield that the spell has put around you. I cast the spell, which means I control the shield, so I can feel if it is doing what I set it to do. The spell works at first and then...whatever hounds you is searching passionately for you, almost desperately. The feeling I'm getting is like a fractured entity trying to remerge all of its parts. There's a force on your side of the shield fighting to reconnect with that entity, like it's magnetized and attracted to that force...calling it in as it's being called. I do not know what this entity is...I have never felt anything like it. I am...afraid to track it."

Essien was already shaking her head, her eyes flicking to Enyemaka's. He was looking at her with some emotion. Her throat closed at the sight of what looked like horror, terror, and pity showing on his face. She knew that she could link with him, but she was as wary of him as he was of her. There was a reason she shouldn't link with him, to read his thoughts and let him read hers without Osiris hearing any of it. She knew she shouldn't, so she didn't, and she dropped her eyes again to Osiris.

The flame on the incense stick had burned down almost to its end. The holy man grabbed another one from the floor in front of him and lit it from the dying flame. The new incense stick was red, and the smoke that rose from it was a thick scarlet color. Essien breathed it in, spices that tingled and blurred her vision. She closed her eyes.

"I'm going to try to increase the strength of the spell with this blessed oil. I'll rub it on your face in symbols of protection. This should keep you safe for as long as the oil is on your skin. An added layer of defense."

She just nodded, keeping her eyes closed, her hands resting flat on her thighs.

The smells of the incense blurred together, layers being added as another stick was lit and then another. Osiris's fingertips touched her forehead, and the oil he spread in a loop that crossed and crossed over itself was cool against her skin. It added another layer of a soft, sweet scent that made her want to lick the oil and see if it tasted as good as it smelled. He spread more of the oil over her eyelids and her cheeks. Then he used a thumb to spread a dab of the oil over her bottom lip. Essien startled away, her eyes snapping open.

Osiris was capping the glass bottle with a rubber cap, then it disappeared into the pocket of his pants. The last incense stick burned, this one a deep purple with silver sparkles making the fire at one end spark and glint. The smell seemed to echo the scent of the oil, sweet and settling over her tongue.

Osiris had been chanting softly the entire time in a language that might have been Xhosa, but Essien wasn't fluent enough to translate what he was saying in clipped and staccato phrases. He said the last words in a language Essien could understand: "May the Mothers bless you and keep you."

Behind him, Enyemaka's eyes darted to the back of Osiris's head. Everyone knew that the holy men worshiped no other gods besides Amun-Ra and his Son turned into human flesh, Heru. The men who were known for wearing white and predicting miracles did not worship the Mothers.

A single tear slid out of Essien's eye, her head bowing over her lap to hide it. She didn't know why she was moved so deeply by that last line of prayer, but something in her heart went soft.

When she had gathered herself, she lifted her head with dry eyes and speared Enyemaka with a cold stare. "What do I need to know in order to burn tonight?"

CHAPTER SIX

◆

THERE WERE RAISED RED BURNS ON HER PALMS WHEN THEY set out by engine to reach the place where she was going to burn their first target. Despite the brutal color and the pulse of pain, the unleashing of fire was a desire beating in her as sure as thirst or hunger. So, it would be nights like this of learning the depths of her newfound skills in the dark of night on secretive missions that caused untold amounts of damage meant to inflict the maximum levels of devastation against an enemy whose name and face she couldn't remember. The spells recast over her that evening were working, and there were parts of her memory that were as blank as slate stone.

Essien had trekked silently through the wooded area around the illegally stolen construction site with a group of rebels who were as silent as she was. They had gotten out of the engines a ways back, to travel on foot. The watchtowers at the edge of the cleared-out space where buildings would soon go up were silent sentinels, occupied by two armed security each.

Easily and effortlessly, the snipers among them separated from their group to set up their long-range rapid fires at the edge of the woods on the other side. Armed with chemical darts to temporarily knock the guards out without killing them. The rest of them continued to their positions at different points around the perimeter of the land. A chunk of the group split off to the left. Enyemaka went right, and Essien followed him.

Sharp bursts that barely reverberated through the air dispatched the four men at the tops of the watchtowers, their bodies slumping where they once stood high up on the platform. A five-note whistle was their cue to draw closer. A set of wire cutters appeared from the bag Enyemaka had carried. He snapped through the fence surrounding the construction site, cutting a line that opened like peeling back a can top. The machinery and stacks of building materials loomed up out of the shadows as they crept inside the fence, keeping close to their bulking size to avoid being seen by any happening eyes.

Enyemaka kept to the edge, taking Essien toward the back of the site, to be sure her flames would incinerate it all. The metal fence surrounded the wooden frames of several different buildings, with unfinished frames starting to be built for several others. There were pitted lots waiting for frames to go up around them. There was an area with a dry water fountain and a white stone sculpture in the middle of a man and woman holding a child between them, their arms raised. Essien wondered where the water was intended to come out.

"Here," Enyemaka's voice directed in the dark. "You can cover all of the site from here."

They were standing in the paved corridor that ran through what would one day become the main street of the business district that had been approved without acknowledging whose land this was and how it had been acquired.

"On your mark," he said, and she felt him retreat from behind her, moving a few paces away, but not abandoning her entirely. "You have the clear to ignite."

Essien approached the door again, key in hand. She put the key in the lock and filled her lungs, holding her breath. She cracked open the door slowly, and the force pushing out from inside of her ripped the door clean off its hinges.

The fire was fierce and overwhelming. It was everything, and she was nothing. It wasn't supposed to be like this. The fire that pooled out of her palms and fingertips was nothing compared to this. The colors of orange and red and gold were mesmerizing, and she was not there. She was nothing but the flame, and it was her own fault for thinking she could contain this element with her human flesh, that she could contain what was infinite into something with only one lifetime. She tried to breathe deeply, but there was just burning and flames, and nothing else for a long time. She heard her name, distant, forgotten, unrecognized with the exultant flames dancing around her head.

WHEN THE FIRE WAS DONE, WHEN SHE'D MELTED DOWN THE fence surrounding the property and some of the trees surrounding the fence, when even the watchtower and any evidence of the security officers' bodies was reduced to ashes, and when at last she turned to look at

Enyemaka, he was on his knees curled over into a ball trying to make himself as small as he possibly could. His rapid fire had melted into a puddle in front of him, the silvery metal still liquid and reflecting the flames. His clothes were burned clean off him, but his skin and body were not even singed by the flames. As she gazed at his hands clasped tightly in front of him and his eyes wide and glazed, she knew there was nothing in the world that would ever make Enyemaka want to be on her bad side.

"IF I DIDN'T KNOW BETTER, ESSIEN, I'D SAY THAT YOU WERE BORN to be a rebel. You have the spirit of destruction in your blood." She was walking back from dining and heard Mansa calling her name. He'd been standing in front of the war tent with a group of other rebels, and there was Enyemaka among them. The look on his face was wary, refusing to hold her eyes when she tried to meet his. He had reason to be terrified, although perhaps he always had before now.

She was frowning before she could stop herself. "That doesn't sound like a compliment, Mansa. I wasn't raised in destruction. I used to be a farmer's daughter before I was a..." What had she been? Before coming here? The space in her mind where a place should have been was empty and yet filled. She stared at Mansa's face as he continued talking, but she was concentrating on that empty space in her head. What did she used to be?

"I can't remember," she said out loud. She shook her head once, twice. "I can't remember what I can't remember."

Mansa was holding up the tent flap with the hand holding his cane and beckoning to her with the other. She followed him into the weakly lit tent interior. The front room of the tent was empty, but Essien could hear voices coming from behind the tent flap on the far wall. She hadn't yet been invited deeper into the space than this front room. She couldn't make out what those voices were saying, but they were loud enough to echo out into the larger space. He tapped over to the table where the map was spread out as it had been every time she had come in here so far. Nothing else about the room was changed.

"Last night, two of my top commanders complained about our strategy. They want us to try a different tactic."

Essien frowned, confused. Mansa went on before she could ask. "They think your flames are too dangerous. And unreliable."

"I apologized for almost burning them up in my fire frenzy. I'm learning this power at the same time that I'm using it. It feels natural, but I don't know what I'm doing. So maybe they're right."

Mansa's smile was wicked, and for a second, his face distorted into something devious and bloodthirsty. "I already overrode them. They haven't been able to get this level of attention or win over this number of recruits for months now. Burning the fields all those years? Maybe we hurt a few farmers here and there, but what you did last night? The reports we are getting so far tell us we're winning."

"What do the reports say?"

"There are military units mobilizing in places they think we are, but we aren't. They're watching the wrong places, and we are already on to the next target."

"Where are we?" Essien couldn't remember much from before, but she knew that she had never been told where they landed or where they had trekked to. She couldn't even begin to guess. They could be right in Igbo State for all she recognized or knew.

Mansa looked down at the map, his hand hovering over several states. He balled his hand into a fist. "It is better if you don't know our exact location. We agreed that you will be kept on a need-to-know basis. We'll tell you about your next targets as you need to know them."

Essien bristled. "It's just like being in the military and working for the President."

A gong shocked her so suddenly that she startled, jumping almost an inch off the ground. Her hip hit the table, pushing it into Mansa's side where he stood on the other side of it. His hands were resting on the table's surface, so he caught himself roughly on the edge.

"It's best you do not think about that, or him."

"Him?" Another gong, this time deep into her brain, like the worst headache, one that seemed to pulse and throb in time to her blood beating.

Essien had her head down almost on the tabletop, trying to stop the echoing sound and growing feeling of pressure.

"I'll call for Osiris," Mansa said to her. His cane tapped deeper into the tent while she stood with her eyes closed tightly, waiting for another throb of searing pain to hit her.

His voice was calm from in front of her, but she didn't open her eyes. "We should go back to your tent. I can reapply the oils there." She couldn't open her eyes, fear and phantom waves of pain still hitting her. She felt a hand at her elbow, and then she was being led. Eventually, she opened her eyes, from fear of falling more than fear of pain. They reached her tent, and she immediately lay down on the cot. She kept her eyes closed.

"A light, ara?" Essien held up a fingertip and thought of the flame sparking just on the tip of her nail. She heard the crackle and pop seconds before Osiris laughed.

"Even while in great pain, you still manage to control your flames. It's remarkable, girl. Don't sell yourself short...or start to doubt. What you are doing here means something to the people. You may not see it yet, but Alkebulan needs you."

Essien cracked one eye open enough to look over at Osiris. His white cap made the deep brown of his skin even more stark.

She whispered more to herself than him, "Maybe what I need is to not be needed."

Osiris frowned and leaned over the cot. "What do you mean?"

She closed her eyes and shook her head. "Nothing."

Osiris began wafting the incense over her as she lay on the cot, moving his hand in circles that she could feel over her head. The smell hit her, and suddenly she felt light and clean. There was a hollowness in her head, but she felt chastened enough not to explore or probe it. There was something her mind didn't want her to know. The spell. The spell Osiris was weaving over her with gently spoken words that she couldn't have understood even if she heard them. Yes, there was something about the spell.

The first time that incense had burned around her she'd been unconscious. The second time, she'd been so angry with Enyemaka, she hadn't been able to pay attention. Now, as the smoke fell, she could feel them slipping away. The memories she couldn't remember. A face—she could see it and almost reach her hand out to caress that clenched jaw, and then it was gone. Wafted away gently on the scent of herbs and clean air.

"Mansa told me you had trouble with the spell today. That it caused you pain?"

Essien spoke with her eyes closed. "It was like my head was coming apart, or imploding on itself, my whole body. Like every time I thought about...something...it's your spell isn't it?"

"It's not supposed to work like that," and even with her eyes closed, she could hear the worry and concern. "It shouldn't cause you pain, Essien."

She had to open her eyes then. It was the first time she'd heard any of them use her name besides Enyemaka. Osiris was still kneeling beside the cot; the incense almost burned all the way down in his hand.

"Then what's going wrong? Why does it hurt every time I think about..." She stopped herself from going further in word or thought.

Osiris stared at the burning incense. "I don't think it's the spell. I think it's... Do you remember when I said that there's something—think of it like a battering ram—banging up against the wall of protection I've put around you? Night and day, since I cast the spell. Eventually...the walls start to give. I think that's what you're feeling."

Essien knew and didn't know what he was telling her. It was like there was a fog of mist around her mind, keeping her from looking off past anything not concerning the present moment. "Do you need me to light another one?"

Osiris extended a fresh incense stick, and Essien carefully lit the end. Letting out only that much of her flame, over and over, felt like she was gaining control over it. The key to the door lock was solidly in her hand. She realized that she didn't know which target they had planned for her next. As soon as she was protected and the spell was working again, she would head back to the war tent to find out.

CHAPTER SEVEN

◆

I N THE CENTRAL JUNGLES OF ALKEBULAN, A FIRE BURNED UN-
restrained and full of rage. It had been months, if the changing of the
seasons was a measure. She'd lost track of how much time had passed between her old life—one she couldn't remember—and this new, rebellious
life fighting for an inherited cause. The skies were once again blue and full
of electric sunshine and fluffy floating clouds. The months in which they
had trekked through rain and mud and even a strange onslaught of sleet
for several weeks at a time had been brutal now that she had time to pause
and think about it. The camp had moved so many times, Essien traveling
along with the group to the different underground villages using hidden
jungle paths. She had lost track of which state she was in and how long she
had been there. She had no technology or even a simple calendar. She didn't
even have a way to tell the time beyond the daily rising and setting of the
sun. It was an amorphous and dreamlike state that moved her from one day
to the next, one campsite to the next, and at some point, Essien realized it
was likely being forced into her by the spells that the holy man had to redo
every day, sometimes several times a day.

Essien didn't need to practice controlling her flames with Mansa anymore; that door and its key were solidly under her control. There was some
small part of her that knew her power was nothing compared to whatever
it was she kept forgetting every day. Still, she knew how to burn now like
she knew how to breathe. It was automatic and innate. She could start fires
with a thought, no need to even point her hands, though she often still did,
just for dramatic effect. She was still slathered with oil and smothered with
smoke every morning and night, her chats with Osiris one of the calmest
moments of her day. In the evening, she was summoned to hear the major
plans they had created without her, centered almost entirely on her flames.

Despite the rebels' protests, Mansa's confidence in her flames had not
let up. Every strategy he had now included her at the center. It was actually
impossible for Essien to be in all the places he wanted her to be, noted by

little dots and stars on his map. Each night was a negotiation of ensuring that she was harming only corrupt Council members, not innocent civilians, that she wasn't destroying farmland unnecessarily, and that nobody, absolutely nobody, got hurt in her fires. It had been six months of practice, and she could turn the flame on and off just like snuffing out a candlewick between her thumb and forefinger. There was no way she could hurt someone if she didn't want to.

The camp was full of more and more people, and Mansa Musa had made the decision to send them to other camps in different states. A group of them had left just the night before, but there were always more to take their places come the morning. For all intents and purposes, her tent was a storage site because she hardly ever slept a full night's sleep on the cot with its bed square of padding and thick coverlet. She didn't have to conduct patrols as the camp was secure and protected underground with only one way in and a drop off a cliff as the other way out. Nobody had asked her to wake up at 4:00 in the morning, when the sky was just barely beginning to accept the sun's ascent for the day, and it was still dark and peaceful.

It was the constant threat of something or someone finding her that haunted her and compelled her to rise. She'd slip on her boots, and take her uniform rolled up into a bundle to the bathing tent with other toiletries she'd managed to acquire since coming to the camp. There was a woman who made and gave away soaps and bathing oils, another who made butters and creams for skin and hair. Still another who always had dyes and pigments in small clay pots to be used to brighten the eyes or accent the lips. Essien had so badly wanted to cultivate some kind of friendship with the smiling, watchful women, but they only ever had the homemade goods to give and little else. After washing and dressing in the bathing tent, she'd make her way to the entrance where the constant guard wouldn't even attempt to bar her exit up to the tunnels that would take her topside. The entrance was obscured from the casual view of anybody who might be walking near or flying overhead by a cove of thick-trunked trees, leaves, and logs piled up on three sides to hide the tunnel sloping off into a dark hole.

A pair of rebels fell into step behind her as she stepped over the threshold of piled twigs, their footfalls almost too quiet for her to detect. With only a slight rolling of her eyes, she stepped into the open air and made her way through the stands of trees. The rebels who were stationed to follow her were different every day, and these two were not ones she even recognized. They sometimes told her their names, sometimes didn't, and Essien had learned to stop asking. There was so much secrecy here, and she guessed that was to be expected when you were a rebel fighting against your own country.

Essien had felt relatively safe before coming here, though she knew there had been danger of some kind. Now, as she traipsed through the forest every morning as far as she could on foot, she had to accept that it wasn't because she was patrolling or making sure there was no danger coming. There was something dogging her, and she couldn't help repeating the holy man's words to herself. Something out there was hunting her, and she had no idea what it was. Or who.

She had not seen any akukoifo; they were as absent as humans were this far up in the mountains. That both saddened and relieved her. She wasn't sure why, but those weightless beings that she remembered from her childhood, that only she seemed able to see, made her think of the Mothers... and the lake...and the man at the bottom of that lake in the center of the jungle where she was never supposed to go. She stared up at the lightening sky through the trees and was almost glad that they had not come to her again here. It was probably that spell, the one she could feel starting to wane from her even now. She felt a memory hovering on the edge of her consciousness like a word she'd needed and forgotten or a premonition of an event she was just about to experience.

She imagined akukoifo floating around her, breezing through her as a whoosh of air. It filled her with euphoria despite everything that had happened. On the edge of that joy, an angry fear crept in, riding on the scent of her abandon to come and stifle it. Her heart beating up against her throat, Essien searched for the smell of that oil that had been swiped on her the night before and the smell of the incense all mingling together. There was no trace of it anywhere on her skin because she had scrubbed her face clean with water and the moisturizing soap bar made from scratch. She quickly thought of the strongest thing she knew: metal, the hard iron and steel of a rapid fire and the hot metallic lightning flash of projectiles. She tried to calm her breathing and her heart, but in that moment, she could feel that force that she was magnetized toward was still obsessed about getting her back.

One second, she was trying to concentrate on the placement of her steps as the path led upward in a steeper and steeper incline with a gray rock face on one side and the trees angling down the mountain side on the right. The next, she remembered his name: Gabriel. Thoughts of the President flashed through her mind, bombarding that metallic glint like flimsy aluminum sheets, and flooding her consciousness with memories of the last ten years of her life. The wall inside her mind wasn't gone; she was just solidly on the other side of it, so that meant some part of the spell was still working at least. President Gabriel Ijikota—that's what that force was that was now barreling down on her without the shields of the spell's double barriers to keep her safe.

She had done her part these past six months to allow these memories to be washed from her mind without resistance. She had not grabbed for them or clung to the life she had lived before she'd decided to escape that hospital. Now the memories were just there again, and a part of her felt a sorrow and a shame so deep it had her instantly rethinking her newfound recruitment to the rebel cause. This was never what she wanted, she realized.

A grasping guilt took the place of that blank, empty expanse that she had only just been able to reach out and stroke without a thought. The lands she had burned lay in ruins that marred the countryside worse than any strip of concrete poured over green grass and flowering trees would have. She had stood adamantly against burning fields if they were too close to a single compound or village, but she had still burned. She had tried to avoid burning the harvests, if they were on land owned by Council Members, but wasn't that in itself wrong, too? What waste to burn crops before they could be reaped. It wasn't hurting the Councilmen as much as it was hurting the farmers, who had worked hard to till and water and weed and tend those harvests for their own well-being and the well-being of countless communities.

As she remembered more and more of what the spell had forced her to forget, she realized that she had no right to burn in an effort to practice her magic or even to harm the President and bring down his wicked nation one corrupt Council Member, one plagiarized piece of legislation, at a time. The rebels should take their fight straight to him, not do their work in the shadows, behind the skirts of Alkebulan's people.

She knew it was madness as soon as the thought circled back around. No matter what power had awakened in her that she had yet to even fully explore, she could feel that the President's abilities dwarfed her own. He hadn't shown her his true self, not really. She had only seen a glimpse of it when she realized what measures he had taken to ensure she would end up in his military, how many systems he manipulated and maneuvered through to arrive where he was, let alone where he wanted her to be. She remembered that vision he had shown her, of a crown he had placed on her head, and it made her recoil with discomfort that she might ever be worthy of or deserve a status as high as that one.

The rebels wanted to fight the President—that's what they had said. They wanted to bring down the empire he was trying to build before it could even get off the ground. But so far, they were only fighting other Alkebulanians. Yes, powerful, crooked ones in positions to wield too much influence, but Essien felt regret for her actions. She didn't want to use her ability to burn fields or buildings. It was wrong, and eventually, it would catch up to her. Eventually, she would be caught. The rebels would have to rework their plans to not include her. She still didn't remember whether she'd ever heard the President mention any interest in world domination, but when you amass as much power as he had, there was only a matter of time before the drive to gain more never ceased.

Essien stopped on top of a rocky plateau at the edge of a clear view. She could see all the way out past the range of dark mountains that were capped in gray clouds around their peaks. The land stretched out in green and gold squares with irregular circles of blue stretched into flashing ribbons. Low-hanging clouds and the gray smear of paved streets and tall buildings off in the furthest distance.

Behind her, the rebels following her were noisy and loud as they reached the summit where she was. Their breathing was labored, their steps heavy. She knew the air up here was thinner and harder to breathe, and they hadn't been coming up here every day for months like she had. She didn't give them a second to rest before she turned and began trekking her way back down to the campsite.

She thought again about the President, the memory of his face and what he had done to her, pounding over her like successive waves, tugging her out in an unstoppable riptide. He was ruler of all the land and wealth in the richest country on Ala-ani. He had turned the continent into a force to be reckoned with. And now that force was aimed at her like a heat-seeking missile tuned to the frequency of her precise temperature.

She made it back to her tent without receiving a summons from any of the scurrying rebels swarming around the camp. The ones who had eventually followed her back took up posts across the path from her tent. She knew another set would replace them when she exited again later. Her boots *thunked* onto the floor, and she fell face down on the cot. She may have slept, or she may have just lain there with her face pressed into the woolen blanket.

With a pang of remorse so deep—deeper than any emotional wound she'd ever been dealt—Essien thought of her nna. His aged face came into view; the dark skin and dark hair like onyx with silver hairs starting to grow at his temples. He had been such a strong man before his fields had been burned, hardworking and tolerant of her with no end. The fire that ripped through hundreds of stadia in his fields had changed his life forever. And hers.

The remorse turned to sorrow, and the sorrow turned to warm, salty lines slipping down her cheeks and absorbing into the coverlet. It was the first time she had felt this devastated by her own actions, to the point that her chest ached, a constricting press around a hollowed-out space between her ribs. She sat up on the cot and covered her face, biting her lips and sniffing loudly to keep herself from sobbing or moaning out loud.

Oh, Nna, she cried silently. *What have I done? What have I caused?*

"You have to let us cast the spells." Enyemaka and Osiris had come to her tent only moments after she had wiped the wetness off her cheeks and dried them on her pants. Her eyes were probably stained red, and she knew her eyelashes were wet and sticking together. Enyemaka cleared his throat as he always did before calling out to her in that soft, gentle voice he seemed to use only for her. Essien had known in that moment what she had to do.

"Not the spells of forgetting. I don't want to forget. I want to remember everything he's done. You can cast protection, but don't remove what I remember."

Osiris sighed and came closer into the tent. He squatted down on the other side of her from Enyemaka.

"The protection spell is interwoven with the forgetting. It is easier to protect you if your mind does not think of what I am protecting you from."

"Then I don't need your protection anymore."

Enyemaka tried to reason with her. "He will find you if he can sense you, Essien. And if he finds you, he finds us. We have to maintain the integrity of the camp."

"Then I should leave," she said, standing up, forcing him to back up a step. The tent was too small for all three of them, even with the holy man still on his haunches, now head height at the level of her stomach.

"Where will you go?"

"Anywhere but here."

"How will you get there?"

"I have two feet and two legs. I am capable of walking out of here you know. Running even, if the ground wasn't so steep."

"I think we should talk to Mansa Musa before you—"

Essien put a hand against Enyemaka's chest and pushed so that he had to step completely out of her way, his hands coming out to the sides to keep his balance. "Then let's go find him right now."

She was almost at the tent flap, her hand reaching out to smack it aside. Enyemaka's harsh grip on her elbow pulled her back from the entrance and around to face him. He jerked her so hard that she tripped over his feet, and he had to switch from grabbing her by only one arm to holding her around the waist and her arm to ensure she remained upright.

The erratic movement caused Essien to feel anger welling up within her, and yet she stilled in his arms. She had touched him first, so the aggressive response was her fault. She calmly dragged her arm out of his hands and angled her body away from him. He let her go, but his eyes were on her face. Osiris hadn't moved the entire time.

"You cannot go strutting into the war tent and tell them that you're leaving."

She tried to keep her breathing even, but it was becoming harder as she decided to get angry anyway, even though she knew she shouldn't and couldn't afford to.

"Then how do I get out of here? If my being here without that protection spell will put the camp in danger, how do I leave, so that doesn't happen?"

Osiris had a grin on his face as he stared up at her. "By strutting into the war tent and telling them that you're leaving."

The anger melted away in the face of that smile. Essien suddenly wanted to pat his head. She stared back at Enyemaka.

"I will not burn another thing for them. I'm sorry if that disappoints you or if it hurts the cause. The rebels will have to find another weapon. I can't betray what—who I am any longer."

Both men just nodded. Perhaps they had heard her muffled sobs through the tent flap before they'd made their presence known.

"You can't be there. Neither of you. If they try to stop me...I won't let anyone contain me...or use me against my will anymore."

They both nodded again.

Enyemaka moved closer. "I would help you."

She was shaking her head before he could finish. "I won't put your life in danger. Or jeopardize your standing with a cause you care for. If they do what I suspect they might do, these people are going to need you both to rally again and keep the effort going."

Osiris frowned. "What do you suspect they might do?"

Essien stared down at him and didn't want to answer. She looked up at Enyemaka and then back at the kneeling man.

"Pray that they don't do it."

Enyemaka reached for her hand, and this time, Essien knew that he was trying to be gentle.

"I didn't mean to make you feel like you had to leave. We can find another way to—"

"I already know how to block. I realized this morning on my walk that I could block him, and he would be on the other side of that shield still, but he couldn't get in. It's not perfect yet because I might find myself on the other side of that wall, but the wall holds."

Osiris stood up. He said, "Let me do the spell one more time before you leave. It will wear off by tomorrow morning, and you'll be well on your way with at least some added layer of protection."

Essien just shook her head. "I might forget why I'm leaving and stay. And then I'd have to have this realization and this conversation all over again tomorrow morning. I don't want to forget again. It is now my duty... and my atonement to remember."

Osiris said, "You have nothing to atone for, Essien. The error and the fault lies with the man who started all this."

Essien turned back toward the tent flap, her hand already pushing it aside, "Tell that to the guilt I'm carrying now."

They couldn't argue with her on that, so neither of them tried. Both men left the tent with her, Osiris telling her to keep the incense sticks in case she might need them. The smell would at least remind her of her own ability to shield. That cool, impenetrable essence of metal; the sleek dangerousness of a rapid fire; the sharpness of steel; the electrical magnetism of copper. It was inside her mind and surrounded her completely. Essien took a deep breath and headed to the war tent.

CHAPTER EIGHT

◆

ESSIEN WAS GLAD THAT ENYEMAKA HAD NOT COME TO THE the war tent. His role in the camp kept him busy and away from her for most of the day, but he had come to her tent every morning for the past six months to make sure she was protected with smoke and oil. He had done his best to speak sense about the proposed targets in meetings without her where her flames were discussed. Nothing that would put her in too close contact with the military, nothing that would put her in too much danger.

Not even a week ago, they'd wanted her to burn a government building on the edge of a heavily populated village; of course she had refused after seeing it, claiming it was too close to the residential compounds nearby. Enyemaka had spoken up then, offering another location, a field that was harvested for the direct use of state military compounds, to avert their attention. The only buildings near that field were those belonging to and affiliated with the military compound, and their surveillance had already revealed that the majority of its sojas were gone on a mission to the north. When her flames spread to the rapid fire manufacturing facility, the sound of projectiles exploding could be heard long after they had fled the scene.

Despite his trying to protect her, Essien knew that Enyemaka was not a leader of any kind here. He was a layman, someone to do grunt work, send messages, make deliveries. He didn't make the decisions; he was barely able to advise the decision makers. But he'd spoken up in that circle of overly armed men, time and time again, only the second bravest thing she'd ever seen him do.

Mansa Musa had looked at Enyemaka sideways at that last meeting, a glance that had seemed to narrow down into evil, but then he'd clapped him on the shoulder so roughly the much smaller man almost buckled at the knees.

"We will have caution," Mansa said. "We will heed these warnings and not bring too much attention to ourselves." Mansa looked over at her, standing somewhat alone in a space against the farthest wall near the tent's

50 WIELDERS OF FLOODS & FLAMES

exit. His eyes had that same watery sheen over them, like his tears would fall down his cheeks at any second.

Essien was glad to have Enyemaka's support then, but she'd known it was only a matter of time. They would ask more and more of her flames. Eventually, they would force her to burn people, in broad daylight even. It wouldn't matter if it was sojas she'd once trained alongside or locals she'd never met a day in her life. They wanted the President's attention, and that would bring him right down atop her head. She wouldn't be able to hide those awful deeds, so she wouldn't even commit them. Starting down that road was asking for the Mothers to damn her soul.

IT WAS A SOLEMN ROOM WHEN ESSIEN TOLD THEM SHE WAS LEAVing. She walked into the largest tent with a practiced flip of her hand against the flap of gray fabric that covered the opening. They had moved the war tent many times by then, shifting their location by a few stadia every couple of days or couple of weeks, covering the markings of their stakes and fires in the ground.

She entered unannounced into a room full of men talking heatedly about something upsetting them all. The room felt hot, like walking into a wall of stale air. They were huddled over the papers on the tables, new sheets of papyrus added to the maps always spread out there.

As Essien pressed closer, moving shoulders and backs out of her way, she saw the same map they'd been using the entire time she'd been with the rebels. There were more markings on the map now, spots further out from where she had been burning the last half year. That meant they were likely going to be moving again. Some of the spots looked like they covered major cities with larger populations than the local villages. Mansa Musa was pointing and pounding down on different spots on the map. He was angry enough that he was standing up, one hand propping him up on the table, and spittle was flying from his lips as he ranted.

When he saw her stepping up to the table next to him, he stopped midword, almost stumbling over himself to pause and get the other men not to clamor to fill the space he left.

"How now, Essien, we were just speaking of you." Mansa Musa always had a prime position right behind the map. Essien noticed that he was wearing the green overcoat and pants of the rest of the men. The shirt underneath was a thin brown fabric with tears at the neck.

All the men were looking at her now. It felt like being blasted with cold, flat wind. She had come to know some of their names, but at that moment, she couldn't recall a single one. Few had introduced themselves to her after that very first meeting, and fewer still had attempted to make a connection of any kind. She had not gotten to meet any of the women in the camp; Essien got the steady sense that they had been told to stay away from her. Now, the men invited to this planning meeting where she was almost never allowed looked down at her as she walked up to their leader and looked down at him.

"I have to leave. My being here has put the camp in danger, and I must leave immediately." Essien couldn't—didn't want to—explain more than that. They wouldn't understand. They wouldn't accept it anyway. The guilt and shame were there again, pressing into a filmy sheen over her eyes that threatened to fall as surely as the water always collecting in Mansa's eyes.

Mansa's mouth first spread into a smile, but it didn't make his eyes any happier. "We can protect you, Essien. Haven't you been safe here with us?"

Essien tried to blink the tears away as she knew she couldn't cry now. Not when she wanted to convince them she was strong enough to handle what she was heading into. "Would you permit me the use of an engine just to the next town over? I can figure the rest out from there."

Mansa Musa's mouth tightened, his bottom lip thinning and pointing toward his chin. In the silence, Essien shifted her eyes to look at the map that she could now see up close. She saw one of the target markers was covering Biafra. There was nothing on the map to indicate where they were, so she still had no idea. Were they in Dogon? Maybe Mbuti or Himba State? She couldn't tell, and she was focused on scanning that map for any sign of the rebel camp's current location.

Suddenly, multiple hands grabbed for her wrists, other arms wrapped around her shoulders, and a foot swiped her legs out to bring her to the ground. Mansa Musa must've given some silent signal she was too engrossed in the map to see. The room was a rushing clamor of hands grabbing her, more hands than were needed from anyone who was near, anyone who could help to pin her hands and prevent her from firing those deadly flames.

For a moment, Essien felt the weight of them all trying to hold her down. She was still too surprised to even start struggling yet. They should have knocked her out like Enyemaka had done on the skycraft that had flown her away from the hospital. They were all too late to stop her.

The fire seared out of every pore of her skin at once, the red and yellow blazing up around her, catching instantly on the hands that were holding her, the legs near her head, all the way up the walls she could see above her. There were screams now, the hoarse cries of men who were already dead and those lamenting their own stupidity as the cause of it.

Essien felt the flames intensify as the fire turned each of them into nothing recognizable. The fire crackled and devoured in her ears, drowning down the sounds of the shouts and yells from further inside the tent, then from outside the tent. The camp must have realized what was burning and that they couldn't stop it. She stood up from the ground easily now, the black soot falling off her in sheets of ashes. She took a deep breath and blew out air that pushed more fire up to the very top of the tent, spreading it wide all the way to the very back.

She walked forward through the flames, her own body a burning, twisting wick of blue and white at the center of the red and orange blaze that raged and grew. Everything around her was covered in flames consuming with a fierceness that felt almost like joy.

There were more shouts outside, and Essien could hear them contemplating whether they should risk wasting the water to try and put it out. There were other shouts asking how many people were inside. Even a shout asking where she was. Essien said nothing and just let her head tilt back with the power of the flames that roared out of her unrestrained. She ignored the sweat beginning on her brow and the smell of burning hair that wafted down to her from the flames above her head.

When she was done, her breath was sharp in her parched throat, her tongue sat stiff and useless, stuck to the roof of her mouth. Still, she smiled. The tent and everything in it had burned into thick, sooty ashes that drifted away in a spread of dust through a suddenly blowing wind. The metal boxes that once lined the walls up to the ceiling had melted down into oddly shaped puddles, the weapons once inside now just quickly solidifying metals. None of the tents around them had been touched by even an ember.

She felt her temperature cool into a light sweat across her forehead and upper lip. She felt lightheaded and had to sit down, stepping over the soot piled up on the ground, crunching bits rolling under her now bare feet.

Essien peered out of the destruction of the war tent; not even the metal girders framing the tent had survived.

Essien stepped out of the whirling smoke and flying ashes between the melted frames of the now destroyed tent into the crowd of people that had gathered. There were gasps and shouts and cries of "Mothers save us!" There were faces gaping at her standing there alone, naked now as her own clothes had incinerated in the first spread of the blaze.

One of the rebels standing closest immediately took off his tunic and tossed it to her. She caught it without reaction and slipped it on over her arms, buttoning the front, so that she was covered to her knees.

She hadn't thought about who would be attracted to the flames, not when she'd sparked them up to keep the men from pinning her. She scanned those faces now and saw Enyemaka and Osiris at the edge, hesitant to come nearer where the burnt tent once stood.

In a surprising display of fealty Essien had never before experienced, and didn't want to explain to herself, all those standing before her suddenly dropped down as one onto their knees and prostrated before her, putting their foreheads to the ground. Some lay flat with their faces pushed into the grass and the mud, the ashes blowing over them as the wind continued to draft upward. As all present kept their heads down, Essien noticed both men and women in the crowd.

Essien bowed slightly in return, the movement automatic and bestowed upon her by years of her mother's etiquette training. She glanced at where Enyemaka and Osiris had been, but they had joined the crowd and lay flat on the ground with them. She couldn't see their faces, couldn't tell if they wanted her to stay or to go. So, she turned, and as she walked forward, the people parted to let her through. When she was clear of most of the crowd, she began to run.

CHAPTER NINE

◆

THE PRESIDENT OF ALKEBULAN STEWED IN HIS UNHAPPINESS. It pressed in on him from all sides, and there was an answering press from inside him, too. Despite presiding over the largest, richest continent on Ala-ani, everything made him feel uneasy and uncomfortable. Before him, from where he stood on the balcony of the highest floor, Alkebulan was teeming and bustling with raw, unfiltered energy. Light seeped out of the ground in rich brown and neon green lines. It flowed up from the sea beyond the land with vibrating glints of blue.

The energy of the nation and the continent filled the air with a shifting, dizzying swirl. He could glide casually over all that motion, fingering through it lazily like a hand dangling from the side of a water vessel. He could immerse himself in it, being torn and twisted by every jagged edge, soothed and comforted by weightless beings. He could shut himself off from it completely, a hardened stone, unmoved and unmoving, as he had done for years.

His vision turned inward from all that frenetic energy to an image, a face. It was a lovely face, dark and serious, with high cheekbones and a glossy mane of curls resting over her shoulders. Her eyes held a flickering red flame in their midnight dark depths if he looked into them for too long.

He felt suddenly that he wanted to see that face before him more than he wanted anything else, more than he wanted the continued position of being President. He would willingly give up all that he had been building for decades if it meant he could have her before him. If it was a sacrifice she wanted, he had his life to offer her for the taking whenever she pleased. But, she hated him. And Gabriel had been searching for her for six months.

With that countenance in a mental picture, he opened the place inside him where he kept all of his power. An energy that rivaled the invisible flood pouring up over the earth and overflowing from the sea. Opening himself up felt like the immediate propulsion of crude oil from hidden crevices deep within ocean rocks.

He allowed the overwhelming pulse of his energy long unfree to mix with the energy that surged up from the landmass beneath him. His skin tingled with the sensation of the purest release, beads of sweat pooling on the bridge of his nose and the dip of his upper lip.

It was a feeling he hadn't felt in a long time; he couldn't remember how long. The mix of his own energy mingled with the energy from the land and the people of Alkebulan, and he felt himself scatter in infinite directions.

He was being pulled by everything around him, as far as the edges of the continent to the north and the south and the east and the west. A mother nursing her newborn son, a father staring proudly out at fields of grain and orchards of trees, a dutiful daughter scribbling equations in a crisp notepad, a rebellious son using handfuls of raw meat to tame a lion. It was an unseen energy, the particles translucent to the eye but felt by every atom in his body.

The tumultuous energy rushed in and out of him unimpeded. He was wide open to receive, like the place where rivers meet oceans, where tectonic plates bulge, where stars swirl around each other and collide. There were grandmothers and grandfathers, aged and wizened, some bed stricken, others slowly strolling through rapidly modernizing villages. There were babies, crawling over the ground, putting bugs into their pink mouths, screaming to be fed at a dripping breast. There were akukoifo, spirit guides, gesturing and waving to him from the air, begging to be let out or let in. He longed most desperately to go to them and rest awhile.

Gabriel hadn't opened himself this wide in a very long time. Always, he held himself and his power clenched tightly, so that no one around him would sense the abyss within him. He had seen the looks on peoples' faces when he'd let his power leak out unexpectedly, how frightened and wary of him they became. Now, the freedom and release made tiny water droplets gather in a layer of sheen over all his skin, and his breathing was fast, even though he stood still. He had to concentrate to focus the energy on the task before him and not simply float in the luxuriant feeling of finally being unbound. He needed to find Essien; and he needed to find her fast.

Essien had been afraid of his power, too. Not so afraid that she'd cringed before him like a submissive coward. No, she had been afraid but brave, standing up to him with an underlying fierceness that she didn't even fully realize she possessed. He remembered how she had gone against him the day he had tried to teach her to execute criminals. How fiercely she had rejected the offer of more power than she had ever dreamed of having. She had wanted to join the military to avenge a wrong done to her family. The heights she had attained were not what she had planned for herself, that much he knew.

He recalled how, the day of the festival to honor her assent in his military, he had wanted her to wear a slip dress and stacks that would have elevated her several inches taller. Something so minor and inconsequential, a uniform as surely as the one she wore as a member of his Guard. She had railed against it, almost as strongly as she had rejected the power he tried to show her she had within. She had balked at the level of control that was inherent to the very role she had signed up for.

Essien was the one prick of pain that made him wince and wish he could go back in time instead of always rushing forward. She had escaped without a trace from the hospital where she had been transported after the accident at the festival. There had been no sightings of her since.

Upon learning of her disappearance, he had overreacted and roared a great shout that shook the windowpanes, sent cracks lining up the walls, and then a great wave of water appeared and filled the entire island compound, flooding everything in it. He had nearly drowned his Guard in his emotional outburst. If he was a lesser power, countless invaluable artifacts would have been destroyed by the flooding. Still, the attendants and cooks and even his Guard cast covert glances his way, worrying about when he might spill over next.

He knew he would have to be more intentional in his search for Essien. The power itself required him to search for her, pushing him and goading him in the static he felt without her. In the six months since, his being had tried more than once to slip away from the confines of his skin to float untethered and high above everything. He was finding it harder and harder to be in his body the longer and further Essien was away from him.

Without physical motion, his hands gripping the balcony railing tightly to keep him planted, he rushed over the people and the plants and the animals covering the surface of Alkebulan. Despite the creation-energy flowing over, around, and through him, all he could sense was a painful lack that made him feel helpless, and lifeless, too. The energy of the land he reigned over and the people who had elected him to reign should have bolstered and strengthened. It typically made him feel an unspeakable joy because it was all his, and theirs, and one day hers. But Essien had left him, gone completely, without a trace, and everything felt less real without her.

That thought startled him solidly back into his body, his consciousness sliding into the meaty, jointed, long-boned cage. He turned to walk back into the office beyond the patio doors, just one of the many in the compound that he had not used in these many months. He didn't even see the light-wood desk with its chair pushed up to the desktop covered in stacks of papers that were starting to spill over onto each other, papers that were calling on him to fulfill his responsibility as President of Alkebulan.

Gabriel had realized, with a quick flash of epiphany that sometimes struck him, that he had begun the process of bonding Essien as his kwere nkwa—his promised—the one his elder mother had told him about. But it was more than that, she was his soulbound, his onye ndu. And yet, no word could fully encompass what Essien was on the verge of becoming to him. He stared down at the pair of brown leather armchairs in front of the desk and then down at the cream and brown rug on the floor, and then back out through the open balcony doors. He stared out until the horizon met the sea, but he wasn't seeing any of it. He had known better. His thoughts rushed far and away, and then back, chasing after the origins of a realization that should have been impossible.

He had never bonded anyone as his onye ndu, in all his years, even though he knew how to do it. His Nne nne, his mother's mother, had taught him, like her Nne nne had taught her before him. She had shown him how to cast the spells, the words to use, the supplies he would need to perform the rituals, the exact steps to take to link his life energy—the very essence of his power—to a person or a place. She had cautioned him in the teaching to be wise and not mark anyone unless they were his promised, his kwere nkwa, that fated woman who would be sent to walk beside him while he led Alkebulan as godhead. Those lofty, preposterous dreams his elder mother had given him, her face and hands gentle but her words fierce.

"She will come to you, when you need her."

He knew that whoever he chose to bind would become a literal part of his being, as connected and closely tied to him as his heart and lungs, inescapable and irreplaceable. As a result, he had not marked anyone yet. Partly from fear, but mostly from great respect for his Nne nne. She had told him roughly, so that he could explain the mechanics of it, could imagine himself doing it, but he had no recollection of beginning the process with Essien.

This knowledge should have relieved him, but it only made him feel sicker. He stepped over the rug with quick steps and yanked the office door open. Two guards were stationed in the hallway, one right outside the door and one at the bank of rises that would take him to any of the floors below or above him.

Down the hall he stalked without seeing the metallic gold floor winking his own reflection in its mirrored surface, a turn, and he yanked open the door leading to his bedroom. Then he was in his closet and pulling off the thin tunic and loose pants he'd been wearing for uncounted days past. He pulled on fresh clothes without bathing. He was moved by something that felt much like shame and frustration with himself. Gabriel felt horribly appalled that he had already begun such a sacred ritual without his or her knowledge. He had not put it together before just now that this grinding ache within him was a result of a bond left unfinished.

He was her superior, her boss, her commander, he gave her orders... there was no way he could...he hadn't let himself realize just how much he had come to depend on her. He needed her to do her job, so that he could do his. He had not thought consciously about bonding her as that would require her knowledge that he could—at the very least, her presence. As he knew it, the spells did not require her willing participation. The spells and the resulting bond would be strongest and deepest if she accepted it and agreed to the bond being placed. Some irrational and uncontrolled part of him had been conjuring up its own plans, plans to one day make Essien a goddess. In his humanity, he had been merely trying to make her a Queen to his King. It was a day that he might never see now.

He stepped onto the rise and descended to the second floor where Antonious and the rest of his senior Guard had their rooms and offices and personal training areas. He could have called ahead for them, but it was no use. He stepped onto an open space with white floors, white wallpaper, and a soft white carpet. The absence of any color made him pause and feel like he had lost his hearing for a second.

The men who were sitting on the chairs immediately stood and snapped into tense stances of awaiting orders. The President waved a hand at them to relax, but he didn't stop to assure them. One of them followed him as he headed down the hall and turned a corner at the end that opened onto Antonious's office space. There was an anteroom with more seating, this time soft blue fabric covered armchairs and a longer gray couch sat beneath a window. The floor was a hard pale wood in geometric shapes. Antonious was sitting at the desk that Gabriel could see through the open office door. He entered and closed the door behind him.

Antonious was an ageless man; he had probably looked like an elderly man in his cradle. He gave off an air of wisdom from the broad jaw, the flat, broad nose, and the high forehead. His hair was completely white with some dark silver speckled in. He always wore gray suits, their sleeves, cuffs, and lapels embroidered finely, and expensive loafers that made no sound. He had been by the President's side for many decades now. Antonious had his own vantage point with another window behind his desk where he could watch all the way out to the very eastern side of the island. Beyond it was a dusky blue expanse where the sky flirted endlessly with the sea. Distantly, Gabriel could just make out the pale smear of the sandy beaches on the mainland. He had built his home on Capital Island, a mountainous, tree-strewn rock hanging off the edge of the continent south of Igbo State, his homeland, to celebrate his heritage. Now it just felt isolated, keeping him even further from finding Essien.

The island still had its own indigenous peoples, who had been considered Alkebulanians since the War of Unification. Their land was left largely undisturbed by the mainlanders who ventured over as vacationers and day visitors, none being allowed to set up permanent homes. The island off the west coast of Alkebulan was a third of the size of Tear Drop Island situated at the southeasternmost edge of the country. Gabriel was the first President to reside on Capital Island, and he wanted to be the last. But he would need Essien for that.

"Did you know I had started to bond with Essien? Did you...sense it on her?" His question was abrupt, but he did not have energy or will for the niceties of polite courtesy.

Antonious seemed confused at his words at first, a frown punching the middle of his forehead into an indent. He put down the gold pen he'd been using to write on a white pad of paper. Gabriel looked down at the notepad on Antonious' clean, bare desk, the notes in a small, boxy handwriting at the very bottom of each line. He couldn't read what was written there, but he hoped that Antonious was drafting some plan for finding Essien. The older man flipped the black folder next to the pad closed and sat back in the gray leather desk chair. He almost seemed to blend into its monotone surface behind him in his matching gray tunic and pants.

"The onye ndu..." Gabriel spoke again. "Did you ever feel it on her when she was around? When we interacted? Did she feel like...like she had been bonded to me?"

A muscle in Antonious' jaw clenched, like he was biting back what he wanted to say. That flinch almost always preceded anything the much older man spoke.

"Do you want me to answer honestly or in a way that will absolve you of any wrongdoing here?"

The agonizing suffocation of helplessness was new to him. Gabriel stared down at Antonious, the shorter, dedicated right hand who was never reluctant to speak reason into his near insanity. He felt himself settle more completely back into the unwashed skin and unshaven beard of his physical body, the result of days if not weeks of searching for Essien without ceasing. Despite the obsession that preoccupied his every waking moment for the last half a year, he had not yet come to accept its constant presence. He sighed a gust of air that sounded almost like a growl.

"I want the truth. I need to know what I've done." He didn't like to admit it to himself even now, but Essien's vanishing had left a vacuum both in his military command structure and in the deepest part of himself that he didn't like to look at very often. He had been only half hearing and part skimming the reports that were delivered to him first thing every morning. The stacks were piling up on his desks in all three of his offices. Essien's disappearance had left a vacancy in the countryside as well with rebels being inspired to resurge even fiercer than ever. He wondered if Essien might have joined them, but shrugged at the thought of it. She loved her country too much to ever betray it.

Antonious simply said, "You already know what I am going to say."

"Say it anyway."

"The day you first met her."

Gabriel's brows went down into the wrinkles that might become permanent if he didn't figure out a way to de-stress himself. He tried to remember the first day he had met her, not with the eyes that had seen her by the lake that first time. Not the day of her hearing when he had just so happened to be at the Council House and passing by in the hallway. He had decided at the last minute to stay and preside over her testimony against the complaint of her parents. They had demanded in multiple letters sent directly to him that she be expelled from the military. They had based their wishes on the orders of a village elder's decree that no girls or women were to join the military or face being exiled. They had begged him to send their only daughter home. Unbeknownst to them, their letters had only deepened his intrigue when he realized who she was. He had not spoken to her that day at the Council House; he had just bored into her mind as she'd answered the long ream of questions meant to determine if she were fit to join his Soja...and eventually his Guard.

Gabriel shook his head, trying to dislodge a memory. Antonious thankfully went on. "That day in the jail cell, after she'd killed three men and admitted to conspiring to kill two others. When you walked into that jail cell and saw her, I felt every single one of your layers of protection drop, even the ones you have up automatically, without thinking. Every spell and shield you had against the magic of others was down when you touched her. You held her hand. She was covered in blood, three different types of blood. You didn't need more of a ritual or paraphernalia than that. It was enough to start the process unconsciously. It's clearly not finished, or she'd be here, but...you likely wouldn't need much of anything else to complete the bond."

Gabriel had sat down in one of the matching brown leather armchairs in front of Antonious's plain dark wood desk. He dropped his head into his palm, his elbow rested on his knee, and he groaned. That was not what he wanted to hear.

"What do I do now? How do I find her?" He asked the question out loud, but he wasn't expecting Antonious to answer.

When the man began speaking, it was Gabriel's turn to bite back what he really wanted to say.

"Ser, you are languishing here, while people have need of you everywhere. You are pining after a woman that may never be yours. Your attendants are afraid to go near you. Even the Guard is hesitant when asked who will cover you each day. Your office desk is piling up with your obligations, presidential and personal. You are in crisis, and you need to gather a firm hold of yourself!"

Gabriel stood. He knew the man was right. Antonious had been guiding him rightly for so long that Gabriel felt the man had risen in tandem. With every promotion and leap Gabriel had earned, the older man had been alongside him making the same strides and gains. Now here he was, sitting in that chair trying not to let his own irritation and anger show. Gabriel just shook his head, not capable of returning the anger.

He turned to leave, too much left unsaid between them. Behind him, Antonious dropped a final remark. "The rebels are spreading. Faster than we can track them now. Entire villages are turning, taking up the cause. And we cannot find them anywhere! It is like they are invisible to us. If you do not act quickly to stop them, Ser, there won't be much your Presidency can do that won't appear barbaric and tyrannical to wrest control from them."

Gabriel stood completely immobile, his eyes on the ground. He pressed against his temples with his thumb and second finger, rubbing in circles to give himself time to think.

"I have been searching for Essien every day since she disappeared. Somehow, she has managed to achieve the intolerable and become invisible to me. The only people in Alkebulan with the power to be invisible to me are likely those rebels.... She must have joined with them!" Gabriel paused, staring down at the ground, his chest squeezing tight against his lungs so that taking a full breath was hard. His chest rose and fell quickly, and he put a hand on the back of a nearby chair.

He went on, still staring at the floor, his shoulders heaving. "With a thought, I can instantly picture every corner and crevice of this continent. Essien must be in a hiding hole or some obscure location that I can't peer into...even though I can see everything without moving an inch from where I'm standing right now." He finally got his breathing under his control, his chest rising and falling quietly. He looked up at Antonious. "When I first saw her, she was just a rebellious girl by the side of a lake in the center of the jungle." The melding place of silver-blue waters rose up before his vision. Gabriel choked and had to stop. He breathed deep, filling every inch of his broad shoulders and considerable height.

"And later, long after that first meeting, I told her the truth...almost all of it. She ran from me, Antonious. That wasn't how I imagined she'd react; no prevision could have revealed that she would try to escape and succeed, right in front of my eyes like a sneaky market thief." He stopped again, keeping the next thoughts to himself even in front of Antonious, his most trusted companion.

He had orchestrated so much to get her near him and to keep her close, but now that connection was broken, possibly forever. He had known she was unhappy with him, that she was angry even, but this felt like a betrayal that he hadn't earned. He had been good to her, he thought. He hadn't been as harsh as he could have been, as he would be if he ever found her again. And he *would* find her. He had to. She might have learned how to block him, but she would not be able to outrun old-fashioned manpower and legwork.

Looking at his right hand over his shoulder, he said, "Prepare one hundred thousand sojas for a nationwide search. Equip them with heat seekers and night-vision sensors, so they might travel when the sun is down. I want them on foot, door to door, inch by inch. I want her found. Do that, Oga, and then you can speak to me again about presidential obligations."

At least he had told the truth. He couldn't focus on anything else except the one most pressing concern before him. He and his right hand didn't have to be at odds on the matter at all. He had always thought Antonious liked Essien. Especially with the way he had appointed himself as kenye-maka, a friend, to help and protect Essien during her first few years in the military. He knew the man would do his best to carry out the small request he had made. He had never given Gabriel reason to mistrust or suspect his loyalty. As efficient and practical as he was, Antonious would ensure his request was implemented easily and quickly. If he didn't, then there were other positions for the man to hold.

Antonious was silent for a moment, staring at the back of his much taller boss. Then he reached over and swiped the phone communicator from its cradle. He pressed a few buttons on the front of it and held it up to his ear. Antonious stared at the ceiling while he waited.

A voice answered through the speaker, and Antonious didn't bother to whisper as he spoke into the receiver: "Increase the current search times ten.... Then send half up from the Southern compounds. It will cover the same area much faster.... I know we need them elsewhere, but I cannot speak sense to him now."

Gabriel snorted and spoke from where he was standing between the threshold of Antonious's office: "When her location is found, tell them no one is to approach her. Notify me immediately; I will be the one who brings her in."

"Make sure she isn't approached when they find her; he wants her alive," Antonious relayed and then replaced the earpiece.

"And Antonious?" Gabriel was staring at him with a hardened look, his eyes shielded by his eyelids. "I think the compound on the mainland could use your presence."

Antonious listened to the hard crack of the President's steps as they led away to the bank of rises, and then silence. Antonious sighed and stood as he began silently gathering the few items on top of his desk.

CHAPTER TEN

◆

GABRIEL WAS SITTING IN THE FORMAL DINING HALL ON THE first floor for his morning meal. The cornucopia of dishes spread before him were all ones that he had previously tasted but hadn't touched again: plantain porridge with coconut milk and groundnut sprinkled on top, chopped fruits covered with a sweet cream glaze, and several black and red teas steeping in warmed cane juice. He sat silently at the table staring at the seat diagonal to his; it was empty and pushed all the way up to the table.

Though he hadn't given it much attention, the newsprints had begun writing steadily about the revived rebel raids. Rebel camps hidden in the forests and jungles of the central states were looting crops, burning buildings, and devastating more than just the local surrounding villages. The burns were causing financial damage to investments that Gabriel himself had been told would bring prosperity to the country. Details in reports that he used to read documenting sales and purchases that were meant to fill their coffers to an unprecedented balance. Gabriel wondered again if Essien had joined the rebels. It would be so unlike her, but her flames...they could cause the level of destruction that was being reported.

The President knew that today he needed to head over to the Council House, to meet with the Military Council. They had called for him some weeks ago, and he had only just now mustered himself to make the trek over the bridge. He had even allowed the attendants to bathe and dress him in clean and crisp black attire that befitted his position.

Gabriel had just picked up his spoon, dipping it into the thick yellow porridge, when a teenage girl flounced into the dining hall. She had reddish skin and even redder hair done in thick locks hanging down to her waist with white and brown cowrie shells worked into the locks near her face. She was wearing a dark blue uwe with sandals, and she was carrying a large, empty woven basket on her arm.

The girl walked boldly up to where he sat in his dining hall and said, "I want to know what you will do about the rebels as President, Ser. My family's native village in Maasai State was nearly torched when a fire spread from the building that was being burned. The roof of my grandmother's own compound caught fire and almost collapsed upon my family living there. We could be heading home to plan funeral rites instead of here serving you.

"You should do something about the crisis in the fields, Ser. I am pleading with you. A president should protect his people. That's your job, isn't it? To make sure Alkebulanians are kept safe? Well, we are not safe, Ser. We are in danger, and you need to do something about it." With that, she had turned and stormed out of the dining room, her basket swinging off one arm. The audacity of the girl reminded him of Essien.

He thought of the girl again when the military chaperone he ordered carried him over the thin bridge connecting the island to the mainland. Of course, he had not been reading the newsprints, and lately, he hadn't been reading his own intelligence reports either. Nothing contained news on Essien's whereabouts, so in his unconscious mind, they ceased to matter.

The city of Lagos rushed by in red, yellow, and brown blurs before he was being escorted into the Council House. The building was statuesque at the end of Lagos Street with several perimeters of sojas gathered in the streets leading up to it. The Military Council had been assembled at his request. In total, there were 12 military councilmen from each state with 144 tribal councilmen sent as representatives from the oldest villages in each state. This Council meeting room was smaller than the room they used for full assemblies. This one had just enough chairs for the Councilmen and one or two others. There were a series of inward facing tables lined up in two rectangles with the one in the middle descending down one step into the black-carpeted floor surrounded by the polished white stone. Gabriel sat at the head of the black wood table, his elbows propped up on the surface. The white paneled walls around him made him feel cut adrift and hopelessly lost.

One of the Council Members, the oldest of them, said, "Eze, we are so fortunate you could be here."

Gabriel nodded but kept his eyes down on the table. "Is there...any news about Essien?" He had to ask, but just saying her name made the seam of his exterior creak open again. He felt himself wanting to slip back out of his body like discarding all his clothes into a pile on the floor. He had been searching for her so intensely it felt unusual to be inside his skin, talking, sitting still in one place. Essien had gone from him in a way that would not have been possible had he marked her completely. That partial bonding he had begun was not enough for him to locate her now, but just enough to let him feel a sickening, unusual weakness where none had been before.

The men around the table exchanged a look, like bouncing a rubber ball between walls.

The oldest member spoke again. "There are other, more pertinent duties to which the President must attend. That is still you, Ser." The formal tone was indeed mockery, and the President knew it. He felt upbraided like iodine on fresh wounds. He made the effort to contain his instant rage, but the pressure from focusing so hard to remain in his body put Essien at the front of his mind almost instantly. He suddenly did not want to be there talking to these men who had been lording over this Council House, some of them for decades longer than he had been alive.

Looking around at them all, their faces were a mixture of beleaguered endurance and veiled hostility. Whatever else they might have wanted to say to him would have to wait.

"Finding Essien takes precedence over it all," he finally said. Even to him, his voice sounded too soft.

Another Council Member spoke up, this one newer and with less military prestige attached to his name. "Ser, we can assure you that the Military Investigations Team is handling her search and seizure. Your part is here. Otherwise, you will exhaust yourself and be no good to us as a leader."

Gabriel nodded, faintly bobbing his head up and down. He and his council did not have to be at odds. He had never liked any of the Council Members from Igbo State. They had stood in the way of one too many of his promotions and initiatives over the last quarter century. At least half of them had wanted to execute Essien after she...

Another Council Member took their turn now that he appeared sensible. "Something has to be done about the raids and the attacks. Businesses and enterprises are being hampered and delayed. The people in the villages most affected are creating patrols of their own to keep the crops safe after dark using large knives and heavy mallets. Nevertheless, the losses for untended farms continue to mount. We sent an economic report of the impact to you; it was reams and reams long. Did you read it and see the devastation that's being wrought?"

Gabriel had to shake his head.

A final member spoke up from the other end of the table: "We have convened a full Military and Tribal Council House Assembly to discuss the matter. Please, Ser, we ask that you be there." A full assembly had not been called since the legislation for presidential expansion had been passed. The legislation that had turned his limited term into a lifetime position. As long as he lived, he would be President of Alkebulan. The full assembly had gleefully passed the law, and Gabriel had let them think it was all their idea. Now he could only nod. There were other things said, but Gabriel soon stood, prompting them to fall into silence, and walked from the room while one of them was still talking.

Before leaving the hall, Gabriel met with a small, nervous woman who he was told held the position of agricultural planning director. One of the many roles that functioned without his notice and often without his gratitude. He was thinking of the girl from that morning when he ordered a delivery of two tons of produce and several trucks worth of building materials to be shipped right away to the impacted villages in Maasai State.

"Where shall we take the harvests from?" A soft but firm question that he knew meant there was little to spare and even less justification for it.

"Donate them from the national harvest collection."

"The national collection is already falling short, Ser. The fires have destroyed more than a quarter of the reserves for feeding sojas...." Her voice trailed off, but Gabriel knew what she meant.

"We'll just have to increase our exports to feed our legions. Don't turn anybody away." The woman nodded and turned to begin relaying his orders.

Gabriel lay in bed that night wondering if his actions today were enough to make it seem as though he were stepping into action and helping, that he hadn't forgotten his role as leader. Perhaps he needed to record a newsreel to play at the top of the morning and the bottom of the evening. The last newsreel he'd recorded had been the day Essien had been presented with her presidential service award. The people might need to see his face and hear his words to know that he was still their President, even if they hadn't seen him for months. Even if it seemed as though he had left them to be devoured. He didn't sleep that night, his exterior leaking open as he lay, and all of Alkebulan rushed underneath him.

CHAPTER ELEVEN

◆

THE ENGINE THAT CARRIED GABRIEL BACK ONTO THE MAIN-land the next day was swift, and the streets of Lagos were soon bus-tling around the vehicle. The floor of glittering black marble stone and the walls of dark wood panels led him into the shocking white expanse of the President's assembly room. Above his head, a balcony teetered on the outer edge of the cavernous room above the main dais at the front on the lowest level. Gabriel was seated on that raised dais on the viewing platform. An-other table of blackwood with a wide-backed cushioned chair that didn't match. The walls usually had floor-to-ceiling windows at spaced intervals on one wall of the assembly room behind him, but today, long, ornate silver and white wall hangings were pulled all the way around, so that Gabriel felt boxed in and suffocated.

The assembly sat in the armchair seats arranged in half-circle rows in front of the viewing platform, lined up all the way to the back of the first level with more curving rows on the second-level balcony. The Council Members were all present in their military and tribal regalia, and Gabriel felt a tinge of pride at the people of his nation gathered. There were the flowing silk agbadas of the Igbo and Yoruba tribes, the stiff skirts and beaded headwear of the Mbuti, the floor-dragging robes and tunics of the Amazigh and Moor peoples of Berber, the colorful yarns and intricate patterns of the Zulu people, the simple black-and-white-lined tunics and skirts of the Xhosa tribe, the ochre-red painted skin of the Himba tribe, and so many other colors pressing into the crowd. They were all present and accounted for, women now joining the assembly through the Tribal Council Member rolls. Gabriel almost smiled at how beautiful they all looked before him with every seat filled. When he remembered that they were likely there to admonish him for his negligence, a muscle in his jaw clenched.

Gabriel tuned back into the fervent speeches just as the Councilmen from nearby Maasai and Bantu states traded places to continue their rant.

"Something must be done!" shouted the man in a blood-red shawl and robes with multihued beads piled around his neck, biceps, wrists, calves, and ankles. He carried a carved wooden staff with him that he thumped on the ground to accent each word. "Burning our crops is inhumane! Do they mean to starve us on our own lands? How can this be? The rebels must be caught and executed to send a message! When will those on high speak for those who are down low? When will you stop them and make this right?"

The man paused, and the Councilman from Bantu State stepped up to take his place. He was wearing a brown shawl and robes adorned with feathers and gold beads that flashed as he moved back and forth, raising his arms in the air as he faced first Gabriel and then the other Councilmen. "So far, these rebels, these traitors to our country, have only burned buildings and our harvest to a crisp, leaving us hungry and dependent on the government for yams and vine fruit to survive. It is only a matter of time before these rebels turn on us, and we lose our lives. If you are with us, Ser, then you must rally all of your might behind us."

Gabriel opened his mouth to respond as the doors leading into the assembly hall began to open. When they did, a military official from the local military compound heaved a lungful of air, as if he had just completed a long run. Antonious appeared behind the man and solemnly closed the doors. Gabriel was irritated at the unprofessional disruption until he heard what the man was saying.

"Almost half the number...of rebels in the Bantu State camp...just disappeared." He was still trying to catch his breath as he walked closer to where Gabriel sat up on the dais at the front of the room.

"What is that to do with Essien?" She was the only explanation that would precipitate someone bursting into this closed assembly. He hadn't heard any good news yet.

The man had caught his breath and went on in a hurried, low tone, trying to speak for only the President to hear him. "We have reports of a woman emerging from a fire, more than fifty of the men being gone. Nothing but thick, black soot on the grass to say they had been there at all. We sent in operatives to search the villages."

Gabriel moved to the edge of the chair, preparing to rise. "Where is she?"

"Reports are vague and uninformative as to where. There were a considerable number of rebels still present on site when we arrived. Almost like they were too shocked or stunned to react. They say she ran off into the forest surrounding the camp, and none of them followed her. There was no trail when the first of our operatives arrived. She could have traveled north or south of the state's borders. The rebel camp had a skycraft, but it was not on site when we arrived. There was just the empty landing patch."

For a second, he had hoped they might have uncovered her exact location. The man said almost half gone, so did that mean there were less than two hundred of them left? They must have threatened her or tried to harm her. She wouldn't have killed them on a whim or for anything less than self-defense. Capturing her would prove to be more dangerous now than it had been at the start. There were other powers he could use to subdue her besides water, but he couldn't use fire. That was her magic alone.

Gabriel blew air out between his lips and said, "She could not have left the country without me knowing, not through any international aircraft with her own credentials."

"We are continuing to search the country and have swept all regions at least once so far. We are beginning a second search from the midline north and south in just a couple days. The remaining rebels we captured are being transferred to a holding facility until their trials and sentencing."

Gabriel stood and stepped off the dais. He put out his hand, and the man reached to touch palms with the gratitude of the forgiven.

"I appreciate the update. Why isn't the search starting today?"

"We dispatched every available soja to the rebel camp, and there is no one else we can spare from their current posts."

"Fine. Send them outward from the camp. They should start by searching the immediate area and moving outward. It's how she would move. We're just not sure of the direction."

"We'll have some preliminary units sent out tonight, Ser."

"Make sure I am notified the minute she is found. And have a travel plan prepared for me immediately."

Gabriel glanced back at the assembly of Council Members waiting for him. They had been covertly and not so subtly eavesdropping, but from the looks on their faces, they hadn't heard anything after the military official lowered his voice. Glancing at the timepiece on his wrist, Gabriel realized that the assembly would run for at least another two or three hours if everyone had a turn to speak. He needed time to process and decide his next steps.

He shifted his eyes to Antonious who nodded and moved forward down the aisle, his voice loud and distracting. The older man would continue the assembly without him and inform him of anything he personally needed to know. Gabriel was in a waiting engine and briskly traveling back to Capital Island before his thoughts caught up to his body.

He realized that in a short space of time, he had elevated Essien to a higher status in his mind than the concerns of the entirety of Alkebulan. She had taken precedence over everything, even himself. This state of being was the lowest he'd ever sunk, lower even than when he made the decision to leave his first wife. Amachi had been a petulant child next to Essien. His first wife had whined about his late hours and his early mornings, his constant travels and how hot his skin always felt against hers.

Amachi had nagged him about their lack of reproducing, and he had shunned her for the same. On the other hand, the girl who had joined his military and taken it for her own was more, less...utterly different. He still struggled to name what she was to him—not his wife and likely never to be. She was a decade and a half his junior. He had already died many times before she was even born. He had no right to think of her in this way, and yet still, he did.

He had made and accepted a decision about her that he hadn't even acknowledged to himself. He had decided that she must be connected to him permanently, a link turned into diamond, an eternal, unbreakable bond that would keep her with him forever. She would never be able to leave him again once he had completed the bonding. She would never be able to disappear or become invisible to him. He would never experience such a feeling of loss ever again.

Once he found Essien—if he found her—he would harden that connection he had begun with her and make it impossible for her to be free of him. He would have her with him for eternity, as it should have been from the beginning, as it had always been from the past, as it would always be in the future. He just needed to find her.

That night, he stayed up long enough to watch the sun rise and turn the sea flaming yellow, the tall tower of stone on the coast of the island a dark gray, and the rippling short grass into dark golden bends leading up to his stone compound. As he took in the multitude of colors and the morphing scape, his mind kept dashing back to the past before jumping forward to the hereafter that might never be.

When Essien had burnt the bodies at the Festival, he had felt the stirring of something inside her like a coiled lash waiting to be unleashed. A power that had no end or form, distinctively hers to wield. A power that she didn't even know she possessed. A power that might one day make his own powers look like flimsy playthings. He hoped she never discovered that power, but upon hearing himself, he realized that wasn't true. He wanted her to become as powerful as she could because that helped to solidify his own power base. He just didn't want her to ever learn to use that power against him.

THERE WAS ONLY ONE THOUGHT IN HIS MIND AS HE LAY ON HIS back in his empty bed staring out the balcony windows. His compound... that island...it had become small and unimportant upon hearing one message about Essien—and not even the message he had been hoping for. He wanted to be on the mainland, out searching for Essien himself. If he could get up into the sky, Gabriel reasoned, perhaps he could help search for her more effectively than on the ground.

Before the paleness of dawn had arrived, Gabriel called for Antonious. He could no longer run down to the rise and descend to the man's office and adjacent rooms. He had to use the communicator to reach him. His response time had grown to half an hour since his relocation to the compound Gabriel had set aside for him in his retirement. The man wasn't retired, not even close, but having him further away was proving both an inconvenience and a necessity. "Order a skycraft for me. I want to move to the compound in Zulu State. I haven't been there in years. Come along, if you're up for it."

Left unstated was his wish to delude himself into believing that flying in a skycraft and moving to the mainland would help him search better than standing there on his balcony would. It wasn't that she was gone or that she was dead; she was hiding from him. Somehow, she had learned blocking without his teaching her. Gabriel felt a chill spread through his ribs and into his lungs, making him feel like he was suffocating. He realized she had already learned what he didn't want her to learn, and it hadn't mattered whether he taught her or not.

CHAPTER TWELVE

◆

ESSIEN WAS WEARING A DIRTY TUNIC AND TOO-SMALL SLACKS that hit almost to her mid calf, when she hopped off the back of the engine she had begged a ride from. Her arms and legs were scraped and scratched in bright red lines, some that seeped. Around her swarmed a chaotic and busy village with large engines lumbering down stone streets, pedestrians scampering around their head-height wheels. Crowded stands and stalls and business compounds lined the walkway with fruits and vegetables freshly picked from the fields. Dine-in kitchens already steamed and smoked as they prepared fragrant foods from the fresh, local produce. There were other services, like travel agents, career placement services, and internet boonas—trendy places to buy seasonal drinks and use the electronics for a small fee.

She saw a woman with a large mane of dark brown hair and a train of children following behind her, each a smaller version of the one before. Essien watched a group of men pull up to the shipping center and quickly load an engine full of boxes and crates with the country's military seal emblazoned on all their sides—a lion's head imposed over an outline of Alkebulan. Essien hurried in the opposite direction.

A few blocks down, she saw a small older man walking slowly with a walking stick, wearing vision correctors. He wore a red shawl wrapped over one shoulder and around his waist with a mantle of black and white beading over his shoulders. His back was hunched, and he walked with a slow contemplation of each step and the careful placement of his stick.

"Pardon, Ser. What state might this be?"

The old man looked up at her from where he had been staring at the ground and smiled the smile of a man seeing a beautiful woman and becoming happy that she had stopped to speak to him. His bright white teeth sat in a face that was a deep mahogany, polished smooth and shiny like wooden furniture. The walking stick was made of a light-colored wood with darker grains running down in lines.

The man kept smiling as he said, "Xhosa State, young one. How did you come to be here? Where do you travel? Have you been hurt? Come to my home, and I can bandage you."

"I was passing through, no need to worry. I'm heading for the next town over," she tried to interject. But the man spoke so quickly and with such authority that Essien found herself following him in the direction she had been walking anyway.

"You seem parched as well. This heat, ehn? Where did you say you came from? The heat can be rough on tourists. They don't expect it; the ocean is right there, how can it be so hot?" He reminded her of her nna nna ukwu, her father's grandfather, a man she had met only as a blur in her earliest memories. She remembered that he was funny, always joking around, and he never stopped talking either. It made her trust the old man almost instantly, not even questioning the wisdom of the impromptu decision.

The man walked slowly as he stared up at her. "I am a physician. Well, I once was. I have bandages and ointment. I live quickly over here. Come." The man's pace sped up, his staff making a tap-tap-tap sound the faster he walked. He took a hold of Essien's elbow to make sure she stayed with him.

"You are burning up. Have you been running? You need eucalyptus and mint."

"I'm fine. My blood is just warm."

"I cannot walk fast, but my compound is here. I am just coming back from my third wife's grave. I like to visit her most. All my wives are buried in the same mounds. A few of my children, too."

They had reached a two-story stone compound with a tall wooden fence all around it. The man tapped through the fence and up to his front door. He pushed it open with a shove of his shoulder, no key in sight.

"Come in; do not worry about darkness, it will brighten soon."

Essien followed the old man through a dark and dusty front room with shrouded shapes of furniture under yellowed tarps. He stopped near a cabinet in the kitchen and took down a basket from an open shelf just above his head. The basket was filled with medical supplies, liquids in glass vials, bandages, gauze, tape, scissors, and even thread and thin needles sealed in thin envelopes. He pointed at a wooden chair next to a round dining table, and Essien sat. He reached for the arm with the deepest scratches.

"Let me see. You have so many scars. How did you get this scar on your arm? Was it an attack?" She stared down at her own arm as if it had just sprouted at the end of her shoulder. There were so many scars marking her skin; she couldn't tell which one he was pointing at.

"I used to work a very dangerous job."

The man used his right index finger to point to the smooth, pink scar from when she was attacked with the machete at the Festival. It's what led to her losing control of her fire and burning all those people. Essien closed her eyes as the feeling of ashes seemed to burn her nose and crumble between her fingers. She moved her arm away with her eyes closed.

"Who would attack a beautiful woman like you?" The old man was working quickly, pulling out vials and lining up bandages and tape. "Forgive me, the ointment stings a little, but it will heal you. I use it on all my aches and pains, and they go right away."

Essien let him quietly work on her arms, gritting her teeth when the dark reddish-brown liquid he dabbed on her scrapes did in fact sting. Then he lifted her leg up on a chair to clean and bandage the scrapes there. Essien let him tape the last bandage and then stood as if to leave.

"I'm sorry you have to leave so soon. I have fried plantain and fish. You like some?"

"I don't want to impose any further, Ser."

The man smacked his lips, "I am Utatomkhulu Kamakhulu, and you will see I make the best fried fish." The man walked over to the farthest cabinet where several platters were resting underneath glass domes with running lines of condensation as he lifted each one. The smell of fried foods made Essien's stomach stretch and yawn. Essien nodded, the reluctance gone, and the man began setting out two filets of fish with a pile of plantain next to it on a wooden platter. He handed the plate to Essien.

"Thank you," she said. The man sat next to her while she began pinching pieces of the fish off the spine and rib bones.

"I have fourteen daughters and two sons, but everybody lives in other states now; two of my daughters have gone all the way to Iroquois. A better country than Alkebulan because of the weather and the landmarks, she says, but I told her I would mash her for telling such lies. No country on Ala-ani is better than Alkebulan, you see."

Essien nodded. The fish was warm and came easily off the thin, translucent bones in white chunks covered in golden brown crisp. She ate bite after bite while Ser Utatomkhulu Kamakhulu prattled on, moving about his kitchen doing absentminded tidying, moving a dish here, setting a cup there.

Essien had finished the plantain and was on the last piece of fish. She slowed, trying to savor each perfectly seasoned bite.

"The fish is so flaky and crispy, yes? Here, take this piece," he said as he put another filet on her plate. "So good ehn?"

She waved her hand. "You've been too kind. Please, save the rest for yourself."

At that, the man reached over and added yet another filet. "I cannot finish them myself. Take two and eat well...You were a soja, you say?"

Essien's head snapped up, but the old man was looking down at his feet, his chin resting on his hands folded over the head of the staff. "Oh yes, yes, I remember. A woman joined the Guard some years ago then. How now, is that woman you?"

She shook her head, and then feeling guilty, nodded once. "Ehn, the people of Xhosa State commend you. Let me bless your hands and your feet." The old man leaned down over his staff to sprinkle little splatters of spit on her, droplets hitting the back of her hand and her leg nearest him. Essien stood, meaning to leave then.

"Yes, I understand, you must go. Take the extra fish and plantain." The old man quickly wrapped more of the fish and plantain into a strip of parchment he peeled off a roll. He then wrapped it into a green cloth bag he pulled from another drawer. Essien shook her head, backing toward the door she could see at the end of the kitchen.

"Yes, take, please, I have plenty more; you should see my garden. I will let you out back, so you can pass through it." The old man moved around her to open the back door. The smiling yellow heads of sunflowers and the grasping vines of red seed fruit greeted her as she walked off the back steps. "Oh, you water my house on this day, young one. Go with the Mothers now. Be watered."

Essien left the man's compound as quickly as she could to avoid being spotted or stopped by anyone else. It was unrealistic to expect no one to recognize her. The old man clearly figured it out in the end, and so would anyone else who stared at her for too long. She walked up the stone street in the same direction they had traveled. She was thankful for the food and the medicine for her cuts, but she still needed to find shelter and figure out what she was going to do. She could not access her money. She had no belongings. She had nothing to her name. She could not go home. She could not go back to the military. She could not stay where she was. Essien knew that she would kill or be killed if they ever found her. And the rebel group might even have spies searching for her, too. She had numerous enemies to avoid, and no idea when or where they might come for her. But she still had a weapon. A powerful, deadly weapon.

She pushed her one free hand down into the pocket of her borrowed tunic. Whatever she was to do, it would require money. If she withdrew Naira from her bank, it would draw Gabriel and his military down on her head immediately. How could she make money?

She was so deep in thought that when she first saw the sign, it took her a second to understand what it meant. Wanted: Human hair for wigs. Inquire within. The sign was in the glass window of a hair shop. She could see a few people sitting down inside. She had heard of women selling their hair, women with long hair that reached their waists and lower. Her mother had hair that reached her thighs. Thick, curly, shiny black hair that she kept braided in oily ropes that she twisted around her head and pinned.

Essien had been growing her hair since she was a teenager. She had also grown into the custom of wearing her hair braided in a bun at the back of her head, low and tight. It made it easier to wear her headgear. She would take the braids down every few days to unravel it and pull out shed hairs. Then she would oil her hair with butter and rebraid it, the same way her mother did when she was younger. She had not measured her hair's length in many years. She had not rebraided her hair in many weeks.

When she had joined the military, she had considered cutting it off in an attempt to fit in better with the other men and make her life easier with not having to braid and rebraid so often. But she had quickly dispensed with the idea, believing that she would not erase her femininity just to fit in. Keeping them looped toward the back of her head was good enough for the cap she was required to wear as a part of her military uniform.

She walked into the hair shop, the sound of bells signaling her arrival. Three women turned to look at her. They were coffee-colored women, with golden streaks in their brown hair and dark stone eyes. Essien thought they all looked alike, maybe mother and daughters.

"Do you need a style today, nwaanyi?"

Essien shook her head and pointed at the sign. "I want to sell my hair. How much?" She felt momentary discomfort about cutting her hair, but she knew she needed the money. If the price was reasonable, she would do it.

"We pay five thousand Naira for one-third meter minimum, ten thousand for two-thirds meter, and twenty thousand for one meter. More if over that, but we've never had that long. We measure, then cut and pay."

Essien nodded and then set down her package of fish and plantain to begin unraveling her hair. She had to remove the pins and then she carefully loosened the braided ropes. Black specks of ashes fell out of her braids as she began unbraiding them. The women's mouths dropped as they watched her unbraiding each thick rope. When she was finished, her hair stood around her entire upper body like a massive fluffy black cloud.

They brought out a measuring rope and held it up to her scalp. They stretched it all the way down to the ends of her hair. The longest strands went past the one-meter mark at the end of their rope. Essien was as shocked as the women. She had not realized that her hair had grown to be so long; far past her hips.

"We wash and dry, then cut. Twenty thousand Naira okay for you?"

"Thirty would be better."

Two of the women looked at each other, frowning, but then the eldest-looking one of the three spoke up. "We can do it."

One woman washed Essien's strands at a metal-bowl-stand, being gentle but firm on her scalp. The suds smelled sharp and clean, like laundry soap. Another one of the women slathered on thick yellow globs of shea butter, working it in until the hair was smooth. She dried the hair using an air blower that sucked the hair tight and let it go straight and flat. Essien stared at herself in the mirror, her hair like a silky black cape around her body all the way down to her knees. It was the longest her hair had ever been.

Two of the women rebraided her hair, in bigger braids this time. Then, the shears came out. Essien closed her eyes. She listened as the snips moved around her head. Her nose stung, and she knew she wanted to cry. Yes, it was hair, and hair would inevitably grow back. Essien knew that and had been growing her hair since she was a preteen. Then, it had been in hopes of one day performing her rites and rituals of womanhood, the secret ceremonies only initiates were allowed to attend. The ceremonies involved weeks of practice and preparation leading up to it. And much of it centered around hair, caring for the hair, styling the hair, growing to understand the science and artistry of hair. It was an important cultural moment. And Essien had been deprived of it. Her nne had been too distraught by her joining the military to go through the ordeal of preparing Essien for them. She hadn't learned those ancient secrets, and now, she probably never would. One of them involved cutting the hair—the proper tools and the process. Now, realizing what was fueling her sorrow, she decided she would not cry over chopped hair. She tried to take deep breaths through her trembling lips and not be so weak. When the hair was chopped, she heard water spritzing over her, and she smelled lavender and rosemary.

"You can look now."

The woman Essien saw in the mirror looked like a softer version of Femi with rounder cheeks and wide eyes. Her hair was a mass of shiny coils hanging just above her ears and only slightly touching her neck at the bottom. She reached up to run her hands over the shortened curls. They felt so soft and light on her fingers. She rubbed the back of her neck and then the front of her head again.

"I finally look like my brothers now," she heard herself saying.

The thirty thousand Naira was handed to her in a white square of papyrus. Essien knew if they were paying her that much for her hair, they were selling it for a great deal more. She had not known anyone who wore wigs, but she had seen newscasters wearing them on nightly news reports and watched them on performers at festivals and one-acts.

As Essien was leaving, she heard one of the women mutter excitedly, "We probably make one hundred wigs, each one thousand Naira." Essien heard the sound of the two younger women smacking palms as the door swung closed.

Essien walked back out into the streets of the village with a better mood. She had Naira in her pocket and food in her belly. Now she just needed somewhere to stay while she figured out what to do next. She thought about going back to ask the women in the hair shop if they could direct her to a rooming compound, but she didn't want to draw suspicion or curiosity. She walked on. The packet of fish and plantain was turning soggy with grease in her hand, so she stopped to finish the rest, sitting on a bench outside an engine repair shop.

She came to a travel station before she found a rooming compound. As she walked up, a large steel engine with a long trail of passenger compartments behind it rolled in. The sound of metal clanging on metal as the smoking engine came to a stop, and people spilled out. Cost of travel was fifty Naira for the next state over, one hundred to reach Igbo State. She knew she could not go home. It was likely that every official in the state was alerted to look for her. Not to mention the operatives the President had likely already sent out searching. Quietly though, she knew he would not use news reports or post missing persons adverts. Just the steady tread of boots over terrain, with one goal in mind: recapturing her.

A man's voice interrupted her thoughts. "Nwaanyi, lady, I have a ticket to Ndebele that I cannot use anymore. You can buy it?"

Essien stared at the young man warily. He was dressed nicely in a clean tan suit and dark sandals. There was an older woman wearing a head-and-face covering standing nearby whose eyes were all for them. *Perhaps his mother*, Essien thought.

"How much?" she asked. If it was less than the cost of a ticket to Igbo State, she would buy it.

"Just fifty Naira. I paid seventy-five Naira, but you can have it for fifty."

SHE BOARDED THE TRAVELING ENGINE, FIFTY NAIRA SHORTER. She would travel to Ndebele, a city in the northern part of Xhosa State. It wasn't a major city, not a metropolis like Mfengu, or even heavily populated like some of the smaller villages, namely Lomwe and Sena. The difference was quaint, neighborly villages that were large enough to give some anonymity but small enough to make strangers stand out. She would try to blend in or isolate herself in a hideout; she wasn't yet sure. She knew that she could not draw attention to her person. There were some who might recognize her even without the hair. She remembered the old man. She would have to be careful; there was only so much help she could take before it drew suspicion or a query. A life on the run from the most powerful man in the country—not one of her smartest decisions to date.

CHAPTER THIRTEEN

◆

THE FIRST PLACE IN XHOSA STATE WHERE THE ENGINE LET her off was practically deserted. There were red stone buildings lined up in front of a gray stone path butted up against a jungle with very few paths trekking into it. It was the perfect terrain for Essien to navigate.

Rather than head further into the town bordering the trees, she turned toward the emerald darkness and pushed her way into it. The sun was still high up in the sky, so she easily picked her way through the bushes and shrubs down near her knees. As she moved along she came upon a flutter of butterflies flitting around in bands of sunlight filtering down through the canopy high above. She also heard the occasional hoots and screeches of birds and monkeys in distant trees, and saw lines of ants carrying chopped pieces of leaves down a tree's trunk. But she neither heard nor saw any other humans.

She walked for a long time before happening upon an empty cove of trees circling around a bare space of ground. The circle was irregular, and there were two thick-trunked trees close together with their roots forming an almost solid ground between them. Essien spun around in the cleared-out space and wondered who had formed the trees in such a way that let sunlight drift down while staying close and sheltered, creating an isolated space in the wider jungle around her. Essien sat down with her back against one of the trees and listened to the sounds of nature, rustling here and there, gentle buzzing, with the sun and the wind covering it all like icing made of a cool breeze and golden color.

It was deep night by the time she picked her way back to the nearby town. The lights out front of red stone buildings let her know which were still open. Loud laughter met her at the door inside one of the first buildings. The room was filled with small tables, more than half of them occupied. A man was sitting behind a waist-high counter covered with mixed drinks swirling around in clear kegs full of ice.

"A drink for the ara?" The man opened a pink mouth empty of teeth. He reached yellowish brown hands for a glass and waved his hands over the jugs.

"Do you have hibiscus fizz?"

The man's smile grew, and he gestured to one of the jugs with a bright red liquid inside. He used a silver ladle hanging into the jug to dip up the liquid with falling streams and chunks of ice.

"Three Naira."

Essien paid with a small bill from the money in her pocket and accepted the drink. She took her first sip standing there at the table. The strength of spirits gagged her, and she stared at the glass in her hand with a grimace wrinkling her forehead and pinching her lips together. The man laughed, staring at her face and then threw his head back to laugh even louder.

"That's nothing like the hibiscus fizz I grew up drinking."

"This is the version for grown-ups. Keep drinking, you'll like it."

She hadn't planned on staying, but she took a seat at one of the tables at the back of the room. She took another tentative sip of the drink and smacked her lips. It was sweet after she got past the shock of the taste of hard liquor. She couldn't name what was in the drink beyond the sweetness of the purple flowers she'd grown up drinking. She'd have to ask her nne one day if this is how she drank hers back then. That sorrow between her ribs tried to expand, but ignoring it, she sipped more of the fruity poison and looked around the room.

The people around the mmanya, the nearly full drinking hall, had gone back to talking to each other instead of staring at her, so she could look around at them now. Most of them were couples, men and women, or two women, out for a night of drinking, dancing, and partying. She could almost tell which pairs were on a romantic date and which were just friends.

The women were dressed up and made up in short uwes. The men were wearing suits or tunics and slacks. Some of the men were grabby, sitting on the same side as the women and holding on to their arms and legs. The women sitting with women were giggly and kept touching each other, too, but more like they were trying to draw everyone's attention than being romantically involved. There was a group of men on the far side of the room at a table playing what looked like betting cards. They were loud, and Essien noticed Naira piled up in the center of the table.

Essien sat there until she finished her drink, listening to the music playing. The drums transported her somewhere else, and she forgot herself for a second. She forgot why she'd ended up in Xhosa State; she forgot why she'd entered this building.

The only thing she could recall was how good it had felt to burn those men, their bodies succumbing to a force that nothing could quench. Essien looked down and realized that her hand around the glass had started to emit small flames, their orange tongues licking around the lip.

She jumped up, shoved her hand into the pocket of her tunic, put her head down, and burst out the door. Upon reaching outside, she took in great mouthfuls of the night air.

Looking around, there were other lights on in front of similar buildings. A crowd of younger-looking teens stood together at the end of the street. Essien's feet took her in the opposite direction.

There were streets intersecting, and she turned down random blocks without thinking. She stared at the sides of the buildings, trying to decipher what each one might be. They stopped being stone and turned into metal and then glass. On the front of one of the glass buildings up ahead, a sign flashed on and off in neon color: Rooms.

Essien hurried toward the building, turning down the street that would take her right up to its doors. The smell of something strong and toxic filled her nose, a harsh, gagging scent that made her recoil. A broad chest behind her head and another one in front of her, two more peeling out of the shadows around her, another face covered up to its nose with just a band of pale flesh around the eyes showing through.

That's when Essien knew that she wasn't safe. She tried to spark her flames, but the smell was making her nauseous, and the man in front of her was wavering from side to side. She felt like she was sinking slowly to the ground. She tried to grab on to something, to find that heat inside her core and snatch it free, but in spite of her desperate efforts, she was unable. Above her, the neon blue sign continued blinking on and off.

CHAPTER FOURTEEN

◆

ESSIEN TRIED TO OPEN HER EYES, BUT THEY FELT STICKY AND clung together. She felt her face lying against something soft and wet. Her arms ached from her shoulder blades, tight and pinned back, all the way down to her wrists, cuffed together and bound to her ankles. It felt like something was wrapped tightly over her eyes and around her head. She knew she was lying on her side, and that she was tied up.

She kept her eyes closed and fought not to move around too much. There was utter silence around her, but that did not mean she was alone. She strained to hear, the sounds of outside slowly filtering in like distant and muffled swishes and whirs. She kept her breathing slow and even, and though her arms hurt terribly, she didn't try to move them.

Nothing around her moved as she tried to open her eyes again, and they slowly peeled open. Utter darkness, not a sliver of light from anywhere. She contemplated sparking up a tiny flame to enable her to see. *What if someone is here and watching me, or what if I'm lying in gasoline*, she thought, feeling the wetness of the floor. Whoever had kidnapped her likely knew about the flames; it's why they'd knocked her unconscious with whatever that smell had been. She remembered the stench of it being harsh and toxic.

Essien tried to sit up, flexing her abs and her back, and she managed to rock into a sitting position. Her arms were behind her, and there was a chain attaching her ankles to her wrists that was just long enough for her arms to rest on the floor behind her back with her knees drawn up almost to her chest. No matter what way she turned her head, she couldn't see anything. She desperately wanted to create a light to see, but she didn't know if she'd rather see what was around her or remain in the dark.

Just when Essien was about to risk a small prick of white light, she heard footsteps thudding closer to where she was. There had to be a door in front of her and a hallway beyond that door.

A bright burst of light hit her full in the face, seeping in around the cloth tied over her eyes. She cringed away as best she could. Those footsteps thudded in heavy and loud right up to where her own feet were chained and tucked up against her butt. She kept her eyes closed, even though she was blindfolded, fear making her mouth dry and metallic. She couldn't breathe let alone smell or hear. It was as if she were trying not to be there.

A hand, not as rough as she expected, yanked her up under one arm. She tried to stand even with her hands tight behind her back. The chain between her ankles was long enough for her to take short, shuffling steps like a waddling duck.

"Your convoy won't be here for another hour." The voice was male, but Essien couldn't place the accent. "There's been another threat while we're waiting, and we're moving you to a different site." The hand on her arm was covered with a glove, and she knew that hard metal prick against her back was the barrel of a rapid fire. Whether it was a legal 5,000-round limit or something illegal from other shores, it would still do the trick if taking her out was the goal.

"If you try to light me up, I'm going to shoot through your spine. Either way, you're dead. Got me?" Essien kept her eyes closed; she didn't want to see where she was or who was leading her out of the dark room.

"I said, got me?" The man gave her a push and she stumbled forward. With her arms tied behind her and her feet shackled, she couldn't catch herself, and she hit the ground on her side, her shoulder taking most of the impact. She groaned as the radiating pain shot up and down her arm and back, but she gritted her teeth to keep the sounds in. She wasn't going to give whoever it was the satisfaction of breaking her or letting them see her hurt. A hand reached down to lift her up again and tightened even further to help her start walking down what Essien presumed was a hallway. The ground was hard and sticky like wood that hadn't been washed recently. There was the hard *thunk* of a step up at the tip of her toes. The hand pushed her up a step and then another one, and she realized that they were climbing up. Wherever she had been, it was down, perhaps a subterranean level. Up the stairs she went without being able to see and having to trust that the hand on her arm would keep her from falling.

The steps leveled out, and she took a deep breath.

She felt hands at her head and then the blindfold was removed; the relief in pressure from her head no longer being wrapped was instant. She opened her eyes as she was led through what appeared to be a large auditorium. Essien knew then that she was in a military compound, although she wasn't sure which. She cursed internally because she had thought she'd come to Xhosa, a state with no compound. There were posters on the walls, a screen projector straight ahead of her, and chairs spread out in rows. It was familiar to her, as Essien knew well the feeling of the orderly, clean military compounds situated across the country, where she had spent her first few years in the Soja.

The next thing she noticed was the man leading her. He was covered head to toe in a silver suit that crinkled and wheezed with each step he took. He was holding the chain connected to her wrists and ankles in one hand. He had a rapid fire held against her side with the other.

Essien pushed away the memories that tried to rise at being back on a military compound. Now wasn't the time. Not now with those chains on her ankles and wrists. She wanted them off. It was an insult, and she wanted to weep with the realization that she was in those chains by choice.

Before she could think too deeply about what she was about to do, Essien turned on the river of flames inside her. For a fraction of a second, she thought they weren't working. She could feel the wind of the fire in her hands behind her back. The chains didn't even settle; she'd have to turn the heat up hotter than she'd ever burned to melt those chains. She considered that she would be naked once she stepped out of flames that hot and gave a mental shrug as she let the flames eat over her wrists and forearms and catch onto the hand clenched tightly around her arm.

It was only a few milliseconds before the fire seared inward, past the supposedly protective silver suit, past the decidedly dangerous weapon pointed right at her, and the man was all but a cascading pile of ash, the rapid fire clattering to the ground, black specks still falling as Essien took a few steps away from him. The chain burned bright red as it slowly began to melt and dissolve from around her wrists and then her ankles. She could feel the heat of the metal against her skin, its near searing starting to sizzle her flesh. She gritted her teeth, shut her eyes, and kept burning.

Slowly, slowly, the felt the chain begin to flex and then stretch. She pulled her arms further and further apart, the metal white-hot now. Finally, the chain stretched and stretched until she could slip her hands out of their links and let them fall to the ground. Parts of them burned and singed through the floor, the metal so hot it melted right through the wood down to the stone beneath.

Essien rubbed her wrists, the skin red and tender, and then bent to pick up the rapid fire the man had dropped. She used both hands to hold it tight and secure it against her hip. The shame of being naked as the day she was born tried to overwhelm her, but she pushed it away like she had pushed away her sadness earlier. She would get out of this situation like she had gotten out of all the others. There was nothing and no one who could stop her. And, with an ironic smile that set her eyes glowing like a banked fire, Essien was happy to realize that she didn't need the rapid fire in her hands to protect herself from anything or anyone. Not even chains could hold her.

There was a counter against the far wall covered with electronics and pamphlets in piles, and the area in front of it was full of armchairs. Fabric-covered seats were grouped in inviting circles, and she longed to sink into one of those deep, cushiony spots.

The front of the compound was a wall of windows with a glass door that showed a clear view straight out to the front of the property. There were engines parked haphazardly, and Essien didn't recognize anything about where she was out over the horizon. There wasn't the familiar ring of brown mountains or the line of green trees leading down to a circle of shiny blue. There was just gravel and then dirt and the sky beyond it.

The growing darkness was misted across with thin streaks of silver white, the sun long gone but not forgotten as the last golden tinge pushed out from beneath the foggy covering. Essien watched the sun die in its bloody orange glory with the rapid fire tucked up against her hip. No one came for her, but she knew they were out there.

She could feel them, not as strong as she would if she'd linked with them on purpose. But there were energy sparks out there that kept shrinking and rising, probably with anticipation or anxiety. They were waiting for her to come out and threatening her to stay in. It was obviously a trap. What were they waiting for? What was she waiting for?

Then she remembered the man who had come for her. She looked down at the pile of ashes that he had become. He had said she had an hour until they came. That meant one thing, or rather one person. They had called Gabriel, and he was likely already on his way.

Essien peered out of those glass windows and knew that if she didn't go now, the President would be here within the hour. That's why they hadn't stormed her inside or brought the building down around her ears. He would want her alive, and if they fought her, she would not feel the same way about them.

A deep breath later, Essien whirled out of the front of the compound in a spattering of broken glass and busted bricks, the roar of a red lion flame rushing behind the explosion. The men who had been sent to keep her pinned down didn't see anything beyond a bright red flash, like that prophesied supernova of the sun. They didn't even have time to pray.

CHAPTER FIFTEEN

◆

H E WAS SURPRISED BY THE INDUSTRIOUSNESS OF THE REBELS as they trekked deep into the jungle and then began their descent into the underground parts of their camp. He was gaping at the subterranean architecture, trying not to show his awe too publicly. These were his self-declared enemies, a group that had been fighting against Alkebulan since before he was even born. He hadn't read many of the reports lately, but he knew enough to know that they were dangerous. That they were damaging both the country and their fellow countrymen. And Essien had been among them for months. Had likely aided their cause up until this point. What point had she reached to both side with them and then turn against them in the same way?

It was a carefully executed destruction, Gabriel mused as he walked around the burned-out remnants of the tent that had been the rebel's war tent, according to the intelligence information being quietly whispered into his ear by a site commander whose name he'd heard when he first arrived but would have to ask for again. Essien had torched it so completely that little remained to even identify what or how many. She must have gotten training somehow, he thought as he craned his head this way and that to take in the pattern of soot marks that licked against the tents on the sides of the wrecked one in the center of them. He glanced around at the crowd of rebels off to one side, kneeling in a patch of sunlight that suggested a happier time was being had.

Looking into the faces of the men and some women who had lived alongside Essien for months now, Gabriel wanted to interrogate them all personally. What had she done here? What had she said? What crimes had she committed? How had she been more useful to the traitors than her own country?

Most of the rebels refused to look into his face, but one of them glared at him with a ferocity that made him want a circle of Guards around the man. But it wouldn't do for the people to see him execute rebels without first giving them a trial. So, instead, Gabriel smirked and walked over to stand in front of the group closest to the man.

Kneeling on the ground, he was much shorter than the others around him. He didn't seem to curve in on himself, shoulders hunched, like many of those next to him. His face was thin and angular, but his eyes caught the light like sunlight on glass windows and shined brightly from his face. A slow smile spread over Gabriel's lips as he stared down at the rebel he now recognized.

"Oh, Enyemaka, how now? Is that you? What a time, what a time. I did not expect to see a former member of my Uzo Nchedo squatting among derelicts. You have fallen further than the height you had to fall." Several guards standing over the rebels, with rapid fires out and pointed, chuckled at his joke.

Enyemaka said nothing, but the scowl on his face sank even deeper, turning his jaw into a hard triangle as he bit back words he likely wanted to shoot at the man. Gabriel smiled and walked closer, squatting down to be almost eye level with him. A guard stepped up close and put the sharp end of their rapid fire right up against Enyemaka's neck. The threat was obvious.

"Where is she?" he asked.

Enyemaka just snarled, a satisfied smirk crossing over his face. Gabriel frowned and stood. He stared down at the man who had once lived in his own home. He ran his eyes over the rest of the rebels there. More of them were looking at him with hostile stares. He probably deserved it for what he was about to do next.

"Take him. Bring him back to the compound. I want him interrogated further." The guard behind Enyemaka leaned down to yank him up. The smaller man stumbled and couldn't get his footing as the guard dragged him away toward the area where they had parked their engines, unable to get them this far into the forest.

The rebels on the ground didn't even react. They didn't try to get away or stop him from taking one of their own. Their faces were turned up to him, and for a moment, he wondered what she would think of him when she learned what he was about to do.

There would be no trial for those who still remained. That would only be used to embolden and further recruit more traitors. He would end this resistance here and now. Essien had already taken care of part of it for him, he realized with a grin. Their leaders were dead by flames and now they were about to die in almost the same way.

Gabriel didn't give it a second thought before he unleashed a flow of water from the air funneling directly into the lungs through the noses and mouths of every rebel on the ground before him. It was neat and almost soundless. They all immediately began to choke and splutter, most of them falling prone on their backs or falling forward in an attempt to retch up the water. Some of them began flopping around on the ground as they were inundated with water, neatly though—there were no splashes or waves. He continued his organized flood while they tried to gag and scream and cough up the water that he was sending down their noses and mouths without even exerting himself. There were gurgles and gasps that choked off, and less of them moved. Still he flooded them, the water now starting to leak out into a puddle around the bodies that had fallen and were still.

One of the Guard stepped to his side; even that movement seemed reluctant.

The "Ser" the man emitted made Gabriel turn toward him. The guard was looking down at the people on the ground. The water continued to puddle underneath them, the dirt darkening as it soaked in. The man was frowning and trying not to, his forehead creasing and then uncreasing as he watched. Gabriel thought of Essien and that scowl she almost always wore. He could count the times he'd seen her smile. She would be frowning at him, too, if she'd been standing there instead. With an irreverent shrug, Gabriel halted the water he'd been flooding. Nobody on the ground moved.

THE TREK BACK TO THE ENGINES WAS QUIET AND SWEATY, AND Gabriel had given the order before leaving to destroy the underground labyrinth. His commander had looked puzzled at first, and then asked tentatively, "Should we search deeper for anyone inside?" Gabriel had shrugged, leaving it up to the man to decide. They'd gotten lucky in that most of the rebels they'd apprehended had been standing plainly in site. They'd secured the area, but they hadn't searched further underground. If the rest of the underground camp was booby-trapped, he risked losing squad members. If there were others inside, they might be armed and prepared to withstand a siege of any length of time. If the camp was connected to a network of underground camps, they might finally rout out the rest of the rebels. As his concern shifted elsewhere, Gabriel left it up to the commander to decide.

The man seemed ill prepared to make a decision, and Gabriel heard him call for the engineering corps to join him on site as his escorts prepared to lead him out of the jungle.

As Gabriel sank into the engine's front passenger seat, his communicator began to alert him. A few swipes on the screen, and he was reading an urgent report. His eyes scanned again and again as his grip tightened around the device in his palm. At the same time, his escort's communicator began to crackle to life with an alert as well.

Gabriel stared out the window, but he wasn't seeing the lush green terrain passing by swiftly. A row of signs for market stalls with fresh produce and then the row of wooden market stalls zoomed by as he stared out. Beside him, his driver glanced sideways at him.

He noticed and said, "If she's in Xhosa State, then she's traveling fast. She must be using the rail system."

"The command to alter our location has been received, at your orders, Ser. We are heading to Xhosa State."

"This engine won't get there fast enough. We need sky travel."

"What of the prisoner?"

Gabriel absentmindedly replied, "Have them send him ahead to the holding facility in Zulu State. He can wait. We'll head to the nearest skycraft transportation center."

Gabriel's forehead slowly began to crease as he tried to ponder the puzzle he'd been alerted to. Essien had been captured by a squad stationed in Xhosa State. He almost didn't believe it. It felt too good to be true, and he was waiting for disappointment to set in. To have captured both Enyemaka and Essien in the same day? She'd get to watch her friend's trial personally. She'd get to see what Gabriel could do to him, and that she couldn't stop him. Reminding her that he could do this to anyone she loved. She needed to be brought under control, and if this was the way, he would use every tool he possessed. There was one tool, a powerful tool, that was eager to be unleashed upon her, more eager than he was. Gabriel gritted his teeth to remind himself to remain reined in. He couldn't afford any more accidental eruptions of his power, especially not in public. He would have to use that power with caution, and only when she was right in front of him. It wouldn't work any other way.

HOURS LATER, THE ENGINE REACHED THE NEAREST TRANSPOR-
tation center. If they had driven straight to Xhosa State, it would have required hours more. The skycraft was efficiently arranged, and he would be
on the ground at the location—a military compound he hadn't visited in
years—in less than an hour. Gabriel was seated and awaiting takeoff when
another alert chimed on his communicator and those of his Guard around
him.

Staring at the report, Gabriel felt another roar of rage wanting to burst
forth from him. He blew out air and read the words over again. It was a cat
and mouse game, and she was the cat. Without even realizing it, she had
just snuffed out and blinded the small ray of hope he'd had. If *hope* was an
apt term for the roiling pressure emanating from his gut, that place right
below his heart. It was useless to give so much importance to one person,
especially one like Essien. But the prophecy...it had been hammered into
him too deeply to ever forget or turn away from it. The prophecy and the
potential power both pushed and goaded him into this state. It was fore-
told, and yet even the Mothers must laugh at jokes of their own making.

The guards were looking at him now, and there was the skycraft pilot
coming down the aisle. *Where to, Ser?* Gabriel could see the question already being asked before he even heard it. There was no use going to Xhosa
now, not if Essien had already escaped—again. To have been captured and
escaped within a few hours of each other had to be some record, maybe
an international one. Other countries kept more prisoners than Alkebulan, and there were debates in international conferences on whether that
was more humane than a total execution rate. There were few criminals in
Alkebulan because offenders were simply executed. Gabriel thought of Essien facing execution again for what would be the second time now. Once,
for crimes she had been forced to commit to save her own life. He had
never held that against her. And now? He would punish her for this crime,
though execution seemed extreme. The country's laws demanded she die,
but he was the President. He could change the laws if they didn't suit him,
as he had, and would again. Gabriel rubbed his chin, feeling the bristles of
unshaven hair poking through roughly.

The pilot was standing right next to him in the aisle now. "We go to
Xhosa State. We might learn something more once we land."

CHAPTER SIXTEEN

◆

FLUTTERING FIGURES OF ORANGE GUIDED ESSIEN THROUGH the forest over several days, lighting on tree branches laden with fruit, hovering over safe crevices in the roots of trees where she could curl up on hard-packed dirt and sleep. Those glowing orange orbs beckoned to her, and she followed them, as if she were in a dream, dazed and unreal, until she found the remnants of a small, forgotten building in the middle of a cluster of trees. Standing outside the faded wooden structure in a puddle of shade, Essien imagined the vast amount of digging in soil and sweating through splinters and sprains that it had taken to build a compound way out here. There were no roads or nearby neighbors. This was the dead innermost acres of the Nkandla Forest, a place she could envision on a map surrounded by green and symbolized with a tree shape.

She shifted to another angle on the other side of the building and saw the compound was more like a roomy shed, with the homemade look of having been built by hand. That wasn't something she had ever done before, nor did she plan to.

Walking around the back of the shed, she examined the windows with glass sparkling in the fading sunlight filtering down through the trees, and she spotted the gathered stones around the base of the building and the front door. Some of the stones were flat and others were more rounded, so it wasn't even all the way across. Essien stepped up onto the front porch and saw the spiders' webs thickly covering the corners and hinges of the door. It hadn't been opened in quite some time, so she finally accepted that at least for tonight, she'd have shelter. She noticed that the orange orbs she had been following through the forest for several sunrises had disappeared.

Taking a deep breath of the twilit air, she grabbed the door lever and pushed it up to step inside the small compound. The room smelled of turned earth and cut leaves. The floor was the same wood as the outside of the structure, the door, and the knee-high bedstead of smooth slabs nailed across one wall with wooden legs added underneath at the four corners.

Next to it, a table about waist-high was built into the wall like a counter with two wooden doors on the front underneath.

Essien wiped the sweat pooling on her forehead and down her cheeks. She held the back of her neck and glanced around. The wood inside was pale and seemed to light up the ever-darkening forest around her. Something about it seemed right, like having stumbled upon an oasis in a desert, and she felt that she had earned the right to it.

It was almost full dark, so Essien didn't go far from the compound as she explored the area just around the building. In a cove not even a half league away, there was an orchard of fruit trees, the sweet tropical smell floating on the wind that rustled under the tree canopies. There were yellow bundles of baby bananas on the ground, the side touching the dirt already rotted away. On the other side of the clearing between the trees were the bright reddish orange of mangoes. Essien gave an excited yip and gathered as many as she could hold in her arms. She grabbed one of the bundles of bananas that seemed just barely ripened.

Back in the wooden shed, she set the fruit on the table. She used her teeth and hands to peel the mangoes, eating one after another standing at the table, the orange juice slipping down her arms to stain the wooden beams at her feet. She ate a bunch of bananas, their creamy, white insides sweeter than any candy she had ever eaten. It was full dark by then. She did her best to wipe the sticky juice onto her tunic.

Outside, a roaring trumpet sounded and then crashing sounds like trees being felled by large bodies surrounded the shed. The trumpeting sounded familiar, but Essien had never heard the sounds of trees and branches being snapped off and knocked over. She was afraid to go outside to check on the source of the commotion, but the sounds grew louder and louder and then seemed to pass by the shed. As the bursts of agitated sounds died down, Essien ducked her head outside the door of the compound shed. Through the trees off to the left where she had come from, she could see two giant gray elephant bulls rearing up against each other, tusks and snouts locked. Essien watched their tussling from the porch, her limbs shivering as the adrenaline filtered out of her system. She said a prayer of thanks to the Mothers that the elephants hadn't fallen on the shed with her in it.

Stepping back inside the door, she examined the lever and realized quickly how to catch the latch and snap it into place, so that it couldn't be opened from the outside. Once done, she sank down on the bed made from slabs of wood. She curled up on her side, her arms and legs tucked up tight.

THE SUN SINKING IN THROUGH THE GLASS WINDOWS AND spreading rainbows around the room woke her up the next morning. The pale wood made the bright light seem like neon rays, and she could see more of the compound now. There was a cabinet underneath the table built into the wall. She opened the door on the front of it and saw a gas burner inside. She also saw two earthenware cooking pots, a water gourd, other earthenware dishes, and wooden cutlery on the top shelf of a wooden rack. On the bottom shelf, she found a thicker blanket made of the softest merino wool, dyed a dark blue with white stars scattered across in thick embroidered thread.

She pulled the burner and the cooking gourd out and arranged them on top of the table. She spread the thick blanket over the bed. The room instantly felt cozier. She stared at the wooden walls, the boards fitted closely together, so that no light or air seeped through. The door fit perfectly in the doorframe, not a thin crack of visible light on the inside. This shelter had been well-made. She wondered about who had done it and left it all for someone else to find. Who had sketched out the foundation in the dirt, gathered those rocks, nailed in those wooden beams, spilled their sweat to bring it to life in the middle of nowhere? And then she remembered those dazzling orange lights that had led her here.

Essien stepped out of the compound and shut the door firmly behind her. She went back to the cove she'd found the day before. In the morning light, she could see the makings of an overgrown, but still producing, garden with red seed fruit and melons and green fingers and yellow fruit and brown and yellow and orange ground roots in tangled vines pushing up from the dirt in patches. There was old, rotted fruit that had not been picked in months, perhaps years, but there were also the new seeds pushing green shoots up from the dirt.

She walked around through that garden for hours, seeing where the seeds and shoots had naturally pushed themselves up through weeds and vines, making a way out of no way, refusing to be choked off from life. Breathing in the fresh light, Essien stared around her. As far as she could see, the orchard garden hadn't been tended in some while. She could still see the original borders of the flowers around the edges and the patches of fruit and vegetables and herbs that had started to mingle.

Essien began to work in the garden, doing a duty for no other reason than it was the natural and right thing to do. She broke off branches from a dead tree to fashion the sticks into shovels. Carefully, she selected the brightest patch of dirt and began digging rows. When the patch was large enough, she went over to a muddy puddle in the shadows of a rock and dug up some of the mud. Worms and creeping bugs scrambled out of the pile. She transferred the wet mud into the patch she'd just dug up, using the makeshift shovels to mix the wet mud with the dried-out mud. Then, she carefully uprooted and relocated some of the still-living plants to the larger patch she cleared out. The mud was wet and rich and full of those squirming worms. Essien repositioned the green leaves into rows with their snaking pale roots that had sprouted down, and she thought of her father.

She had hated gardening as a young girl and teen, hated it with the silent grumblings of ungrateful dissatisfaction. She had been forced to leave school for a year after her father's accident in the fields, and she had resented her parents for forcing her to do it. She hadn't missed school or her few friends there. It was the idea that her brothers had been allowed to live their lives freely, and she had to do more than they had ever been expected to do.

Never mind that two of her eldest brothers had enlisted in the Soja as soon as they turned eighteen and were sent on military campaigns that took them out of the country to Iroquois, which is how they'd ended up meeting their wives. She had at least been allowed to return to school for her final year and had attended military academy for two years before enlisting officially at the age of twenty.

She felt ashamed of herself, the guilt burning over her scalp like the fire that could easily spark up at just a thought. To think that she ever hated gardening, the sustenance of life, that she had ever resented her father or considered it a burden to help him in her family's garden.

The feel of the dirt on her hands made her ache for home. Her father would have been ashamed of her for destroying hard-working farmers' livelihoods with fire, like the terrible events that had almost cost him his life so many years ago. Essien hadn't thought about the fires and the burning in years, but the shame grew now as she thought of what she had mindlessly done. It had been selfish and thoughtless. She had been those things.

There was no doubt that Essien would have to pay for those transgressions. She prayed her Nna would never know what she had done. She would not be able to bear the look in his eyes or what he might think of her if he were to know. She knew that he would have been proud of her for finally realizing the harm she had caused and fleeing to avoid any more destruction. She wondered if she might ever see her Nna or her Nne again. Squeezed in a hug between the two of them seemed like the best place in the world.

THERE WAS A CLEAR STREAM OF WATER A LEAGUE OR TWO AWAY from where she had found the small compound. She found it while trekking up the steep side of a hill convoluted with trees but clear enough at the top to see a full vista of the state. The village in the valley below was on the outskirts of a much larger city on the opposite side of the mountain from where she had come. She could see the demarcation between the village with its shades of reds, greens, and browns and the city with its silver, black, and blue hues.

Turning back to the stream, she stared at the water flowing like liquid glass, transparent and showing all the way to the sandy, clay bottom. The stream came down from a hidden precipice in a rock cliff, a rushing flow, not quite as strong as some parts of the Nahla further in the northern part of the country. She dipped her hand in, and it was cool and refreshing. She drank the water from the side of her cupped palm, tentatively sipping. It tasted like the spring water you could buy in glass bottles with silver caps at the fancier markets.

She sat down on a rock that jutted up and out from the side of the hill. The sun had heated it to an almost too hot temperature. Essien sat there, watching the golden sun move across the blue expanse like a constant clock. She waited there for a few minutes, lying back on the rock to rest her eyes for a bit. When she opened them again, her mouth had grown drier, and she felt thirst like a scabby film over her lips. She did not feel any sickness in her belly, so she went down to the edge of the stream and put her lips directly into the stream to drink more. She drank until her stomach felt heavy. She was sure that the water was safe, but still she waited. She waited for what felt like the entire day, lying back on the rock with her eyes closed. She tried to focus on her breathing, and it felt like she was spinning around and around, off the side of that hill and up into the sky. She put her hands flat on the rock, palms facing up, and let herself spin. It felt like she could spin herself right up to Igbo State.

She thought of her father as she breathed deeply. She wondered if his smelling herbs were still being burned and if they had improved the condition of his lungs at all. She thought of her mother left to care for her father alone and wanted to weep. She thought of her brothers, each of them married to beautiful women and fathers of lovely children that Essien wished she had gotten to know better. She wondered if Femi had gotten married; she had not heard news from him in too many years. As the many thoughts zigzagged through her mind, her eyelids grew heavier and heavier, until at last Essien fell asleep.

When she awoke and opened her eyes again, the sky was a dark indigo, the pricks of stars and the glow of planets making bright circles in the sky. She felt fine, no presence of a single physical pain. This both shocked and pleased her.

Essien sought out the water gourd that she'd previously seen inside the compound shed and subsequently filled it to the brim with the quickly flowing water. She capped it with the plug and carried it back down the hill to her compound. When she drank from the water gourd, it tasted fresh and sweet.

Essien went back to the stream the next day when the sun had risen again. She followed the stream where it tumbled down the hill in the opposite direction and ended at a short cliff that turned into a waterfall that blew away in a mist down into an enclosed section of a larger river. Essien let her eyes trace the river below and saw that it opened into a lake, oblong and reflecting the sky like a mirror. At the far end of that lake, another river snaked off into the distant brown, green, and blue horizon.

Essien hiked down to the lake, picking her way through more faint paths where feet had trodden before but not in a while. When she reached the lake at the bottom, she stood looking out over its mirrored surface. The river churned at the mouth, the water plumbing up over large gray rocks. She noticed flashes of silver under the water and realized they were fish. She had never been fishing but as with many who have never fished, she imagined she might catch a fish quite easily.

She slipped the extra tunic out and formed it into a bag net, closing the end with a tight knot. She opened the other end of the bag she'd made and waded into the river. She held the bag just beneath the surface where the river rushed through. Several fish swam by. Quickly, she snatched the bag up out of the water. The first few times, she caught nothing. Then, she caught a small fish, too thin for her purposes. She let it go but kept trying.

After at least an hour of missed attempts, Essien caught a fat, wriggling fish that smacked its tail against her arm and tried to squirm out of her homemade net. She held the open end of the net closed and high-stepped out of the water, where she beat the fish against a stone with two firm *thwacks*, and it lay still. She looked around her immediate area and soon found a jagged rock that she subsequently used to scale and gut the fish. She also smashed off its head and fins, and then used the rock to peel out the spine and bones. When the field dressing process was complete, she washed the edible fish parts off and carried them up to the compound in one hand, while she held the wrung-out tunic in the other.

Back at the compound, Essien used one of the earthenware pots on the burner to stew the fish—chopped up in water with herbs, green vegetables, and red seed fruit she snapped off the vines on her way back to the compound. She had even dug up a thick tuber of yam and a small yellow ground root that she peeled against a stone, soaked, and boiled with yellow ground root. The pots bubbled and roiled, and Essien felt a sense of peace that belied the true danger she was still in.

She marveled quietly that it was the first meal she had ever prepared for herself and herself alone. When at last it was finished, she dished up the fish and the yam and used one of the spoons to have her meal. If Femi were there, he would have remarked on the fresh quality of the food despite the lack of seasonings and salt. Essien ate all of the fish and had only a small hunk of yam remaining when she was done. With her belly full, and thoughts of her brother on her mind, Essien curled up under the thick, soft blanket, feeling content for the first time in her memorable history, and drifted off to sleep.

THE NEXT MORNING, SHE AWOKE TO THE SOUND OF MILITARY ENgines barreling through the village center just a few leagues below her. She recognized the familiar metallic grinding of their engine sounds, and the husky shouts of commands and directions reached her even through the leagues and leagues of tree covering.

She could see them from up on top of the hill when she went to get water. She peered down into the valley, her eyes furtive and skittish. More engines followed yet more engines, a line of them proceeding into the village where she had not dared to go. They were probably sojas sent by Gabriel to find her. They were probably distributing her picture even now. They might come marching up this hill on foot, peering into every crack and crevice along the way. If she stayed, they would find her. If she ran, they might still find her.

Essien sat down on the bed that somebody had made with their own two hands. She looked at the heaps of mango and bundles of bananas on the table waiting for her to devour as her morning meal. In the distance, the low-pitched buzzing of engines was a foreboding sound to Essien, seeming to grow closer and closer. She quickly packed up what she wanted to take into the tunic bag she used to fish. There wasn't much for her to pack: The blanket was coming with her, the knife and the gourd also to carry water, and the fruit she had gathered the day before.

As she stepped out of the wooden compound, leaving everything else behind, Essien paused in the doorway. If she ran now, she would be running forever. There was likely no end to this flight.

Essien shut the door tight and set off heading in the opposite direction of the villages below and where those engines had gone. She would have to travel north, deeper into the forest, over the hills and through the woods, avoiding the roads entirely. She didn't even have a map to guide her. The footpaths she'd been traveling on often barely allowed her to safely pass. She set off quickly before fear could seize a hold of her.

It had been over half a year since she'd escaped that hospital rooftop. Would there ever be a time when the President wouldn't be searching for her? Had she thought he would forget about her? She had hoped at least. There was probably no distant future that she could run to where he wouldn't be looking for her. And yet, still, she ran.

CHAPTER SEVENTEEN

◆

GABRIEL STEPPED FROM THE ENGINE ONTO A PAVED DRIVEway. The compound standing before him was modern, made of light stone with a flat roof of red clay tiles. The windows were small and round. There were cacti in square pots along the pathway leading to the door, a rounded entranceway with intricately designed tiles bordering it. The front entrance was already open, and the man standing in the doorway had to duck to step through without hitting his head.

The man had a timid smile on his face. His dark blue tunic was unbuttoned and flapped open over a white undershirt. His pants matched the tunic, but they were wrinkled, as though the man had been lying down. He stepped onto the front porch, and the smile dropped. He came to the edge, and Gabriel stepped up on the first step.

"Stop right there," the man said. "I know who you are."

Gabriel smiled, his benevolent grin. "Then you know why I am here."

"I do," the man said, nodding. "I can't help you. I won't help you."

"You don't know where she is then?" Gabriel was at the top step and still moving forward. The man backed up a step, giving him room, without realizing it.

"If I knew where she was, I would advise her to stay as far away from you as possible. Your military has almost gotten her killed how many times now? Do you want to finish the job?"

"Nifemi, let us have this conversation inside, out of the heat."

"The house isn't air conditioned. It's as hot inside as it is out."

"I can feel a breeze coming from the door." Gabriel glanced into the doorway. There was a little girl peeking around the doorjamb. She had a golden-brown color on her cheeks and her braided hair. Her small head darted out and then in. "How old is your daughter?"

Nifemi jumped toward the door and slammed it shut. The little girl had scampered away as he leaped. Gabriel laughed at the ferociousness on Femi's face. He wouldn't take it personally. Here was a man who understood family. He understood what it meant to secure and protect. He could be brought around to see reason.

"I'm staying just south of the border in Zulu State. It was a nice drive coming up to Igbo State. I got to see more of the countryside than I usually get to see. I must say that I enjoyed it. Would you like to visit my compound in Zulu State? We can have the conversation we need to have back at my compound. I can have a skycraft prepared if you'd prefer?"

Femi spit over the edge of his porch. Gabriel felt drops of wetness hit his face as the dry wind suddenly kicked up. Gabriel reached up to wipe his cheek, and he stared into Femi's eyes. The man was large, taller than Gabriel by a couple inches. Gabriel had not brought many of the Guard with him on this trip. He still thought he might win Femi, Essien's brother, over with niceness and cordiality. He did not want to resort to force just yet.

"Why don't you and the entire family join me? It would be fun for you and the wife. I'm sure your daughter will love it. Your baby daughter probably won't remember it, but you can take pictures. The compound in Zulu was newly renovated, so we have plenty of room."

"I will not let you take my family as hostages." Femi's teeth were gritted, and he had balled his fists. Gabriel signaled softly with a wave of his fingertips for his Guard not to step up. He knew the aggression in Femi would make them move forward, but he did not want the man to turn violent. If he did...

"Your sister is the most important person in the world to me," Gabriel said, opting for truth. "I am worried about her. There are people out there who mean her ill, who wish to harm her, and through her, me. I need your help finding her. Please help your sister. Help me for her sake."

Gabriel had walked all the way to the top of the wooden porch, and Femi had backed away with each step he'd taken. He was almost in the doorway he had closed moments before. Behind him, the door opened. A woman with a kinky golden yellow Afro and sandy brown skin stepped through. She had on a dark red tunic dress that hit her at the knees. Her face and feet were bare. In her arms, a baby was wrapped tightly in a light cloth. The little girl hung around her mother's knees, almost tripping her as she walked.

"President Ijikota," the woman greeted him, bending her knees slightly and ducking her head in the provincial habit of bowing to tribal royalty. "My name is Obechi, Chichi to my friends. Femi and I have been married for five years. In five years, I have not met his sister once. She did not come to our wedding. She could not come to any of our first-year festivities, because why? Because you. She was serving in your military, and we do not even know if she received our invitation. I have come into her family, and she does not even know me. I have given her nieces, and she does not know their names. The big one is Nnamdi, and the small one here is Chinasa. When you see Essien, would you tell her that she has two more nieces now? They would love to meet her. Their father has not talked to or seen his sister since before his daughters were born. You can't understand what that might be like, President Ijikota, as you have no siblings. Neither do I. I can never know what it is like, but Nnamdi and Chinasa will know. I imagine my two girls would be devastated to go so long without contact between them. Oh, Mothers, her nna isn't doing well. Perhaps you might send that message to her, too. We saw him last at Equinox, and he wasn't doing well. Mothers, may he live long enough to see his daughter again."

CHAPTER EIGHTEEN

◆

FOR SALE OR RENT, IT WAS EASY FINDING PLACES TO LIVE IN Bantu State, where growing populations meant growing neighborhoods and a welcomed element of anonymity. Taking advantage of the anonymity, Essien seized the opportunity to ride further out of Mbanza-Kongo with a mother and her two sons. The two sons were small, one still in swaddling blankets who eyed her with innocent curiosity. The woman had the dusty hands and clothes of a farmer. The empty food crates in the back of her truck attested to it. Essien talked little, but she handed the woman ten Naira for the ride and jumped out as soon as she was sure they were in a small village in Bantu State.

There were tan stone buildings with brown stone pathways out front. The sand was a dusty backdrop blowing gritty, dry wind that came in from a distant shore. Essien went first to an internet boona. When she opened the door and noticed teens filling every available spot, the aroma of sweet, fizzy drinks and burnished coffee met her. She got in line to order a tea and waited for a spot to open.

There were newsreels for her to peruse while she waited. She scoured the local newsprints for available rooming compounds, sneaking a peek at other pages to see if there was any news about her. Nothing screamed at her from the front pages, so she settled her shoulders a bit and stopped glancing around as much.

Later, she went on a few tours of homes that were walk-in and crowded with other visitors, like everyone had gotten the same idea to move down south at the same time she did. Some compounds in an old neighborhood were small and cramped, while others in newer developments were large and squat.

At one location she'd found in the ads section, a young man in a fresh shirtfront showed her around a cramped and musty room that wouldn't break her dwindling pockets. But the smell of wet, rotting wood and the screech of a neighbor's kids in the front yard kept her searching.

She traveled through so many neighborhoods, each of them different. The villages were marked by large, old compounds usually surrounded by wood or stone fences. The newer cities had more multifamily residences in compounds that towered up four, five, six floors, some even taller.

Essien sat on a large rock perched at a crossroads leading into a newer neighborhood and watched the people coming and going. There weren't many trees, creating a sense of open air and space. She saw lots of teens and children in different school uniforms hurrying to catch motor buses that rolled up to a stop across from the rock, one after the other. Drifts of their conversations reached her, and their words were so foreign to her she couldn't understand if they were talking about going to a party after school or competing in a wrestling match. She tried to imagine herself living peacefully in that place with its orange-brick paved streets and compounds made of paneled wood instead of stone. She couldn't see herself there at all, and it made her feel uneasy.

What if there was no life for her outside of the military? She stilled at the thought, everything around her going invisible and silent in her mind. She couldn't understand how to get beyond feeling like she was prey running from a predator. Gabriel was sending everything he had after her because magic had failed him. It was only a matter of time before he found her. She dropped her head, momentarily frozen with pain at what her own actions had caused. It wasn't just guilt but sorrow for what she'd lost and anger at herself for not knowing any better, not being able to see into the future far enough. She sighed and stood from the rock, dusting dust and rock fragments off her backside. Upon further consideration, this neighborhood wasn't right for her; it had far too many people.

It took her four weeks of living in different rooming compounds to avoid drawing too much attention before she found a home she could afford, which would obscure her comings and goings from nearby neighbors. The home was more a bungalow than a compound, with no gates or fences or secondary structures, but it was surrounded by thick forests that were uninhabited for stadia out. She recognized it as home when the owner—an elderly, wizened man wearing a dark brown tunic over matching pants and sandals—directed her to follow him up the long curving lane that led to the front door.

It cost way too much of her remaining Naira, but it isolated her in a wooded lot, hidden just beyond the curve in a road, far outside any city or village. She made the landowner take cash for the transaction and only completed a handwritten bill of sale, which he had to copy twice, so they'd each have one. No banks or courts were involved. She told him he could keep the home in his name, and he delightedly agreed. She had a signed copy of the transfer of ownership, using her mother's family name rather than her father's and her first name initial only.

Still, she knew it was a stupid decision on her part. She had watched her father sell land with a member of the Tribal Council, an elder of the community, and a broker from the accounts holder always present. "I always ensure the validity of the sale," he had told her.

There was no way to protect her sale except by the neatly written papers that they'd both signed. There were no witnesses and nobody to corroborate that they'd made the deal. The old man was a grandfather and had been married for over sixty years, he had proudly shared. It would have to be enough. He had even offered to bring her furniture over from his storage for free. She had offered to pay him, but the old man had waved her away and said he'd return the next day.

She celebrated with a cold bottle of palm wine at the rooming compound's food shop. She stared around the first-floor dining room with its hushed guests at square tables in the darkened space. She sipped slowly, savoring the drink that she had never really enjoyed drinking before. She stared at the opaque liquid in the glass with foam bubbling over its top. Though she couldn't imagine drinking it every day, the feeling of relaxation that slithered through her core and into her limbs made her mind flash onto Gabriel's face.

With a flare of magic in response, Essien tightened those protective layers around her mind and waited for her heart and her breathing to slow. She gave a toast to the table runner as she downed the rest of the glass and left the remainder of the bottle for anyone to finish. She had accumulated only one canvas bag worth of belongings; the rest she left in a donation box for someone else to make use of. She slipped out of the rooming compound and hired an engine to take her halfway out to a side road, and then she walked the rest of the way.

Inside the small cottage-style compound, she opened all the windows: two in the front room, one in the washroom, and one in the back bedroom. The walls were a dingy off-white and the floors were brown wood. She could feel the breeze of fresh air curling after her as she searched through the small closet beside the indoor washroom, finding a broom, a wooden bucket, a bottle of vinegar, and clean rags that seemed freshly washed and wrung out.

She used the broom to sweep out collected dust and bugs and insects. She brushed the corners of the ceiling to drag down thin sweeps of old spider webs. She used the bucket filled with water from a spigot in the kitchen and splashes of vinegar to wash the windows and walls inside and out. The vinegar made the off-white walls brighten up instantly.

She used the offensive smelling mixture and the bristles of the broom to clean the floor, scrubbing hard in places where the wood had dust encrusted. *How long will this be home?* she thought as she stood in the open front doorway and wiped dripping sweat off her temple.

She tried walking to the city soon after she moved in, and it left her almost dying with sweat, and exhausted, with heavy packages to carry back. After that dreadful excursion, she'd found a small two-wheeled engine sitting in front of a repair garage, with brand-new tires and only minor dents and scratches. She paid for it with the last few Naira she could spare from her remaining funds and didn't request a bill of sale. No paper trail—best to stay invisible and undocumented as much as possible. The engine started up right away, and she drove to the markets with quick speed using the basket in the front and the cargo storage area underneath the seat to store her purchases.

Throughout it all, in the back of her mind, an unacknowledged threat dogged her every step. But it wasn't the dwindling Naira, now down to three digits.

A FEW WEEKS AFTER MOVING IN, SHE WOKE AFTER THE SUN HAD already risen for the morning. It was the first night in many that she had slept so completely. If she dreamed, there was no memory of it. The stuffed pallet and wooden frame that was donated by the old man was comfortable enough for a night's rest, but she couldn't linger there. She had so much work to do to keep herself busy and her mind occupied.

The cottage was still mostly empty even with the items she'd received the day after moving in. There had already been an old-fashioned iron stove, the kind her grandmother had probably used, that required her to light pieces of wood to blaze underneath pots and pans set on top of a wire grill. There was a large, dented copper pot, a set of chipped clay mugs, and a stack of clay plates.

The old man had come back with two muscular grandsons early the day after she'd moved in, saving her from sleeping another night on top of her clothes spread out on the floor. He'd delivered the bed and covering, a wooden table and two chairs, a rug for each room to warm up the bare wooden floors, and one pillow armchair that she sank deeply into. She had even gotten a set of dinnerware and a cast-iron skillet with the rest of the donated furniture. She'd also kept the copper pot and the dishes that were left behind. His promised deliveries made, the old man waved away her profuse gratitude with wrinkled but strong hands as he and his grandsons left.

The second night in her new home, Essien made a bubbling soup of stockfish and green root vegetables that she ate over slightly crunchy, undercooked rice because the pot had no suitable lid other than using one of the plates. At night she slept underneath her dark gray merino wool blanket and looked out the window at a dark sky full of crystalline sparks. She felt cozy and safe. She felt protected by an invisible blanket of anonymity. There was no way Gabriel would find her way down here. The closest military compound was in Zulu State. Essien couldn't imagine any reason for the President or his military to be in Bantu State. It was another state that did not have a military agreement. Just like Xhosa State, Bantu did not have a single military compound within its borders, but the Soja and the Uzo Nchedo were free to enter the states at will.

Essien remembered the history of those intertribal wars, the battles that had been fought by fierce warriors, and the compromise that was reached after the War of Unification. Only Bantu and Xhosa States had managed to establish local defense protocols that made the military there unnecessary. The Military and Tribal Councilmen from Bantu and Xhosa States were thought to be so formidable that some states often waited to see how they might vote on legislation to follow their lead. In Bantu State, she had felt sure that she might yet escape the President's notice for the length of time it would take him to forget her. She knew it had been delusional even as she thought it.

His bonded, the holy man, Osiris, had called her. She had no idea what that meant, but she felt dread weighing at the bottom of her stomach knowing she must find out. She'd served in Gabriel's military and then joined his guard as a compromise after her life was spared. At what point in that time he'd bonded her, she couldn't even begin to think. Maybe he'd put something in her food. Even though he had never harmed her, she had never felt she could truly trust him. There was always that feeling of a predatory animal being contained just on the other side of unbreakable glass. The unsettling thoughts continued, and though she tried, Essien slept fitfully, tossing and turning, unable to get comfortable.

CHAPTER NINETEEN

◆

ONE MORNING NOT LONG AFTER SETTLING IN, ESSIEN DE-cided to eat a meal at one of the food shops lining the road leading into the city. She was tired of the walls surrounding her, and she wanted to be near people again. She had been alone for over a month, working with her hands in the dirt to cultivate the garden she had started.

This morning, she had smelled the doughy scent of fry bread drifting in on the wind and knew that a food vendor had set up shop close by. Not even a few stadia past the curve in the road leading to her home, she saw the food stall, already attended by a line of three, and a fourth straggling up to join the end of it. There was even an area of folding tables and chairs underneath a canvas awning that flapped against the stakes holding it into the ground. She ordered fried brown roots and pounded yam with spicy stewed red seeds. It was the cheapest meal, costing just six Naira—her financial resources almost down to double digits.

One of the table runners brought her a gourd of fresh coconut water and left it on top of a newsprint on the table. Two words on the edge of the paper made her move the drink to read the rest: Armed and Danger-ous. She flicked the pages out and saw the full headline: Missing Military Official, Considered Armed and Dangerous. Accompanying the headline was a twelve-by-ten-centimeter photo of her face in military regalia. Essien remembered the day it was taken. She was not smiling in the photograph because the photographer had told her not to. Her hair was braided in a single thick black rope under a dark red cap that dangled over her shoul-der and disappeared past the bottom of the photo. Her shoulders looked sharper with the black mantle of the shirtfront. She stared at her own face, done fierce and stern. She calmly looked around the dining area, her eyes catching those of the shop owner.

The wizened old woman nodded at her and continued stirring the steaming contents of her pots. Essien kept eating, slowly chewing and star-ing out into the street as people passed, some looking curiously in at her, others not noticing her at all. She thought about the cottage in the woods that she had just dumped the majority of her cash funds into. It would take more time for her to sell it again. Where else could she go where newspapers and the threat of her past could not reach? The answer, unfortunately, was nowhere.

She casually covered the article as she skimmed the other stories. She was surprised to read a headline announcing a rebel camp raid and capture. Essien continued to read the entire length of the column across the front page, ignoring the story about herself right alongside it. After skimming the words for names, and finding none she recognized, she went back to the beginning and read more slowly.

As she feared, the camp she had spent half a year hiding in had been raided. Because of her. Sojas had been dispatched to the area after smoke from the fire was reported by an official who had just happened to be passing nearby. They'd managed to navigate to the labyrinth of underground tunnels and camouflage tent cities that was characteristic of every rebel camp. A mysterious flood drowned 120 people, men and women alike, some of them pregnant. That was too many people to list out. Just one rebel had been captured and would be facing trial.

She stopped reading and refolded the paper. She flashed onto Enyema-ka's face and wished she had a way to contact him. *Please don't let him be one of the drowned,* she thought. A mysterious flood, an unexplained flame. Her nose stung, and she kept brushing her fingers together to remove the feeling of gritty ashes. She folded the newspaper as small as she could and tucked it into her pocket. She tipped a few extra Naira for the paper and left quickly.

As she arrived back to her cottage, taking a long, winding route away from the road leading to her home, through the woods around the back way and up to the back door, Essien admired the great marula tree spreading its thick branches and spindly leaves wide in the field next to the structure. That tree had stood for over a thousand years, the previous owner had told her, and had been standing since long before Alkebulan was a country. Other trees with sharp, spicy smells surrounded the small cottage, hiding it from view until one had walked the long, winding road to its very end. Her engine barely fit in the clearing beside the massive tree without being scraped by branches. Essien hoped it would be enough to hide her. She then remembered she had lemons and honey on the counter.

Inside the closet-sized washroom, she mixed up lemon juice and dusty red clay from the hills behind the house with half the bottle of honey. She used the red mush to dye the curly fuzz of her hair a coppery orange that clashed sharply with the cool blue undertones in her deep brown skin. Staring at herself in the mirror, Essien practiced smiling, pulling the edges of her mouth up so high her eyes squinted closed. It felt unnatural and nothing like her. She looked again at the face staring blankly out from the front fold of Bantu State's largest newspaper. If she smiled, she was a completely different person than the woman in that photo. If she smiled, she might not be recognizable at all.

Essien began waking up at five in the morning again. She'd lay on her bed, the pallet soft, but not luxurious. She'd let her mind wander, but not too far out of bounds. She tried to think of all that she was grateful for and only some of what she missed. She was alive, and unconfined, even if that didn't exactly mean she was free. Her thoughts would turn as they always did toward the one subject she still had to put up mental blockers against. As she lay on her pallet, she'd run her hands along the seams and edges of that wall, feeling for any weakening spots. She'd patch them up, using her thoughts of sharp, hard rapid fires to bind her thoughts to herself. *It's still working,* she always thought. *I'm still undiscovered by him.*

Eventually she'd get up, but for those few moments, it felt surreal that she could decide not to get up right away if she chose. She had tried venturing back into the local village, but every stare and glance back, every double take and double back, made her paranoid. She didn't want anyone to recognize her familiar face. She had already been captured once, and she couldn't risk it again. She might not survive another encounter with any of the boots Gabriel had searching for her even now. The last time she'd gone into the village, she had jumped at shadows and expected the worst when a shopkeeper had suddenly pulled out their communicator to speak to someone the moment she entered their store to purchase fabric. Her mouth grew dry, and she could barely whisper out that she wanted two yards and a length of rope. She hadn't gone back into the town for at least a month. Or had it been two? She'd lost track of time again.

Essien feared that ultimately someone else would see her and know exactly who she was. She was terrified that that person would then be forced to grapple with themselves on whether to report her or not. Even worse, maybe they wouldn't need to debate at all. Maybe they'd have no qualms and go straight to the nearest government building to turn her in. Then Gabriel would be on her head before she could even realize it, leaving her without enough time to run. So, she stayed in the cottage or the forests behind it most of the time, not able to overcome the stifling fear that seized her at the thought of being kidnapped again. She vowed to go into town only when she was desperate for some item or wanted to search again for a way she might make money, anonymously. She had already vowed never to enter the bank building with its glass sides you could see into from the other side of town.

Despite her restlessness, she found plenty to do around her home and the surrounding lands. Climbing up onto the roof from the attic, she mended a leak by replacing broken boards with new ones still yellow with resin and resealed the cracks with thick putty. She cleaned out the roof's gutters, dispersing a bird's nest full of torn paper and blood ticks. She made curtains out of yards of cloth she'd purchased and suspended them up over the windows with lengths of rope nailed to the wall. She tended the growing plot of fresh fruits and vegetables, digging up weeds that scrambled away from her and tried to bury themselves deeper. She picked a plump red seed fruit from the vine and ate it to test its ripeness. It was sour and chewy, but she swallowed it down. Almost ready, she thought.

On her way back from tending the garden in a clearing between the trees beyond the small compound, she noticed a field of wildflowers bloomed a stadia or two behind her house. She stopped her trek home and traipsed between the trees to pick flowers: the pale pink of Hottentot's fig, the delicate white of seeplakkie and wild foxglove, the sunny red of Barberton daisy, the curled green of monkey's tail. These she wove into a basket and placed on her table. Her nne had taught her how to weave baskets from flowers.

She longed to call her up and ask her about Nna and tell her about the garden she was growing. Her mother would never believe that she had started a garden on her own and was planting and weeding with nobody forcing her. Essien had hated tending her family's garden. Her brother Femi never had to weed or harvest, she always complained.

Essien smiled at the colorful basket she'd woven as she ate her small dinner of warm rice and spicy vegetable stew. The next morning, small green buzzing insects were climbing all over the basket, squirming specks on the pretty flowers and leaves. She threw the flower basket out the door and used the heel of her boot to squash the bugs that had dropped onto the table.

CHAPTER TWENTY

◆

AFTER A COUPLE MORE WEEKS OF GOING NOWHERE, ESSIEN used a map of Southern Alkebulan to locate other towns and cities, smaller ones. There were larger cities of course. Zulu State was to the southwest, the southernmost part of the country; Khoisan State was to the southeast; Bantu State was just to the north of Khoisan.

Within Bantu State, smaller cities were much harder to locate on the map, and villages were not even printed at all. She knew this was one of the states where rebels had been headquartered, but after she had burnt up so many of their leaders, there was no way of knowing if they had dispersed to other places.

Essien traveled on the engine following the back roads that took her through villages leading to the larger cities, hoping she'd find a small, unmarked city on the way.

Thorn was a city situated on the road north of her small abode, and it wasn't on any map Essien had perused. It was closer than the larger cities but had a smaller population with just one local medical center. She decided to stop there.

Essien walked through the center of the town with its black jasper stone streets and considered the plate glass storefronts. In one store, there were pressed embroidered uwes for sale, tall boots with a high stack, and a silver sewing machine. A shop clerk beckoned her inside the dress shop with elegant ringed fingers and showed her an emerald-green uwe with sparkly gold patches on the shoulders. Essien ran her fingers lightly over the slick fabric and told the shop clerk she had no special place to wear it. She had to say no to more beautiful gowns before she could slip guiltily out of the shop.

Essien continued strolling and decided that the people in the lower part of the country smiled more than they did in the north where Essien was from. Maybe it was the weather, warm and cool breezes blowing in from two oceans, the sun setting later and with more fancy. Maybe it was the open land, the white sand beaches only a few steps away from the end of any street. Maybe they only smiled because she did so freely, hiding herself in plain sight.

Before returning home, Essien left a doctored name and an employment inquiry with hotel managers, retail shops, and the lone law practice in the town. She left out that she'd served in the military and the President's personal Guard. She used her mother's family name instead of her father's. She didn't use her first name at all, just the letter E, as she'd done when buying the small compound. She didn't include a calling number either as she didn't own a phone and wouldn't want to get one that could give her location away. For necessary communication, she had created an inbox for electronic correspondence and checked it as often as she dared go into the cities, always at a local Web boona. While there, she'd sip red rooibos tea with sweet cane milk. On this particular visit, Essien noted that both the retail shop manager and the lawyer sent her a formal message letting her know they were not seeking new candidates. The hotel manager never responded at all.

Passing on from Thorn, Essien drove an additional one hundred stadia to get to Soja's Inn, a town that had started as a military training compound, until the military had been forced to move elsewhere with the agreement several centuries ago. Since then, the city had transformed completely into a small-scale metropolis with an impressive university, technology firms, and two large-scale farmers who supplied food to the entire city and surrounding areas.

Essien sat in a boona, searching the Web for news about herself, sipping her rooibos tea long gone, and trying to watch the people around her without being too obvious. She was truly anonymous. Nobody even looked her way. The women here had a certain looseness and freedom, their clothes scant with bright colors and their laughs loud; the men were friendly and talkative, too, holding doors open and stopping random women to compliment them. Essien stood out from people that she could tell were locals, but there were enough people who looked different just like her that she didn't draw too much attention. At a table behind her were a group of people who looked like they might be from Yaxia, with the straight, cape-like dark hair and the language Essien could overhear as they chatted in between ordering. Definitely travelers to Alkebulan by the sounds of their conversation that she couldn't understand at all. Essien knew that Gabriel had only just begun allowing travel between the two nations a mere decade ago. These were the first visitors from that nation that Essien had gotten to meet personally. She thought about her cousins, the daughters of her Nne's sister, and wondered if they were enjoying their own travels in the East. Oh, what an adventure it would be to freely visit them and explore that part of the world.

When her eyes scanned over them, she noticed a young Zulu girl sitting at a table with an older woman who was watching her. Essien smiled, drawing her cheeks up wide. The woman smiled back, just a small flex of her lips, and the girl dropped her eyes. Essien knew the dangers and the risks of being recognized, but she couldn't remain locked away forever. And she couldn't survive much longer either if she didn't start bringing in funds.

The garden behind her small compound was finally producing the beginnings of a harvest, but it would be months before she was bringing in enough to live on, possibly even years to have a steady and reliable source of her own food stored away. Essien sighed. She was both grateful that she had grown up being taught the intricacies of crops and annoyed that her life had been reduced to this. She had once stood beside the President. She had been destined to build a queendom and sit on a throne. And now, all she had to show for all her hard work was a fear so deep it kept her wound up tight as a coiled snake and just as deadly. Whatever the risks, Essien knew she had to take them. If she were caught...she'd cross that bridge when it came.

Essien crafted a slightly more honest employment inquiry, including that she was a farmer's apprentice and had weapons training. She kept her mother's family name and added the number of a quick voice phone that she'd bought off a teenager at an electronics stand for twenty Naira. She left this updated inquiry with several departments at the Soja's Inn University and with a tech entrepreneur who she met randomly at an internet boona where she learned within the first few exchanges that he was born in Igbo State and had sisters who looked like her. As a result of the communication, she finally got two interviews.

To prepare for them, Essien had the dressmaker in Thorn make suits for her on credit. The dressmaker was more than glad to trade gossip with Essien, and in exchange for the camaraderie, she made Essien two suits on credit until she had received her first pay.

"You must have blue," the woman told her when Essien asked for black.

"Let's do both." One dark blue with pants, the other black with pants.

"What about this?" The dressmaker held up a skirt made of dark gray material with fine, shiny black and gold threads running through it. Essien ran her hand down the fabric and appreciated its texture. She knew she'd never wear the skirt anywhere, so she had to shake her head.

Both suits fit her as well as her military uniform had. With all the military had taught her, she had at least appreciated impeccable dress. She knew she could distract from the brightness of her dyed hair with serious attire—at least she hoped to. If she didn't begin working soon, she would be completely out of money and have to access the funds at her bank. That would almost surely bring Gabriel down upon her before she could even spend one cent of Naira. Essien hadn't planned on needing to risk her freedom within barely a year of being a civilian. It made sense for her to save the money in her bank accounts for longer term emergencies. Going to the bank would announce exactly where she was, she was sure of it, so that wasn't a real option—not yet.

THE INTERVIEW WITH THE AGRICULTURE AND RURAL DEVELOP-ment department at the Soja's Inn University showed the most promise. She spoke with a panel of three professors in an empty lecture hall, the front dominated by a transparent board before rows and rows of seats with retractable desks.

Two men and one woman sat at a table in the front of the room. The men smiled when she shook their hands, one becoming self-conscious about the length of his jacket sleeves. The woman waved her to sit down with a flippant gesture that instantly made Essien feel defensive. All three had similar yellowish-brown coloring with both the men and the woman's hair cut low. All three of them spoke only Kinyarwanda and English.

Professor Mulekatete, the woman, asked the questions as though she were bored of the answers before she even heard them.

"What do you know about the Unathi Agricultural Production and Regulatory Enforcement Act of 1905? How would you go about implementing a countryside agricultural census? What do you think about commercial farming and the proliferation of industrialized farmers in the AmaZulu and AmaXhosa Collaborative?"

When Essien was done answering, Professors Hakizimana and Rusanganwa asked Essien follow-up questions, smiling and saying, "Yes, very good."

After all their questions had been asked, Professor Mulekatete finally smiled, and the spread of her teeth made her deep-brown skin shine. "If hired, you will become a consultant for the school's newest addition, an agricultural technology school. Our mission is to properly instruct men and women in new farming methods. With our next candidate's help, we aim to improve farming efficiency and sustainability across the country."

They asked if she had any questions. Just one: "Is the school government run?" All three of them started laughing, and Essien didn't join in. She couldn't see what was funny about her question.

Professor Rusanganwa spoke up. "The school operates largely independent of oversight or external control. We hired our own school Director, whom you will meet if we decide to hire you."

The three of them exchanged a look again, and then the woman said, "You are our best candidate so far." Essien smiled at each of them in turn, keeping the smile on her face as they concluded the interview with a tour.

The hiring panel took her around the campus, showing her the granite buildings and the marble statue of the university's founder, a man of proud Nguni heritage, whose eldest father had made his fortune building sailing ships and navigational equipment in the 900s. After the military compound shut down centuries later, the man's inheritors had used some of his passed-down wealth to purchase the land and turn it into a beautiful campus with functional academic and research buildings occupying a discreet position in the city's most prestigious neighborhood.

Essien also learned that the university had started as an apprentice-style academy for shipbuilders and sailors to learn proper ship building and sea navigation; more and newer schools had been added over the years since its inception. The school of agriculture was surprisingly the newest.

Professor Rusanganwa looked around at the university buildings with his lips pinched into a proud smirk. He said, "People did not need to come here to learn agriculture. They learned it from their families who learned it from their families all the way back. But we're always learning new things, especially as imports from other countries increase. So much produce we've been able to cultivate in the last fifty years is because of our increase in imports from the Iroquois Nation, Ka Pae Aina, and Ayiti alone. The research we're doing now would not have been possible a century ago."

"You know we started as a military compound centuries ago?" Professor Mulekatete asked her with the second smile she had seen throughout the interview. "There is an amazing exhibit in the visitor center about the military's history and impact on the nation. Our Tribal Council was able to negotiate a treaty during the War of Unification that included no military compounds would be built within our borders or in Bantu State. Would you like to see the exhibit?"

"I'm sorry, I have a second interview shortly after this. Can I come back and visit later?"

They were more than happy to let her leave. They each shook her hand a final time, pumping her arm harder. She knew she would be hired for this job. She was a fool to take it and an even bigger fool not to take it. There was just eighty Naira left in her change purse. She needed the income and had accepted as much. Assuming a job on a fake identity felt somehow safer than walking into the bank and asking to withdraw funds from her account. She had to work, but she had a limited skill set. Working for an agriculture school had to be the least expected route she would take.

THE MEETING WITH THE MAN WHO OWNED THE START-UP TECH-nology company took place in a multistory glass building in a circular courtyard of other glass and stone buildings. He had greeted her at his office door, smelling of an expensive scenter with a rushed and urgent tone in his voice. Right away, she knew he hadn't been interested in the years of weapons training listed on her inquiry.

"It's Uche, please, call me Uche. Mr. Nwabueze is my father."

"Then you must call me Eziamaka."

The man's eyes when they looked at her seemed to sink down into slits that conveyed something to her without saying it.

"Such a beautiful name. You have to tell me, where is your mother from? Eh-heh, and your father, what did he do?"

Essien lied again and made up a story about being born in Iroquois Nation and only returning to the homeland as an adult, to explore her roots.

"But your family is still in Igbo State, yes?"

"Everyone died when I was twelve. My mother, my father, my sisters, all dead."

"My condolences. You must be in want of new family bonds, then. Are you dating?"

Essien had smiled, so as to remain unrecognizable, but she knew she would not be getting hired by this man as she said, "I am engaged to be married to a man from Iroquois. Early school sweethearts. He is there now renewing his travel documents. He'll be expatriating to this country in a couple of months to join me."

At that news, Essien knew the interview was over, but still the man kept talking. Essien just nodded and smiled wide, and tried not to give away that she had lost all interest. He wanted to know if she would be having any children soon.

Behind the man's head, a screen projector depicted footage of a scene that stopped Essien's breath in her throat and removed all pretense of paying attention to Uche. There was Enyemaka, his short stature making him instantly recognizable. His hands were gripped behind his back by the Guard walking him briskly into a dark stone building with a black plate glass front. Essien stood up from where she'd been seated across from Uche.

The headline under that repeating footage was damning: "Rebel to be tried and executed." Essien tried to breathe and felt her chest squeezed tight. She had to get out of there.

"I'm sorry, I have to go." She had lost any sense of where she was and why, so she was completely herself as she stepped away and began walking toward the door. Uche caught up to her, even put his hand on the small of her back as he walked her out of his office and thanked her for dropping by. He didn't seem to have any idea who she truly was or why her mood had changed so suddenly into one of hopeless terror.

IN THE FRONT OF HER MIND NOW, GABRIEL SURFACED AGAIN AND again, swimming through her conscious thoughts, chasing her through living nightmares as she made her way home through city traffic. She wondered how the President might react to finally learning where she was, if he would come to her immediately or send someone in his place. If he would be overcome with righteous anger or relieved that she was safe.

He had Enyemaka. Gabriel was putting him on trial. If anyone had been a friend to her, it was Enyemaka. Essien couldn't let him take the fall for all that the rebels were trying to do, had done, what she had let them use her to do. Maybe Enyemaka had already spilled where he thought she might be. Maybe Gabriel already knew where she was, and he was simply biding his time until he came to her.

Somehow, she knew that wasn't like him; if he found her whereabouts, he would come to her himself—and immediately. She only had to think about them to know that her blockers were still solidly in place. There was no way he could have found her. But he had Enyemaka.

Enyamaka had saved her when no one else could or had even known she needed saving. He had gotten her out, helped her escape. Maybe he'd done it for a selfish reason, to get her into Mansa's grip. Maybe he'd also put her in danger, more than once. Maybe he was even to blame for what had happened in the rebel camp...and before, when she was still just a Soja in the military. Enyemaka wasn't perfect, and he'd hurt her, too. But that was back when they were both working as Gabriel's Guard together, before Enyemaka was kicked out. Kicked out by the President, more likely. To keep him away from her? To stop him from doing what he had planned to do? To keep him from destroying any chance of the prophecy coming true?

She tried to remember that conversation she'd had with Enyemaka. He'd tried to warn her. He'd told her in so many words that Gabriel was not who she thought, that he wasn't a good person. He cautioned her that spiritual and mystical forces were at play, moving her into position like a piece on a chess board. And she'd known; even then, she'd had some suspicions. That underneath his friendly grin, there was a depth of cruelty that the President kept hidden. Hidden even from her. But she knew it was there; she had felt it as she sat next to him at his dining room table every night. She tried to remember how she had felt back then. About Gabriel, her position in the Guard, and...everything else. She couldn't put herself back into the mind of young Essien; it was too foreign to her considering all that she had done since. But Gabriel had been honest and tried to tell her. Of course, she'd been afraid, and paranoid then, too. She had rejected the truth he had tried to get her to acknowledge. She had refused to accept it. A human did not become a deity. Not even in this world of flames pouring out of her fingertips or floods in unnatural places. It wasn't like now though, when her head was on a constant swivel, and she was always waiting for Gabriel's hand to clamp down on her shoulder out of nowhere.

Those emotions had dogged her steps every day of being with the rebels in their underground lairs, too, falling into a sort of background static that couldn't distract her from what was in front of her. Eventually, both the fear and the paranoia disappeared into a dull undercurrent of noise with first those spells to make her forget and then encompassed by her own constant thought of metal. A thick, solid, weighty wall of protection around her to keep her thoughts away from Gabriel at all costs.

As Essien ran her mind over these months, the most she could get from this time after she had gotten away from the military and gone into hiding in plain sight were snapshots, moments frozen in time, disconnected from everything that had come before and would come after.

What Essien remembered most was the color brown. From the darkly tanned and multihued browns of faces that stretched from pale ivory and shiny gold to deep umber and midnight black, from the greenish khaki brown and deep ochre in stadia after stadia of fields covered in the crops that kept Alkebulan rising.

Her favorite moment in the snapshots that flowed past during her reminiscing was the shoots of green that sprouted out of all that brown and grew tall and bushy or thin and viny. The crops that would grow into colorful pyramids that she would never get to see sitting on her counters and being chopped and added to her meals.

The snapshots from the brief time she had spent in that cottage got blurry, and it was as if the days rolled all into one, a monotonous rumble of the day in and day out of an anonymous life. Never letting anyone get too close to the real her. She had never stopped looking over her shoulder all the time, never stopped reinforcing those shields around her mind. The feeling Essien got from those times wasn't peace. She wasn't at peace. It would be artificial if she were because the fear never left. There was no way she could hide forever.

And he had Enyemaka. She hoped he wasn't dead already.

Taking a deep breath, Essien dissolved the shields in her mind, pulling down the walls of metal she'd carefully constructed around her thoughts over these months, and whispered out loud, "Gabriel."

CHAPTER TWENTY-ONE

◆

LIKE A VISION UNFOLDING IN HER MINDS' EYE, ESSIEN SAW GA-briel's face for the space of a series of heartbeats. He was shirtless, stand-ing beside a bath in a compound she did not recognize or know. Her eyes got distracted by the sight of his bare chest, the strong pectoral muscles straining across his chest, carved down his abs, and bulging from his arms. Then she saw the woman smiling up at him. A woman with tawny skin, like gold and red mixed with deep brown, was kneeling before him, helping to slide his legs out of slacks. Essien recoiled from the image, pulling all of her blockers back in place with the mental clank of armor. She shut the link down tighter than it had been before, wondering if it was too late.

It was full daylight out, but Essien suddenly felt tired. Her arms and legs were heavy and weighted. She couldn't tell if she was exhausted physi-cally or mentally, but it was as though she hadn't slept in days. She went to her front door, her steps slow and more labored than even after a long run. The sun poured in through the front window, lying in a square on the floor in front of the armchair. Essien wanted to stand in that patch of honey on the floor, but the effort to take another step was too great. So, she turned, taking the same slow steps into her bedroom. She knew it was early, the sun was still out, but she couldn't shake how sleepy she was. She lay down on her pallet bed and went to sleep.

As Essien slept, the President made an appearance in her dreams. He stood in her bedroom doorway, and she awkwardly beckoned to him with hands chained at the wrist. Then he stood at the end of a long hallway, and no matter how long she walked—with feet weighted by stone blocks—he never got closer.

Just before she woke, Essien dreamed that Gabriel had lain down in the bed next to her, and she felt the release of her chains falling off. His skin was like warm velvet against her fingertips as she reached for him. She woke up feeling saddened and depressed by the walls around her, and the mood remained dark when she realized it was still only nighttime on the same day. She rolled over and knew she would only regain contentment when she drifted back into sleep again. Her stomach emitted a howl of emptiness, and Essien sighed, pushing herself up.

She moved to stand inside her bedroom doorway for the space it took her to realize that the buoyant anxiety she had felt earlier was still there. Her muscles were already twitching, and her mind began to run in an endless loop of hypotheticals. She didn't turn on any lights as she moved to sit on the armchair in the front room, forgetting her hunger entirely.

The moon slid in through a skylight in the ceiling. The old man who sold her the compound had told her he'd installed that skylight himself because there were only the two windows in the front room and the one in the back bedroom, but none in this middle space between. The muted light fell onto her head and into her lap in a metallic blue that made her feel like everything she wanted was just inside the reach of that circle. She felt as though she had stepped into an alternate mode of being, one she couldn't understand.

She had no idea what it was she should be feeling sitting beneath a moon that shined so brightly in darkness. She put her hand out and let the light pool into her palm, the darkness slashing her at the wrist. She thought so many things sitting in the dark that she became one simple thought, pulsing in her head, pleading with her for some channel of translation that she knew she could not give it.

Since the escape, her life had become a day in and day out hustle. She had almost forgotten how she ended up here, and that ultimately, she couldn't stay forever. She kept thinking of the simplicity and order of that small little cottage and the growing garden out back.

Now that Gabriel had seen her, it was only a matter of time before he came. It wouldn't even do her any justice to try and run again. Another hidden spot in another anonymous city wouldn't save Enyemaka. It wouldn't free him of whatever torture Gabriel might inflict upon him. She closed her eyes and shuddered to think of it, glimpsing bloodstained walls and piles of ashes around her.

Maybe she could leave Alkebulan for good. There were boats that would sail her to Lutruita, and from there, maybe she might end up in Nihon. She had always said that she should leave the country, but she had not yet done it in all these years. She wondered to herself why and whether now was as good a time as any. Sitting on the edge of the couch, her eyes finally able to see in the dark, she couldn't figure out how she would ever move from that spot.

I can't think like this, she told herself, standing up finally. It felt like struggling through chest-high water trying to stand and step away from the armchair. She felt even more exhausted than she had earlier. She could at least turn a light on, so she wouldn't be feeling so morbid and unenthused in the dark.

She switched on a lamp. It felt like her arm moved in slow motion, and her fingers couldn't quite grasp the light chain. She needed to gather her essential belongings and pack. She had more items now than she had when she'd first moved in. She'd have to leave it all behind, but she wanted to be ready before they came for her. A glance at the clock showed it was already close to sunrise. She'd sat in the dark for hours, and yet it had only seemed like a couple of minutes.

Essien must have dozed off sitting there with her legs curled up into a ball. Something woke her up, but she wasn't sure what. As she lay listening, she heard a creaking sound emitted from the floorboards behind her. She shot up out of the chair and then crouched, so she was somewhat hidden. In the dark, Essien saw two figures with the distinct length of rapid fires pointed in her direction creeping into the front room through the archway leading from the kitchen. Essien briefly realized she must have left the back door unlocked. A silly, potentially fatal, mistake. The men both wore the familiar all-black of the military uniform. Their faces were covered by reflective helmets, and Essien wondered if they had come to kill or capture her.

The two men were on the other side of the armchair now, staring down at her. Their rapid fires were still pointed in her direction. One of them shifted their rapid fire muzzle down toward the floor and stepped forward as if to grab her, as though she would go peacefully. They should have shot her as soon as they'd seen her if they believed that was the case.

Essien looked at the two men, sizing them up. The taller one had his rapid fire still pointed at her, while the second man was slowly reaching for her, like she was a stray cat they wanted to lure into being captured. Essien saw it all in the second she had and knew she would be shot if she resisted. She saw the flash of sparks and the silvery-gold projectile that would dart out.

Essien's body responded without her mind having caught up to it yet. It wasn't a blinding rush of speed or a quick snap of reflexes. Essien used her magic like flexing a hand to land a solid punch right in the middle of a moving target. She felt her shields break again as she snatched at all of what made them man: the expanding and contracting of their hearts, the electrical firing of their brains, the blooming and collapsing of their lungs. She had never done anything like it.

One minute she was afraid of being shot, of a bullet rocketing right toward her face, and the next, the rapid fires they held were a scattering of dust in the air, and both men were face down on the ground and not moving.

This magic had come out unexpectedly, not fire or water, but something else entirely; a matter of her life or her death, and she had chosen to live. It seemed to be a specialty of hers: thwarting death.

Someone knocked on her front door, hard knocks, each one feeling as if it was pounded through her chest that made her instantly snap out of whatever trance she had been locked in.

The peephole showed four men, all tall, wearing matching dark uniforms with matching dark helmets that obscured their faces completely. She pressed her forehead to the door and knew who it was the way she'd known that she wouldn't get to sleep this night in peace. She didn't need to see the black, red, and green flag pins on each of their jacket lapels to know who they were and why they were outside her door after midnight. That surreal aura she'd felt all evening dissipated from her with the shaky rasp of her breathing.

She heard murmuring voices through the door and lifted her head to look through the peephole again. There were five men standing outside her door now, a fifth one having joined the four and moved up to stand directly in front. Essien jumped back from the door, quickly recognizing who the new man at the door was.

Even though she'd called him here, she hadn't thought he would arrive this soon. She'd thought for sure she'd have at least a day, maybe two, to get used to the idea that Gabriel knew where she was and was coming for her. Seeing him there almost made her want to vomit.

"It's Gabriel, Essien." As if she didn't already know.

Her intention had been for him to come—she hadn't planned on running—but now, realizing it was too late for that, that all her options were gone, she wanted to scream and punch. Instead, she took a breath, to keep the flames under control.

She opened the door with a snatch of her arm. The President stood on her covered portico surrounded by a few of his personal Guard. He was smiling confidently, his hands in his pockets, bouncing gently on his heels. She peered around him, three engines squeezed in the dirt clearing, six other men posted and alert.

"May we come in?"

"Your guards already did." She flicked a hand at where the two men were on the ground, still quiet and not moving. She almost hoped she'd killed them, then immediately felt bad for thinking it. It was not their fault. They were simply doing their jobs, following orders, just like she had, and so she had to accept that they were not to blame for this encounter.

Gabriel spoke to the men around him softly and then stepped over the threshold. Essien slammed the door behind him without meaning to.

"What are you angry about?" he asked.

"Where is Enyemaka?" She would try to be brave. There was a reason she'd called Gabriel; he'd just come much too soon, but she could rally from that unexpected hitch.

Gabriel stared her up and down, moving his eyes from her head down to her toes and said, "You look well. Civilian life suits you."

"Is Enyemaka dead? Please tell me if he's dead."

"What would you give me for the information?" he said, smiling at her as though they were playing a friendly game of mancala across a table.

She almost said, "Anything, everything." But it wasn't true. Clearly, she wasn't willing to give up her freedom. That price alone was more than she could bear.

"I saw Enyemaka on the news. I know you've arrested him. I don't know why I thought you might negotiate with me."

He stood inside the door, staring at her. "I'll hear your negotiation terms."

She was shaking her head. "The minute I saw you standing at my door, I knew that calling you here means I've likely ruined his life...and mine. I've made it worse." She shouldn't have discounted that cruelty that she knew was inside the President. She shouldn't have believed for a second that having her back in his grasp would be worth the price or worth more to him than freeing Enyemaka.

His smile slipped a little. "I came to try and make the situation better." She didn't believe him.

"Then tell me where Enyemaka is, give him to me, and then turn around and leave. Forget you ever saw me. Or this place."

It was the President's turn to shake his head. "I'd be doing us both a great disservice if I did that, Essien." He took a step further into the room.

Essien took several steps away, so that the armchair was between them.

The President was wearing a simple black overtunic and slacks, his usual attire. He was wrinkled at every bend, like he had been sitting for a while. His hair had grown out, longer and spreading around his head in tiny, shiny springs.

"I sent up that signal for you to come. I knew you were coming. In fact, I wanted you to come, but I didn't think you'd come this soon. I thought I'd have a day or two."

"At one point this year, I thought I would never find you. When you made the connection this afternoon, I knew you might try to run again. Even though you basically put out the welcome mat and screamed, 'Come and get me!' So, here I am."

She shook her head. "I couldn't move. I thought I was in shock or...torn. I should have run. But I knew you had Enyemaka. I want to see him, please. Please tell me if he's alive or not."

Gabriel shook his head, like a zebra shaking away a fly. "I have been flying on a skycraft to get here all night."

"I'll come with you willingly. I won't fight. Just release Enyemaka, please."

Gabriel studied her face quietly. His eyes roved over every inch and line, settling on her lips.

"I came to take you back peacefully, Essien."

She stepped further away from him, having to remember the two men passed out behind the armchair right before she put her foot on one of them.

"I have a life here. A life not connected to any military or politics or—"

"You fool yourself. You are where you are because of me; you are what you are because of me. Everything you do is connected to my military and my politics." He had moved around the couch. She stepped back in front of it, but knew it wasn't enough distance. He could still reach out and grab her from there.

"I didn't want that job anymore. I didn't want to work for you anymore. I asked you to let me go."

"When I left the hospital, I thought you would accept the inevitable and submit to me. I never thought you were capable of mutiny."

"You think I'm a child."

"You were a child when I met you; it's impossible to think of you any other way."

"If you think of me as a child, then why do you want me? What about me says 'chase me to the ends of the earth'? And don't you dare bring up that damned prophecy!" Enyemaka's words mocked her now, standing there with Gabriel inching closer and closer without taking another step. Enyemaka had tried to warn her, and she hadn't listened. She hadn't been ready to hear a word he said, had grown defensive and emotional when he'd spoken plainly. In the end she had tried to heed him, but it was too late. Now it was too late to save him or herself. And the President had Enyemaka.

"If you free Enyemaka, I'll—"

The President cut her off by interjecting, "Lie to me to get what you want and look for the first chance of escape once he's free." Essien didn't even try to deny him. So the President continued. "Whether you realize it or not, Essien, this is exactly what you asked for and have received. When you threw your mind open to me, you basically begged me to come and retrieve you. And here I am."

"Gabriel, don't you understand that I can kill you?" Her voice faltered. She didn't have time to wonder if she could do it. Take out her President. The one man she had been training to protect and serve for years now. She had to believe that she could. Looking him fully in the eye, she tried to put that surety into her words: "I will take your life—and all the men outside, I will take their lives, too. If you won't give me Enyemaka, there is nothing else to discuss."

There was a small lift of a smile at the corner of Gabriel's mouth. "And that's why I want you to come back willingly."

"I won't. Not without you agreeing to free Enyemaka."

He grinned at her, still standing on the other side of the armchair. She hadn't stood too close to him on instinct.

In all the years she'd known him, he'd never let her see what it meant for him to truly exist in his power, to be as he is in truth, without hiding any part of who and what he was. Not like he did now, standing on the other side of the chair that barely came to their knees. She watched him from a few feet across and knew that if he wanted to, he could physically disrupt everything in the room, and everything inside her, without moving from his spot.

CHAPTER TWENTY-TWO

◆

S HE COULDN'T GET HER LUNGS TO FILL COMPLETELY WITH AIR, seeing him like that, glowing with his almost-power that came from outside and inside him at the same time. It made the skin on her arms feel itchy and crawling. A translucent shimmer of silver-blue light pressed outward from behind him and spilled around the edge of his smiling teeth.

She could see it now, an oozing of power that dripped off him and into the room, making the edges of her vision waver and grow faint. She saw him across from her, then she blinked, and she was back at the silver lake. She was under the water, sinking down, down, down beneath the surface of the lake, and then there was a hand.

A hand pulling her up to stand on top of the water. The man made of silver-blue water. As the water dripped, sliding down his cheeks and chin, the face became Gabriel's, and she stared up at him with her mouth hanging open, eyes growing wider the longer she stared.

Essien blinked again, and he was behind her, his face in her hair, which had grown out to just past shoulder length, and his arms, if she could call them arms, were wrapping her up and pulling her in. She felt the snap of static electricity as his skin touched hers, and then she was falling backward into him, not his body but that sizzling of power that made the air around them expand and then contract with the snap of rubber.

One minute her back was pressed up against his chest, his arms holding her tight, and the next something inside of her chest was slashed open to take in everything she'd spilled into.

She let out a shriek as she fell into him and began to drown.

It felt like she drank him into everywhere he touched her, or she slipped into him like a funnel, and he poured all that electricity into her. She knew this was power he'd not used in a long time, power he didn't even need anymore, as he filtered it in slowly, slowly, so she didn't overflow and truly drown. He knew she was taking him into her; he knew she couldn't stop and hadn't meant to start it in the first place. He held her tighter, knowing that this draining was all his idea now, even though at the start it hadn't been.

She felt sweat dampen her temples, the bridge of her nose, her upper lip. There were sharp electric sensations trailing up her arms and down her legs. She tried not to make another sound. Emotions just barely grazed her consciousness, a sorrow that dug deep, a happiness that floated her into the air, an anger that gritted her teeth against her inner cheek and made her taste the salty sweetness of her own blood.

There were memories, too. Memories that she had never lived: Gabriel rising above her, Gabriel's face shining like the moon behind his head, Gabriel splashing her with silver lake water, Gabriel walking beside her through a garden with crowns glinting atop both their heads, a smaller version of Gabriel toddling along behind him.

When it was over, when she'd taken only the power he didn't use and not a drop more, when she felt herself settle back into the room with the harsh tumble of granite stone boulders off a cliff, she opened eyes that hadn't been closed, and Gabriel was still standing on the other side of the room.

"I came to take you back, Essien," he was whispering. "And you are going to come with me."

"No, I am not." She felt wobbly, like her knees might give out beneath her. He smiled—a flexing of his cheeks not showing any teeth. She was still stubborn, even facing her end.

"You are coming with me. You don't have a choice."

"What laws are you enforcing?" She knew she couldn't fight him; she felt her defeat like the lingering tingle of his jaw against the side of her cheek. She couldn't just lie down and accept it.

There had to be some way out of the punishment the military thought she deserved. Whatever he'd just done to her, the punishment hadn't even started yet. She was starting to tremble with the unused adrenaline shaking as her muscles tensed against what was about to happen.

"I could recite the laws you've broken, if that would get you to come willingly, but it won't...will it?"

She shook her head. "What about Enyemaka?"

Gabriel grinned. "I considered keeping him alive. For your sake. In the end, it was too much trouble. His group might try to break him out of any prison I send him to, and there are no prisons in Alkebulan."

The words hit her in the chest and left her breathless for what felt like a stretch of time without a future. "What did you do to him? Please say you didn't kill him. Please."

Gabriel shook his head. "I killed him myself. Right before flying here." He was grinning now.

The scream Essien let out displayed the immense horror and loss she felt losing someone she had grown to care for. It announced her recognition of the grave miscalculation she had made, and how it would cost her everything. He had done it to hurt her. There was no other reason beyond causing her pain. She stared at Gabriel's face, her mouth still open. She attempted to talk, but instead only mouthed words. Her throat was dry and tasted of ashes.

"I am going to fight you, Gabriel." The words tore her throat coming out. She knew now that this was a fight she would not win. "You and all your men outside will be dead before tonight is over. I will bring this house down around us if you make me fight you. You killed Enyemaka, and now I am going to kill you!" She felt the flames spark up in her palm. She hesitated, not sure if she could even allow herself to kill the man she called President.

HE'D TRIED EMPOWERING HER BY LETTING HER TAKE SOME OF his very own power. He felt the bond was complete now, its thick, surety coiled around his heart and wound just as tightly around hers. Whatever he'd expected, the rage sparking up in her eyes and licking at her fingertips showed that it hadn't worked. She knew she couldn't beat him, but she was still going to try.

She was always bold and ready to fight; that's what had made him offer her positions no woman had ever held. Empowering her was proving futile, he realized, as she opened her fists and prepared herself to attack him with flame. They both stood still in her living room: him trying not to scare her, her trying to decide if she should strike first or wait....

He considered his options: He could send in the seven men he'd brought with him under strict orders not to harm her, only to capture her. They would all die.

He could leave her here and catch her unawares at a later date, but not too late because she had already proven herself elusive and difficult to catch. Both of those options guaranteed that all of his men would die, or most of them. He glanced down at the two men, still slumped on the floor, not a sound or movement the entire time he'd stood there. He could reach out and check if their hearts were still beating, but if he moved again, he wasn't sure what the woman across the room would do.

But there was a third option, one he had hoped she wouldn't force him to choose.

He didn't want anyone else dead, not in this country compound with her battered engine out front and her short career in backyard gardening. He also couldn't give her time and opportunity to escape him again.

Essien had watched his face as he stared at those men on the floor, thinking about what awful thing to do to her first. She was prepared to die, that much she was certain of. When Gabriel finally raised his glance to look at her, she taunted him, "Make your move."

So, Gabriel chose the third option and flexed himself into that power he'd poured into her and let her take. She screamed before the invisible mass of his energy even hit her. She tried to throw flames at him, to become a flame to burn them both up, but she was too late. The cascade of electric particles thundering into her lifted her off her feet in a halo of static and then ground her into the floor. There wasn't an ember anywhere for her to grasp.

Her bones felt like the press of a thousand mountains crashing into her and through her, only her mind told her that it didn't hurt; wave after wave of euphoria scalded through her mind and made her muscles unable to control themselves as they fought to scramble off her bones and dissolve into the wood and the dirt and the air.

"What does it feel like for you, Essien?" Gabriel said, panting and looking down at her from above. She couldn't even speak, so she screamed.

"I know it doesn't hurt. Why are you screaming?"

She was on the ground and rolling back and forth, her entire body convulsed against itself, and her mind kept insisting that it felt good even though she knew it didn't.

"Essien, I can do this to you all night. I can do this to you even if I were in the Capital, and you were here. I could make you feel like this whether you were in the room with me or not. Come home with me, Essien. I will not ask again."

He stopped long enough for her to roll over, sit up, and try to stand. She couldn't do it; her muscles were still twinging, and her entire body shivered as though she were cold. There was not a spark to draw on anywhere inside her.

She spoke to him with her head lowered, still trying to catch her breath and calm down. "What did you just do to me?"

"I gave you myself, in the truest sense of the word."

She was gasping, "How can you do that?"

"There is much about me that you have refused to learn, Essien. I want you to come with me, so we can both learn about each other."

"You already know everything there is to know about me. You were able to find me, way out here, and come to me the minute you found out. And you just...did something to me...something I can't even... *What did you do to me?!*"

"I gave you myself, Essien. I made you a part of me."

"*What?!*" She was still feeling those shivers and sparks everywhere on her body, and they were coming from him. She had not the slightest clue what they were or how he was able to do this. She had felt this minor sensation before, the strike of nerve endings down her arms, but that gentle sting wasn't even close to what he had just shown her he could do.

"If you would prefer, Essien, I want to learn to love you because right now, I must say, I do not."

"I never asked you to love me. I never asked you to notice me. I did not ask you for any of this!" She didn't say that she had never planned to fall in love with him, her superior commander, following all of her best judgments, and the bitter taste of his revelation would stick in her mind. It shouldn't matter to her at all, and yet she would think about it again and again for a long time afterward. She made herself stand up from her living room floor now that he wasn't assaulting her beyond the laws of metaphysics. She still felt brave, like she could call his bluff. Maybe he wouldn't throw her in jail and melt the key. Perhaps she could convince him to let her go or leave her alone.

"Please don't do this to me, Gabriel."

"I've already done it. You are coming with me."

"I didn't want to be a guard or a soja anymore."

"You owe Alkebulan another fifty years, Essien."

"I can force you to turn this into a war. I can—" She had been prepared to throw every weapon she had at that moment, but he knew what she was planning to say and wanted to silence her once and for all.

For a space of twelve minutes and thirty-six seconds, he filled every part of her body with his power. It was as though he reached inside her body the way a glove covers a hand, and flexed his fingers, tightening all her muscles at once. Her blood ran hot right below her skin, and she screamed hoarsely, exhausted. He possessed her completely, and he made her body into a pulsing, writhing, scrambling organism on the floor.

She was on the ground staring up at him again, and it was hard for her to talk around her heaving chest and shivering limbs. He could see her trembling uncontrollably, even though he was holding back his energy, with difficulty. That part of him that lay like a pool of magic in his gut wanted to join with the part of her that she had taken. He held it back.

"Don't make me just leave, Gabriel." She knew that leaving the military without permission and without following protocols had been illegal, but if this is what he could do, he was never going to let her leave even if she had asked and followed the proper steps.

"No." His eyes hadn't left her face once. "Your trial date was set the minute I notified the Military Council you had been located. We need your presence to conduct it."

"I'm going to tell them the truth. I'm going to tell them that I'm being forced into political captivity by the President of Alkebulan, so he can kidnap me and force me to ransom my soul for his carnal pleasure."

Gabriel laughed and did that thing with his power gently; he filled her up just barely to the brim, the static charge lifting hairs on her arms. She didn't want to feel that electric fullness again; she didn't want that much of him that far into her and spilling over the edges. He eased back from her in power but moved closer to stand over her.

"If you think that this is sex magic, Essien, then I must make sure I have changed your mind by the end of it."

"Or confirmed it."

Gabriel just shrugged, a half smile still on his face.

If she tried to fight, Gabriel could kill her, or paralyze her long enough to tie her up for transport. He wouldn't leave her be, not when he knew where she was. She had been delusional to think he would leave her to a life without him. It had been naive to believe he might trade Enyemaka's life for hers. It had been worse than wishful thinking. With everything she knew and had done, it wasn't safe for her to be anywhere but with him.

She tried desperately to think of any plan of action besides the one she seemed destined to take. No new ideas occurred to her, as they hadn't over the previous months of her exile. She couldn't go to the news boards or criminal investigations or any of the presidential initiative agencies like the family services office or even her own brothers and their families.

Everything was controlled and infiltrated by the direct authority of the President. She had no idea what he might do to her family if she involved them. No one could help her with this. She couldn't even help herself.

She turned just her head to stare at him. The light of the moon lit the space behind him with melancholic finality, and his entire face was in shadow. She didn't say okay or let's do this; he didn't say anything either.

"You are an evil man." She said each word slowly and tried to fill each with all the rage and hate she felt but could not show. The chains he had bound her in were invisible but no less tight.

Gabriel stilled, like a snake about to snatch its prey between unhinged jaws. "You'll apologize to me for that one day."

EVERYTHING WAS LEFT IN ITS PLACE. SHE LET HERSELF GLANCE around the cottage one time but made it brief. She exited the front door in front of Gabriel who held it open for her.

"She killed Ajou and Nzuzu." Gabriel said it with no inflection, just the facts. Like he wasn't appalled or upset. Two of the guards peeled off to enter the cottage behind them, the door closing with a solid click.

She stood there on her small front porch, waiting for Gabriel to say something, but words never came. He reached for her, and though she flinched in surprise, she allowed him to grip her upper arm and use it to steer her toward the waiting engine. The guards around them silently fell into step.

Driving down the long road toward the closest city with a skycraft transportation center, she knew she might never get to see these streets again. She might never get to experience life on her own, with no one to answer to except herself. She would never again be in control of her life and what happened to her.

Though she had vowed to be stoic and strong, she quickly brushed away the wetness that slipped down her cheeks and watched the moon whip in and out of her view. She was too upset and blinded by her tears to notice the faint outlines of figures floating in and out of the clouds above their engine. She was too focused on the sorrow and despair sitting next to her to notice that akukoifo, those celestial beings from her childhood, were visible to her again. She couldn't see anything else beyond the disbelief and despair. Anything could happen to her; the rest of her life was at the mercy of the President's whim.

PART II

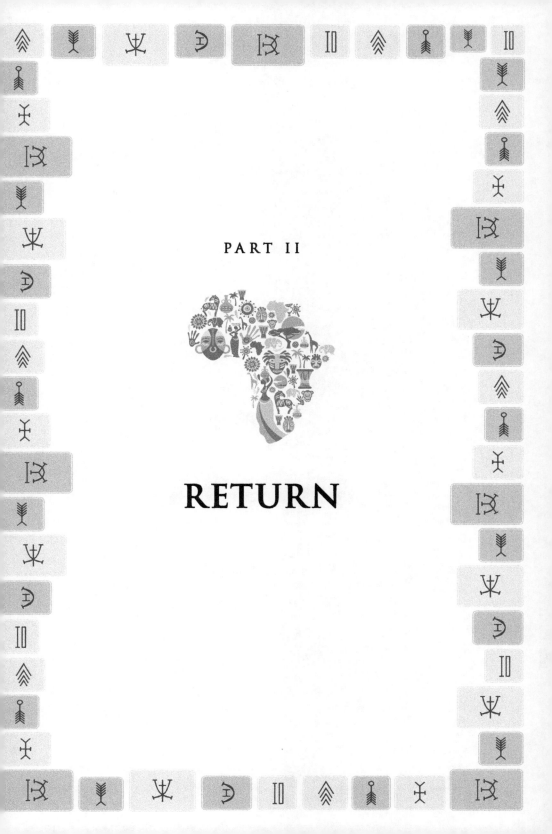

RETURN

CHAPTER TWENTY-THREE

◆

I T WASN'T A REAL TRIAL FOR HER CRIME OF LEAVING THE MILI-
tary without permission, nor was it a trial for aiding and abetting rebels
without cause. They didn't ask her to enter a plea to any charges, and they
presented no evidence against her. They didn't even hold the hearing at
the Council House. Instead, the entire Military Council was convened on
the Island, but Essien knew as she watched the procession of engines make
their way up to the top that the entire proceeding was all a ruse, and there
was some other purpose for the meeting that she did not yet know.

This time, the trial was held in a large room in the President's compound that Essien had never been in, nor did she even know of its existence.
It was behind an obscured door that looked for all intents and purposes
like a bookcase in the President's office. The door swung outward with one
of the red books as a door handle and led up three sets of stairs to a balcony
and a courtyard in the middle of the building. There was a large meeting
room off the courtyard with low fabric-covered chairs and tables and attendants standing at intervals around the space.

The low couches were arranged in small groupings of three or five, sitting on embroidered floor coverings with muted lighting hidden in the
walls. The walls were covered by a dark jeweled wallpaper that brought out
the emerald, ruby, and gold in the fabric of the chairs.

The President was seated casually in one of the couches when Essien
was brought in. She hadn't seen him in the day and a half she had been back
in the compound.

He was leaning on the arm of a Military Official from Zulu State with a
short glass of an amber liquid held casually in one hand. There was a stick of
smoking herbs in his other hand, the lit end twirling smoke up into a cloud
of thin script around his head.

Essien recognized other Military Officials seated in different arrangements around the room. She didn't like the air of intimacy in the room.
Like something had just been discussed prior to her arrival, something that

concerned her, but which they weren't going to tell her until long past when she needed the information. Essien looked back at her escorts, who had stopped at the door and took up posts on either side of it. Realizing that she needed to tackle the situation head on, no matter how unfamiliar, she made a beeline for where Gabriel was seated.

He didn't look up at her as she approached, even though she could feel him feeling her. For one dizzying moment, Gabriel let her see what he saw. Her storming across the carpeted floor in her boots and guard uniform, the only clothes that had been in the closet on the floor she'd been assigned to in his compound.

The scowl on her face made her seem angry, even though she wasn't. She was very carefully thinking and feeling nothing. She stumbled as Gabriel pulled away from her, and she was inside her own head again. She was seeing out of her own eyes, and it made her feel nauseous.

Knowing that he could step into her head or pull her into his whenever he wanted made her feel unprotected and vulnerable. Maybe that was Gabriel's goal. To keep her off-kilter, unbalanced, so she would do whatever it was he wanted without question or challenge.

There was an empty seat right next to Gabriel. The next closest seat was a few clusters over, near one of the oldest Council Members still serving. As she looked around the room, Essien saw that Gabriel was looking up at her and sipping slowly from the side of his short glass, pursing his lips and pulling in his eyebrows as he swallowed.

Essien was standing at the edge of the floor covering underneath the group of seats. She made her way to the only available seat and had to cross over one Council Member's legs to reach it—her hip practically landing in the President's lap as she sat. Essien looked up to note that Gabriel had a slight smile on his face after observing her.

Essien whispered to him, "What kind of trial is this?" Gabriel chuckled and took another sip before responding.

"This is not a trial." Essien waited for him to go on, but he took another sip.

"Then what is it?" Her eyes flicked across his face, jumping back and forth between his eyes and his mouth as he sipped his drink.

"It's a campaign," Gabriel was still whispering. The other Council Members were leaning away, talking loudly to each other, pretending not to hear or listen in on their whisperings.

Essien felt dumbfounded. To her knowledge, there was nothing for either of them to campaign for. He'd already appointed himself to a life-long position, so there were no more political positions for him to aspire to. Essien let her eyes scan over his face and then shift to stare around the room. The only time all the Council Members were gathered in one place was to either punish a criminal and hand down an execution sentence or to approve new legislation.

"Does this have to do with your plan to make me a Queen?" Gabriel smiled at her, all of his teeth seeming big and white behind his lips.

"The people demand a Queen, Essien," Gabriel leaned his arm against hers. He felt so hot, and she wondered if she felt as scorching to him as he did to her with that small graze against her skin. "I intend to give them one to put on their throne."

Essien pulled away. "Don't the people have to decide?"

Gabriel gestured around the room using the hand that held his glass. "Who do you think these ones are, Essien? These are the people." He chuckled and inhaled a puff from his smoking stick. He blew the air out, and it circled around Essien and seemed to flow into her lungs.

"I don't want any part of whatever you're planning. Even when you offered it...I couldn't see myself as Queen."

"I've had a vision, and I know you've heard of the prophecy." Gabriel whispered the last word, leaning in toward her as he did, so that his breath touched her face.

She leaned even further away. This meeting already felt too intimate. She glanced around at the Council Members who watched them without watching them, the glances sidelong and furtive.

"I don't want to speak about any prophecy, Gabriel."

"Oh, but the prophecy speaks of you," he said. "The prophecy has spoken of you for millennia. A queen to rule over Alkebulan where none has reigned before. A queen to usher in a global empire."

"Global?" She wasn't whispering anymore and had to remind herself to keep her voice low. "Alkebulan is the largest continent on Ala-ani. What need do we have to venture anywhere else for empire?"

"The world has opened up so much to us through trade and travel. What if our international relationships were of greater significance? What if we joined with other nations politically? To create a universal nation?"

"With us in charge? Me and you?" Essien tried to let her incredulity be obvious by the loudening of her voice and the way she stared straight at him. She was still leaning away from him, her arm propped up on the back of the seat they both occupied. She started to feel the imperceptible sense that he was leaning slowly toward her.

"What do you want me to do?" she asked Gabriel as she looked around the room. "I don't seem to have your penchant for mass hypnosis. I couldn't get this room to see me as their Queen, let alone an entire planet's worth of people."

"Then you'll have to use your words to persuade instead of your...other weapons. Convince them."

"Of what?" she let her voice rise, just a little. She'd thought he was joking, when he'd asked her to be his Queen. She thought he'd been trying to torture her. There was no way he was serious. She was his subordinate. How could she become Queen without marrying a King? Essien shoved the thoughts away even as the warmth of the realization spread up her neck and made her scalp feel tight and tense.

Gabriel leaned in even closer and made a show of sniffing her before whispering, "That you were born, bred, and trained to be Queen."

"How do I do that? How do I convince them of something I do not even believe?"

Gabriel shrugged. "I thought you might have some ideas. It's you who will be sitting on a throne before them. They'll have to call you Eze Nwaanyi. Give them a reason to. Show them why you deserve the title."

Essien looked down at the glass in his hand that was now just ice blocks in a thin remnant of amber liquid.

"I don't deserve it, though, do I?" She kept staring down into her lap, her hands clasped and still. She was trying not to feel the ashes gripping her fingertips in a permanent vise.

Music started to play, a thumping bass that made vibrations push up from the floor and into the couch legs. She let those sounds fill her, hearing the percussions and strings and horns flow out from a speaker that was as hidden as the lights. She felt like she was swaying side to side as she sat.

"If nothing else, you can sit still and look pretty," Gabriel finally responded. "That's all you have to do for now. The legislation is as good as approved."

"What legislation?"

Gabriel just waved the hand that was holding the drink. Essien stared at his side profile and contemplated how much she would now be excluded from knowing. He didn't trust her at all anymore, not in the ways that could help her to plan ahead and make some kind of decisions about her own life. Her access to the outside world was so limited, she didn't even know if she'd be able to contact her parents or visit her brothers in other countries. Essien blew out all the air in her lungs and stared around the room again.

She noticed the more pointed glances her way and the conversations through the sides of mouths that she might not decipher their lips. She also noted that she was the only woman in the room.

"Can I have one of those?" she asked Gabriel, flicking her eyes to the almost empty drinking glass. Gabriel smiled a wide smile that showed all of his big teeth and flicked his hand in the air. His action was immediately met by an eager attendant holding a glass bottle of the same amber liquid.

"A drink for the ara, please." The attendant produced another glass and poured it full to the brim with frozen cubes floating from top to bottom. Essien took the glass and didn't want to drink it. Her parents had always kept wine and elixirs flowing at parties. Her father drank more often than her mother, sometimes downing entire bottles of malt. She had been allowed to sip palm wine on her twelfth birthday and again when she began her menses, but those were small and private times.

Now, she noticed that the Council Member from Berber State was watching the glass, and the Council Member from Igbo State had turned up his nose when she accepted the drink. Essien put her lips to the edge of the glass and let the tiniest sip hit her tongue. It was spicy, this drink. It burned her tongue and her throat and made her eyes water. It wasn't the sweet and sour flavor of palm wine or the sweet and fizzy swallow of hibiscus fizz. She pursed her lips and sucked her tongue to get the aftertaste to go away.

Gabriel leaned harder against her, his shoulder pressing into her shoulder. "You like it?"

"Help me understand why you drink this stuff every day." She wanted to put the glass down. A taste like smoke spreading over her tongue made her mouth taste disgusting.

"Finish the glass and then tell me how it is."

Essien frowned. There was no way she would finish the entire drink.

"Mr. President, may I have a word?" A Council Member had joined their grouping and was standing just at the edge of one of the couches. Essien didn't recognize the man, but Gabriel seemed to. He straightened his posture and stretched his legs out in front of him more fully.

Gabriel nodded but didn't say anything to encourage the man.

"As a new Council Member from Dinka State, I must express the disagreement of my constituents. They have informed me that it would be sacrilege to approve this legislation. I cannot in good conscience agree to support such a move to a more dictatorial political system."

Gabriel hitched his thumb at Essien. "Does she look like a dictator to you?"

The Council Member opened his mouth and then closed it, staring at her and then over his shoulder at the men who were watching him in the seating area across from Gabriel's. The man opened and closed his mouth again. He let his eyes flit over Essien, and then he turned quickly back to Gabriel.

"How does a dictator look when they are first being handed inordinate amounts of power? Perhaps they look just like her. I am not interested in waiting around to find out. I will have to vote no. I wanted to warn you that many of us will be voting no. We cannot in good conscience approve this legislation. Not at this time. Not under these circumstances."

Gabriel nodded and then contemplated the contents of his drink. He waved his fingers in the air, and the attendant hustled right over. Gabriel held up his glass to be refilled. When his glass was full, he took a sip and glanced over at Essien.

"Anything you can say to assuage the Dinka's fears?" Essien recoiled at Gabriel's language at the same time that the Council Member ruffled.

"My name is Councilman Deng. Please use this name for me, Mr. Ijikota. Let us keep respectful."

"You called Essien—the first woman to join my Guard—a dictator. You started off rude. I thought we were being rude going forward."

Essien wanted to stop this because she knew where it was going. She did not want a fight at this meeting, which was in some way tied to her and whether she would ever actually become Queen. If these were the fights being had about it already, she knew already what a burden the role would be.

"Councilman Deng." She only had to call his name once before he halted whatever he had been about to retort. "I apologize on behalf of the President. It was rude to disrespect your state and your culture. I'd also like you to realize that as Queen, I would never act except in the best interests of the people. And you are the people. Tell me what you want to make this a reality, and I will give it to you."

Gabriel put his hand around her forearm, gripping it. He may as well have put his hand over her mouth or hustled her out of the room. She had said something he didn't want her to say, but Essien hadn't said anything she didn't mean. The Council Member's face softened from hostile to agreeable, and he seemed to relax. He stared down at the ground, his eyes making patterns on the floor that she couldn't track.

"Is there anything I might do that would make you approve the legislation?" Gabriel's hand on her arm tightened, almost to the point of hurting her.

The Councilman looked up at her then. "Might I speak with you in private?"

"No," Gabriel said.

"You may," Essien responded at the same time. She turned to frown at Gabriel. Then, like pushing aside a curtain, he seemed to step into her mind. If she knew what the legislation was, what it said, she'd be able to respond to them more effectively. Part of her was angry with him for his reluctance to share with her, when there was nothing she could ever hide from him. So, she let him see her plan. She wanted to try and convince the man to approve the legislation. If she could convince him, she might be able to convince all those he spoke for. If she could convince them all, she might have more freedom as a Queen than as a former guard on house arrest.

Gabriel ran his eyes over her face and then settled for looking down at her hands. They were gripped tightly around the glass in her lap. She knew he still wanted to say no, even though saying no would make her ascension to the throne much harder than it needed to be. If she could woo them with sweetness, there would be no need to use violence. If she could make them like and respect her, there'd be no need for him to do what the core of him was seething to do.

Essien set her drink on the low table, stood, forcing Gabriel to release her arm, and motioned for Councilman Deng to lead the way out of the gathering room. Their steps were muted across the carpet. Essien looked around the room and managed to deliver a faint smile that just barely made the edges of her lips quirk upward.

Gabriel signaled to her escorts, and they followed her out of the room. It was much quieter in the hallway where a tan tile floor led out to the courtyard open to the honey blue sky above. The door was closed, but Essien knew that Gabriel would know what they discussed, even if they left the compound completely.

Essien smiled, to disarm the man before her, and then she crossed her arms. The Councilman stepped close to her, his shoes almost stepping on the toes of her boots. She wanted to back away, but instead she uncrossed her arms and put her hands on her hips.

"If you promise me that you won't go through any marriage ceremonies with the President, we will sign the legislation tomorrow."

Essien was so surprised she let her real emotions show before she could hide them and pretend she didn't feel what she felt. She wanted to laugh in the Councilman's face and declare that she would never marry the President, not in this lifetime or the next. She wanted to slap him for presuming that she would let the President connive her into agreeing to a marriage with a man she loathed and could not ever deign to love. She wanted to retreat to her floor of the compound because this was the third warning she had been given not to marry him.

In the many years she had known him, Gabriel himself had only brought up the subject twice. Every time, she had rejected him so resoundingly that he could only laugh her off. Yet, Enyemaka—oh Mothers—Enyemaka had been the first person to warn her against the very same thing.

Don't marry the President, he had said what felt like several lifetimes ago. *You'll ruin the world*, he had warned. She'd had other warnings, more solemn warnings, from the Mothers, even. Essien had tried to heed them all, but it was like brushing frantically at spiderwebs and still feeling them clinging to her arms and legs. Essien shivered, and the Councilman reacted by stepping away.

"If you can make me this promise, I will crown you myself."

Essien wanted to lie to him. She had the lie all lined up on her tongue and ready to slither into his ear. She remembered Gabriel gripping her arm, cautioning her.

"I am a member of his Guard. That is all I am to him. What assurances do you want besides that?"

Deng shook his head, closing his eyes in emphasis. "That is all we want. You have to declare it in front of everyone, and then we will approve. You could do it here and now, if you wished."

Essien was already shaking her head. "This was supposed to be a trial. Didn't you hear? My second so far. I was accused of leaving without permission, evading recapture, and helping the rebels damage the country. There is no way the President would..." Essien stopped and couldn't say the words.

"Appoint a criminal as Queen and then marry her? Yes, he would. He would indeed. That is his plan."

"I do not believe that is of immediate concern. The more important matter is that it's not true. The President is my boss, and that is what he will remain. I answer to him. There will be nothing more, and there will be nothing less."

Deng scoffed at her. "Do not play as if you do not know. A woman always knows when a man wants her. She can ignore it, or she can embrace it and welcome the attention. You seem to be embracing it."

Essien shook her head. "I can make him want something else."

Deng laughed a hearty, merry laugh, and Essien smiled at him despite herself.

"You will push him into the heart and arms of another woman, then? Let him marry another instead of you?"

Essien nodded. "If that's what it takes, yes. I cannot announce that I won't marry him, but I can make sure he marries someone else instead of me."

Deng tilted his head to the side, and he looked genuinely puzzled.

"A woman who was in love with a man would not do something like this."

Essien shook her head. "You're right. A woman in love wouldn't."

The Councilman stared at her face, seeming to study all of her features separately and then together. He seemed to like what he was seeing because he smiled.

"I will take your word then, and I will approve the legislation. I cannot speak for others who are adamant that you make a declaration, but I can speak for Dinka State in this."

Essien put out her hand. The Councilman touched palms with her, and then he held her hand with both of his and touched his forehead to the back of her hand. Essien let him do the same with her other hand. She'd never seen someone show respect in this way, but somehow, she had known to give him both her hands and hang them passively as he touched his forehead to them. The Councilman then let her walk in front of him as the escorts opened the doors for her to enter, the meeting thus concluded.

CHAPTER TWENTY-FOUR

◆

WHEN ESSIEN RE-ENTERED THE MEETING ROOM, THE SPACE seemed to be filled with chaotic energy. Angry conversations were rising, voices clashing against each other, bodies moving toward and away from standing huddles in defiance and rebellion.

Essien looked for Gabriel and could not see him right away. She saw his Guard, spread around the room, some against the walls, others spaced between the seats. Essien's escorts were on high alert, too. One minute casually holding the door open, and the next they were pushing her between them and readjusting their weapons.

"Gabriel?" Essien called around the wide shoulders of her escorts.

"Looks like we have a stalemate," she heard Gabriel's voice rise over the other angry tones.

"What happened?" Essien called. It felt weird talking to Gabriel without being able to see him. A small flexing of her own mind, and she was able to envision him before her. He was standing within the protective circle of his Guard, and a cascade of red stained one side of his neck and his hands. All the Guard had their weapons out. Essien knew then that the Councilman from Igbo State had attacked Gabriel.

Catching the President unawares, he had pulled a long knife from his tunic and pressed it against Gabriel's throat. Gabriel had laughed, making the knife press into his skin and cut his flesh. Gabriel had then stood up, displaying to the man the uselessness of his knife. The Guard had subsequently dogpiled the man, stomping on his leg and breaking his jaw. Some of the other Councilmen had been riled up at the brutality shown toward the quickly disarmed man and began shouting down the Guard. The room had quickly devolved into pandemonium.

Essien touched the shoulder of the escort in front of her. "Let me pass," she said. The two men looked at each other and then stepped aside, their weapons still at the ready. She wove her way through the crowd, finally reaching the man being held on the ground by two guards. The knife was being held point down by a guard nearest the tangle on the ground. A barrier of guards seemed to hold everyone else back. The Councilman wasn't trying to get away from them at all. He held his leg with one hand and his jaw with the other. Essien kneeled in front of him.

"Why did you do it?" she whispered.

It was hard for the man to talk as he writhed back and forth in pain. The guards held him down by one shoulder and the other uninjured leg. Essien put a hand against the arm stretched down to feebly hold his knee and then stared into his eyes. She could hear his thoughts loud and clear: "Alkebulan will have no one for a Queen, not even you, one of our own. Alkebulan will never bow to a monarch, not even ones from our own lands."

Essien nodded. The man's thoughts kept flowing, pouring into her mind as she touched him. "As an Igbo woman, you should separate yourself from his perversion, return to your ancestral homes, and make alms to Amen-Ra for your transgressions. This man will never be allowed to take control of our lands without a fight. We will fight him to the death! His and yours!"

Essien nodded again. She glanced over at Gabriel. He was staring at her. He had heard everything she had heard. He had not known the man's mind, but those thoughts were no surprise to him. Essien stared at Gabriel, his thoughts revealed across his face, and because she was still hooked up to him, she felt him or heard him or simply knew that he wanted the man dead.

He was planning to have his Guard execute the man after the meeting ended. He did not want too many eyes to see, but he would be sure to spread the news to all the others. It would send an important message, although a deadly one: resist us and die.

Suddenly, Essien's hands were aflame. She hadn't meant to start the flames, and she fought to tamp them down. The control she thought she had gained was suddenly gone, ripped away by the power put inside her by Gabriel. She gritted her teeth and tried to lift her hand from where it had the injured man gripped. She let out a sob as she realized she couldn't stop it. That the magic wanted out, and it was being controlled by an entity completely separate from her. She was touching the Councilman, and it was already too late.

As her hands flamed, so did his entire body. The fire ate over his skin faster than it could ignite his clothes, the red and yellow teeth spreading over his bloody mouth as he tried to scream with his sleeves only just beginning to smoke. One second, he was a man staring up at her, and the next, he was a body of flame, blazing bright and hot.

There was a cry of fear and horror as the other Council Members saw what she had done, and then a receding as they all stepped back, away from her. She distantly heard the rushing patter of boot thuds and then the door bursting open as more of the Guard poured in, armed and ready for whatever enemy had been roused inside their own walls. She was still trying to pull her hand away from the area of the Councilman's body—where she could feel remnants of skin and muscles and bones already rendering down into flaky ash.

The fire consumed the man quickly after that, turning him into the same dusty consistency that seemed to cover her fingertips and rain down onto her skin. The man's demise was nearly silent due to his inability to scream around his ruined jaw. Despite the conflagration, the floor underneath the man's body remained intact and without any evidence of even being singed.

When all of the Councilman had burned down, quicker than a bonfire had time to collapse upon itself, Essien squeezed her fingers through the fine gray powder of what had once been a man. She squeezed and squeezed those ashes, feeling the texture and cringing the more her fingers brushed against each other. She then dusted her hands off and stood.

Essien glanced around and saw that she was in a protective circle of her own. Guards had formed around her facing outward with weapons drawn and at the ready. When she stood, they stepped away and into rows. Essien saw that the Council Members were a collective body of fear and revulsion. They were mostly afraid, but some of them were intrigued. The terror made their hearts beat faster and sweat dampen their armpits. Essien had a sudden realization that she wanted the onlookers to be afraid. If love and respect wouldn't work, then fear seemed to be quite effective. Essien soon recognized that the words entering her mind were not her own. She stared down at the pile of what used to be a respected man and still felt powerless in the chains that Gabriel had locked around her mind. Yet for everyone else? She was the force they were terrified to ever reckon with. She turned to look up as someone stepped next to her.

Her eyes went first to the slash of blood at the left side of the President's neck, perfectly placed to have killed him. The cut showed white beneath the blood seeping out into the collar of his tunic. The black color saved the red from being more obvious, but even looking up at him, she could see where the blood had stained down over his shoulder and chest. She stayed standing next to the pile of ashes and staring up at him.

"I'm sorry," she whispered, her throat full and choking. "I thought I had it under control. I begged them to train me, but...there wasn't time."

Gabriel looked down at her with an emotion in his eyes that she couldn't read. It wasn't one she'd seen before.

"Your control was almost perfect, but I can train you, Essien. The offer has always been here. I can help. If you let me."

A rustle of bodies moving to the ground en masse made them both look away from each other. It wasn't just one or two, but nearly all of those in the meeting room fell to their knees at once and put their foreheads on the ground, even the guards. Essien's breath caught in her throat, and she didn't know what to do with her suddenly sweating hands. She looked back at Gabriel, and he had the smallest lift of a grin at the edge of his lip. He held his hand out to her. Essien stared at those offered fingertips and then back up to meet his eyes.

It was compassion—that's what she saw staring at her from his eyes. He was pleased with her, despite how guilty she felt, but he also had pity on her. Perhaps if he had sympathy for her, he wouldn't spend the rest of her days seeking out new ways to torture her. Perhaps if he could help her to learn true control, then it wouldn't be this false pretense of having the flames on a leash. Essien took the steps she needed to meet that hand with her own. He gripped her fingers tight, sliding his to interlace with hers. That one gesture felt both fated and fatal. The Guard led them out of the room. The Councilmen remained with their faces to the ground as Essien and Gabriel were ushered away. As they were escorted over to the bank of rises, Essien wondered whether the trial that wasn't a trial had absolved her guilt or revealed it.

CHAPTER TWENTY-FIVE

◆

THE PRESIDENT WAITED UNTIL THEY WERE IN THE RISE, JUST the two of them with one guard each. He turned to her and crossed his arms. She automatically crossed hers, too.

"That went terribly. It couldn't have gone any worse."

"You said it wasn't a trial."

"You shouldn't have offered them anything. Either they obey, or they face the consequences until they eventually obey. Obedience is the end game, not their satisfaction and contentment."

"You can't be serious. If you want me to do this, then it has to be done my way. It would be better for me, and for them, if they voted willingly, Gabriel, of their own mind."

"Is that why you killed a man in front of them?" Essien could detect the faintest heat under those words.

She shut her mouth of what she had been about to say. She let herself take a few breaths before she replied. "I already apologized. Would it help if I said I didn't mean to?"

"I thought you had trained when you were out there with those rebels, burning up my countryside. Knowing they didn't even bother is puzzling. Who wouldn't want all of their weapons at their strongest?"

"*You* wanted that man killed. *You* wanted him dead, so how do I know your power, that power you put inside me, didn't kill him? The job you wanted done is done. You should be thanking me for making it possible for you to do your job again—isn't that what you said?"

"Did you think about the impact as you did it? Did you consider that these are men who like to make the newsreels? What you have just given them is a centuries' worth of scandal."

"I'd do anything to take it back."

Gabriel blew out all the air in his lungs and dropped his arms. He turned back to the rise doors as they opened onto her floor. There were so many floors in this building, many which Essien did not have access to.

When she'd first come, she thought there'd been just five, maybe six, but now, she hadn't the slightest clue how many floors were in the building.

She looked forward to the slide of doors closing on her alone in the long white hallway that was hers and hers only, with its thick carpets and textured silver and white wallpaper. The one place in the compound where she could go and be alone, as alone as she ever could be again. All the rooms were hers, visited only by the silent and near-invisible attendants who glided in and out to clean and deliver supplies.

She wanted to continue the conversation with Gabriel, but he had never come to her floor before, and she didn't know if this was something else that was not allowed.

Essien kept talking as she stepped into the hallway. "There are people in this country who despise me because of what I have already done, what they know I am able to do. There are people who will despise me because I was in your military and your Guard. The things I did while I worked for you." Gabriel's frown deepened a V between his eyebrows. "There are people who will now despise me because I worked with the rebels. Imagine adding fuel to that fire and telling them I have no idea what else I might do accidentally. This knowledge could upend everything I thought I knew about this country. I would be beyond any criticism or reproach. There would be nothing and no one above me, except you, but only we would know that. I would be above the laws of this land. I would be—"

"Their Queen!" Gabriel's voice was loud and harsh, but his face was blank; none of his features told her anything about what he was thinking or feeling.

"You want me to go around piling up ashes? Look what has made them submit to me. I would have to use brute force to get their full submission. I could do it. Part of me wants to do it. Part of me would love to unleash that side of me onto the world. But I don't agree to reign like this. I have to be able to live with myself. It would work. Mothers help me, you might get your empire after all. But I won't. I can't."

"You could do it. You will."

Essien knew that Gabriel was planning something even beyond what he had shared with her, that he likely always had something coming down the pipeline to shock or surprise her. He had thought out every detail in minute description to paint the vision of him and her as the King and Queen of Alkebulan. It was preposterous and ridiculous to shift the rise of democracy into the descent back into monarchy. Other countries had monarchies, but that particular government had never taken hold on their shores. The closest thing they had were the tribal elders back home in the villages, men and women who sat sternly at the gatherings of their descendants—but even they were powerless in the face of the Tribal Council.

Now the continent was united in some semblance of togetherness, a nation that worked for its people, and, after hundreds of years, it could all be undone by one person...two people, if she did what Gabriel wanted.

"You can taste it, Essien. The power. It's spilling into your mouth and running over your lips. You drink and drink, and you are afraid of your drinking. It is your duty and your obligation to be Queen."

Essien smirked. The President was a master manipulator, and she never had been. She would have to learn to be if she were to deal with him as an equal.

"I could say the same to you, Gabriel. You drink too much. At every meal? And the taste? Does it not unsettle your stomach?"

His face didn't even register that she had made a joke. "A lot of things I am required to do are unsettling. You will be responsible for securing the vote from the Tribal Councils for the legislation. Your travel has already been prepared; you need only accept and get into the engine waiting for you downstairs."

He was moving so fast. Essien stilled as his words settled, and she realized she wouldn't even be allowed to get comfortable. Those rooms she had left largely unexplored the last time she had lived here were now to be even further from her use. She hated to admit it, but sleeping on a cot and a pallet when she had a plush mattress that could sleep eight people here was the one thing she regretted.

"I will not lie to them, Gabriel. I will not manipulate them the way you manipulate me. I don't want to kill them when I have the choice. I will not harm them, just to achieve your aims."

"You already have. The attendants are probably cleaning up those ashes now. You didn't even ask the Councilman's name. How do you know he wasn't related to either of your parents?"

Essien choked on her rage and anger as she held it back from being let out against him. She wanted to strike him and bring pain to him. She wanted to levy some words, any words that would strip him of that smugness, that need to control through any means, even hurting her.

Gabriel went on as though she weren't trying to decide if she would lash out or cry. "You will travel to an assembly of every Tribal Council in all sixteen states. You will hear their exhortations, and you will quelch them. You will manifest your considerable show of force, in whatever way you'd like, and make them approve of the vote. If there is violence to be done, you will do it. Once the Tribal Council has voted, the Military Council will have no choice but to comply."

"As Queen, you cannot order me to do anything."

Gabriel smiled, a small flexing of his top lip. "And yet, you are not Queen at this moment. Maybe one day you will be. Until then, go."

Essien stared into his eyes for a flinch of tenderness, but there was none. She stood just outside the rise, the doors still open with both guards standing at attention.

"If I go now, the talks will not go well."

"Then don't talk. Act."

"I don't want to murder them, Gabriel. Do you know how awful it feels? How much of a burden I would be forced to carry with me afterward? I can't go into their tribal lands and slaughter them. What would that make me?"

"A Queen! It would make you their Queen, Essien! Stop fighting against what you already are!"

"I don't want it if that's the cost. I don't want to kill people for...a throne! Saving your life or mine or the lives of innocent people is one thing. Doing this the way you want it done would make me a monster! Worse than any invader who tried and failed to destroy us from outside our lands. Because I know better." She turned to walk away, ending their conversation.

She felt him come up behind her. Gabriel gripped her arm, stopping her and pulling her closer to him with a swift jerk, so that she landed against his chest with her hands pressed between them. Her eyes leapt into flames as she looked up at him. He was smiling.

"I said I would help you," Gabriel whispered into her face, his breath blowing over her bottom lip. "If you show up where I need you, I will take care of the rest."

Essien tried to snatch her arm and pull away from him, but his grip was like a vise keeping her pressed up against him.

"I will not let you use me to assassinate your political enemies."

He let her arm go, but he didn't step away. Essien walked further down the hall leaving him standing just in front of the rise.

"Fine, I won't force you. You'll make the decision on your own when you're ready." Essien rubbed her arm and didn't say anything. "I'll cancel your travel plans for now. Let me know when you are ready to commence with them." Gabriel stepped back into the rise and watched her as the doors shut.

Essien was alone when she went down to dinner that night. She followed the scent of roasting meat and red vine sauce down the hall to the dining room where the Guard usually ate at smaller tables buffet style. The room was indeed full of guards; they seemed less than their usual number but still abuzz with their typical chatter and commotion. They only glanced at her sideways standing in the doorway, no one willing to look at her full on.

She returned to the larger dining room where she once ate dinner with the President every night and saw food had been laid out. She ate the red beef stew with pounded yam, hot and doughy. She devoured the mango, eating almost all of the platter meant for two. She drank a small glass of palm wine. She sat staring at the painting on the back wall for a long time after she finished. It was an abstract one, the same painting that had been hanging when she'd first arrived. Smears and blotches of beautiful brown colors in various shades that didn't quite make an image of anything she could interpret. She tried to remember how many years ago since she'd first sat staring at that painting, and her mind couldn't process how much time had passed. Was it only four years ago that she had first come? Perhaps it was closer to six now? She didn't know if she was waiting for Gabriel to show up suddenly, though she wouldn't admit it to herself if she were.

He came into her mind while she was sleeping that night, and it wasn't a dream. The feeling of his power all over her body made her tangle herself in the sheets and roll off the bed hard onto the floor. It snapped her awake, and she could feel the stream of him into her whether she wanted it or not. She screamed out loud until her throat felt hoarse.

He didn't care about her protest and continued with his invisible action inside that door that had creaked open and now allowed him in further than he'd ever tried to force his power to go. He waited for her to relax and accept it, but she never did. She huddled on the ground with her head on her knees, shivering and trying to keep herself from falling over.

He admired that she had so much strength to hold herself in one pose and not flail around like she had the first time he did this to her. He thought about trying to hurt her or make her scream, but he didn't want to use his power like that. He was trying a tactic he hadn't tried before: getting her to like him. As silly as that sounded coming from his own mind, he knew it was true or else he would have already done what he wanted to do, and she'd have been screaming out murder.

"Please, please, please, Gabriel, please, stop, please..." He heard her, and he almost didn't care. He kept it up until he'd had enough of it, until he'd almost overrode that submissive begging, unlike her tone that made it sound as though she were crying. He eased away from her, and she finally let herself roll over onto her side, breathing heavily. She knew she couldn't stand up yet; she covered her face with her hands. Gabriel breathed out over her body as gently as he could. She shivered again and started to curl up.

"Essien, you should let yourself enjoy it." He spoke into her mind, and he knew that she heard him as though he had spoken out loud in the room with her.

"Never," she replied aloud.

He sighed over her again. She let it wash over her without one twitch, closing her eyes to concentrate on that space inside of her that he'd made, that made her his in some way she did not have words or past experiences to describe, that she herself had only just discovered she could relate to. She'd tried fighting against him, running from him, and it hadn't worked. She was back here; and she would likely never leave. There were no five-year or ten-year terms with him. Not this time, not ever again.

It was ironic that in that moment she longed for the opportunity to serve in Alkebulan's military. Yet what she really wanted was to be far away from here, anywhere else...there were so many other countries where she could run, if only she could escape. Whatever it might mean, she'd give almost the entire time stuck here with him to be back in the military doing something useful, not reduced to an uncontrollable shudder on the floor that felt too weak to run, too exhausted even to stand.

Having been recaptured after not even a full year of civilian living, she had grown to appreciate the freedom of the military. Though she was conscripted the moment she signed up to serve, she'd still been allowed to move freely in and outside of the military compounds. She traveled more in the military than she ever had in her life. Now she would never have privacy or autonomy again.

He'd done something to her, something it shouldn't be possible for him to do, and now she could never leave him. Oh, the fire and the fury if she tried. She was surer to fail now than to get away safely. He'd found her once, and he'd find her again. It would require her to assume an entirely new identity. Maybe if she accepted the campaign he so fervently wanted her on, she could find a way to become invisible to him again. But he was still in her head and heard all of those thoughts spelled out for him inside the firing of her brain. He let that pyrrhic torch inside her blaze up again, controlling it so that it only traveled down her spine to curl her toes. She wasn't thinking about escaping anymore.

CHAPTER TWENTY-SIX

◆

THE NEXT NIGHT, STILL NO GABRIEL. ESSIEN WONDERED IF he'd been called away on some emergency that she wasn't supposed to know about. Perhaps more rebels. Then she wondered if maybe he was hiding somewhere in the compound, to make her think he was gone. That didn't seem like him. If he were on the Island, he would demand she have the evening meal with him like he always did.

She didn't know what he did with his time outside those evening meals and thought resolutely that she would make a note of finding out the next time she was with him. If she were to be Queen in truth, she'd need the same daily reports and briefings that he received. She hoped she wouldn't forget that sense of justice that the rebels had inspired in her. Maybe burning property wasn't the right way to go about it, but as Queen, she'd be compelled to use her power in service of those people who had been wronged. She knew what some on the Military Council were doing, but how many, she didn't know. If she could identify proof, then it would be her literal job to stop the corruption and rout them out. But if Gabriel was in on it and helping men on his Military Council to defraud people of their land... Essien sighed, and it heaved her shoulders up and down. She hoped Gabriel had been as clueless as she was. She drank two glasses of palm wine while she contemplated how long he might be gone.

It was another two days of her dining alone before anyone bothered to tell her that the President had gone to an international conference in Ni-hon, and she would not be seeing him for another seven days.

She closed her eyes and thought of his face, his jawline always clenched into a hard square, those eyes like liquid ore with flecks of shining light, his hair in waves and whorls across his head.

She saw him standing on a crisp green lawn surrounded by trees covered with blooming light pink flowers spreading their fragrance in a scented wash of changing seasons and newness.

Standing next to him was a woman with flying strands of black hair that kept brushing over his nose and lips every time the wind blew. Essien couldn't see her clearly enough to make out more and realized that Gabriel was blurring the image. He was pushing her out of his head, putting up blockers in place that felt like the slamming shut of a steel door. She couldn't get past it to see him again.

Essien stood on the balcony outside the large bedroom on her floor and felt a roil of sickness spread into her stomach. She waited for her feelings to become smaller and smaller pricks. This was jealousy of course, but she knew it was misplaced. There was anxiety about his safety of all things. There was even a bit of hurt that he would leave, be gone this long, and not care to tell her when he'd return. It was utterly upsetting to her that she had been virtually kidnapped only to be shunted into a cloister while he gallivanted wherever he pleased.

She tried to get angry thinking that he was likely still manipulating her, leaving to make her do what he wanted to be back in his good graces. The anger kept sliding away and being resolved by something else that whispered, "Forgive him, he's not wrong, he'll make it okay." She shook her head.

When did I start caring what he thought? she wondered. It was embarrassing and awful to admit, but she wanted him near her. It felt like a hollow place was carved out inside of her, a deep, hollow pit echoing with how empty it was inside. She didn't like feeling that way with him attached to it. She had never felt such a deep and earnest yearning for anybody else on earth. Was this what it felt like to love and be in love? Essien put her head down on the balcony railing. She knew it was a curse tied to that power of his coiling and stretching inside her. It had to be. This wasn't love. She knew she had to make sure it never would be. For the sake of this country. For the sake of this world. Her limbs seemed to shudder as she stood still with her head pressed against her arm.

Lifting her head, Essien glanced down and saw a group of guards circling ominously underneath the balcony window. She stepped back inside and closed the doors. She decided to ignore the sting of isolation and loneliness, even though she was surrounded by people. Being shut out like that felt like rejection and abandonment, but she chided herself for thinking it. It was just a conference. But she'd always wanted to visit Nihon. Her Nne had even wanted her to go east and study medicine. She wished he had invited her. Why hadn't he invited her? And the woman? She wouldn't let herself think about it. She tried to convince herself that it shouldn't matter to her at all.

Finally deciding that she needed to do more than remain snuggled in the large bed in the largest bedroom on her floor, she made herself go down to the mgbati and exercise. There were about half of the guards remaining in the compound, and she suspected they were present for her, to keep her inside the bounds in case she got any ideas about escaping now that Gabriel was gone.

This was a test of her forced loyalty and his guards' ability to keep her safe. "Safe" meaning controlled and inside his compound until he sent for her. She recognized most of their faces from her time in the compound before. If she thought deeply, she might even remember their names. She saw a palbino straining to lift heavy stones as the muscles in his legs gripped and corded. For a second, she was back in that clearing with Akpari and Keesemokwu standing over her with knives. For a moment, she saw a fountain of blood splash down into her eyes and mouth. Essien shook her head hard and closed her eyes. When she opened them again, she reminded herself: Every pale-skinned man was not Akpari or Keesemokwu. That would be impossible because she'd killed them.

She breathed deep and reminded herself where she was and what mountain loomed before her. Even still, these were just men, not dead men come back to haunt her. Just another guard who happened to have been born with no melanin. He wasn't attacking her or out to get her. Essien took a deeper breath and stepped up to a running lane on the track.

She spent as much time as she was willing in the mgbati, allowing her body to move through the paces and remember what it felt like to train this hard again. When sweat edged her features and soaked her tunic to her back, she strolled right out the front doors of the compound. A small group of guards hurried to follow her, failing to make it look casual enough that she was sure Gabriel had ordered it.

The sky was bright, the sun like a gong being banged over and over above her head. She welcomed the heat against her skin, her arms seeming to burn in the light. As she circled the compound from the front around to the back, staring out at the landscape of the mountainside or up at the empty windows, the sun rose higher, and the temperature rose with it. Lap after lap she walked, taking her time, moving aimlessly, pretending that she didn't notice the string of black shirts trailing behind her. The sun reached its peak, and Essien finally retreated inside to the rise and back up to her floor. She was welcomed by the silence of the soft white carpets and the textured wallpaper covering the walls all the way down to the end, interrupted by two doors on the left and three on the right.

The door at the end of the hallway on the left was the larger bedroom, the one she'd inadvertently been sleeping in since returning. It was the same stark white as the hallway: the walls an off-white; the floor white wood; all the furniture white; the floor coverings, a fuzzy white; the bed coverings and pillows, a soft, luxurious white; the armchair that could seat two under the window, white. It was like being inside a vacuum. The room in between the two large rooms, connected by a door, was a washroom as large as the bedroom with a massaging tub set into the floor, a shower with two heads, a vanity with bulbs around the glass, and a closed-off alcove where her clothes were stored. The room closest to the head of the hallway was a smaller bedroom with a smaller bed meant for one, a desk facing out the window with a chair and a side table next to the bed. There was a small alcove in the wall for a single shelf of clothes. That was the room Essien had chosen when she'd been just a guard.

The three rooms on the opposite side were the hardest for her to enter because they reeked of how much wealth had gone into building this compound. The room closest to the bank of rises was a library, her very own, with thick titles that she had only glanced at from the threshold with the door still open. A set of cushy tan chairs and a light brown rug filled the middle with a set of gold marble pedestals on one wall. The other two rooms were a dining room and sitting room combo with a connecting door. In the sitting room, there were instruments on more golden marble pedestals around the room including drums, timpani, a balafon with rubber mallets resting on top of the flat keys, a marimba, fiddles, and several lutes. Essien also noticed glossy sheet music on stands. The rooms on the right looked like museums, picture-perfect settings that nobody used or lived in. Essien started keeping those doors closed.

As the days passed, Essien took her morning and afternoon meals in the dining room on her floor—the food delivered to her with a chime of the rise bell—the scent usually wafting into her before the attendant called her to eat. It was dinner that she had grown accustomed to sharing with the President while she was a guard. After several nights dining alone in the empty, cavernous hall, it was dinner that she finally asked an attendant to begin serving her in her own dining room until the President returned.

"And when might that be?" she asked, making her voice light and only slightly probing. The attendant hurried away without answering.

The seventh day they'd told her came and went, and Essien ached to know that she was counting each day as a painful absence. It made her sick—of herself most of all. She wondered if she had missed some message or forgotten something he'd said. She knew he'd been displeased by her refusal to immediately obey his orders. What he was doing with this government was so new, and Essien still hadn't read the legislation he'd had his advisors write. She had no idea if a Queen had to obey a President, but as it was, she didn't. He hadn't pressed her, not really. She didn't have to do anything she didn't want to. Essien decided she'd stick to her word as she went down to the mgbati for her daily training.

On the twentieth day, absentmindedly, and with hunger gnawing at her insides, she had traveled down to the dining hall on the first floor. She walked almost all the way to the head of the table before she realized what she had done, and then staring down at Gabriel's empty seat made anger and hatred balloon to cover up other, more desolate, hopeless feelings that were right beneath.

She wanted to reach out, through those channels that he had implanted in her. But the door he'd made into her mind, and her heart, was so solidly locked, she couldn't find any crevice to sneak in through. She leaned against that door, putting her ear up against it, but she got nothing back. Not even a sound or sensation that he was on the other side of it. She knew she had once owned a communicator, but where it had gone, she had no idea. Perhaps she had left it at the hospital. Half-heartedly, she wondered if he'd have come to treat her as a captive if she'd never left. She wondered if he might have kept her at his side instead, a permanent sidekick. She couldn't bring herself to regret leaving. Not when the desire to leave still thrummed through her, even sitting there pining after a man that everything in her told her she should hate and despise. And she did. But she couldn't. Not with that power floating around inside her. His power. And yet he'd left her alone.

Essien did not come down from her floors again for several days.

On the twenty-fifth day, she walked right up to the group of guards stationed at the doors of the mgbati, watching her every move while she exercised.

"Excuse me," she said, trying for polite. "Do any of you happen to know when the President will return?" It felt like such a humiliating experience, having to ask them about the President's whereabouts. They stared down at her with looks that ranged from curiosity and interest to disdain and dislike. She'd never gotten the sense that the guards disliked her, so that was new. She'd known they were afraid of her, but it had never occurred to her that they might not like her. She stared hard into the faces of the ones who were frowning and giving off a sense of negative emotions. She barely even heard when one of them finally answered that the President's schedule was posted clearly on his calendar in his office, if she cared to have a glance at it and answer her own question.

"Thank you," she'd said over her shoulder. She took the rise back down to the first floor. Gabriel's office was on the first floor down the hallway from the front door but before the dining hall and auditorium.

Essien tried the doors to Gabriel's office. She rattled the knobs back and forth. Neither would open. She pushed against the door panels as she turned, using her shoulder to push, too. Locked. She knocked once, hard. No sounds came from inside. She turned and put her back against the door, looking up and down both sides of the hallway. Several guards watched her from the end of the hallway. Seeing them there made her anger spike again.

She marched down the hallway heading straight for them. She tried to remember their names as she drew closer. They weren't carrying weapons where she could see, but they were dressed in the black-on-black uniform.

She stood in front of them and put her hands on her hips.

"Tell me when the President will return."

All three guards shrugged.

"Don't you talk?"

One grinned, and Essien knew she didn't like that kind of smile aimed at her. "Antonious keeps the President's schedule; we're either assigned to his protection or not. I wasn't assigned to his protection."

"What's your name again?"

The guard grinned. "You wouldn't remember my name from the one time I told you."

"What did they tell you your job would be when they hired you?"

He was still wearing that grin. "To serve the President and all his house."

"I'm a part of his house. Can you get me into his office?"

"I don't have the key."

"Who has the key?"

The guard shrugged again. His grin was slipping now.

"Probably Antonious. We don't."

Essien sighed and glanced at the other two guards.

"Either of you want to tell me your names?"

The taller of the other two guards spoke up. His voice was like an echo at the bottom of a well, "We were ordered not to cavort with you." He pinned the grinning guard with a hard stare.

"Cavort? He ordered you not to cavort with me? When did that include not giving me your names? Are you all to be nameless and faceless? A nameless, faceless black blob?" Essien threw up her hands, turned on her heel, and stomped over to the rise. She ground her teeth together waiting for the rise to reach her. *What a terrible man,* she thought. *What a terrible, horrible man!*

On the twenty-eighth day, Essien awoke to rain pounding against the windows and the sides of the compound. She opened the balcony doors and let the sounds of water drowning the world fill the room. The ocean and the sky were combined to form a single gray sheet that hung over everything. The rain fell in a continuous pour that couldn't decide if it was cold or warm. Maybe it was the humid air pushing in around the wetness.

She spent the morning going through her training, pushing herself a little harder on each round. She attempted to lift the heaviest stones she'd ever hoisted, and her muscles cramped. She did it, bearing a fierce grin around the room. She was drenched at the end of it and welcomed the fall of hot water down over her head in the shower. Every part of her body was sore afterward. An attendant entered as she was braiding her hair with shea butter and oils. A woman in the same black-on-black uniform of the Guard. She bent to gather her used clothes from the ground.

"Is there anyone here who might give me a therapeutic massage? I think I might have strained myself too hard today." The attendant glanced at her for a second, nodded once, and then swept out of the room. Essien hoped that meant someone would come to help her soothe out the kinks in all her muscles. She had just finished braiding her hair when another set of female attendants arrived bearing a collapsible table, oils in glass jars, and a steel bowl full of hot stones. They set up toward the end of the hallway near the window. Sunlight fell in a square just in front of the table.

One attendant started to disrobe her of the cream-colored silk dressing gown she had slipped into out of the shower. It was the only dressing gown in the wardrobe she'd been provided. Essien stepped away from the reaching hands, shaking her head. The attendant patted the table, a surface padded with white sheets and a blanket. She motioned for Essien to take off her own clothes and lie down under the blanket. They both turned and began to fuss with the other supplies they'd brought. So Essien dropped the gown and quickly slipped underneath the sheets. She smelled burning incense, something herbal and calming.

The attendants' hands were soft and gentle. The oil was warm, but the stones were hot enough to feel near scalding. They pressed the hard stones against every muscle in her body, even pressing them against her toes and the bottoms of her feet. After a while, the heat felt just right. By the end of it, her eyes were closed, and she was floating inside that abyss full of power. She stared into it, trying to get her arms around all of it. There was too much for her to hold, but she kept trying. She fell asleep. The sounds of the attendants rustling around to gather their supplies woke her. She had even started to drool a bit from the relaxation. One of them handed her the robe from the floor, and she sat up with the sheets pressed against her chest. Once the dressing gown was tied into place, she slipped down.

"Thank you," she said. "That was wonderful." And she meant it. She felt she could sleep more, so she entered her room and climbed into her own bed. Then there was nothing except the drone of drip after drip of rain. She grew restless lying there while the sun moved toward the horizon and tried again to push against that door in her mind. Locked still, like the door to his office, like the names of the guards who followed her everywhere.

Essien knew the tears that were falling were a release and not an embarrassment. They didn't mean she was weak or wrecked, she reassured herself. They didn't mean she was failing or going back on her word. The gloom and doom wasn't her, not really, and had nothing to do with Gabriel either. It was the rain. And that damned massage.

CHAPTER TWENTY-SEVEN

◆

ESSIEN HAD BEEN ON A SKYCRAFT FOR THE FIRST TIME AS A child when she had traveled with her parents to meet her cousins in her father's village. The trip to Berber State had been an adventure for her twelve-year-old self. She had gotten to ride a camel and camp out in the desert in transparent domes under the constellation of Osiris. She had ridden on a boat along the edge of the Aur River, watching its glassy surface shine a light of optimism on the day and her future. She had visited the pyramids, some of them with gold and diamonds encrusting their very tops. She had stared up and up at the Sphinx with its proud, regal, half-human stature. The face, beautiful and whole, seemed to stare down at her, reminding her of the women she saw all over Alkebulan. She had thought she would eventually move to Berber State when she grew up, as fascinated as she was by life in the northeastern-most state, its connections to the nations across the Mesopotamian Sea most especially.

The skycraft Essien was on now had better amenities and was a better flight overall, but Essien didn't feel optimistic or full of light. She felt dark and dreary, all of her hidden behind a veil of blank stares and one-word answers. She felt like a mannequin, a fixed thing paused in its motion for a forever-frozen moment and placed in a location not of its own choosing. She felt void of energy and substance. If being manipulated by the President was a skill, then she seemed to have a keenly successful penchant for it. She knew he was doing it, and still it had worked.

She had agreed to lead this campaign, finally, reluctantly, after thirty-one days of near solitude in the compound. The preposterously absurd campaign that would hopefully end with ratification of laws to make her Queen. A campaign she was to lead alone. Of course, there was still the Guard to watch her. There were still the attendants, quiet and barely pausing to hear her special requests before they were gone. She never had time to even ask their names. They were women and men, and she'd have thought their tongues were cut out with how rarely they spoke in front of her.

There wasn't much ceremony or circumstance to Essien's acquiescence to Gabriel. He was not present for it, and she had to knock on those doors that blocked her from entering his mind the way he could enter hers. Knock, and knock again, and then wait patiently for him to ease the door open just a crack to let her in. He had kept his background faded, and she'd gotten only the sense that there was music and sunshine and laughter. She could see him standing in a white shawl and robe that was held in place at his right shoulder with a gold and onyx pin. He was wearing an unusual color that she had never seen him in, and she pressed against that layer of hardness that kept her out of him completely.

"Where are you?" she asked before she could stop her tongue.

She forgot for a moment why she'd contacted him because of the discomfort she was now feeling as she realized it and wanted to change her mind. She knew she wouldn't, couldn't. Not after he had shown her precisely what not doing what he wanted would lead to—being left alone, isolated, cut off from the world, and unsure if he'd killed anyone else important to her besides Enyemaka. And yet. Despite the discomfort and disdain, she stayed there, hovering over him in her mind's eye, trying to see more of the environment around him. Something in her was parched and starved for sustenance that only Gabriel could give to her. She felt sick at the thought of it.

She was surprised that he answered, *"I'm on the islands of Cyrene, in the city of Grecia, if you must know. But we'll soon be headed to Iroquois, another leg of the conference of international leaders. I am unsure of when I will return, though I have heard how important that information is for you. My schedule during this time of year is always busy, more so now. Unpredictable, too."* He wore a smirk, and she knew it was aimed at her. He was moving away from where he had been because his background was now darker, still blurred, but there was a sense of silence beyond him.

Cyrene? Essien wondered at the cluster of islands in the Mesopotamian Sea just to the north of Alkebulan. She had never been, though she had heard of it in different ways growing up. A nation of people called Greeks, who had sent its scholars to study in Alkebulanian universities for centuries, its own schools back overseas growing and thriving because of it. And Iroquois? Essien wouldn't ask, but she wanted to. Here was another country she had longed to visit since she was a young girl. A nation where she had family waiting for her to finally meet them. And he was going without her.

She blurted out, *"What use am I to you if you do not bring me to these conferences? Shouldn't I be there, too? Aren't I to be a leader of Alkebulan as well?"*

His smile grew bigger. *"I take it you've finally decided to accept my orders? You're ready to start your campaign?"*

Essien tried to calm her disgust and anger enough to admit that she had finally agreed to go on his campaign.

"Can you prepare travel plans for me?" she'd asked, the words just thoughts swirling from her consciousness to his. *"And I'd like copies of the legislation to read. I can't convince them to pass a law if I don't know what it says."*

He stopped smiling abruptly and then gave just one slow nod.

"Will you meet me on any stops? Or will—" Before she had finished uttering her second question, the President was wiped suddenly from her vision. One minute she was staring down at his face, his background blurred out, and the next, she was back in her own head. She couldn't see or sense him at all. She pressed against those steel doors, closing her eyes to imagine banging and kicking and then hammering against them. They remained locked, and she had no idea what he was doing or thinking on the other side.

Essien made herself turn away from the despair at the bottom of that abyss that opened up right at her feet. Instead, she let that coiled pit of power unwind a bit. She let it slither out in a tiny tendril that played like a flickering coin spinning between knuckles and fingers. Essien felt almost like herself again by the time the attendant came to inform her that the engine was waiting to take her to the aerial transportation center and that a bag had already been packed for her. She was also handed a portfolio that was half a foot thick, and she flipped through the first few pages to confirm her suspicion that it contained the legislation she had requested. She smiled, realizing two could play the manipulation game.

Essien was to take a solo tour across Alkebulan that might last three months, or it might not be over until a year from now, and she was to have no breaks in between. The schedule they handed her mid-flight was jam-packed, and there was only time to sleep at night. There wasn't a moment of additional rest planned into the agenda of events. Essien put the stack of papyri down on top of the portfolio she had set on the empty seat beside her. She would have to make time for her own freedom, she realized. And she would.

She was only a third of the way through reading the legislation, but already it had caused a straightening of her spine and an elevation of her chin. She wouldn't be powerless as Queen. Oh, no, this legislation granted her an inordinate amount of power. Power the President didn't have. The power to build and to destroy, without needing anyone's permission. She had power over the cultural events and activities of the nation, the educational pursuits of the citizens, and the power to convene a full council of both tribal and military, whether the Council Members wanted to appear or not. She had the power to investigate complaints from individual citizens and establish her own agencies to handle public matters of concern. She also had the power to gather funds and to provide funding for diverse strategies and plans of national interest.

Eventually, she'd had to close the file and put it aside, to close her eyes at the way her imagination sped ahead of her into the future. She could see it. Alkebulan, like a shining nation set up on a cloud above a hill. A place where everyone aspires to be. It was a unique feeling. Before, she had felt completely mired by the chains Gabriel had wrapped her in, limited by her past as a soja and a guard. Now, she could see eons ahead into a world where she was long gone, but where she would forever have imprinted her mark. She wanted that world. Aiming to be a soja or to join the Guard had been a paltry, pale comparison to this exuberant mission. She would take it on; she would embrace it. Whatever plans Gabriel thought he had, this legislation would be her protection against them.

Almost as soon as the skycraft coasted to a stop, she heard the beating bassline of drums and shouts of greeting songs. The thumping sound rose up into her feet as soon as she stepped down to the ground. The Fulani people were welcoming her with dance. She could see the groups of dancers, likely their best troupes sent to the transportation center to greet her and shower her with music. The sounds and moves were so different from anything she had ever seen, likely adapted from the local tribes and customs.

Over time, as each skycraft landed, Essien found that she had grown to appreciate and expect these welcomes. The gathered dancers offered her an entertainment that was bright and exciting; it made her feel a moment's worth of contentment, forgetting temporarily what she had arrived to do. So, she could stand before them smiling slightly, tapping her feet and swaying along if the music sank deep into her bones. At some point as the dances and the music settled to an end, a group detached and came forward out of the crowd to approach her. Sometimes, she knew it would be a tribal elder and their selected advisors. Other times, she knew it was an appointed military councilman, ones whom she recognized from her own time as Guard.

In Fulani, they sent a mix of both councils. The military councilmen were in the usual military attire, black-on-black overcoats, tunics, and trousers. The Tribal Council wore the garb of their culture, some of the men in dark robes, others in all white with white head coverings. The women wore simple bright white uwes or white skirts and wrapped tops with a rainbow of embroidery over the chest and at the waistline. They all had their hair in some variation of round puffs or thin braids that sculpted their heads into elegant shapes. She'd never had her hair braided quite like that and admired the hairstyles as greetings were shared and names were provided, palms touched, and then she was herded by them all into a waiting engine for her first of the endless chain of meetings.

Traveling through Fulani State, she saw the mix of architecture delineating the type of building. The homes were economical, made of dark gray palms built in a conical shape, some small with several clustered around a center fire pit and others larger and dominating the center of a clearing. The business buildings were plain tan stone or ornately decorated with colorful geometric patterns in squares or black and white triangles. The religious centers were white, pale stones with domed roofs and open-air courtyards. The retail and entertainment centers had newer architecture, glass structures with windowed walls slanted directly toward the sun, square bricks in tiers all the way up to a small top floor.

Essien kept her eyes outside the windows while Timbuktu University streaked past. Her head whipped back around to hold her glimpse. Its stone towers and terraces could be seen even as the engine sped away. She hoped she'd find time to visit the hallowed university grounds. Though it was largely a religious university, it was on the verge of expanding into other disciplines. Essien wondered if she might tip that balance over into opening up the colleges to anyone who wanted an education, whether they desired to be a religious leader or only a trader or health professional. As it was, the unofficial apprenticeship style of learning kept so many people, especially women, out of some professions. The thrill of knowing that she could change that course through her own policies made her smile to herself. While her eyes greedily drank in all the architecture around her, her mind was calculating and scripting how she would make her own declarations.

The engines stopped in what looked like the middle of nowhere. There was a tent with open sides set up next to the mouth of a cave. A group of people milled underneath the tent, staring down at something on the waist-high table. Even from the engine, Essien could see that they were all wearing smiles. She climbed out of the engine by herself, and the guards fell in line around her.

The older woman who led the group walking toward her was elderly, but she didn't use a staff. Something bright and shiny glinted near her face, reflecting the sun in every direction and obscuring her face in a golden halo. When she finally drew close enough, Essien saw that the elder woman had gold earrings in the shape of layered half-moons dangling off each ear. The gold looked freshly poured and pounded into the shapes. The woman's head was covered in a bright red and black covering that blended in with the bright red and orange of her robes, which billowed around her as the wind blew. Her skin was a smoky brown, her eyes intelligent dark orbs. The way she held her chin and her arms let Essien know that she was the tribal elder. The other people walking behind her seemed more ordinary in plain tunics and pants, a few of the women in bright skirts. The elder commanded a presence and a power that Essien instantly noticed and felt.

When she got close enough, the elderly woman dropped into a bow, one low enough to the ground that Essien feared she might fall forward. The people behind the elder did the same, with a few of them lying flat with their faces down on the ground. Essien never knew how to react to these displays, so she did what her mother had trained her to do. She returned the bow, and as she lowered herself, she decided to sink all the way down to one knee. She held the pose briefly, her eyes on the ground. When she rose, the elder and her people began to rise, too.

"Welcome to our lands, Eze Nwaanyi. We have waited long for your arrival here."

Essien was shocked into silence as the old woman wrapped her into a hug and pressed her tight. The old woman's body felt light and hollow, and Essien was afraid that she would break her if she squeezed too hard.

"Thank you for welcoming me," she said. She was even more surprised to find that her throat felt clogged, and her eyes burned. That's when she realized that she had expected to have to fight her way through every step of this campaign. She hadn't expected to receive respect and sweetness from dear elders the minute she met them. She had expected them to scold and reject her. Yes, this was just the first state, and Essien still might have trouble getting all the states to accept her campaign. But beginning with a welcome wasn't the worst way to start. Essien tried to reign her emotions back in. She couldn't help the smile that showed she was pleased.

"I am Amina Nana Asma'u, but my loved ones call me Kabbo. I will be your guide during your time here in Fulani."

Essien's head cocked because she recognized part of the name, "Say that name again?"

The elder smiled. "Yes, you guessed correctly. I am descended from Nana Asma'u. All the women in my family bear her name. All the men are named after Usman Fodio."

Thinking back to her lessons from her Upper Levels, Essien recalled what she had learned of Nana Asma'u, the daughter of Usman dan Fodio. She had been a legendary Princess, skilled in poetry. The poems she left behind were collected in several volumes stored at the Muséon, a museum in the great library in Berber State. Essien remembered that they had been allowed to flip through one of the volumes. The poems were words of inspiration and politics, words of wonder and even some romance. She tried to remember more of Nana Asma'u's life and drew a blank. Lucky for her, a living descendent was standing right before her.

With a wider smile, Essien said, "I am even happier to meet you now than I was. I studied your ancestors in school, but I can't recall everything I learned. I would love to hear some of Nana's original poems while I am here."

Taking Essien's arm in hers like they were close girlfriends, Amina steered her over to where the others had gathered underneath the tent. She had a wide grin on her face, too.

"I haven't had someone to speak of poetry with in some time. The Center of Oral and Print Traditions wasn't included on your itinerary; neither was Timbuktu University. That's where originals of my elder mother's writings are kept. The Muséon has other publications in their collection, too, but the University has the bulk of her unpublished works. The Center also has the entire works of Yeɗi Sanba Booyi, another Fulani poet you might like. There are even some of the writings of Usman dan Fodio, my elder father, but of course, they are not in favor any longer."

Essien nodded. Like Mansa Musa before him, Usman dan Fodio had been another of Alkebulan's historical figures who had not agreed with the establishment of a united nation. Even going so far as to declare war against the first President of Alkebulan, Sigidi kaSenzangakhona. Usman had wanted to spread his religion into the government of the country, a foreign

174　　　　　WIELDERS OF FLOODS & FLAMES

religion that had spread from Mesopotamia and taken hold in the northeast first, like all the other religions did, too. Usman dan Fodio's attempt at spreading a religious holy war across Alkebulan had almost been successful, but the first President, known to the people as Shaka, had organized and trained a formidable military, the Sojas and then the Uzo Nchedo, who changed how warfare was fought in those days. Under Shaka's leadership, Usman was defeated, but he remained under captivity until his death of old age in Igbo State. Known for being ruthless, Shaka had shown mercy when he could. Essien thought of Gabriel and Enyemaka and turned to Amina with a forced smile.

"If my guards will allow it, I would love to visit both the Center and the University. I hope you can help me finagle them if you see them resisting." Essien pursed her lips and gave a conspiratory glance at the guards who trailed behind them.

Amina squeezed her arm even tighter and said, "I'd be happy to. I could do no less for my Queen." She paused and then said, "I think I am going to like you even more than I had thought, Essien."

She carried those words with her as she was introduced to the rest of the gathered group of wizened tribal elders, each of them holding a walking staff and centuries of knowledge. She listened as they began to speak to her in spills and flurries that she focused on and tried her hardest to remember. Some of them spoke Igbo, which had only been a common tongue for a few decades. The rest of them spoke a language that Essien did not immediately know. Of course, she was familiar with Fulbe and Pulaar as dialects of the native tongue of the Fulani elders, but whatever they were speaking today was beyond Essien. She gladly noted another language that she needed to add to her growing list to learn. At some point after that first day of her campaign, she asked a guard to carry around pads of papyrus for her and pens that she might have paper to keep track of the information received, and the promises she made.

The elders began telling stories, and Essien was just as enraptured. She forgot where they were, standing next to the entrance to an underground cave that she hoped no one would make her enter. The elders began to weave tales of times past, stories of the beginnings and endings of cities and villages and rulers long gone. When one stopped to think, another chimed in with their own storytelling, and Essien felt giddy with the passions of her youth as she mentally cataloged those new tales. She wouldn't ask the guards to write these down. She knew she'd remember them. Eventually, some began to tell stories of akukoifo. Essien realized right away that these were stories that she had never heard before.

Someone realized that they had gotten completely off-topic and tried to steer them back to discussing the fresh discovery of an iron ore lode in the walls of an underground cave. They moved the group to stand near the edge of the entrance. Essien could see inside where miners had constructed scaffolding and girders leading down and down inside the cave. There were naked light bulbs strung up along the ceiling showing the way as they dipped and turned, falling out of sight.

As Essien stared into the depths of the cave, a shiver pulsing through her, Amina said, "The God of Iron and Metal and Metalworks was said to have mated with the Mothers to produce the akukoifo. He found them irresistible, unlike any other females on Ala-ani, above or below it. They were a proud couple, birthing their offspring, who burst forth into the world shiny and new and never seen before. Oh, the mischief they got into with their proud parents unable to keep them in line. So, it was the God of Iron and Metal and Metalworks who called upon the aid of both the man at the bottom of the lake and the woman on her sun throne to help him tame his own offspring. It wasn't the Mothers or the various Gods of Alkebulan, who controlled those celestial beings, but the God and Goddess of Alkebulan. And they still do."

That story made Essien glance up and up to the blue covering the sky over her head. There, the faint floating figures that were always above her now. They stayed far away from her, none coming as close as they did when she was younger. Just seeing them up there, floating around and dipping down, made her feel somewhat nostalgic. She knew it was always futile to spend time longing for the innocence of her youth. One could never go backward, only forward. Still, she remembered how they had pestered her, one akukoifo in particular. She remembered how it had felt to touch one of those celestial beings, like dipping her hand into tingling waters. There was nothing else like it. She couldn't remember the last time she had seen an akukoifo up close. She was still staring up at the sky when the elders' stories moved on to more earthly matters.

After all their stories were told, another elder mentioned the next meeting. And so, there were the demands to be heard, and she had to listen to those, too. As the guards maneuvered her back into the engines once again, she thanked Amina and the other elders with warmth and smiles. She had enjoyed their time and would be adamant about making stops that weren't on her itinerary, even if she had to pull rank to do it.

The engine took her next to the Fulani Council House. The floors and wings of the compound were made of dark brown stone with stark white pillars and window trim. The floors were a smooth dark brown marble that echoed through the empty halls. They took her through empty hall after empty hall to the central Council room. They pushed open wooden doors to a room that stretched out in a circular shape. It had a circular dais in the middle with a single armchair and side table on it. The dais was surrounded by circles of padded wooden seats leading outward in wider and wider circles. Every seat was filled. The Councils were seated in a mixed arrangement with no discernible difference between Military and Tribal members. They were all wearing different-colored robes, some bright with embroidered patterns, others dark brown or white. There were others who didn't fit into either category sitting in the very front row and the very back rows. Essien tried to guess that these might be journalists or some other public representatives.

The guards stuck close around her, closer than they had been when they were in the countryside. She was led to the very center at the front of the rows. She hoped they wouldn't make her sit on the dais. Being the center of attention would come necessarily with her position, but there was no need to begin the formalities so soon. She hadn't felt this nervous when Amina had called her Eze Nwaanyi. She clenched and unclenched her hands; she flexed her toes in her boots, new and still snug against her feet.

She took the seat they pointed her to, the one up on the dais, and she made herself sit up straight, her shoulders back, her hands folded in her lap. The room was filled with the rustling of movement, but nobody spoke. Essien cleared her throat and wished for water.

Before she could turn to figure out who she might ask, a guard stepped forward holding a tall glass vase of water with a smaller drinking glass. Essien poured her own drink and sipped the full glass. She refilled it to the top and let it sit on the table beside her right hand.

More introductions were made as each individual, each interested party, stepped forth to present their speeches. As she listened to them all, she realized they had prepared what amounted to a response on her claim to being Queen. As their words flowed relentlessly, she knew that they weren't challenging her right to rule. Not a single one of them. Each of them came to the center of the floor before her and laid out their pleas for her as their Queen. They didn't toss alms or give her accolades. No, they each called her to actually be their Queen. By the end of the line of speeches, Essien had begun to smile and nod.

There were everyday people from Ouagadougou, Wolof, Tenkodogo, Mandinke, Yatenga, and every other city around Fulani State. They introduced themselves by their family names, and Essien gave them her full attention.

The activists hailed from Sokoto, Ghana, Senegambia, Maasina, Songhai, and so many other cities that Essien knew she could not pinpoint them all on a map of the state. Their speeches rattled on, and she tried to listen to every word. When she caught her mind wandering, to thoughts of Gabriel or imagining being asleep in her comfortable bed, she'd snap her attention back to the face of the speaker and hope her own expression didn't show her confusion or embarrassment.

There were military councilmen who stood up to speak, and Essien classified them as politicians. She knew they lived the closest to the council house right there in Timbuktu, as required by law. What she hadn't prepared for was that they, of all the groups, seemed the most at odds with every one of the other subsets of the population. They had been on campaigns of their own and knew exactly who she was, what she was. They had likely attended her trial. As she listened to them speak, she knew that what they wanted from her were assurances that Fulani State would be like Bantu State, free of encroachment from either her or Gabriel. She began to frown as they each spoke, none of them giving her the chance to respond. As they droned on and on, one after the other, she had to listen and know that notes were being taken on what was said. She hadn't expected trouble to come from the military councilmen. But she should have. Where the other speakers had been deferential and genuflected an appropriate amount, the politicians did no such thing. Their faces were arrogant before they ever said a word. Essien knew that this might be her most effective obstacle to sitting on the throne.

After Essien heard what the politicians had to say, the scientists were much easier to listen to. They were from everywhere, and some of them were even from other states selected to represent the interests of their various associations in Fulani. Essien listened as they listed numbers and facts, using data to paint a picture of their demands. Her head spun with all the figures and tables they showed her, trying to keep the details straight. *And this is just the first state*, Essien told herself as she focused on a column of numbers meant to tell her just how much expanding the iron mine would cost and how much it would yield and the revenue she could expect to collect for any number of funds she could establish. Essien began to grow tired, and the interested but solemn look on her face slipped. She had to school her features from looking bored or showing just how tired she was.

When the mothers stepped up to speak, they were such a mix of ages that Essien almost didn't believe some of them actually had children. The ones that shocked her the most looked young, like Ngozi had looked when Essien had seen her last with one baby on her back and the other one almost ready to be born. The youngest mothers standing before her probably still had small nursing babies. Others of the women were much older, needing canes to help them walk to the center of the circle. Essien leaned forward in her chair to hear these ones. They spoke with such passion and conviction, naming all their children and their children's children. The oldest was able to name three generations after her. They didn't know that she didn't need to be convinced to give them whatever they wanted or needed. Their message was the same as many of the others: Educate the children of the nation, ensure they had food, employ their parents, and support their entrepreneurial efforts. They were demands Essien could already hear herself saying yes to.

After the mothers, there were the medical providers who cared for the sick and mended the ill. They spoke of how they risked their lives on a daily basis by helping battle illnesses that would decimate the population if allowed to spread. They called themselves the lifesavers of the state and the country, and yet they lamented having to travel overseas for advanced and specialized study. They presented figures on how many of them did not return to the country after receiving their medical certifications. Essien's mind was already traveling faster than she could, and this was another goal to add to the growing list.

If Alkebulan was to compete on an international stage, as Gabriel wanted, then ensuring that its educational system was top tier in all the disciplines would be an essential first step. Nobody should have to leave the country to obtain an education they needed to work in Alkebulan. It made Essien wonder about the extent of the problem beyond the two options she had known: religious study or military training. Had this dichotomy sent parts of the population into the arms of other countries? If she could help different universities expand their offerings, that would solidify her influence as Queen before she had even ascended the throne. She would be starting her reign on a positive note, and there would be few who could stand against her with the kind of support she'd receive.

Essien wished for the meetings to be over that she might begin making her own plans, thinking of what they had already said, wondering how she might leave space for the demands that other states would surely make. A glance around her showed the line waiting to speak dwindled down, but there were still several speakers to go. The Guard remained on alert surrounding the dais and at various intervals around the Council room. A glance out the window showed the sky had darkened, but there was faint light showing the sun hadn't yet set. There would be no time to visit any other sites today, she realized with a slump of her shoulders. She had hoped she might at least go to the university.

After the health professionals came a group who supported and backed up the claims of all the rest. It was cream on top of the porridge to hear what the educators demanded. Their pleas were eager and earnest. They had even more data and figures to show on screen projectors. The faces of Alkebulan's children were large and magnified, their hopes and dreams laid bare. Essien's heart seemed to swell inside of her. For those young, beaming faces, she would do and give anything. Staring at those faces, she knew she had found the ones for whom she'd be willing to sacrifice everything. For a moment, Essien wondered how that love and tenderness might be translated to children of her own someday, were she to have them. She had never felt this level of care for her brother's children, so it was curious that she felt it now. When she joined the military, she hadn't ever planned on being a mother. When she'd been elevated to the Guard, she had declared it impossible. Now she knew where she stood on that position. She'd never be a mother. And yet, Alkebulan's children would be like her own.

Finally, the speeches were almost over, and there was one final group waiting to speak. She would have known them from anywhere, even walking past her on the street. They seemed to have a general dustiness about their skin and clothes. The farmers spoke with slow, steady, and firm voices. They laid out their own figures and numbers. Sketching a different kind of image for the nation. Land, land was gold, and land was king. Without land, there were no crops, and without crops, there was no fuel to feed the nation. No food to fill the bellies of those children of Alkebulan. The farmers were so humble, and their demands were more offers of service than making the case for more of anything. Yet, watching them each simply state their piece and step aside for the next, Essien knew this group that stood before her last had the greatest demands of all.

As Essien listened and signaled with her hands or her face, the guards taking notes for her covered pads and pads of papyrus. The demands included promises and guarantees from her, as she listened and nodded, which she had them be sure to write down, with an emphasized glance or a pointed finger, so she would have a note to remind her to enact those promises she had made. Some of the promises she could keep immediately, sitting before them with the desire to agree and acquiesce wafting in exuberant waves from her smiling face.

After they had all finished, after the last farmer trudged back to his seat, another of the tribal elders began to close out their assembly and invite them to the next gathering. Essien wasn't listening as the Councilmen and elders and others began to rise and disperse, some standing around chatting, others immediately gathering their notecards and portfolios to exit the room. Essien sat waiting for someone to direct her to her next destination, her mind not in the room at all.

She seemed to float absentmindedly as Amina bid her goodbye until the next morning, and she was led back down those empty, echoing halls to the waiting engine. The sky was a deep purple with streaks of magenta and indigo when they set out for the nearest military compound. The pads of papyri were on the seat next to her, and Essien set her empty hand on top of them to keep the stack from spilling over. There were so many ideas and plans churning through her mind, and yet she knew there was something she didn't have to wait to do.

One knock on those steel doors in her mind this time before the door was opened, just a crack. This time, Gabriel's background was just as noisy as before, but she couldn't tell if he was inside of a building or outside. The blurred images seemed to be moving, so she wondered if he might be driving somewhere.

"Any good news, Essien? How has Fulani been treating you?"

All it took was one brief explanation that did not require words of any kind, only thoughts and sensations. She watched Gabriel's background as she spoke because his face told her nothing. He listened, and she rushed on, not pausing to take a deep breath for fear that he would interrupt her. With one brief nod from Gabriel, she knew that what she had asked for would be done. In the days that followed, there would be military engines filing into the cities of Fulani one after the other in a stretching line to deliver supplies and materials that had been asked for, and even sojas from local compounds to help coordinate and organize the labor that was needed.

"Is that all?" Gabriel asked. His background was still, so she knew that he had been moving, but now he was stopped.

"Are you in Iroquois yet?" she dared ask him. She fully expected him to wipe their connection clean and shut the door in her face.

He smiled. *"You would love it, Essien. Even the air here breathes a little differently."*

She let her disappointment show as she dropped her head and began to pull away from him. She was closing the door before he had a chance to.

"You couldn't have gone on your campaign and come to Iroquois at the same time, you know. And besides, you'll get to see this country one day, too. I promise. The partnerships I'm building now will be instrumental in the near future. Just watch. And don't look sad. You're on the trip of a lifetime. I hope you can act like it."

"Maybe if I had an agenda that included some moments of rest and not just meeting after meeting."

"Of course. What did you have in mind?"

Essien perked up. *"Timbuktu University. And Amina suggested I visit the Center for Oral and Print Traditions."*

Gabriel smiled now, and it felt like the sun had risen just for her. She shook her head to clear the feeling, pressing her lips together to avoid smiling at him. *"The University is one of our national gems,"* he said. *"Oh, the library alone is worth every Naira of upkeep and maintenance we spend each year. I can't say I'm familiar with the Center you mentioned. You won't receive a single objection from me or your guards to visiting these locations, if you wish."*

Essien did not quite believe him. He ended their meeting with a wave of his hand. Back in her own mind and body, she could feel the engine slowing down.

She shifted her gaze outward as they rolled slowly into the military compound, the black iron gates parting to let her convoy through. It was fully dark now, and she couldn't see beyond the bright yellow spotlights that pointed directly at the engine and didn't illuminate the surrounding darkness. The engine had pulled right up to the front doors, and she was let out at the doorstep of a multi-floored dark tan building with rows of square windows on each floor. There were sojas on patrol on the compound walls, their back-and-forth trek taking them around the top of all four sides of the stone wall surrounding the compound. She didn't see any other sojas or commanders as she climbed the few steps leading up to the dark wood front door.

Her stomach chose that moment to remind her that she had been traveling all day and had not eaten. But, unfortunately, the late hour meant that dinner had already been served and cleaned up.

With her stomach rumbling, the Guard led her down hallways where she could hear the murmur of voices and the thud of steps just out of her sight. They traveled up sets of stairs, down hallways, and around corners, until finally, she was deposited at a door into a small chamber designed to be occupied by one person. The door was opened for her, and she stepped inside to glance around the plain, stark room. The chamber contained only a bed for one, and a chair and desk, upon which she noted a covered tray and glass vase of water. There was also a shelf next to a sink with a mirror above it. She avoided looking at herself in the mirror during her glance around the room. One guard set down the stack of her papyrus pads and the portfolio with the legislation she still needed to finish reading on the desk. Another set down the canvas bag that had been packed for her, likely containing a few changes of clothes for different occasions, on top of the bed.

"Your schedule has your departure time in the morning. Someone will be on duty all night, if you need anything."

Essien just nodded, her eyes on the tray. As the door clicked closed behind her, she was already lifting the wooden lid off the tray, the steam and scent of fresh food wafting up to her. The main dish was a stew of some kind with chunks of tender meat, square bites of some root vegetable with a crunch, and small pearls of a grain she'd never had before. The dish was spicy and flavorful, and she was left scraping her spoon against the wooden bowl to get every morsel. There was a warm flatbread wrapped in a cloth that she used to mop up all of the leftover sauce. She downed all the water in the vase, not even bothering to use the glass.

The canvas bag had only a thin white shift for sleeping. She shivered as she climbed between the thin bed covering. The bed square at least was soft, and she sank down into it. It made her miss her bed back at the President's compound. Lying on her back with her eyes closed, Essien tried not to think. She was so tired that her limbs felt heavy and boneless. She hadn't thought about where she might sleep, so she was glad that Gabriel's plans for the campaign included everything she did not have to think about. Her only challenge was to get through the meetings tomorrow and carve out space to visit the locations she had at the top of her list. As she drifted off to sleep, Essien wondered what Gabriel was doing. She was too far gone into her dream to feel the anger as she remembered that he had traveled to two of her top destination countries without her.

When she awoke the next morning, she discovered that the canvas bag that an attendant had packed for her contained no more uniforms besides the one she had arrived in. Instead, the bag was packed with more uwes. The dresses were made of silky fabrics in light colors. So were the underthings. There were no tunics or trousers. At the bottom of the canvas were two pairs of matching flats. Essien threw the shoes down. If she had checked the bag herself, she would have washed out her uniform the night before and worn it again. Better yet, if she had packed the bag on her own, she would have packed her uniforms, at least the tunics and loosely fitted pants that were comfortable and matched what the Guard wore. She had no desire to stand out, especially not in pastel colors and thin, short dresses. Though she had gotten used to being unarmed, she would never grow used to dressing like a civilian.

When Essien stepped out of the room, the two Guards were already standing at attention. She didn't recognize them from the day before, so she knew they had changed shifts at some point in the night. She nodded at them both and let them lead her to join the larger group of guards waiting for them on the first floor.

The day outside was bright, but the sun was hidden behind clouds, so the brightness didn't shock her as soon as she stepped foot outdoors. The drive back to the Council House was quick. She didn't realize how close the compound was. She was unloaded briskly. The Council House seemed full to bursting today. There were people milling down every hall, gathered in every room and office off the hallways, and filling every seat in the Council room. Every one of them wore a smile, wide and big, aimed at her in particular. Their smiling faces made Essien smile in return, the grin making her feel a sense of excitement where before she had been feeling only apprehension and irritation.

Essien pulled at the hem of the simple light gray uwe she had finally selected as the Guard led her into the room and to the center of all the rows. This time, the table on the dais had a large book flipped open to the first page. Next to it was an ink pen with a delicate tip. Essien's breath shook as she breathed in, taking her seat behind the table.

She saw another elder from the day before stepping forward to begin proceedings.

"Today is a momentous day for the people of Alkebulan. Today, we will cast our vote to establish or reject the Quorum Upholding Enactment for Establishing the Nobility Act. With the passage of this legislation, we will usher Alkebulan into a future that is as bold as the first woman to join the Guard, and the first woman who will lead us. Let the vote commence. Each Council Member will sign their name to the role electing their choice to approve or reject the legislation. The first Council Member, please."

Each Council Member came forward, one at a time. Some of them looked at her with those smiles still plastered across their faces, infectious and beaming. Others avoided looking at her, and she knew immediately how they would be voting. For everyone that signed to vote down the legislation, there were two who signed to pass it. Having to watch each Council Member step up to the dais, grab hold of the pen, and sign their decision was awkward and uncomfortable, despite how many seemed open and cheerful. She wished she didn't have to watch so closely and so publicly. She tried to keep her breathing even because there were pictos capturing every second of this moment. Each signature inspired a rush of clicks and whirs and murmurs as news reporters documented it all.

Essien had been concentrating so hard on her breathing that before she knew it, the end of the line was suddenly before her. The last signature was placed. She hadn't been paying attention to who signed on which side. She hadn't been keeping a tally at all. Now, she stared around the room, unsure of how the vote would swing. From the front row, she saw Amina beaming up at her, the old woman's face transformed into something youthful and innocent. That sort of joy was life-changing.

Three tribal elders came up to the dais and began handling the book. They ran their fingers down the signatures, counting each one again and again. A third count was taken, and then they each finally looked up at her. With straight faces, they pronounced with one loud voice:

"Naija stand up! Alkebulan rise!"

Behind them, the voices of everyone in the room, even the guards, chimed in as one accord, repeating the words so loudly the windows shook in their frames. "Naija stand up! Alkebulan rise! Naija stand up! Alkebulan rise! Naija stand up! Alkebulan rise!"

As the words reverberated through the room, Essien's arms and legs began to quake. She pressed her hands flat against the table to keep herself from vibrating up out of the seat. She kept breathing, deep breaths in and out, so she wouldn't bolt from the chair. She didn't know if she was to speak now or if the vote was over. She knew she had won, whatever winning meant when she still had fifteen more states to go.

There were a few more words spoken by the three elders to end the ceremony, and the book was closed and packed into a locked metal box, carried between two guards out of her sight. The Council Members rose, and those who had voted against her were the first to leave.

The guards' looks at her were expectant, so she rose and followed their path out of the Council room.

Back into the engine, her one familiar companion, she was quickly traveling down the stretch of road away from the Council House. Essien saw a glimmer of diamonds as the sun reflected on water.

"Wait. I want to see the river. Can you bring me? Whichever that one is; it seems closest." The guards exchanged glances.

"Your next stop is the University. Then the Center. You're scheduled to leave the state after that."

"Oh." She wouldn't complain too much. She was going to see the University! She had heard of the fabled hall of learning since she was a little girl. Everyone wanted to attend Timbuktu. Until they learned that they could only study a few limited subjects. When she had been so obsessed with joining the military as a young girl, it had never occurred to her to go into studying for ministry of any kind. Besides that, acolytes of the Mothers didn't need to go to school to study, and that was the only religion Essien had ever known personally. The others were taught in Cosmology, as cursory introductory subjects, but Essien had never read any of the holy books of the other major religions. She made a note to check Gabriel's library for copies; she knew he'd have them.

Timbuktu University loomed up out of the horizon. The city of brown and red and yellow stone buildings had stone streets that were narrow and cramped, forcing the engine to move at a snail's pace. Not to mention the people—students and instructors—crossing into the street at every intersection. They passed a red stone building with square windows arranged in patterns on each side. The peaks and turrets of the different floors spread over several stadia. Other buildings of various sizes and heights surrounded the largest building, angling off on different streets and alleys on all sides. The engine stopped, and a group of people were gathered on the steps of the school waiting for them. Sankoré College was printed on the sign above the red stone building.

The men and women pressed forward to meet her. There were so many palms to touch, so many names to listen to and try to remember. Essien noted the mix of faces, the features revealing that these were people from all over the world, not just Alkebulan. And yet, they all spoke a common tongue.

The man who stepped forward last was a deep clay brown with small, shiny dark curls in a receding hairline and thin features. He introduced himself: "I am Hammadi Diallo, the Director of the Astrotheology program here at the Sankoré College," He wore a dark blue overcoat with matching blue slacks open over a white tunic; his shoes were black loafers with silver buckles. There were straps of leather around his neck and wrists with chunky silver medallions woven into the straps. They made a slight jingling noise when he raised his arms up to shout, "Welcome to Timbuktu, the greatest university in the world!"

Essien grinned at the man's palpable excitement. "I am glad to be here," and she meant it.

He adjusted his overcoat and rubbed his hands together. "Shall we escort you on a tour?"

"Yes please!" Essien didn't hide her exuberance as she pressed her hands together and clasped them tightly. Finally, she was getting to do something she had longed to do.

Hammadi cast a sidelong glance at the guards who prepared to fall into place in front of, beside, and behind her.

"Do you need this much protection? Surely, they could walk behind the group, couldn't they?" The guards were already shaking their heads.

Staring at each of them in turn, Essien patted the Director on the shoulder and said, "It's okay. They follow the President's orders." Hammadi nodded and seemed to accept it because he shuffled the group, including the guards who kept anyone from getting too close to her, into the nearest building.

White marble floors stretched down hallways leading in all directions off the entranceway. There were classroom doors off each side of the hallway, some opened with the shouting lectures of instructors pouring out. Pictures, images, photographs, and glass-covered artifacts adorned every wall and rested atop every pedestal positioned along the hall. There was even a mosaic on the ceiling depicting a pastoral landscape scene of herdsmen tending to their goats, camels, cattle, and sheep. Essien bumped into the shoulder of the guard in front of her and had to switch to paying more attention to walking than staring up at the ceiling.

It's like being on holy ground, Essien thought. *These are hallowed grounds*. All the scholars' feet that had passed through those halls, sat at those desks, all the lecturers who had given lessons at the front of those classrooms. It dwarfed Essien's mind to think of all the knowledge that had been generated and the ideas that had germinated there. The works that had been created and spread to other parts of the country, and the world, too. It was like walking through history. Essien remembered the demands of so many of the Fulani locals. How they had essentially begged her to revolutionize the university system in Alkebulan. She thought about the power she might soon have to bring their dream—now hers—to life.

As her guides led her through hall after hall, crossing outdoor courtyards and plazas, to reach silent libraries stretching into cavernous spaces designed specifically to hold all the precious texts, Essien contemplated her role in making education more accessible for average Alkebulanians. The activists and educators had a strong point, and she couldn't find a single point of disagreement. The challenge would come from the leaders and supporters of this famed institution, Essien already knew. She knew she had to convince them, and that they'd be a promising initial ally. She only had to convince the key players, like the Director walking just ahead of her, and her plans were as good as realized.

"What can you tell me about the astrotheology program?" she asked, walking quicker to keep up with Hammadi's quick, jerky steps.

His whole face brightened as he launched into an explanation, "Oh, we've been established here for at least three hundred years, one of the oldest disciplines offered. My job is to study the implications of space travel... not just the financial costs, or the cultural achievement, but the spiritual and ethical considerations, too."

As Hammadi answered her questions, the tour circled through a few more halls, exiting through an archway to enter another building, the guides explaining how the third largest building on campus, the Sidi Yahya School, had been most recently renovated to add a theater on the lower level. Now, the University could host its own productions instead of needing to rent out local venues in the city. Essien listened as the guides rattled off the latest productions and the newest student-written plays that would be starting in the upcoming season. Essien couldn't recall if she'd ever seen a play, not even when she had been a student in school. She didn't think the skits put on by inexperienced students under the force of overly enthusiastic teachers counted. It was an experience she'd like to have, she realized, even if she had to do it alone and as an adult. She started to giggle at the thought of Gabriel sitting for hours watching a play about falling in love and praying to a God for romance. Essien's smile drooped when she realized that the President might be more interested in the subject than she was.

She saw that their tour had stopped at the back of a large lecture hall full of students with an instructor flipping through images and blocks of text on his screen projector at the front of the room. A few heads darted around to stare at them, but most kept their heads focused on the lecturer while their hands scribbled notes.

Cheers erupted from a classroom down the hallway. As the tour group passed by, the Director stopped and ducked into the noisy room to find out what all the excited clapping and shouting was about. He came back out with a broad smile, the excitement in the room having contaminated him that quickly.

"They have just successfully put a manned vessel into orbit around another sun! Anyanwu 4507! This one has nine exoplanets, just like us!"

Essien pressed into the space in the doorway. Inside the room, the students, men and women, were crowded around several screen projectors as information from one of the computers broadcast a live diagram. It showed the vessel, a metal contraption that looked like a rotating helix, spinning in a trajectory around a glowing circle in the center. Other panels and instruments on the screen lit up and emitted beeps, flashing different numbers that meant something to everybody in the room. The excitement was contagious because Essien was smiling at them, too.

"Would you like to hear a presentation?"

But they were already guiding her further into the room with their arms outstretched, and the excited students were still smiling, but now their smiles and happiness included her. It was almost like they didn't care that she had just been introduced as Eze Nwaanyi, their future queen, nor did they really register who she was. They were all so excited to tell someone about their research, their voices rolling over each other as they fought to get in their details. The students were a variety of ages, all of them young and different shades of brown. They wore the style and dress of professionals, so it was a mix of foreign fashion from overseas and stylish versions of their traditional tunics. Essien laughed at their clumsy attempts to tell her about the research all at once, and they finally allowed one voice to speak at a time.

They had finished explaining the new metal alloy they had to create to build the vessel that could withstand extreme heat and long-distance travel. Now they were explaining the new designs they had manufactured by hand to ensure swift space travel, moving faster than the speed of light. Essien's mind was spinning even more than it had when she was a student trying to understand her own science lectures. Essien asked, "But how did you conduct your research here? Is the University not reserved for religious studies?"

The students' smiles grew bigger as they all exchanged glances. "Astronomy is one of the oldest disciplines of study here. Mapping and studying the stars and planets *is* considered a religious study."

Essien burst out laughing, and a second later, so did everyone else. "I bet the religious leaders who helped establish this university did not think of that exception."

One of the students, a tall male with his hair in long, thin locks, said, "Oh no, the imams had no idea we'd be learning how to send people into deep space. They thought we'd just be training up the next generation of religious leaders. Little did they know what the future would bring."

Essien questioned them more about their project, asking how she might help support them and their program in the future.

One of her tour guides was able to chime in and answer, "Having other science-based programs across the country would help expand our research, producing new innovations, ones we can't even imagine. Think of what a University in KhoiSan or Dogon might produce for the future of scientific advancements."

Essien nodded. "I would like to see this program expand. I would like to see what Alkebulanian genius can produce when it's allowed to freely express itself."

The mood in the room stayed excited even as the guards signaled to Essien that it was time to go. As the engines carried her away from the University, Essien had already grabbed one of the papyrus pads that were always around her now and began scribbling down notes of ideas she had. Essien finished her final thought and glanced up. Her face fell when she noted the engine had pulled back up to the barracks.

"What about the Center?" she asked the guards who were always seated in the front, two of them. There were more guards in the engines in front of and behind her.

"We don't have time. We stayed too long at the University. Your flight to the next state is in a few hours."

Essien started to pout and then remembered herself. "Take me into the city. I said earlier that I wanted to see the river. Never mind about the

Center; I can come back to see it. But what about Amina? She'll be waiting for me." The thought of finally making a friend and having someone to talk to was ripped away from her, and she vowed that she would come back to the state as soon as she could.

"The other meetings on your agenda were notified of your schedule running off. They won't be expecting you." The gruffness and finality in the guards' voices reminded her of Gabriel. They must have learned it from him.

"Either way, I want to see the city. At least for an hour. Look, it's just over there."

The guards exchanged a series of nonverbal messages, and then the engine switched back on and began to maneuver toward the body of water she had spotted off on the horizon.

IT TURNED OUT TO BE A RIVER, A LIFE-SUSTAINING BODY OF WATER snaking through the city and its surrounding villages with bridges across and footpaths or roads running alongside it. It turned out that the city of Timbuktu was located just off the Joliba River—the river's great rushing waters having many different names depending on the region of the nation one was in.

To truly know the heart and beat of a place, Essien liked to go back to its beginnings. The early start of a place always began near its waters' edges and spread from there. It was also the only time she'd get to be around people who weren't guards or Council Members or elders who would make demands of her.

She watched the river from the height of a bridge as water vessels carrying local passengers and tourists alike floated past underneath. Birds dipped here and there, their beaks darting into the water, their wings flapping them away with a catch. There were shouts and honks from horns, screeches and squeals as engines of all sizes sped through the driving lanes. An oasis of green amid the concrete jungle was a botanical garden with sweet floral scents floating on the breeze. An open-air plaza with the smell of spicy incense wafting out was a temple of one of the popular religions, the bowed and kneeling figures of worshippers visible from within its halls. A group of adolescent girls in thin braided hairstyles giggling together outside of a clothing store with a provocative outfit on display in the front window. The sounds and sights and smells of the city lulled Essien into a sense of anonymity that was both thrilling and relaxing. She was just another Alkebulanian out for a stroll. Never mind the circle of black surrounding her at all times. She hurried her pace along when people began to notice her, stopping to stare.

The vendors along the main roads greeted her with smells that made her mouth water. She hadn't eaten yet, once again, so her stomach gave a twinge of emptiness. Standing next to a mobile vendor stall, she watched as the man wearing yellow robes and a straw hat pinched off a ball of dough, packed it with a spoonful of orange and yellow filling from a bowl, twisted it closed, smashing it into a crescent shape in his palms, before dropping it into the hot oil. The pastry bubbled and roiled in the oil before floating to the surface, crispy and golden.

Essien watched the vendor make several pastries like this. He then bagged three of the fresh, hot pastries into a paper bag and handed them to her with a smile. Essien jumped to take the offering, holding the bag with both hands. Oil stains were already spreading up from the bottom. Essien turned to look at the guard nearest her.

"Would you oblige my purchase with whatever coins or Naira you might have? I know the President will ensure you are reimbursed." She pulled a pastry into the top of the bag and used the sides of the paper to hold it without getting her fingers greasy. The guard made a face, but he reached into the pocket of his overcoat and produced a bill of Naira to pay the vendor.

The first bite of the pastry was piping hot, but the sweet and tropical filling was quickly swallowed down. The next bite was even sweeter, the heat no longer as painful on her already scarred tongue. She finished the first pastry in two more bites. The second, she savored, walking away from the vendor, but only at a stroll, in case she wanted to go back for more. The second pastry was soon gone, but she was full. Her tongue was also coated with the remnants of the filling. She handed the paper bag with the last pastry to the guard who had paid for her. With a small smile that lifted only one corner of his lips, he accepted the bag with a nod of his head. Essien watched him pull the last pastry out and devour it with one bite.

She laughed out loud, not being able to stop herself. The guard licked his fingers and looked at her with one eyebrow cocked.

"We're still nearby if you want more," she said pointing at the vendor who noticed and waved at them.

The walk up the streets was slow and casual. Essien stopped at each vendor that drew her stomach, pointing at some treat she wanted to try. As she did not have access to any money and only one way to obtain her own, she knew full well that without the guard's support she wouldn't have been able to buy herself anything. The guard who had lent her money at first seemed to have deep pockets. He didn't begrudge her the ones and tens and twenties that he slipped out of his pocket and into the hands of vendors waiting to be paid for foods that she had already begun munching.

Essie had long ago spent the Naira she had earned from chopping off her hair, and any funds she had in the accounts paid to her as a soja and a guard could only be accessed by entering one of the local offices. There were offices everywhere, likely even here in Fulani State. But the methods Essien had to undertake just to stroll along the riverbank in public before being herded back into the engine and back to her endless string of meetings was enough to make her not even broach the subject of gaining access to her own financial accounts. Still, the option kept nudging her to take it.

On the guard's Naira, Essien ate her fill of the local cuisine, including fried shrimp on sticks, spiced fish in foil, and fura da nunu, a spicy-sweet fermented milk and millet drink over slushed ice that was cool and refreshing. She walked for some time afterward, soaking up the sights, until the guard indicated it was time to go. As in, moving on to the next state. Having experienced the feels and sights of the city and taken in the delicious foods, she didn't complain as several guards hurried her to the engine, which subsequently took her back to the military compound to gather her canvas bag and retrieve the portfolio and papyrus pads already filled. She was then ushered back into the engine and on to the transportation center where she had arrived just a few days prior. *Had it only been two days? Or had it been three?* It had felt like weeks ago that she'd first landed in Fulani. She knew that she would make a way to return and visit the Center. She hoped Amina might join her on that visit, too. The Guard carried her canvas bag and her stacks of papyruses onto the skycraft. With a sigh, Essien followed them onboard without looking back. Seated in a row by herself, Essien flipped open the portfolio holding the thick legislation bill to continue reading from where she had left off.

CHAPTER TWENTY-EIGHT

◆

LOOKING OUT THE WINDOWS OF THE SKYCRAFT, ESSIEN thought her eyes were deceiving her. From over the tops of the heads of the crowd, there were tall men hopping up and down, the height they were able to achieve taking them up higher than the head of the tallest person standing there. Essien's mouth gaped as she descended from the skycraft and was led over to the group of jumpers.

The other people in the crowd were chanting and clapping and stomping their feet in time to the jumps. Each of the men was wearing red robes that stopped above their knees and simple brown woven sandals. They each carried a thin wooden staff. The jumpers shouted something as they jumped, seeming to compete against each other for the highest jump. Essien watched in awe as one man became the clear winner. His jumps were the ones that took him far over the heads of the tallest of them standing there.

Around her, Essien lost sight of the smiling faces as they chanted. All she could see was the impossibly tall man walking toward her with a grin on his face that was all for her. He towered over her, but he wasn't the tallest man among them. Like the rest of the men who crowded around them, he had mahogany brown skin and a low-shaved head, wearing the traditional shuka cloth, with its red background and thin red and white lines criss-crossing it, wrapped around his middle and draped over his shoulder.

"I am Koinet Nyaga. I have won the battle to be your escort while you are here." He wasn't even breathless or sweaty. His face and every limb was long and thin, his features and fingers graceful and elegant. He wore light blue and white beads on several necklaces around his neck. He held his hand out from between the folds of his shawl, and they touched palms.

When Essien went to pull her hand away, Koinet curled his long fingers around her wrist, flipping her palm over to face down, as he pressed his forehead to the back of her hand. His skin was warm and seemed to cling to her hand as he rested against her for several seconds before pulling away. Essien pursed her lips to stifle her smile, and she took her hand back as soon as he loosened his grip. Others had done this greeting with her before, but something about his fingers wrapping around her wrist made it feel different.

"Pleasure to meet you, Koinet. Where did you learn to jump like that?"

The man smiled, ducking his head like he was suddenly shy. "We are born with this athletic ability. Even our toddlers. And you should see our women run. Their long-distance running times set world records." The people around him chuckled and began to chime in about the legendary physical prowess of the Maasai.

Not to be distracted, Essien said, "I assume you have tons of meetings planned for me to attend?"

Koinet nodded, his smile gone. "I've never seen a tour schedule so packed. And it doesn't include any of our more enjoyable attractions, the ones actual tourists come to see. They didn't even include the reserve on your agenda. But how can anyone, let alone someone vying for a throne, not be shown a tour of the reserves?"

Essien sidled closer to him, already liking his passion. "Do you think you might help me wiggle it in?" She batted her eyelashes, too. The look on Koinet's face told her that whatever charms she had worked on the man, even if she didn't seem willing to use them at all on Gabriel.

"Absolutely. I'll consider it my one true purpose while you are here. If I have to carry you on my back, you will see the reserves."

Essien returned his smile, ignoring the ripple among the guards around her. "Then I will hold you to it, Koinet."

"Please, my friends call me Koi." Then Essien was noticing how white his teeth were, and how pink his lips were, how soft they looked. She turned her head away from the feeling, one that felt all too familiar. She'd always noticed Gabriel's teeth first, then his lips, even when he wasn't smiling.

"Koi, then. Lead the way."

He nodded, adjusting his shawl around his shoulders and holding out his hand. His fingers were so long and fine. Essien glanced at the guards, who knew more about her than she often liked. They were watching her. She stared back down at that hand. Koi waggled his fingers, his smile growing bigger. His confidence seemed to boil off him. He had won the competition, he was the highest jumper, and as far as he was concerned, that had earned him rights and privileges. One of them was reaching out to hold her hand, such an innocent gesture.

With a smile of her own, Essien reached out to take that hand. Even though it looked fine and elegant, his fingers were rough and calloused, his grip strong. Koi pulled her closer to his side as he led her through the crowd. Around them, the gathered people began to chant, a song in Swahili and then in Maa and then finally in Igbo. Essien was surprised when Koi climbed into the engine after her. No one had ever ridden with her in the back before. She had to move her own luggage and belongings out of the way to make room. The guard who slammed the door after him gave her a look that made her suddenly feel like she was about to betray Gabriel.

A frown dented her forehead. There was nothing she owed Gabriel. He had no claim to her, regardless of and contrary to what he might think. And besides, it was just an engine ride over the valley to the Council House, most likely.

Koi looked around the engine as the wheels began to roll them away.

"So this is what it looks like from inside one of the President's rides. Feels rich."

Essien chuckled. "Do you not own vehicles here?"

"Yes, of course, the rich people. I was not born rich."

"How did you come to be working with the Council?"

Koi's delicate hands smoothed over the seat between them. "My father is a businessman. He owns several eateries and a chain of pop-up street vendors around Loikop and some of the surrounding areas. He started out as a chef, if you can believe it. He studied in Celte for a few years after he finished his Levels, and then he returned to Maasai with what he had learned and started his first eatery. He was the first to manufacture and sell the Maasai blood sausage. Then he started franchising his name for others to use, and that's how he started the chain. The Tribal Council offered him a seat to represent Maasai State, and he implored them to give it to me. That was almost ten years ago now."

"Is your father still a businessman?"

Koi chuckled to himself. "He still travels to his office in Nairobi every day, complaining about the traffic all the way."

Essien fell silent, thinking about her own father. She wondered if he had seen reports about her on the news reels. She cringed a bit inside to imagine what they might say about her. Maybe not now, but a few months ago, surely the reports were scandalous. A member of the Guard turned rebel sympathizer? It wasn't a tale anyone in Alkebulan was used to hearing. Oh, the rebels weren't new. But people who supported the rebels usually came from activist families, or simply people who felt they had been wronged by the Council or the State or the President, even. There were few who were as heavily entrenched in the military as she was who had turned on the power structure and became traitors. She didn't think she was a traitor, but she knew there were people who would believe that based on the surface-level facts of what they heard. But if they knew the prophecy, the one that kept dogging her even when she tried to ignore and get away from it... They'd probably be a lot more sympathetic toward her behaviors over the last year.

Koi was asking her a question, and she hadn't heard a word of it. He repeated, "Is your father a military man?"

The scoff Essien gave hurt a bit. "No, far from it. My father owned land and produced a harvest to feed the people in our region."

"Oh, your father was a farmer? What an honorable profession. My nne always said that farmers and teachers are the most important jobs; they both plant seeds for the future."

Essien nodded and turned her attention outside the engine where the ride was slowing down to a crawl as the texture underneath the wheels turned softer, like looser rocks or chunky sand.

Most of Maasai had stretched past without her notice. Now she saw that the landscape was red rocks and orange-brown dirt stretching out beyond the dark stone buildings to plains with sparse green patches and spindly-topped trees. There were more blue-green mountains far off in the distance to the west. Beside her, Koi chattered on, not noticing that she was no longer paying attention as she tried to take in the new environment.

The building in front of her was made of speckled red bricks, three floors with curved walls surrounding all the sides and black iron gates barring the paved driveway. There were other buildings, one of similar size peeking behind the left side of the building, and another smaller building off to the right on the other side of the driveway. Essien could hear the sounds of pots clanging and see steam wafting out of the open doorway.

As she had come to expect, there was a group of people gathered at the entrance. More joined them from the engines that had traveled with her from the transportation center. Essien stepped out of the engine, staring up at the hulking building.

Koi helped her with more introductions, using his hand on a shoulder or an excited leap to introduce her to people he particularly liked. Essien thought his father would be among them, but they were all Tribal Council members and other local representatives. There were even a few visiting diplomats who were being provided lodging in the Council house lodgings.

Essien was led into the building and right away, she noticed how run-down and in need of repairs the compound was. The floors were cracked and splitting, some spots weak and buckling as their group passed over them. The cracks continued up the walls, some of the slashes in the paint traveling all the way up to the ceiling. There were light bulbs out in the string of lights hidden along the ceiling edges. The door frames they passed were chipped and dented. Essien began to feel bad, thinking about that golden floor in Gabriel's compound, the unused instruments in her library.

They led her into the largest Council room, and Essien's jaw dropped. How had this State not received any of the overflow of wealth? The floor was bare wood, the same cracking and blistering slabs as the rest of the floors. The chairs were mangled, glossy wood, the kind that could be folded and stacked. There was no padding, and Essien imagined they weren't that comfortable to sit on for how long she knew sessions could last.

Koi's confidence and pride hadn't decreased at all. She wondered what he saw when he looked around. All she could see was lack and what they didn't have. At minimum, they deserved a better Council House, one that matched the splendor of the one in Igbo State. She hoped the rest of the Council Houses across Alkebulan weren't in such disrepair. This was something else she needed Gabriel to know.

As the smiling faces ushered her through the remaining rooms on the upper floors, Essien tapped on the mental door that kept her connected to the President no matter where she ventured.

"Yes," just his voice, in her head. Where normally she could see him standing before her, all she could see now was the same blackness she saw when she closed her eyes. *"It's me, Essien. What do you need?"* Somehow, he had limited his output to only the sound of his voice, no sight.

"You must be somewhere you don't want me to see." Essien's attention narrowed as she wasn't seeing anything in front of her. *"Are you in Iroquois? Is that why you're hiding where you are?"* She was just far enough in his head to know instantly that she was correct. He was silent, just the wispy sound of his breathing deepening as he took in air.

"If you feel guilty about leaving me behind, then you can stop treating me this way. Anytime you'd like, I could be at your side."

"I thought you didn't want to be at my side? I thought being as far away from me as possible was what you wanted."

The tour of the Council House was circling back to the main chambers. Essien remembered why she had contacted him.

"Have you seen the Council House in Maasai?"

Silence. She waited, and when he didn't reply, she went on, *"It's the worst one I've ever seen. It's in serious need of renovation. You can't have been here recently, there's no way. If anyone on the Military Council had known the building was in this state, surely they would have reported it and requested the funds, right?"*

Essien wished she could see Gabriel's face as he finally responded. *"Tell me what is needed, and I will have it done."*

She thought she would feel more optimistic at getting him to agree so quickly. So why did she feel disappointed and the bitterness of what felt like defeat?

"If it was that easy, why didn't you have it done sooner? This building looks like it has been neglected for decades."

"I have only been President for eight years now, not even ten yet. I admit I have not been to every Council House. That is an error on my part, and I am glad you are there to finally remedy the failure for me. As Queen, I would expect nothing less from you. Taking up the slack, picking up the ball when I drop it." She heard a smile in his voice and knew he was about to say something he thought was funny. *"Did you finish reading the legislation yet?"*

"Not yet. I'm almost halfway through. It's really wordy. Did you write it yourself?"

"Oh no, I had the help of my advisors. The final version has dozens of different fingerprints on it. I'll await your thoughts once you're done reading it. Do you think it'll be before all the States ratify it?"

"I hope so."

"Has there been any resistance? I know you were worried about that."

Essien was surprised that Gabriel kept the conversation going so long. He usually heard her requests and had cleared the mental link before she could say all that she wanted to voice. If she weren't foolish, she would have thought he missed her.

"I've experienced no resistance at all. I think I'll get lucky and be done with this campaign by the end of the month."

Gabriel laughed, a deep chuckle that seemed to rumble from his chest. She wished again that she could see his face and enjoy the sight of him laughing like that. The blackness in her mind was the same emptiness.

"Gabriel," she said.

"Yes?"

She shook her head. *"Never mind. When do you think the renovations can commence?"*

"*As soon as I can have materials and supplies ordered and shipped. Perhaps by tomorrow at the latest. I'll make a few calls and start the cheetah running.*"

"*Thank you,*" she said. She waited for him to say something back and then realized he had already disconnected.

Essien tuned back into the present and saw Koi's concerned face staring down at her.

"Are you okay?" his smooth forehead was indented by worry lines. It made him look several decades older.

"Yes, sorry. The busy schedule has just made me so tired. What were you saying?"

"The Council meeting is scheduled for tomorrow. We have a meal prepared for you. Then your guards will transport you to your barracks from here and give you time to yourself this evening. There are some beauty contests and sports competitions scheduled for the night's entertainment, if you feel up to it." By the look on his face, Essien knew Koi hoped she would attend.

Essien smiled. "What's for the evening meal?"

Koi grinned even wider. "Traditional Maasai cuisine."

He showed her through to the dining hall. The long room at the back of the compound had several clusters of low, round tables spread throughout the space with cushions for seats around each one. Koi sat down at one of the tables and indicated the spot next to him. Essien sat down to his right. The Guard stayed standing on all sides of her table, so that they loomed up over her from behind.

"Couldn't you stand over there?" she asked, looking up at the three behind her and pointing to the wall next to them with a smile. The Guard didn't reply, but they did reshuffle their positions, so that two of them stood near the wall looking out over the room and only one of them stood directly behind her and a few steps away.

Koi showed her how to use the steaming towels in the steel bowls next to each place setting to clean her hands and arms. Then, the first portion was brought out, a brass bowl of some congealed red liquid that was shiny and lapped up the sides of the vessel. As soon as the drink was set down before him, Koi had already brought it to his lips and was taking great gulps, not even pausing to breathe. Essien lifted the brass, feeling the warmth of the soup through the metal. Essien put her lips to the edge and took the tiniest sip. The liquid was as thick as it looked, thicker than the fura da nunu she'd had in Fulani State. It was hot like soup, and the flavor was both faintly sweet with a slightly salty aftertaste at the same time. She took another bigger sip, trying to identify the meat or vegetable that was in the soup. There weren't any other textures in the soup, just the thick red liquid with its strange, almost metallic taste. Essien smacked her lips after taking a mouthful, not quite sure if she liked it or not.

Koi was done with his soup and had set the empty dish back onto the table beside her. He smiled at her, his teeth stained red and glossy.

"What is this?" Essien asked. "I don't think I've ever had anything quite like it."

Koi's smile grew bigger. His tongue was stained red, too. "Boiled blood and yoghurt drink."

Essien gagged; she couldn't help it. She slapped a hand over her mouth to hold back the liquid that gushed back up into her mouth. She forced herself to swallow it down, looking around the room. A guard saw her desperate glance and set a glass of water down next to her. She downed the clear liquid, swishing the water around in her mouth as she did. She glared at Koi.

"I thought something like that would be mentioned ahead of time. *Blood?*"

Koi's smile took over his cheeks, pushing them up into his eyes. "We drink it for special occasions. Is it not a special occasion?"

She just shook her head and held up the glass over her shoulder to signal for more water. The guard took it and refilled it two more times before the next course was brought out. Platters of beef, some of them raw and drizzled with honey, herbs, and spices, others sizzling with a fresh grilled searing of the same spices and honey on top of the meat. The smell of the cooked beef mingled with the smell of the raw beef and the taste of the blood in her mouth, and she knew she wouldn't be able to eat anything else.

"Raw meat to go with the blood?" Essien knew she was being rude by the stares that others at the table threw her way. She had been raised to accept and eat whatever was placed before her. It was just that warm, bloody soup and raw meat had never been placed before her. She kept drinking her water as Koi served himself from both the raw and cooked beef platters. Essien noticed that the raw beef went first, and after everyone had been served except her, there was only the cooked beef left.

"Have some," Koi tried to put a few of the smaller slices onto her plate. Essien waved her hand at him. He shrugged and piled more onto his own plate.

"Please tell me there's no dessert course."

"There's no dessert course, but there is a final stew course. And, you'd be happy to know that my father trains the cooks here at the Council House. These are dishes and recipes straight from his kitchen, which were passed down to him from my nne and nne nnes. I grew up eating this way, and look how I have turned out." Koi raised his arms up alongside his head, using the move to flex the lean muscles that bulged slightly from his arms. Essien rolled her eyes and then gave him a mischievous grin to go with it.

For some reason, that still didn't make her want to eat anything else. The final stew was brought out in a larger brass bowl, and from the deep red color, Essien knew it also contained blood before Koi turned to her with his face grimacing like hers had.

"Okay, the stew has a blood base, but it's delicious, and you can't even taste it." Essien shook her head and tried to wave her hand in refusal, but an attendant still set one of the bowls in front of her. This red soup was chunky with brown, light red, orange, light yellow, and even green chunks floating around in it. Essien knew it would be polite to take at least one bite, so she picked up the spoon and stirred around the contents of the bowl. She brought a spoonful to her mouth and schooled her features not to make a face no matter what it tasted like. She chewed and chewed, and realized that he was right—it was delicious. She took another tentative bite, getting more of the chunks that she knew were stewed beef.

"See? Blood is good, right?" Koi poked her with his sharp, thin elbow. Essien set the spoon down with a clank. Her stomach roiled up, and she frowned at him.

Doing something Essien had never thought she'd do, she turned to the guards just behind her, seeking refuge.

"I'm ready to go wherever my next stop is."

Overhearing her, Koi leaned over. "Will we see you tonight? The dancers and competitors will be crushed if you do not attend."

Essien looked back up at the guards, "Is the entertainment on my schedule?" The two she could see in front of her nodded, adjusting their rapid fires in their arms as though the news made them uncomfortable, or they disagreed with it.

Essien gave Koi a smile. "Then you may yet see me after all." She patted him on the shoulder, feeling the strong muscles through the layers of his shawl and robes. The smile he gave her seemed to make the darkness pressing down outside recede a little.

The silence of the engine ride was a relief to Essien this time.

The barracks where the sojas and commanders stayed when not on patrol or active missions were just as dilapidated as the Council House. Staring around in near disgust, Essien didn't know how to ask what had happened. There had to be some reason that nothing had been maintained, even though she could tell that there was a great deal of care. The sojas she met gathered around her, seeming proud and eager to serve. It was like they didn't realize what they were missing out on or even knew how neglected they were. They likely hadn't seen what the other Council Houses looked like.

The sojas at the compound touched palms with her, one after the other, fighting over who got to greet her first. The guards were on high alert, and she didn't know why they were being so stern. The sojas were smiling and giddy. From their snatches of conversations that she could just barely understand, she knew there was a patrol on their way back to the compound, but they hadn't returned yet. Essien could overhear the sojas laughing and chatting about how the returning sojas would not believe who had graced their presence this evening.

The guards stepped in, literally putting their bodies into position around her, and she was escorted up to one of the upper levels and her accommodations—a set of private barracks usually reserved for highly ranked commanders. The other sojas she passed along the way gawked openly, catching sight of her quick and almost secretive march down the halls and into her designated quarters. It was almost like now that her time was up on the daily schedule, the guards wanted to ensure that no one else saw her or spoke to her at all. Essien tried to drag her feet and slow them down, to be sure that the sojas could get a look at her. From the wide eyes and the halting in mid-word, Essien knew that many of them recognized her from just the few seconds they were given an opportunity to view.

The door they finally stopped in front of was peeling and seemed swollen at the bottom, like the floor had flooded, and the wood had gotten wet. Maybe that's what had happened to the Council House, too. A flood had swept in and ruined the flooring and the walls. Maybe it happened every year, so they didn't bother to repair it after a while.

The guards let Essien know that she was to stay in the room until they let her out, then they closed the door and took up their positions in the hallway. Inside the room, Essien changed out of the silk dress into another of the cotton shifts meant for sleeping. She then sat on the bed and flipped the heavy portfolio open into her lap. She was almost done reading the legislation. She had read through all the responsibilities of the Queen, she'd gone over the rights, she'd even read through the supporting roles and agencies she would need to establish. The end of the legislation listed out how the position of Queen intersected with the position of President. Essien flipped ahead to those pages.

She read for hours, having to stop and take notes to be sure she understood what she was reading. She put a finger on one page and flipped back to an earlier page to check something else she recalled. Eventually, she reached the end of the pages and lifted her head to stare blankly at the wall across the room from her bed. Her mind was reeling.

At the culmination of the legislation, Gabriel had made sure to include a section that provisioned the President's role as separate from the Queen's. There was no mention of a King anywhere in those final lines. Instead, Gabriel had delineated that while the Queen would have assumed and implied power and control over the domestic and national affairs of the country, the President's domain would expand to include responsibility over the international affairs of the country. Its relationships with other countries, for travel and trade, comradery and commercial enterprises, were now solidly under the President's control. It referred once to a separate piece of legislation, called the Kingdom's International Nobility Governance Act.

Essien shut the portfolio and let it slip from her hands to thud onto the ground. The pieces in her mind were gathering into an image; if she stared hard enough, long enough, cocking her head this way and that, she might finally start to see what the picture painted.

So that was his plan, she thought as realization hit, clear and crisp as a winter morning. That's how he was going to use her ascending to the throne to eventually prop himself up. She was suddenly fuming, the anger turning to nausea when she realized she could do nothing about it. Once she got the QUEEN Act passed, the KING Act was almost guaranteed. In fact, Gabriel might ask her to present the legislation to the Councils herself. How long had this been his goal, she wondered. For how many years had he been scheming his plans and devising his paths to lead here. She couldn't say that he hadn't been honest with her. He'd told her exactly what he planned to do, many times, even when she'd been a guard. It was her own fault for not believing him and listening to his words.

There was a series of three soft knocks on the door, and Essien startled. She hadn't expected visitors tonight. She hadn't planned on attending the evening's festivities with Koi, but she'd wanted to be discreet by not telling him. She looked down at the dress she'd thrown on top of the canvas bag after removing it earlier. She debated slipping back into it before answering the knock and eventually decided on getting dressed.

"One moment," she called. If the guards were on the door, they would have handled anyone who didn't have a right to be there.

Of course, just like she predicted, Koi stood at her door with a lopsided, childish grin on his face.

"Hello, my Eze Nwaanyi," he greeted her. She couldn't help smiling back, suddenly feeling bashful. The title sounded so right and appropriate, coming from him. The way his voice dipped down into an intimate husk. Like it had been his idea to crown her in the first place.

"I came to escort you to the pageantry." He held his hand out to her, the perfect gentleman. Essien didn't hesitate, taking his hand and letting him lead her out of the lonely room. Finishing the legislation could wait. Essien deserved a bit of merriment, however false or superficial it might be. The guards took up their positions around her.

"Pageantry? Like beauty pageants?"

Koi smiled a tight-lipped grin and nodded his head enthusiastically. "That's exactly what they are. Have you ever seen a Maasai beauty pageant?"

They both loaded onto the engine that was pulled around to the front of the compound. The gates were opened to let them through, and Essien noticed at least two more engines following behind them.

"Does the jumping contest from earlier count?"

"Right again. Are you sure this is your first time in Maasai?" His smile let her know that he wasn't serious.

"I paid attention in lessons during Levels," she said. "I made sure I learned everything in geography class, history class, and anthropology class."

"The education system in Igbo State must be better than the one in Maasai."

"Are the subjects taught in school not standardized across states?"

Koi shook his head, "I'm no expert on the education system, you'd have to speak to different Council Members than me, but I've learned enough since filling this role to know that it differs from state to state."

"How so?"

"Funding, to start. Some States have more funding from the national coffers. Maasai gets next to none."

"Why?"

Koi shrugged, "Long-standing misheld beliefs that the Maasai do not value education the way other cultures do. They say we are nomads who build temporary, always moving villages, who train our children to live simple lives, but did you know, my ancestors have been dwelling in the same valley for hundreds of years? Did you know all of our children, boys and girls, are trained in cultivating and pastoralism? Did you know one of my elder fathers helped transform the traditional Maasai architecture into its modern adaptation that uses baked bricks instead of dung plasters and wood molds? The houses you saw coming into Maasai from the transportation center were designed by my elder father, based on a simple idea: What if we built our compounds the same but differently? Too bad, the process is now too expensive for the average Alkebulanian to afford. So, even though we move with the weather and the seasons, with our hunting patterns, and we do train our children to live in harmony with the land, we always come back to our ancestral grounds. And we never go far."

Essien forgot all about Koi as her mind rotated; something he had said triggered other thoughts she had been having since Fulani. She could not bear the thought of some children not receiving the education they deserved, simply because they were born in a different state, or in a poor, subsisting family instead of a rich, elite one. Essien thought the Councils, the President, and her, the Queen, should do all in their power to provide a basic foundation for every Alkebulanian, regardless of family ancestry or wealth. That baseline should include a standard education, and not just for children, but one for adults, too. Her plans to open up the disciplines offered by Universities and to create new schools and colleges were suddenly thrown wide open. Adding schooling for every Alkebulanian would further revolutionize this nation. Essien vibrated with that familiar feeling of excitement that arose every time she began to plan for the future with purpose. With her leading, if Gabriel didn't get in her way, the people of Maasai wouldn't be neglected any longer.

She tuned back in as Koi said, "But I'd like to hear more about your life in Igbo State. What were your schools like there?"

"I got an exemplary education in Igbo State, and they definitely taught us more than where each state is on the map, you know."

"They clearly didn't tell you anything about our cuisine."

Essien tilted her head, a whimsical sparkle in her eyes. "No, I can't say that they did. I think the food in Maasai is something that should be advertised on every newsreel."

His laugh was so jolly, and she grew transfixed with the way he threw back his head back and laughed so freely. She could clearly see the knot in his throat bobbing up and down. His eyes grew shiny and wet as he finished being amused and looked back at her.

"Hey, blood has so many nutrients. Perhaps it's why we can jump so high. Maybe those researchers at Timbuktu can research us next. Everyone in Alkebulan will be on a diet of blood and raw meat before the turn of the year."

Essien shook her head, grimacing as she did. "I'll make it my life's mission as Queen to keep that from ever happening!"

As the engine reached its destination, Essien turned her attention to where they had arrived. To the left, there was an open-air plaza strung up with colorful lights in the trees scattered throughout the patio. Underneath the merry lights, there were tall tables, and lots of tall people standing around them. There was a live band up on a stage at the back of the plaza, their instruments already emitting a lively tune that made Essien want to move her feet to the beat. Beside the stage there was a cleared-out dance floor area with space in the middle bordered off by colorful ropes. Around the ropes were padded wooden stools for sitting. People were standing near the ropes in small clusters. On the far-right side of the plaza was a vendor behind a wooden bar top selling colorful drinks she could see swirling in large glass vats. Behind the vendor, other workers hustled in and out of the unseen kitchen bringing out sizzling platters and steaming bowls.

"Good, we arrived before the pageant. I'm sure you'll be given a prime viewing spot!" Koi's eagerness was infectious, moving Essien to quickly exit the engine. A warm wind hit her from all sides, and she let her arms and shoulders relax into the feeling of being held by the air. The guards stepped up around her, and they all followed Koi onto the plaza.

When one group of people about Koi's age saw him, they threw up their arms, started clapping, and shouted out gleefully, "Koi-Koi has arrived! And he brought his new lover!"

Essien immediately became embarrassed, heat speeding up her cheeks, over her forehead, and searing down the back of her skull. She stopped abruptly in the circle of guards and contemplated turning back around, getting back into the engine, and leaving the party.

But Koi said, "This is the future Queen of Alkebulan, show some respect you ilmeeks and ildorobos!" It was the first time she'd seen Koi feeling anything beyond happiness and joy. He was angry, his nostrils flared, and his fists were gripped into hard stones. She kept walking toward him, wanting to thank him for defending her, and not knowing if she even needed to.

Essien's eyes went back to the table of people. They were an equal mix of men and women, but all the men wore red robes and shawls, while all the women were in more color than that. All the men's hair was low cut and somewhat shaggy, but Essien noted the differences in their features. The women wore their hair in intricate braided styles she had never seen, some of them with shaved edges, others with long braids weighed down by beads and shells.

As she ran her eyes over them all, they exchanged glances among themselves. One woman kneeled to the ground, holding on to the table to support her. The others followed her, bowing at the waist, the neck, and a few doing the dramatic face-down lying on the ground bow that Essien realized she preferred. Everyone she encountered needed to know that she was Queen. So what that she hadn't yet seen three decades. So what if she had never undergone any maturation rites. The only thing that mattered was she had clawed and fought, and yes, even killed her way, to the top of this country's political structures. She hadn't planned on being here. Nothing in her deepest, darkest dreams had ever prepared her for this. But here she was. And by the Mothers, they would respect her.

They all mumbled their apologies as they rose. Koi turned to her, and he held out his hand. Essien didn't want to take that hand. She stared and stared at it until he dropped it by his side. His smile didn't waver at all.

For a second, she regretted coming entirely. Perhaps putting this event on her schedule so late in the day had been a mistake. She'd already been shuffled around since the early morning. For a second time, she considered returning to the military compound. She looked at the faces of the guards around her. For once, none of them was looking at her. They were watching the people on the plaza, as more and more were crowding around the bordered area. There was the motion of people from an entryway into a building behind the back of the stage, a painted face peeking out.

Koi exclaimed, "Oh, the pageant's about to start. Did you want a drink?"

Essien quirked up an eyebrow. "Will it have blood in it?"

All the tall, tall people at the table burst out into laughter that instantly made the mood lighter and easier to breathe through.

"No blood in the drinks here, I promise." Koi led her over to the vendor and placed an order for her. She watched the vendor dish up a light amber-colored drink into a tall glass. When he handed it to her, the outside was chilled. She sniffed and smelled sweet and perhaps floral notes. She took a tentative sip, just enough to rest against her lips and the very tip of her tongue. Sweetness burst into her mouth from just that tiny sip. She sipped an actual mouthful, swallowing slowly.

She smiled at Koi and the vendor. "No blood!" They both laughed. Essien drank more of the drink, taking huge swallows that finished the glass while Koi watched her.

"Whoa, whoa, whoa, Eze Nwaanyi, slow down! The honey mead is sweet, but it's also very strong! One glass will put you on your ass!"

Essien set the glass down and emitted a burp that she quickly covered with her hand. "What will two glasses do to me?"

Koi gave her a devilish grin. "Let's find out."

The vendor set the refilled glass in front of her with a warning, "Sip it slowly, or you will need to be carried out of here. Koi-koi here doesn't look strong enough to do it." Koi was just good-natured enough to laugh, but Essien knew he was strong. His arms where they peeked through his shawl and robes were corded with muscles that flexed up and down his arms as he moved. And his thighs were probably the same underneath the layers of robes. Essien shook her head minutely, admonishing herself for ruminating at all about his thighs.

People were flowing into the area around the dance floor, the border keeping them from stepping onto the floor likely meant for the performers. At a signal from someone near the front of the stage, Koi said, "Your seat is ready." They and the Guard moved to an area near the back of the dance floor space. A chest-high table with three chairs was set up, and Essien climbed up onto the one nearest the dance floor. From there, she could see the dance floor clearly. To her left was another cluster of tables with three chairs at each. As she watched, other women wearing beautiful, billowing robes in blues, greens, blacks, and white fabrics sat down. She could also see into the entranceway of the building behind the stage. There was a curtain that was flicked out of the way to reveal a line of what Essien at first thought was painted ladies.

Before she could ask Koi what exactly the pageant would entail, the band started up again with a fast, thumping bass and all eyes went to the entranceway. A line of tall, exuberant men came out, only at first, Essien had thought they were women. Each of them had their face painted with makeup in bright orange, white, and other colors that magnified and distorted each of their facial expressions. The men's faces changed rapidly; the emotions they were feeling likely not matching the faces they showed. Exaggerated happiness, overdone suaveness, hyper excitement. Mixed in with the face pulling were jumps, leaps, and footwork formations that showed off their athleticism and their dancing skills. To the left, the women at the tables murmured among themselves and moved their own bodies to the beat of music from the band.

An announcer began to speak, and the men lined up at the back of the dance floor. She couldn't see where the announcer was speaking from, and she knew they were speaking Maa, another language she had only a rudimentary understanding of. She sipped her drink slowly, being careful not to let the growing mental fog and swirling lights become any more unsteady than that. The announcer began to call each man forward to perform their own section of face stretching and physical dexterity. The women at the tables made noises that sounded like approval and appreciation, some of them raising their hands or standing up and walking up to the barrier or ropes when a particular man was called forward.

Koi leaned over to her, one hand covering his mouth as he whispered, "This communal ritual was actually adopted from the Wodaabe, a Fulani tribe that migrated here to Maasai State a few hundred years ago. Some of us here have Wodaabe ancestry, so carrying on this tradition is important to us."

"Are the women picking the men?"

Koi nodded. "The men perform for the women over seven days, and the women decide which of the men they like. Since tonight is the final night, at the end of the night, the women will pick the man of their choice and if they make a connection, their families will begin preparations for their marriage. It is not the only way, but we have been doing it this way in our village for many generations. My mother picked my father because she said he had the best smile."

Essien smiled. Since she had never planned on marrying, it had never occurred to her to find out the specifics of the Igbo marriage rituals. She knew her Nne would lament this fact until the end of her days. But she shouldn't be too sad since her sons had given her wives, and if Nifemi hadn't yet, it was only a matter of time before he did. At the thought of her own family, Essien felt something tight and too large for her skin to contain stretch outward from her chest. What a relief it would be to enter her family home and sit at her parents' feet. She wouldn't unburden herself by telling them anything that had happened to her. She would simply sit and marvel that they were her parents, and that they had loved her, even when she hadn't thought they did. She suddenly didn't want to be around other people any longer. That quickly, the Guard had become more than just her limitation; it had become her way out of anything that made her uncomfortable.

Essien stood, and the entertainment had reached its fever pitch as the paired-off couples began dancing together in rows with the men on one side facing the woman who had picked him on the other side. Essien reached out to touch Koi on his back, getting his attention. The way he turned to her was expectant and hopeful, like he had been turning to her like that for their whole lives, waiting for her to tell him what she needed, so he might deliver it to her promptly. Staring down at him, Essien knew more strongly than she ever had what she was giving up, what she had already sacrificed. She would never have what his upturned face offered, and if she wasn't already feeling low, the weight that settled into her would have ground her into the dust.

"I–I have early meetings tomorrow, as I'm sure you know. I should leave."

Koi's smile immediately turned into a frown. "But you didn't finish your mead." He picked up the glass and lifted it up to her.

"You finish it. I think if I drink any more, the guards will have me in their arms."

"I thought I was going to be carrying you in my arms."

The feeling that tingled through her made her want to lean into whatever those words represented. Whatever this feeling was that made him so appealing when she'd just met him. Essien made to step away, and he quickly stood with her.

"Please allow me to escort you back?"

She knew she should say no. The guards were perfectly capable of getting her safely back to the barracks. In fact, she didn't need him to escort her around anymore at all. Koi was dangerous in ways that Gabriel wasn't, couldn't be. Whatever she felt for Gabriel, she knew it wasn't real, it wasn't her, and she wouldn't have chosen it if she had the choice. The feelings starting to bud in her chest for Koi were real, they were her, and they reflected something true about who she was. She valued sincerity and humility. She appreciated power that knew its limits. Gabriel was none of those things, and he never would be. If Koi was what she wanted, when she permitted herself to want anything, then Gabriel never had a chance at all.

Essien started walking away from the dance floor, back through the plaza. Koi, taking her lack of an answer as an affirmative response, trotted after her. He was still carrying the glass she hadn't finished. As he caught up to her in the circle of guards, he tipped the drink back to guzzle its leftover contents down his long throat.

The engine ride back to the compound was silent; Koi, obviously sensing the change in her mood, kept quiet the entire time. Essien didn't wait for him or the guards as she hopped out of the vehicle the instant it stopped outside the entrance to the military compound. She noticed the line of engines already parked off to the side of the driveway out front. There must be a shift in her Guard happening as soon as she made it safely back to her room. She walked quickly up the stairs, pushing open the front door and leaving it open behind her. She could hear Koi's steps following closely after her. She was practically running by the time she got to the stairs that would take her up to the room she'd been occupying. The guards were trying to edge around Koi as she marched down the hallway, to get between her and him, but he was so eager that he didn't seem to notice.

She got to the door and then waited for him to reach her. He did, almost out of breath. She opened the door to the room and pulled him by one wrist. The guard closest to the door opened his mouth to say something, but she slammed the door before she could hear it.

Koi had finished a spin around the room and had walked backward into the middle of the space. He crooked one of those long, thin fingers at her. She took one step forward, two steps, three, and he loomed in front of her close enough to touch.

She sighed, and as she did, he leaned down from his great height, down to her height, and she lifted her face up to him as he did, so that the kiss he gave her was a kiss she wanted. His lips were rough and scratchy, but when he opened his lips, his tongue was soft and eager. Essien let her hands rest against his chest, narrow but muscled against her palms. She pressed her hands flat against him as he brought his hands up to hold her face. One hand held her jaw, and the other moved to hold her around the back of the neck, pressing her into him. She stretched up onto her tiptoes, giving herself to the feeling of his mouth without a care beyond the darkness of the room and the sound of their breathing.

There was a knock on the door, hard, two knocks and then three. Essien snapped away from Koi's lips, but he didn't let her go. It seemed that the hand on the back of her neck tightened.

"Were you expecting anyone this late?" he whispered into her mouth. She shook her head, but she stepped down to stand flat-footed. They both stared at the door. She didn't make a move to answer it. If it was anyone who didn't belong there, the Guard would have stopped them. What if it was the Guard? Had they knocked because they knew Koi was in here, and they wanted him out? Were there some other orders from Gabriel that prevented her from having friends or even consorts? The anger that always seemed to be there now flared and with it a heat that threatened to come out to play. Essien knew then that she couldn't afford to keep getting angry. The more she did, the less control she'd have over her flames. Koi finally let her go, staring down at her.

"Do you want me to answer for you?"

She turned her back on him and stepped to open the door on her own.

Of all the people it could have been, the one standing there hadn't crossed her mind in the least.

"Good evening, Essien. Too bad I missed the beauty pageant, but I see I'm just in time for the afterparty. May I come in?"

She stood frozen in the doorway, one hand on the doorknob, the other hand pressed against the wall next to the door. She felt Koi step up behind her, and it seemed to give her strength or resolve where before it had all leaked away.

"Koi was just leaving," she said, and even to her, it sounded weak and lame.

She stepped to the side and let Koi step around her.

"Ser President!" he said, his voice going up into that excited, eager tone he must be known for. Koi extended his hand so far forward that Gabriel was forced to take it. The guards were just at the edges of the doorway, seeming to bristle at Koi as they had all evening. Essien could only guess who might have tipped Gabriel off to Koi being in her room.

Koi's eagerness was met with a stoniness that was unusual from Gabriel in public. She stared up at him, smirking, and crossed her arms. Here was one of the people who he served as President. Was he going to ignore that bright, bubbly personality right in front of him to keep glaring at her?

"Pleasure to meet you, young one, but the hour is late. I have important matters to discuss with my..." The pause was noticeable enough for Koi to step further out into the hallway, so he could look at both of them at the same time. "My former guard," Gabriel finished. It was his turn to sound lame and weak. She hadn't been just his guard in a while now.

"Of course, Ser President." He turned to Essien and took her hand. Gabriel's eyes widened, and he switched to glaring at the side of Koi's head.

"Essien, I will return tomorrow morning to escort you to the meetings at the Council House, as planned. I hope you enjoyed getting to see some of our culture here in Maasai. Sleep peacefully. Tomorrow will be an even busier day."

She and Gabriel both watched Koi's tall, graceful figure receding down the hallway and disappearing down the stairs. When Gabriel looked back at her, his upper lip turned up in a slight sneer.

"Kissing him?" he hissed and advanced toward her, entering the room and flinging the door closed behind him. "He is a member of the Council you will one day rule. How reckless and irresponsible of you!"

"Jealous?" she threw over her shoulder as she turned into the room that would never be her home. The portfolio of the legislation lay where she had dropped it, and the canvas bag still had the night clothes on top that she'd thrown off.

"You are here for one purpose, and one purpose only. No part of your mission includes making yourself overly friendly, stooping to the level of the locals, promising what you cannot deliver, or being what some part of you wishes you still were: a village girl with no concerns beyond the ones right in front of you. You're *not* that village girl, you never were, and you will not attach yourself to village boys! When that boy comes back here to escort you tomorrow, you are to maintain the distance that the status of your role demands." He was so angry that his shoulders heaved up and down, and his lips were hardened into a thin line.

Essien flopped down onto the side of the bed. "Did you drive all the way here just to tell me that? I thought I wouldn't see you on any stops."

Gabriel stepped closer to her, moving to stand right in front of her, the tips of his loafers in between the flats on her feet.

"Hear me when I say this, Essien. You are to be Queen. If you've finished reading the legislation, then you know what that means. Who you wish you were no longer exists. If you do anything...*anything*...to bring shame upon your new reputation—"

"I have murdered dozens of men, Gabriel. What reputation do I have to protect? Don't talk about honor to me. I've already been dishonored the minute I used that rapid fire you shoved into my hands."

"The rapid fire you accepted and embraced like the lover you wish that boy could be? If you want romance, Essien, here I am. Come to me." Gabriel stood up, rising to his full height again.

Essien's eyes snapped up to his, and she knew he would see and feel how much she meant her next words. "Never. I will never feel for you what I've felt for *that boy* in just one day. You are not him. And *you* never will be."

A vein in his jaw throbbed; a muscle in his neck stretched; his eye twitched.

She plowed on. "You showing up here? Like this? To say these words? Because you can? What would be the point of loving someone like that? I wouldn't have chosen to if I had a choice."

He leaned down, bending at the waist and putting his hands on his knees to hold him there, as close to her face as he dared get. "You have the choice now. And you will not go any further with Koi. If I suspect or sense that you are debasing yourself with him, or anyone else you meet on this campaign, I will have him stripped of his titles, his land, his family's land, and any inheritance he had hoped to gain. His family will be penniless, and no one will give him heirs."

Essien's voice was a croaking whisper when she said, "You can't do that. He is nothing to me. Why are you so afraid of him? What threat does he pose to you, the President of the country?" She stood up, forcing him to back up, and walked toward him, then tripped on the tome of legislation still on the floor where she'd dropped it earlier. "Or, should I say soon to be the King? What trouble could you possibly foresee in someone like Koi?"

Gabriel didn't answer. He ran his eyes up and down her body, and then rested them on the portfolio on the floor. "You should get some sleep," he finally said. "Busy day tomorrow."

Essien watched his back leaving and felt the loneliness that had momentarily receded seep back in. "Do you want to cut me off from all life, from anything that makes life bearable? Because you're doing a great job of it. First you leave me alone in that mansion for weeks, to punish me for not doing what you want. Then you cut me off from making friends with any of the guards or attendants who work for you. Now, you block me from anyone who wants to befriend me on this damned campaign! What's the point of any of this if I am to be miserable the entire time?" She realized she had been yelling. She quieted, and then said to his still turned back, "No matter how much you use your power to force me to love you, beneath it, I will always hate you, Gabriel."

He stilled, but then his hand was whipping the door open and he stormed out. As he strode down the hall, she heard him tell the guards,

"She is not to have any guests in her rooms." She had to slam the door closed herself. If she were wearing her boots, she would have kicked the portfolio, stomped on it until the pages ripped and tore. If she had any strength of will, any true power of her own to use against him, she would use it to leave. The crown and throne be damned! She threw herself on the bed and stewed in her hopelessness.

Essien slept like the dead, then woke to sharp knocks and brusque shouts of the time and how much of it she had to get ready. When she opened the doors, dressed in another one of the silk dresses that were packed for her, this time a light blue that matched the sky, the guards on duty had rotated back to familiar faces. She smiled, despite herself. She was then immediately herded back through the military compound, where more sojas who had heard the gossip about her arrival had gathered to catch their own glimpse of her passing by. She was quickly deposited back into an engine, the doors slammed, and off she went to her first stop. By the agenda she kept tucked in the back of the portfolio, she knew they were to visit all of the ancestral villages along the way. Essien sighed deeply and loudly, hoping that the morning meal would be provided at some point in the first destinations.

CHAPTER TWENTY-NINE

◆

GABRIEL DECIDED THAT HE LIKED TRAVELING OVERSEAS AND admonished himself for not undertaking it sooner. His plans for Alkebulan had finally diverged to this moment, and it couldn't have come at a more perfect time. In half a day, he had traveled from Iroquois to Alkebulan; in another half a day, he had traveled back again to continue his conference agenda where it had left off in the nation to the west. He knew back home that Essien was poised to step into her queendom, and soon after, he would join her on a throne of his own. He stared around him at the new environment and let the smile creeping across his cheeks freely spread. He wasn't prone to whims or fancies, not when he had an entire nation back home to lead. But being here, in Iroquois, made him feel like he had entered a land of fantasy.

So many names for the nation also called Turtle Island. So many who had wished they could rule its prosperous, plentiful lands. Their Parliament, made up of people indigenous to the land, functioned so efficiently, too efficiently. Their military, trained by Alkebulanian warriors hundreds of years ago, when the Iroquois nation had needed neutral, foreign aid the most, spread across the full continent, from north to south, even its coasts and shores patrolled. Gabriel admired what he had seen so far, the military demonstrations not even showing him the full might of the country's entire defense. It was a wonder what the nation had been able to do in half a millennium with just a bit of support from their allies across the Ethiopian Sea. The treaties and trade agreements between the two countries had withstood the challenges of time since then. As a result of that alliance, the people of Iroquois were safe and sheltered—they had almost no concerns or cares. It was obvious in how their small children played outside alone; the way the doors of their peaked, rounded, or terraced homes remained open to any visitors; the way markets and takeaway eateries were left unattended, and payment was based on the trust system. Gabriel knew Alkebulanians were honorable people, but even they had to deal with criminals like petty market thieves or even the occasional rage murder. But to know that the nation didn't have to deal with rebels from within made Gabriel grit his teeth and wonder where they had gone wrong.

It bothered him immensely, and he realized it was jealousy. Almost like that nasty feeling that had made him want to snatch Koi, the tall, thin young man he'd found in Essien's room, and shove him through a wall. He hadn't, of course, but the desire had been so strong, he'd had to slip his fisted hands into his pockets to prevent it. Now, here he was all the way across the sea, and she was back in Alkebulan. For a second, he wondered if he had made a mistake in not inviting her to travel with him.

Despite the distance, he never had to fear that she would escape him again. He had made that impossible. But, where the people of Iroquois were safe, his people were not. And the threats? He didn't know for sure where they were coming from, though his advisors had gathered their suspicions. Reports, the ones he had started reading diligently again, were not painting a positive or easily solved picture. The rebel groups across the countryside kept shifting, altering their methods, changing their locations, so that the more they seemed to hone in on a target, the further he seemed to be from actually putting a stop to their reign of terror across Alkebulan. He thought he'd captured them all, routed out their underground lair, what he'd hoped was their headquarters, and burnt them all out. Now, reports told him that was not only inaccurate; it had obscured a much bigger problem. Bigger than burning crops or importing foreign high-capacity rapid fires into the civilian population's hands. So far, the reports were just rumors, and they hadn't found any more proof. Just a few cases of illegal weapons years ago. The people he'd left in charge of the rebels' underground hide-out hadn't bothered to do any searching, they'd gathered no evidence, and again, it was his fault. He'd told them to figure it out while he'd been so eager to get his hands on Essien again. Those rebels she'd been among had been homegrown, but there were other groups, splinter groups, of whom there was a growing suspicion were foreign-backed. But which foreign country, Gabriel only had rumors and gossip to go by. He'd need much more than that if he was to actually do something about the problem.

Standing in the sparkling room, the Parliament's Chamber House, with its merry tinkling of string music, he tried to shake himself out of the dark mood. He'd thought these bitter days were beyond him. Essien was by his side again, he was progressing toward his life's goals beautifully, and yet...he still felt uneasy and unfulfilled. Snorting with derision at himself, Gabriel swallowed down the dregs of the sap wine he'd been handed as soon as he'd entered this hall with the rest of the international leaders. It was lighter than palm wine, but tasted just as strong as the amber elixir he especially liked. He could feel that his vision had narrowed down to a sweep over just three people in the room, and the way he obsessively cycled through those three people let him know that the wine's effects were taking hold.

The first person was the current Parliamentary Leader of Iroquois Nation, a woman named Jigonsaseh—not her real name, she'd joked. Her lined face and stark white hair were signs of her age, and her wisdom. The strength in her wizened hands was obvious when she held on to Gabriel's arm and made him look at pictos of all her grandchildren. He had noticed that she was not quite so familiar with the other leaders, not even the ones from the lands south of Iroquois Nation.

The second person he kept finding excuses to observe was Akai Yoshinobu, the daughter of the Shogun of Nihon. He had met her before, on his previous trip to Nihon many months ago. She intrigued him. Not because of the way she looked, so physically unlike Essien or any of the women in Alkebulan. Her skin was a translucent eggshell color, her hair, straight black strands that hung heavy around her shoulders like a shawl. But it was the way that she wasn't just Nihon-jin, she'd told him with a wicked smile that had made him think reluctantly of the woman who had led his Guard. When he'd asked her to elaborate on her background, she had said simply, "Guess." His advisors had only told him that her mother was from Iroquois and had passed away during childbirth. They were unable to ascertain any further information about her background. In contrast, her educational background was easily accessed. He'd learned that she'd even attended a university in Alkebulan, which is how she had come to learn the common tongue and to speak it with such dexterity. It had made him feel a fascination for her that was alluring and a bit dangerous. Again, Essien rose to the front of his mind like a phantom scent, but he knew instinctively that just like Essien, Akai wasn't the kind of woman who would shower herself in his pity or his attention. He kept watching her hoping he'd find some clue as to how he might approach her, respectfully.

The third person his eye kept tracking to was Gunther Schmeisser, a stocky man with a broad set of shoulders covered in animal pelts and a tartan cloak. He was from Alemania, a nation that Gabriel had long suspected of providing weapons to rebels. But he didn't have enough proof. When he'd been introduced to the man at the first of these conferences by an emissary, he'd gotten the sense that Gunther was just a representative proxy for a politician who couldn't make the first week of the conference. The more he'd spoken to him, trying to find some common ground with a man who was very different from him, the more he'd come to see him as an oily weasel who spoke from both sides of his mouth. He overheard the man talking to the Sapa Inca, the Chief of Tawantinsuyu, a country in the western part of Abiayala, the continent to the south of Iroquois. Schmeisser had been bold and brash in telling him that Alemania's trade agreements were completely open and focused on building new partnerships with nations south of Iroquois. Later, he'd overheard the same man telling the Chief of Kalinago, an island nation to the northeast of Tawantinsuyu, that Alemania's trade agreements were locked for the next fifty years. Gabriel didn't mind lying; it was the sloppiness and easily verifiable lies that made him dislike and despise the man.

Never mind that the rumors surrounding who was arming the rebels kept circling back to Alemania. Again, Gabriel needed hardcore proof before he could bring his demands and accusations to the government of Alemania's notice, asking them to reveal who had sent those weapons to be found in an obscure rebel camp in the middle of Alkebulan. He had worried then that there would be other weapons found. So far, they hadn't found any more, and his fear of the rapid fires that held double the capacity of weapons they manufactured for strict and limited military use had dissipated. But something about seeing the dishonesty had reawakened Gabriel's suspicions and made him avoid the man after those introductions while keeping a close eye on his movements around the room.

There were other leaders, at least one from every country and nation on Ala-ani. None of them struck Gabriel's radar the way those three did. He'd been cordial and polite, asking the requisite questions, sharing his own relevant stories. When he could, he stood alone off to the side observing everyone else around him. He had already noted which of these leaders would be most instrumental for the next phase of his plan.

The massive, sprawling complex where the leaders were to reside while in Iroquois was a modern wooden and glass structure built right on the beach, the crystal blue waters situated on three sides. He had a clear and unobstructed view out over the ocean like a sparkling blue sapphire right at his feet. While the other leaders conversed casually in short sleeves and sandals, Gabriel looked out over the water and imagined what Essien was in that moment doing.

He didn't have to imagine. With a small opening of that place inside him, he could shuffle around like rummaging through a basket. There she was, faint at first, but as he pressed inward, his vision of her grew as clear as though she were standing right in front of him. When he peeked in on her like this, she had no idea he was watching and hearing everything she did and said. He knew she didn't feel him in her head in that moment by the longing glances she kept throwing at that boy, the way she would sigh, shaking her head, looking down, away, and then finding herself staring at him again. She never stared at Gabriel like that. When she didn't want to look at him, she didn't. He knew she would think him an intrusive overlord when he did this, if she knew he was doing it.

"Is there something you'd like to say to me?" Gabriel was snapped out of his introspection by the playful voice speaking his own language. He was already smiling by the time he connected with the honey brown eyes of the Shogun's daughter.

"Oh, plenty, actually." He skimmed his eyes over her legs, long and barely covered by the short pink and yellow silky wrap dress she wore. His eye trailed over the pattern up to her neck, the open space where he could see more skin, rounded and covered in a shimmery pink powder. Gabriel met her eyes, and his dimple deepened.

"Like what?" she cocked her head to the side, and for a second, he saw Essien standing next to him. There was a cluster of wooden wicker chairs shaped like palm fronds with padded cushion backing. He sank down into one of the chairs, his legs outstretched toward her. She followed his lead, slipping into the chair across from him.

"Well, how did you compare your studies in Alkebulan to those at the other universities you attended?"

Something about her smile shrank a bit. She put a thin, long-nailed finger up to her lip, while she cast her eyes up to the ceiling in thought.

"Besides our own universities, my father recommended two nations for my study: this one and yours. I came first to Iroquois, attending two universities here. Then I came to Alkebulan and found that I didn't want to leave." Here, her nose wrinkled up, so that Gabriel thought she looked precocious, like an imp. He had no idea what would come out of her mouth next. "I'd love another reason to stay now that my studies are over."

"What were your plans for your studies? Did you have your eye on taking over your father's position?"

She shrugged. "I did not. Nihon outlawed hereditary transfers of power over three hundred years ago. I'd have to be selected for the role by the same process my father underwent, as all Shoguns do. I also hadn't served in my nation's military, so I am not yet eligible."

"What role do you serve now?"

She held her hands out, palms up, fingers splayed out wide. "None. My father has freed me of all obligations that would ordinarily be placed on a firstborn. He is the free-spirited sort, if you didn't know. He wants me to follow my heart, whatever that means."

Gabriel pretended to frown, his eyebrows creasing together in the middle of his forehead. "What terrible advice," he said deadpan. "But do not tell him I said so." Akai laughed, the sound like flutes playing in the wind. "How is it you come to be here then? It is a conference for international leaders, no?"

"Then you might say I came as my father's translator and diplomat. He is often too softhearted for his own good. He tells me to lead with my heart, and yet one can't rule a nation that way. I do not act in any official capacity, but I'd say I have become my father's closest advisor."

Gabriel nodded. "Then you must be incredibly valuable to him. I have someone who serves a similar purpose, but she doesn't do it with any joy."

"Hmm, she must have been forced into it then. It's hard to do anything joyfully when you did not sign up for it."

Gabriel shifted and then sat forward on the edge of the seat, "In some ways, she did sign up for the role. In other ways, I admit it might have been a surprise to her."

Akai pursed her lips together. "If my father forced me into some official position in his government, I do not think I would enjoy it anymore. This way, I get to travel as freely as I please, and there is nothing that will be left unattended if I am not in Nihon." She paused, and the way she batted her eyes up at him, he braced himself. "Did you know my permanent home is in Igbo State? Yes, very close to Capital Island. Too bad I haven't been to see it yet."

At her words, and their meeting the reality in his mind, the dual images of Essien walking around with Koi and this lithe, devious woman sitting before him, he tipped his head back and laughed up to the ceiling. Other leaders around them turned to stare. Gabriel didn't care. He was thinking of Essien and Akai in the same room. Essien would sense his attraction immediately. She'd be pissed, jealous even, but she would cover it up. It might even send her more fervently into the arms of another man. Any excuse to avoid turning to him, as she was fated to do anyway.

He glanced at Akai, and she had been watching him the entire time. He gave a slight shake of his head, staring into the empty glass of sap wine.

"I think I have had enough to drink for the day. I need fresh air. Pardon me." He gave her a slight incline of his head and rose from the seat. Seeing his tread across the hall, his Guard fell in around him like the well-trained squad they were. He didn't look back, but he knew that Akai watched him leave the room through the glass doors on one side, walking down to the beach below. He also knew that if he stayed out there long enough, eventually she would follow him out.

CHAPTER THIRTY

◆

DESPITE GABRIEL'S WARNING FRESH IN HER MIND, WHEN KOI arrived the next morning, Essien couldn't see his excitement as anything other than endearing and sweet. But it was like everything Gabriel said began to cast a shade of color over her eyes, influencing her thinking as the day wore on, until his thoughts were hers. The way Koi clapped his hands and laughed so loudly started to irritate her, when before it had been appealing and made her feel joyful, too. The way he bounced up and down, like he wanted to be leaping up in the air instead, made her want to put physical space between them. Twice, he seemed like he wanted to talk about last night, and each time, she turned away from him or changed the subject abruptly. When they stopped at the selected site for the new military compound, Essien elected to have the on-site commander lead her through the tour.

The commander was a short, stocky man from Mbuti State, only a few inches taller than Essien. He had a patch of hair at the end of his chin that he kept massaging between his thumb and forefinger. He introduced himself as the commander, and Essien was fine with that. After the close familiarity she'd experienced with Koi, titles and roles were a good way to keep herself a step removed. Then Essien began to wonder if the commander had a wife or any children, if he had been called back into active duty to serve his President, and his Queen. As she worked up the courage to ask him what his family name was, she accepted that it would be impossible to keep herself completely separated from the people around her. She was supposed to care for them, to understand their concerns and work to address them. And in the process of doing so, what difference did it make if she found herself attracted to the men or wanting to befriend the women? As Queen, it was her prerogative, Essien thought to herself, as she followed the commander around, and vowed to be nicer to Koi—even if she now had Gabriel's admonition creeping into every thought.

The commander showed them around, pointing out the spaces being laid out for different buildings, pointing out engineers and architects who would be responsible for ensuring the designs for the new Council House fit the environment. He introduced them to sojas who had newly arrived and directed different groups to various tasks around the muddy site who came up to them with tools and materials in hand. The sojas were from all over Alkebulan, called from different posts and positions on the strength of her request to Gabriel. Essien admired the efficiency and noted that she could potentially use checking on her various projects being completed as an excuse to come back to the states she most wanted to revisit.

A long engine arrived on the site, chugging white smoke, pulling up behind Essien's convoy of engines. Koi turned to her with a smile and then looked at the commander. "Would you take on some Maasai warriors as trainees?" The commander watched as some of the tallest men Essien had ever seen stepped off the bus carrying their staffs in one hand and tools in the other. Koi went on, "Those are morans, Maasai's strongest warriors. Can we offer their help that we might learn from your work here?"

The commander stared at the men as they gathered in a group right beside the bus. He unfolded a piece of paper from his pocket and glanced over it before saying, "They'll need boots, pads, and helmets. Pardon me, Eze Nwaanyi." Then he jogged over to the group of men over double his height and began assigning them to a soja responsible for helping direct a truck of new materials where to unload.

The site tour over, Koi led Essien back to the engine, and they continued their trek around village after village, introducing her to elders and young adolescents, taking her in and out of different agencies and organizations that were local to Maasai State. Throughout it all, Essien felt strongly that Gabriel had put those negative thoughts into her head on purpose. She knew he could access her memories, show her his memories, and give her visions of lives she had never experienced. But being able to sense when she was starting to feel any strong emotion toward another person felt creepy and invasive. Then she began to worry that he had felt Koi kissing her and been inside her head while she'd been comparing them. Maybe Gabriel had seen something in her thoughts and feelings toward the young man that showed him more than she realized in that moment. Essien shuddered sitting in the back of the engine heading to their final location of the day, the Council House.

Koi placed a hand on her thigh and patted her. He took his hand away quickly and said, "Don't worry, Essien. I am confident the vote will be successful for you. You have already done so much in just the time you have been here." Essien just nodded, still focused on her breathing and unable to come up with anything to say back to Koi's genuine faith in her.

Essien ignored the shabby interior of the Council House and focused instead on the faces of the people. As she was led into their Council Room, she stopped Koi, who was heading toward the front of the large, high-ceilinged room.

"I'd prefer not to sit up front while everyone votes." He paused, glancing up toward the front, then nodded and sat down next to her in the very last row. The voting roll was carried into the room and placed on the table, still locked in its box. The heavy book was taken out, its pages were turned, and a pen was prepared. One of the elders made the ritual announcements, and the voting began. As each member stepped up to sign, Essien looked everywhere around the room except at those signatures and where they were being placed.

The hall was silent. The dry scrape of pens on papyrus, the murmur of soft voices, the rustle of movements into and out of seats, up and down the aisles in between. Some of the Council Members threw fierce, celebratory smiles her way. She wished she could feel that way about the vote taking place. When it was Koi's turn, he reached over to squeeze her arm before taking his place in the line. After signing his vote, he was directed to sit in a row near the front so that he was seated with other Council Members.

Essien knew it was over when a group of three began reading over the votes and the names. They glanced down for only a second before they smiled and turned back to look at her while one of them waved her forward.

Essien took a deep breath and walked up the middle aisle toward the table in the space at the front. She glanced down at the rolls and what she saw made her reach out and run her fingers down the list of signatures, a smile spreading almost instantly over her mouth. Every signature was on one side of the voter tally; under the column for rejection of the legislation, there wasn't a single signature. Every Council Member, both Tribal and Military, had voted in favor of her ascension.

Essien felt like she might cry or combust on the spot. She kept taking deep breaths to make sure she didn't do either while all around her the chants announcing her win rose up, "Naija stand up. Alkebulan rise. Naija stand up. Alkebulan rise! Naija stand up! Alkebulan rise!" Everyone was on their feet. Essien saw shiny eyes and damp cheeks. In that moment, she knew what they felt because she finally felt it too, and only her continuing to breathe slowly in and out kept her from shedding tears of happiness with them. *Two down, fourteen more to go*, Essien thought to herself.

She looked over at Koi, and his face was awash in an enormous grin. He ran toward her and picked her up with his arms around her waist. She laughed with surprise and then wrapped her arms around his neck as he spun her around in the open space of the floor. The other Council Members were shouting and hooting, some of them starting to sing a song in the Maa language that was loud and forceful, exploding the room in a collective display of celebration. Her win was truly their win, she realized, as she thought of the projects starting even now to construct a new compound and to bring new universities to the region. Looking around her, at everyone celebrating her win, Essien knew that whatever happened in the other states, this reaction alone meant that she had already won.

CHAPTER THIRTY-ONE

◆

DRIVING IN THE ENGINE THROUGH STREETS SHE'D NEVER seen, it was shocking to Essien how much Hausa State looked and felt like Fulani State so far. Mostly the buildings, looming up alongside the highways and roads. Here, the designs and ornamentation on the sides of residential and business compounds were ornate and intricate with colorful swirls and geometric patterns engraved or painted into the sides of walls and doors. There were more intricate designs around doorways and windows, and at the very tops of buildings serving as trim around the roofs. She even saw more of the buildings made of dark brown stone with white trim. The only difference between Fulani and Hausa States so far had been the absence of any greeting songs and dances. She had stepped off the skycraft to a small group of lavishly dressed Council Members who stood silently waiting for her to join them. The men and women were in sumptuously designed robes, wrappers, and scarves in deep colors and bright patterns.

One woman who instantly caught Essien's eye had on a lavender wrap over a fitted skirt and top made of the same material. There was a darker purple design running over all of the fabric that seemed to shimmer in the sunlight as the woman moved. She wore silvery stacks that peeked underneath the hem of the skirt. Her hair was braided into an updo that swirled and coiled around her head, thin silver rings worked into the strands here and there. She eyed Essien up and down, her face looking bored and unimpressed.

Essien had managed to secure her uniforms when an attendant had come to replace her canvas bag with fresh luggage just before leaving Maasai. She stood before them wearing the black-on-black uniform of a simple loose tunic, loose-fitted trousers, and the lighter overcoat that didn't make her swelter in the heat. She'd replaced the flimsy flats with her black boots, their thick soles thudding around when she walked. The uniform wasn't anywhere near as elegant as the robes the Council Members wore before her, but she was comfortable, and she felt like herself.

"Greetings, Essien, of Igboland. Enter Hausaland and take sustenance. May Hausa State be as true to you as you are true to us. May your wits protect you as much as your magic does." The words seemed odd to Essien, but she smiled like she was supposed to.

"I am eager to see what Hausaland has to offer the Queendom."

The woman with the lavender outfit that fit her so well and looked gorgeous against her deep, ink dark skin then spoke, and her voice was dusty and seemed full of thunder. "It is your Queendom that is here to be tried and tested by Hausaland."

Essien nodded, eyeing the woman up and down openly like she had done earlier. "Yes, that too. I hope I pass." The woman's lip twitched, like she wanted to smile but kept herself from doing it. Others stepped forward and the familiar roles played out.

As they escorted her throughout the different districts of Hausa State, Essien listened while her guide filled her in on bits of history and lesser-known facts about the state. He shared the legend of where the Hausa people had originated, a tale that Essien had learned in one of her anthropology classes during Upper Levels. She let the man go on with his explanation.

"And so, Bayajidda, the prince from Baghdad in Mesopotamia, married the Queen, Daurama of Daura, leaving his wife and son Biram behind in Bornu. From the Queen, the six sons of Bawo were born, and also the seven sons from Karbagari. Today, we have the seven districts of Hausa State, one for each of Bayajidda's sons by marriage, and the seven ancestral villages for the other son born from a woman not his wife." Somebody in the group snorted at the man's convoluted words. Essien knew the legend, so she knew exactly what was being left out.

She let the man's words stir up her memory. She had visited Hausa State on overnight school trips more than any other state in the country. It was to the north of her home state, not even a full day's engine ride. She had never known anyone from Hausa that took the legend seriously.

She asked, "Do people here believe in the legend of Bayajidda?"

Essien had learned the names of her guides, but after Koi, she made a point of not getting too close. She let them talk, asking questions at points when she was curious. But she kept their conversations surface-level. Now, she wished she had a name to use for them.

The guide's face went from smiling to frowning, "Please avoid letting anyone hear you doubt the legend of Bayajidda. It is as important to Hausa people as the religious beliefs of the holy men or the other faiths." Essien swallowed her next question and nodded. She hadn't grown up hearing creation stories for her nne or nna's family tribes. She'd known her father was Berber and her mother was Igbo. She knew her nne had grown up worshiping the Mothers. If her nna had a religion before, he would have adopted the religion of his wife and her tribe. Even still, Essien could not remember learning any other origin or creation stories beyond those of akukoifo and the Mothers.

"I'll be sure to take the legend seriously, then."

"Every year, there are reenactments of the legend of Bayajidda that bring more visitors into Daura than any other time. There are costumes and songs, pageants and competitions, art showcases. Oh yes, the Hausa show respect for their founder, and they continue to honor his legacy no matter who rules these lands."

She felt like she needed to apologize for even asking but didn't. The openness that Koi had inspired in her might not be the best approach as Queen. She didn't quite know how he had gotten past her natural reticence, anyway. He must have had some magic of his own. The fact that Essien was states away and still thinking about him said enough about the attachment she'd allowed to grow so quickly. She had known saying goodbye to him would be difficult, that he'd want to make some profession to meet again, so she had quietly slipped out of the Council House while they were all still celebrating with glasses of honey mead for everyone.

She couldn't risk making those kinds of attachments everywhere she went. Not if Gabriel would keep stalking her and bursting in on her if she tried. Not if they couldn't go anywhere beyond those stolen, hidden moments in the dark. She hadn't seen or heard from Gabriel again since that night he'd come to stop whatever he had suspected might happen between her and Koi. The door between their minds was still barred from her access. As the days of her travel continued, Essien vowed to refocus once again on her mission: Get the legislation approved and she could return to her life on Capital Island. Get the legislation approved and she could start keeping the promises she had already made as Queen. Get the legislation approved and she would have more freedom than this.

IT WAS THE EVENING BEFORE THE HAUSA COUNCIL'S FINAL VOTE. After a long day of meetings and listening to demands, her guide had returned her unceremoniously to the barracks, this time a long, skinny room that barely fit the bed, desk and chair, and table for a hot water kettle and a few pods of tea leaves. Essien had long ago stopped hoping for luxury. Perhaps once she was Queen, she might be able to demand better accommodations. This might be something else Gabriel was restricting from her until she had succeeded at her mission. It would be just like him to make her suffer on too short beds at near collapsing military compounds. The major compound in Hausa State needed renovations, too, though not as badly as the one in Maasai State. The need for repairs was about space more than anything. In one meeting in the days before, she'd heard that there were sometimes up to ten or twelve different sojas in a room meant for four. The commander had begrudgingly agreed that another compound in Hausa would provide more space for the currently enlisted sojas and enough additional room to house another five or six squads of sojas.

"Consider it done," Essien had said with arrogance. But, when she knocked on Gabriel's door in her mind, he hadn't answered. She'd waited, knocked again and again, but no answer. The thrill of panic and fear that shot through her made her heart beat like she'd been racing. She couldn't quite catch her breath, and she tried to get a handle on the instant feeling of foreboding that seized her. The kind that made her stomach hurt and threatened to come up into her throat.

The day had progressed to other meetings, so she was forced to focus on the present and not worry too much about Gabriel and why she couldn't reach him. She was back in the engine. Hausa State's residential areas and its villages, its retail and entertainment district intermixed with its business and government district. They drove through one of the familiar brick villages that turned into stone buildings with the intricately engraved walls on all sides. Off in the distance, tall glass buildings shimmered in the sunlight. The engine stopped in front of one of those glass buildings with multiple floors stretching up into the clouds. The doors were made of glass, too, and swished open as people walked toward them.

The guards led her in and the group of health professionals that met her on the first floor were all wearing different colored uniforms, one-piece coveralls with long sleeves or long-sleeved tops with pants that tucked into each other.

She was introduced to the senior doctors, the junior doctors, and the trainees. They were men and women, most of them Alkebulanian, who worked as medical professionals. The tour took her around each floor of the building. Essien insisted on walking closer to the inner walls, so she didn't have to look down as each floor went higher and higher. They let her view different medical wings and operating rooms. She could hear the squawking of newborn babies in the wing for new mothers. The tenderness Essien felt watching the babies with their mothers, some of them offering their bundles up for Essien to hold. She couldn't reject such an offer, so she smiled as pictos snapped and captured her holding other people's newborns. As she handed them back, Essien could have sworn she felt a small twinge of a sappy emotion. Holding a bundle of her own seemed both foreign and fascinating. It wasn't possible though. Guards were bound to the President and having a family automatically disqualified anyone from serving in such an elite role. She knew that made sense because of the demands of the role and the dangers. Still, having infants around the Compound might give it a lighter mood than it had while she had lived there.

Essien could only ever remember being inside of a hospital once. She had ridden in the back of an emergency engine with her father when he'd been hospitalized after the fires. The fires that destroyed hundreds of stadia of his land. Afterward, those fields that had burned produced significant harvests, probably from all the ash fertilizer, and her nna had made back the money he'd lost. But he never fully regained his health. As Essien looked in on ill patients in the wing reserved for the sickest ones, she hoped her nne was still alive and prayed a silent request to the Mothers, something she hadn't done in a long time, that she'd get to see him again soon. Then she wanted to leave that wing as soon as possible. But she couldn't figure out how to do it without making more of a fuss than she wanted to. The medical professionals around her were sharing their facts, pointing to different pieces of machinery in different rooms, pulling aside other workers to stop and answer questions. She couldn't hear anything around her discomfort and desire to leave the area where she could hear faint wailing from people in mourning over dying loved ones. Essien realized that she'd been slightly afraid of medical centers since her father's accident with the fires, seeing them as places where people went to die. After the Mothers had helped save her father's life, she hadn't had to return to a hospital since. She realized that she hadn't been sick or ill herself in a long time. And though her nne had not gotten better, no one else in her family had fallen sick either. Not that she knew.

The group tour brought her to the final wing of the hospital where the patients who needed surgeries were hospitalized. They each took turns explaining to her how so many surgeries had originated in Alkebulan, leading to foreign doctors coming to study in our hospitals to learn our methods. From giving birth to multiple babies at once, safely and without losing the mother, to brain surgeries that alleviated pressure on the brain for people with severe, debilitating illnesses. Essien stood in awe from a viewing platform above a live demonstration of a pioneering new neonatal surgery method. The doctors, the most senior on the hospital's staff, were operating on a set of twin babies while they were still inside their mother's womb. Essien couldn't look for too long, realizing that despite the carnage she had seen and caused, seeing a woman helpless on a table, listening to all the contraptions and devices beeping and flashing around her, something about it unnerved Essien. Perhaps it made her consider her own mortality. Maybe she was already in a sour and depressed mood from thinking about her father and the accident that had almost killed him. It might have been something else entirely. When she looked over at the Guard standing closest to her, they knew that look. So one of them stepped in, signaling to everyone in the tour group that Essien had her next meeting to attend. It felt a bit abrupt after all that they had shared with her, and Essien tried to do better than that.

"Please, if there's anything the hospital needs, I am here to listen to your demands."

One of the senior doctors spoke up, "Just don't forget about us when you take Alkebulan into the future. Remember who keeps her going when no one else can."

Another doctor, a woman, said, "If we had sister hospitals across Alkebulan, we might be able to disseminate our new methods much easier. Now people have to travel to our hospital here for our innovations. It would be a blessing to every citizen if we had a network of doctors at hospitals across the country."

Essien turned to one of the guards and said with a smile, "Please write that down."

After that, they all wanted to touch palms again before she could leave. Finally, she was escorted back down to the first floor, and the Guard took over with getting her back to the waiting engine and safely inside. She didn't have to ask them where she was going next. She'd looked at the schedule for the day closely. She had one more stop and then a visit to the Council House at the end of the day. Essien suddenly felt so weary that all she wanted to do was go back to her barracks at the closest compound and sleep until the end of the trip. Let them take their vote without her. She lay her head back against the seat and with the jostling of the engine over the road, she was asleep in minutes.

When she opened her eyes, her head had slumped down sideways against the window. Outside, the engine had stopped beside what looked like a jungle. The Guard sat in the front seat, patient, quiet, and still. When they saw that she was awake, they stepped out of the engine and opened the back door to let her out.

"How come neither of you woke me?" she asked, covering a yawn and stretching her arms over her head.

The guard standing next to her shrugged his massive shoulders and said, "You looked like you needed the rest."

Essien peered around the clearing they were in. On one side was what looked like an overgrown jungle. As she looked closer, she could make out wooden stakes driven into the ground and covered with vines from top to bottom. In between those stakes were patches and rows that stretched further into the tangle of greenery and dangling fruit. On the other side was a complex of orange stone buildings with red tiles on the roofs. The building directly in the middle was the largest with at least three floors. The other buildings were of different sizes and shapes with two stories and rectangular; others one story and circular or square-shaped. There was nobody gathered at the base of the stairs leading up to the front door that was green with a window at the top.

The guard led her into the building, holding the door open for her. Essien entered and thought she could smell paint or what smelled like rubber balls. The hallway stretched all the way to the end of the building with doors leading off the hallway. At the end of the hallway, another set of doors with windows opened onto a grassy courtyard and other buildings across the other side of it. Children darted back and forth across the window, and Essien could hear their shouts and laughter floating through the closed doors. To the right, another set of windows and a door made of glass opened onto an office. The walls were painted light blue, the desks were yellow, and the child-size chairs were red. The carpet on the floor was a mix of those colors in abstract streaks on a white background. On the walls were life-size paintings of children in various poses—some running in a race, others spinning in a circle, others jumping ropes, a few sitting under a tree with books in their hands. A woman sitting behind one of the desks glanced up at them and smiled when they entered. The other desks were empty.

"Hello, you must be Essien." Her voice was like a birdsong melody. She came forward in billowing red robes with darker red embroidery across the fabric that extended up in a head covering and down all the way to dangle on the floor. Her hair in two braids hung down to her hips in front. She held both her hands out. "I am Rashidah Gbadamosi, the Director of the School for Active Learning and Transformation. I am so glad you were able to join us here. Have you had lunch? Our instructors are just sitting down to their afternoon meal."

Essien's stomach chose that moment to growl and remind her it was empty. While some of her meals were planned, most were unplanned. Ensuring she was fed didn't seem like a consideration that was made when her schedule was planned. If she wasn't included at the Council House for meals or didn't find ways to go into the city for food at vendors, Essien suspected she likely would have starved on this trip.

"I'd love to join you all."

Rashidah escorted Essien down to the dining hall at the end of the hallway with the Guard trailing around and behind them. The Director's voice trilled on, pointing to the colorful murals and signs on the walls. Some of the displays were student work, and others were posters with friendly messages. Rashida pointed out classes that were in progress, older students with their heads and shoulders hunched over exam booklets, their hands frantically scribbling sentences across the page.

"Our Level Six students are testing to see what schools they might attend for Upper Levels. Here in Hausa State, their options are endless, if their families have the money. If they don't? They'll be forced to get jobs working for other people or start businesses for themselves or go into their families' trade. We try so hard to keep our students enrolled as long as we can, but we end after Level Six."

Now she had Essien's attention. As they entered the dining hall, Essien made a note to ask more questions and to be sure one of the guards took the details down. The dining hall was a large, airy square with windows on all sides open to the courtyard in back and the other buildings on the other sides. At one end of a long table closest to the kitchen, the instructors were serving themselves from wooden bowls and platters.

Rashidah clapped to get their attention and smiled wide, gesturing to her with both hands. "Our esteemed guest will be joining us for the afternoon meal." One of the lunch attendants set more place settings. Rashidah turned to her with a frown.

"Will your guards be joining?"

Essien looked back at them. The six behind her gave her blank stares. She realized that they never ate when she did. They must have to wait until their shift was over to eat. It's probably why there had been no consistent plans for her meals. Like the guards who starved all day, they likely expected her to do the same. Come to think of it, when she had been a guard, she had only ever had her early morning meal before going out on any assignments or patrols and her evening meal after the day's training and missions were over.

She smiled sweetly at Rashidah, shaking her head. "They prefer to starve all day. Keeps them focused." One of the guards chuckled a bit, and several of the instructors smiled.

Rashidah sat, and Essien sat next to her. The bowls and platters were passed down. Several of the larger bowls contained mounds of fufu. Essien was pleased that she recognized something. The other bowls contained different-colored stews. One was orange and lumpy with flecks of green. The other was red and lumpy with oil puddles settled on top. Rashidah dished spoonfuls of both stews into a bowl and set it before Essien.

"This one is baobab leaf soup, and this one is orange vine fruit soup. You eat it with fufu."

Essien took one of the mounds of smooth white dough from the bowl as Rashidah handed it to her. Essien was familiar with this kind of meal, as she had grown up eating fufu and soup or stew. In fact, one of her favorite meals to eat was pounded yam with stock fish soup. She pinched off a piece of the dough, and it was warm and stretchy. She dipped it first in the orange stew, picking up a chunk of meat with the dough as a carrier. She put the whole piece into her mouth and was instantly hit with spices and savory herb flavors. It reminded her of ogbono soup, minus the sliminess of the okra her mother used to put into it. She could see that everyone at the table was watching her.

"It reminds me of soup my mother used to make," she said.

An instructor at the end of the table, a man with a short Afro and wearing a plain tan-colored tunic said, "There is so much overlap between Fulani and Hausa and Igbo cultures that I'm surprised we managed to become separate states when this nation was being founded. We could have been one big conglomerate state."

The instructor sitting next to him, a woman with her hair braided down into thin braids close to her scalp and a black and silver embroidered tunic, said, "What would we have been called?"

"HausIgbolani State?" the instructor offered, throwing his hands up as though he were also confused. The table erupted in laughter.

Essien said, "That would not have gone over well for Igbos or Fulanis, I'd imagine. We had enough trouble with the smaller tribes and the religious zealots trying to form this country into a united whole. That would have been borrowing more trouble than we might have been able to overcome."

A different instructor, a man who towered over everyone even sitting, put his hands up in the air, the sleeves of his long-sleeved blue tunic pushed back, and said, "As a history teacher, I must challenge that assertion. Are you saying that Alkebulan wouldn't have existed if Fulani and Hausa hadn't been given leadership over their states?"

Essien shook her head. "I spent a lot of time studying the history of this country, but you may know more than I do. From what I understand, the Fulani and Hausa were two of the largest tribes in West Africa, and they'd experienced centuries of conflict leading up to the War of Unification. It didn't make sense for any new government to not factor in that conflict and do what it could to ease and eliminate the problem, if it could. And would you say the conflict has been eliminated?"

The instructors all looked at each other. Rashidah looked down at her plate. The guards stirred, stepping a pace to either side of her, maybe just to remind her they were there, which meant to remind her that Gabriel was there, too. She didn't think she'd said or done anything to ruin her new reputation yet.

The instructor was solemn as he said, "Every month, our Council Members meet to hash out their arguments and disagreements over the State's plans, its direction, hell, even its decision to seat you on a throne. So no, the conflict has not been entirely eliminated." The man stared at her for a second longer. No one else said anything in that silence that stretched on.

Rashidah clapped her hands again. "Afternoon break is almost over. Let's finish our meal. Essien, you still have to meet the students. And they've prepared a special presentation for you!"

THE PRESENTATION TURNED OUT TO BE OUTSIDE STANDING NEXT to that thicket of trees that at first Essien had thought was untended woods. As the students of all ages, from six up to fourteen, led her around the orchard and garden, Essien saw up close that the life brimming off every vine and branch was anything but unattended.

The students crowded into the garden, their heights putting some of them down low near the shrubs and bushes, while others were taller than Essien. Many of the girls wore head coverings that matched their school dresses, light blue and white. Some of them wore headbands in front of tall puffs, others had their hair in intricate braids around their scalps meeting in a braided ponytail or a twisted bun. The boys were in similar uniforms, white collared tunics with light blue pleated pants or shorts. All the children were equally excited, jumping or running from place to place, shouting over each other with excitement. They showed her where they were growing seasonal patches of fruits and vegetables, the colorful fruit peeking out between the green leaves and vines. They showed her where they were cultivating new plots within the garden for the next season's plantings. The freshly turned ground was a darker color, the dirt smooth and mixed up within the patches. They showed her the baskets and baskets of produce they'd picked already as a part of their daily classes in the garden.

Rashidah told her, "These plants provide all the school's meals with so much excess we are able to donate the extra to local residents and charities with a daily list of deliveries. If we don't get rid of what we pick every day, it will go to waste here. There's just so much of it."

The students finished their presentation and wanted to take pictures with her. She felt inspired and proud, standing next to them as she went through the motions of standing in front of the mounds of dirt that would be the new garden plots, then standing with the arms of several children wrapped around her with pleased, satisfied smiles on their faces.

As she prepared to leave, she asked Rashidah, "I am here to be of service to you. Is there anything the school needs?"

Rashidah took her hands. They were soft and smooth, like she'd never handled anything rough a day in her life. "You have already done so much, just by being here. Our students will remember this day for the rest of their lives. That is more than enough."

Essien stared down and then asked quietly, "Would having a universal education system help this school? Or other schools in this state? In Alkebulan?"

Rashidah stilled, but then she gripped her hands even tighter and leaned in close. "I would open schools all over this nation if we had universal education. I would open a school for Upper Levels and guarantee admission to all of our students who complete Level Six here. Oh, Essien, you remind me what it is to be an educator. I haven't taught in a classroom for young students in decades. All of my teaching is for my instructors now, but for the first time in a long time, I am inspired to think outside the little universe I have created here." She stopped and looked down at where she was still clasping Essien's hands.

"I had heard that you had agreed to almost everything the States demanded so far, that you had asked for almost nothing in return. Why?" Rashidah looked up at her, piercing her with a soul-searching stare that seemed to lay her bare. Essien wondered if the woman could actually see down to what was inside of her. The truth of the matter was that she would do anything to have her freedom again, but somewhere along the way, she had stopped pretending. The people of Alkebulan had revealed to her what she hadn't seen from inside Gabriel's shadow.

"I am happy to give you what you want, to agree to your demands because you are my people. There is nothing you could ask that I wouldn't agree to." Rashidah was staring deep into Essien's eyes without looking away. Essien had only ever experienced eyesight this intense once before. Then she'd been forced to kill the old man.

Her voice was a whisper that Essien could barely hear: "And if we asked you to fight against the President at every turn, to stop whatever he has planned for this country, and this world, is that a demand you would grant us so freely, too?" Essien leaned back, but Rashidah's grip on her hands were like claws now, digging into her skin. She noticed the gold sparkles around her eyes and the small curly hairs around her hairline.

"Let go of me, Rashidah," she whispered, not yet willing to let the guards know that Rashidah was not who they thought.

Her grip got tighter; the tip of her nails seemed to sink into her skin even further.

"Tell me the truth first."

Essien sighed, letting the increasing aggression ease out of her. "Somebody already beat you to that particular demand."

Rashidah's smile was starting to come back. "Are you saying that the promise you made to Councilman Deng was true? He is a known liar, so outside of Dinka State, few of us believed him."

"Us?"

She shook her head but whispered with an even lower voice, "Those of us who know the prophecy, who have been tasked with protecting this land from what that prophecy says will be our fate if we don't."

"I've heard enough about my fate and what some prophecies from thousands of years ago said. I've been told too many times now that if I do what Gabriel wants, the world will come to wreck and ruin. I've heard it before, and I'm doing everything I can to make sure that doesn't happen. I'm trying to make my own fate and my own lane in history."

Rashidah's nails eased up from her skin, her grip loosened. She let Essien's hands go. On all sides of her, she felt some tension leave the guards as they settled their shoulders and shuffled their steps. They'd been on high alert the moment Rashidah touched her, even if they hadn't heard a word she said.

Rashidah put her hands on Essien's shoulders and leaned forward. She planted a soft, dry kiss on Essien's forehead. "Then Hausaland blesses you, and the Mothers keep you."

ESSIEN TRIED AGAIN TO CONTACT GABRIEL WHEN SHE HAD A MOment alone in the back of the engine between destinations on her schedule. She tried knocking hard and firm against the door that usually let her into Gabriel's mind when he allowed it. For months when she'd been among the rebels, she had kept Gabriel from entering her mind by blocking him. She couldn't do it completely on her own at first, so she'd had help from Osiris, the holy man who knew spells of protection and had protection oils to smear on her. But she'd learned, and she'd been able to keep him from sneaking into her mind. Now though, with that hole he'd made into her soul, she could never block him again. Yet, he still had the power to keep her out of his mind whenever he wanted. It wasn't fair. Add in that she felt genuinely terrified, and there was nothing specific except that blocked door in her mind.

Leaning forward into the space between the two front seats in the engine, Essien asked, "Is the President okay? Has anything happened to him?"

The guard who was driving answered, "The President is fine as of our daily update this afternoon. What makes you ask?"

She sat back. "Why doesn't he answer me then? I've been trying to reach him all morning."

The guard in the second seat turned to look her up and down. "Reach him with what communicator? You didn't ask to borrow ours."

She shook her head. "Can one of you get a message to him for me? Tell him I'd like to speak with him." The guard in the second seat reached into one of the pockets on his overcoat and pulled out a slim silver rectangular device. It was one of the latest communicators with its colorful pixelated screen she could touch to dial up whoever she wished to reach. She was already shaking her head as the guard tried to hand her the communicator. "Not like that."

The guard frowned. "Then how else would you reach him?"

She'd never talked to Gabriel on a communicator. She always used the mental means he had given her. It would feel weird to talk to him where she couldn't see him, like that time she'd contacted him, and he'd kept his background completely blacked out. It had felt weird then, too.

"You call him and tell him for me, please."

The guard put the communicator up to his ear. "Tell him what?"

"To contact me." The guard shook his head, like she was being silly and he didn't understand her at all. Maybe she was.

Someone answered because the guard said, "Is the President available? She wants to speak to him about something. Didn't give me a message. Said to tell him to contact her. No, she doesn't want to. I don't know why, she just doesn't. I tried it already. Just give him the message. That she wants to talk to him. I know that already, but I'm just giving you the message she gave me." The guard hung up, and Essien wondered if the message would even be relayed to the President. It hadn't sounded like it.

They were pulling up to the military compound then, and she had no choice but to get out and return to her room. And now here she was, alone in the small room with walls that felt like they were closing in. The President hadn't reached out to her yet. Tomorrow was the vote, and she hadn't spoken to him since the night she'd seen him. After he'd thrown Koi out and damn near bit off her head for even entertaining the young man seriously. Perhaps he was ignoring her as punishment, like he usually did. She snorted and lay down to sleep.

When she opened her eyes again, it was still dark out. She sat up, her heart pounding. Something had woken her up. She threw back the bed covering and walked to the door. The lights in the hallway were out. She quietly opened the door and peered out. The hallway was empty with no guards standing right outside. She knew that two guards stayed outside her door each night, no matter what. She looked up and down both sides of the hallways, but the moonlight leaking in from the skylights above wasn't bright enough to let her see all the way to both ends.

Essien quietly closed one door and turned inward to try and open another.

"Gabriel," she whispered into her mind. Her own voice echoed back to her. Darkness. Silence. Nothing. She quickly fumbled around in her canvas bag to pull on the trousers and tunic she'd taken off earlier. She fell on top of her boots trying to search for them, but she got them pulled on. *"Gabriel! Please!"*

Finally, she heard and felt and saw the door give way. It was dark wherever he was, too. He was in a bed, lying on his back, the light pink sheets around him rumpled and pushed down to his waist. Essien didn't have time to think about anything else beyond what was going on in this compound.

"I think something's happened," she said in a rush. *"The guards aren't outside my door, and all the lights are out. I'm worried. I've been worried all day."*

Gabriel was sitting up and swinging his legs over the side of the bed where he was. Behind him, she saw the prone figure of a woman lying on her side, her bare ass plain and visible for her to see. Essien let that sight distract her. She stopped, and the nasty feeling that started to bleed up her throat was worse than the fear she felt right under it. Something had happened, possibly something terrible, and she was worried about who Gabriel had in his bed. Just like he was worried about keeping anyone *out* of hers.

Gabriel said, *"I can't sense my guards who were stationed on you tonight. Or any of the other guards with you at the compound. They weren't supposed to change over until the morning. The morning guards won't arrive for a few hours yet. I will try to reach them through my communicator and send you backup. Stay in the room until another guard arrives, Essien."*

But she was already easing the door open and creeping out into the hallway.

"Essien, go back into your room!" Gabriel was standing now and pacing around, then his steps took him out of one place and into another with more light. He must have been truly agitated because she could see a wall of windows with a patio outside suspended over an expanse of turquoise blue water. As Gabriel moved around the space, Essien could even see white sand beaches in the distance and a shiny, sun-reflecting city in the background.

The hallway she moved down was pitch dark, and having the brightness of Gabriel's background in her head made it even darker. She knew she could create her own light, but as she moved cautiously on tiptoe down the

242   WIELDERS OF FLOODS & FLAMES

hallway, she had no idea who might be watching and waiting for her to do just that. She crept down the hall in the opposite direction from the main stairs. She knew the main stairs opened onto a central hallway that ran the length of the building with a few turns at one end. If an ambush was being set up, she would do her best not to walk right into it.

Gabriel was cursing in her head. *"Nobody can get ahold of your crews on site, Essien! Listen to me, please—that means you have been compromised! We have to assume the guards are all dead. That is the only reason they would disappear and go radio silent. Essien, did you hear me? You are not safe!"*

Essien stilled at the end of the hallway. All the other doors along the way remained closed and quiet. She hadn't seen any sojas on this floor the entire time she'd been here, so she assumed the rooms were emptied. She had no idea what might have happened in the time since she'd fallen asleep. She didn't want to imagine that the guards who had been keeping her safe and taking care of her over the last few weeks were no longer living. That was not a thought she was willing to entertain.

She ducked just a sliver of her head around the corner at the end of the hallway, so she might see if anyone was there waiting for her. The doors along both sides were closed and at the end of the short hallway was another set of stairs. Crouching low, she made her way slowly and quietly to that stairwell. She walked at a sideways shuffle, so she could look back and make sure no one was coming behind her. She wondered where the rest of the sojas were, if they were all playing their part in whatever plan was being orchestrated against her. Essien cursed herself for being so trusting and not seeing the signs. Still, though nothing had happened yet, the lights being out wasn't that shocking, but the guards being off their posts and unreachable was alarming. They wouldn't have abandoned her without being relieved, not without a good reason. And if Gabriel couldn't reach them either?

He was still ranting in her head, and now she heard a soft voice in his background. It distracted her as she reached the head of the stairs and peered over the railing to the first floor. The voice, a woman's voice, seemed to come closer to Gabriel. Instead of paying attention to what her eyes were seeing, and her ears were hearing, Essien was straining to see a face that went with that soft, gentle voice. Gabriel seemed to realize what she was doing, and his background was suddenly blurred again. She couldn't even see him clearly anymore.

"Essien, please don't get hurt," he said, his voice resigned but still panicked.

"I'll try not to, but can you quiet down, so I can concentrate?"

"What are you going to do? I've called for backup, and they'll make it to you from the nearest compound in less than thirty minutes."

"I can't do anything if you don't stop talking!" she hissed.

His voice went silent, but she knew he was still there. She couldn't see anyone on the first floor from the landing. She knew she couldn't stand there forever, waiting for someone to rescue her. Eventually, whatever had happened to the Guard would reach her. She said a prayer to the Mothers that they weren't dead.

Back down the hallway, around the corner from where she had come, Essien heard a creak and a thump. Adrenaline thrilled through her, making her fingertips feel tingly. Without thinking, she leaped over the railing and down from the landing to the next stair level below, landing softly on her hands and the balls of her feet. She edged quickly down and around the final stair landing. The door leading into the end of the long hallway was closed. She walked the rest of the way across the short hall and put her ear against the door. Nothing, not a single sound. Above her, another creak in the floorboards. Someone was coming closer down the hallway above her.

Essien quietly eased the door open, peeking out as the crack in the doorjamb widened. The hallway she could see was empty, so she squeezed through and closed the door softly behind her. The square alcove at the end of the hallway was clear. There was another door leading outside to the left and the hallway leading back up to the front of the building straight ahead around another corner. Going outside seemed less safe because there were too many wide-open spaces and not enough cover.

Taking a deep breath, Essien eased around that corner slowly, using first just one eye, then half her head, and then slowly, her shoulders and the rest of her body. There was another corner and then she'd have a clear line of sight up to the front of the hallway. Her heart was beating so hard against her ribs, it felt like her ribcage flexed outward with each pump. Her breathing was loud in her ears as she strained to hear both ahead and behind her.

She edged up to the last corner and slowly eased her head around. Her eyes flicked up and down the hallway taking in everything, and then she ducked back around. She had a hard time catching her breath then, her lungs suddenly panting and struggling to get air down. She wanted to spark up her flames and send them razing up the hallway to burn everything she had seen. She thought about slipping out the back door and maybe trying to circle around to the front.

Around that corner, the hallway was filled with a small army of men in white robes, their heads covered by white caps. Sitting at the sides of two of the men were two pairs of lions on short, thick chains. In front of them, down on their knees with their arms behind their backs, mouths gagged by ropes that cut across the back of their heads, were her guards, all twelve of them who had been on site. They were still alive and breathing, but Essien was terrified that she might fail and cost them their lives. She tried to calm her breathing and couldn't, her shoulders starting to heave as her terror overwhelmed all her training. It wasn't fear for herself that made her unable to control her reaction.

In seconds, Essien had seen what there was to see in the hallway and realized that her usual tactics of burning everything in sight wouldn't work. She couldn't burn everything in the hallway. It would kill her men, the guards who were good people to have around her, who had taken care of her and made sure she was safe. She said a prayer of thanks that they were still alive and a prayer for guidance that she wouldn't accidentally kill them.

In her mind, she knew that Gabriel had seen the situation and was relaying the details to her backup.

"They are just five minutes out, Essien," he was saying to her. *"I told them to come in hot but quiet."* She knew he was nervous and afraid for her.

"What rebels are these?" she asked him, her mouth still as she communicated to him mentally.

She felt his confusion and how disappointed he felt with himself that he didn't recognize the men who had taken over the military compound, seemingly without any resistance. Before they could figure out how this had happened, they needed to survive. Gabriel sighed, *"I don't know. They don't look or sound like the rebels you were among in Bantu State and that area."* His voice was low and choked, like he was keeping himself restrained and holding some part of him in check.

Essien stood up from her crouch. At her sides, her hands sparked up in red and yellow flames that crackled and popped, sending silver and gold sparkles to bounce across the floor.

"Please, Essien, backup is on the way. Give them five minutes."

She thought about heeding his words. She thought about waiting for help to arrive, for others to come and rescue everyone. Five minutes was a long time to stand there waiting. She didn't know what they wanted, but her death seemed the most likely. They would get tired of waiting, too.

Eventually, they'd realize she wasn't up in that room, if they hadn't discovered that already. Anything could happen in five minutes.

Gabriel and Essien's eyes widened at the same time as they both saw the man step around the corner, his rapid fire rising to aim already. One second Essien was raising her hands up, the red and gold flickers getting brighter. The next, Gabriel had reached into her and through her and the man in front of her clattered to the floor, his rapid fire rolling out of his hands.

"Move quickly, Essien. They'll have heard that."

She took a deep breath and flung herself around the corner.

The lions leaped first, their roar seeming to tear her eardrums. Their claws were huge sharpened daggers as their paws slashed for her. At the same time, she could sense the men moving in behind the wild animals, their arms extended in length by curved daggers that whined through the air.

As she set her flames to burn with exception, there were two things she made sure to consider. One was that she didn't want to burn the lions, just incapacitate them enough that they couldn't attack her. The second was that she didn't want the guards to be hurt or injured by her flames.

She saw the first lion's paw slash over her head as she ducked, and the second lion smashed over her head, missing her entirely, going flying to land behind her. She heard the crack and crash of wood splintering. She didn't see the hind legs of the first lion continuing to slash down low, out of her line of sight. So that even as her flames turned into a fiery wind, blowing the men back from her end of the hallway with embers that whipped and snapped, she felt the rip and tearing of her flesh as one of the lion's back paws scratched at her outer left thigh.

She groaned and cast up a wall of flames that engulfed the space behind her. The lions rolled over each other in a heap, their sharp talons gouging lines in the floor as they scrambled back toward her. The flames reared over them, and they both cowered back from the heat. They slunk back and forth in front of the flames, a paw extended to bat at it, but they both eventually backed into a corner. Essien knew the flames wouldn't keep them back there for long.

In front of her, the army of men had not come closer through the flames. Essien felt a trickling down her leg and looked down. A puddle of blood pooled near the inside of her foot. The puddle wasn't that big; as she watched, the red liquid began to seep around her heel and follow the lines of the tiles to spread behind her. Essien looked up suddenly as a thin silver blade whizzed by her face.

Suddenly, her attention widened to take in the entire hallway. The flames behind her had risen to tickle the ceiling. In front of her, the men in white robes were yelling words at her that she couldn't understand. It wasn't the common tongue or Hausa or English. It sounded like some dialect of Arabic, but it wasn't quite that language either. The men brandished their daggers, their curved edges gleaming, slashing them around her, showing their dexterity with the sharp weapon.

The sparks on her hands began to erupt and drop globules of flames onto the ground. At first the flames just burned harmlessly, bubbling on top of the floor's surface. Essien walked forward, raising her hands at her sides, her fingers gripped like claws. The holy men, because that's what they were, she realized, formed a barrier at the end of the hallway.

Then Essien heard Gabriel's voice in her head. *"Backup is incoming. Stop playing with them, Essien. Either take them out or stand down and let the backup handle it from here. Decide now."*

Essien took another step down the hallway. One of the holy men still at the far end of the hallway shouted something, and then he was gripping the back of one of the guard's necks and yanking him up to stand in the middle of the hallway. The man shouted something again, but Essien didn't understand. She tried to open herself, letting all of her exterior leak open. The flame behind her shot up, folding over to burn along the top of the ceiling that began to singe and turn brown and then black and then gray. On the floor around her feet where the sparks had been floating, now they began to smolder and singed the floor everywhere they touched.

Several of the holy men looked up at the ceiling and then down at the floor. The flames were growing. The entire end of the hallway behind her was burning, the flames starting to cast their own wind behind her. Essien didn't dare take her eyes off the hallway near the front entrance.

The man gripping the guard's neck said something else and moved the machete in his other hand forward in a slashing motion. Essien heard that awful gurgling sound over all the shouting and roaring and saw a fountain of red explode up and then tumble down to spill all over the floor. The red gushed and gushed.

Essien screamed, shrieking out, "No!" She threw her hands forward at the same time. The flames followed their direction, so that the holy man's hand was suddenly on fire. He noticed as he swung the knife down again, and he shook his hand. He let go of the guard's ravaged neck and tried to beat the flames off his wrist. The flames were already moving, eating up his arm, starting to crawl up over his shoulders. The man dropped the machete, its metal clanking loudly against the stone tile floor in the already noisy hallway. The guard fell forward onto his face and side. His hands were still bound tightly behind his back, so he couldn't catch himself or do anything about the blood that was still pouring out of the wound in his neck. Essien scanned the rest of the hallway for the rest of her Guard while the holy men were distracted.

Two things happened in that moment: The first was that the ceiling above them began to crack and shatter, bits of burning wood and insulation starting to come down like fiery rainfall. The second is that the door at the front of the hallway exploded with a wall of black sweeping in. The wall of black poured over the white robes of the holy men, and they panicked then. About half of them dropped their machetes to the ground and put their hands up. Some of them tried to fight, taking swings that connected with the hard metal of rapid-fire muzzles. Sharp eruptions from the rapid fires, and the still fighting holy men dropped one after the other.

The last group of men, the ones who hadn't given up, turned toward her. Essien was still frozen in shock while the life in the guard's eyes faded away. She wasn't paying attention as the last cluster of holy men, armed with machetes freshly sharpened, surrounded her and raised their machetes to strike her all at once. They were all killing blows. Essien couldn't take her eyes off the guard's dead eyes, and a hot line fell from her left eye. She looked down as the tear dropped off her cheek followed by another one on the other side after that. She noticed the puddle of blood had now spread underneath her left foot and was creeping over to her right one.

Suddenly, she smelled and felt Gabriel all over her, like he'd stood just behind her and wrapped her up in his arms. Then his voice in her ear: *"Dammit, Essien!"*

The next thing she knew, Gabriel had taken a hold of her like he never had before. She knew then he had given her the illusion that his control over her had limits and didn't extend beyond her mind. In that moment, Essien knew that had been a deliberate deception. He hadn't wanted her to know just how far and how deep that power went, and he hadn't wanted her to remember just what he could do using her power mixed with his.

One second, she was standing there looking at her own blood puddled around her feet, at least a dozen machetes coming down upon her. The next, her flames erupted from her body like the epicenter of a hydrogen bomb. The hallway was filled with blinding white light. Their machetes turned to liquid metal, their robes incinerated into ashes, their bones and skin were obliterated into nothing where they stood.

When the smoke cleared and the dust settled, Essien stood there panting, holding a gash in her outer thigh, staring at the backup guards as they rushed over to help the guards on the ground in gags and ropes. Essien looked around the empty hallway as the gray billows began to disperse. Even the lions' carcasses had been turned into just stains on the tiles.

CHAPTER THIRTY-TWO

◆

E SSIEN DREAMED OF HER ELDER BROTHERS SITTING IN HER parents' front room when she walked in. They each sat on a stone chair up on a dais that was so tall that they towered way above her. As she walked closer to them, she looked around for her parents. First, the front room was empty with not a single piece of their familiar furniture, and then it transformed into the hearing room in the Igbo State Council House. Now her brothers were military councilmen, all five of them. They wore the full military regalia of the highest status, silver and gold stripes on their black mantle. In the rising theater of seats behind her, the families of everyone she had ever killed filled the rows. As she looked up at them, their faces changed from sadness and tears to anger and rage. She snapped her head around.

In front of her, her brothers spoke to her with one voice: "Every death you have caused, directly or indirectly, will be taken against you, and you will pay."

She was shaking her head and trying to speak. "I've already paid," she tried to say. But no words would come out. She kept trying to speak, her mouth growing dry. She walked closer to them up on the dais. The dais seemed to get higher and higher the closer she got. Then it transformed into a stage beneath the dais. On it stood a line of men. She kept walking closer, not realizing yet who they were. She got to the foot of the stage before she saw that lined up on the stage, in several rows from one end to the other, was everyone she had ever killed.

There were Akpari and Keesemokwu at the front of the line, and the other man she had killed right after them. She wailed and covered her mouth, even though she knew she was being dramatic. They couldn't hurt her, she tried to tell herself. They were dead, and they couldn't hurt her. Then Akpari stepped off the stage and came at her in a pale yellow and red blur. She screamed and tried to back up, but the people in the audience were right behind her now, forming a barrier that kept her from moving away from the man she had already killed running toward her.

She screamed even louder and threw her hands up over her head to shield herself as best she could. Then she was standing outside the tent in the rebel camp. The flap flickered, like someone had gone into the tent just seconds before. Essien moved forward to follow, and the flap suddenly flew up, and there was Mansa Musa running toward her with a curved dagger clutched in each of his hands. She screamed again, the sound ripping out of her throat. She turned to run, and then she was standing in front of the dais and her brothers at the top of it.

"Your crimes will be displayed before everyone, and we will judge you." For each death, a red slash appeared across her skin. For each kill, her arms and legs became more and more covered with slashes. Some of the blood leaked in constant drips onto the floor. Suddenly, a pit of sand opened beneath her feet, and she was sinking, down, down, until she was armpit deep and still sinking. She pleaded with her brothers to forgive her, but they were so far up that she couldn't even see their faces anymore. They ignored her pleas. Then they morphed into Gabriel, all five of them wearing his face, and he was stepping down from that great height into the sand pit next to her. He snarled into her face, "I told you this would happen. I told you that you'd be disgraced. I knew your reputation wouldn't last." Then she was floating through water, clear and warm. The Mothers were bathing her, their hands gentle and firm against her naked skin. As she stared, their faces shifted from one to the other, turning from golden brown to pale cream to midnight black to shadowy brown to purple-blue. Essien relaxed and closed her eyes as they dipped her beneath the water and held her under the surface until she stopped breathing.

Essien startled awake. Her eyes flew open, and she rolled over to scan the room. The soft blue sunlight of early morning poured in through the balcony window, and she could hear the soft peals of music coming from some room in the compound.

She sat up in her own bed on her own floor in the President's compound on Capital Island and felt sorrow well up into the space of her consciousness. This was the moment she hated. The moment that had kept her stuck in her bed for the last three weeks.

It had been three weeks since the incident in Hausa State. Though she'd been unable to force herself back into another engine, the campaign for the QUEEN Act legislation to pass had gone on without her. The days that had passed were a silent, blank space now as she thought back over the time since.

Taking a deep breath, she contemplated as she had done for each day over the last three weeks. She should get out of bed. She could practically feel her muscles starting to atrophy. She should find the nearest attendant and demand they arrange travel to the next stop on the campaign. Deep inside, Essien knew that what she needed was to go home to her parents. Something in her felt broken and wrong; something she had thought would always be strong and capable was no longer working the way it should.

She had seen people die before, so figuring out why the latest round of deaths had paralyzed her so deeply was another unanswered dilemma. She smoothed her hands over the bed coverings, the soft texture reminding her that she was still alive. Everything else might have gone to ruin, but she still had breath in her lungs. That had to count for something.

On other days, she had gotten out of bed and sat in the chaise near the balcony. But then she hadn't been able to move from that spot. Food was still brought to the dining room for each meal, but she made no move to walk across the hall. The attendants started bringing a tray into her bedroom and putting it on the table beside her bed. Sometimes, a few bites were all that she could manage. Other times, the trays sat on the table untouched all day.

In the front of her mind, Essien kept seeing the guard's throat being slashed, rewinding again and again to pinpoint the exact moment when she should have released her power and didn't. It was her fault the guard was dead. She could have saved him, and she'd failed. Every time she closed or opened her eyes, she kept seeing that moment. The flames were up and ready to fire, and she'd held back. And now a guard was dead. She hadn't even known his name because Gabriel had forced them not to tell her. Groaning what sounded and felt like a sob, Essien lay back in the pillows and pulled the bed covers over her head.

Outside the window, the sunlight brightened into a metallic silver and then a honey gold as the day progressed. There were sounds and movements all over the compound, some on Essien's floor, too. Down below, she could hear sojas coming and going in engines that arrived every hour. Essien could hear the engines rumble up to the compound, stop, and then lumber away after some time. Somewhere, the music continued, floating into her buried under the covers like a barely felt wind.

Essien came to know that the days were passing because the food on the table beside her bed eventually disappeared, and a new meal reappeared. Most days, she stared at the food on the tray, and nothing like hunger or thirst reached her. Because she knew she needed sustenance or she would die, she would eventually work herself up to taking sips of the tea, rooibos, the red smoky drink she'd come to love living in hiding in southern Alkebulan. Every other day, she managed a few spoons of porridge or a bite or two of rice. Then, she'd remember her sorrow, her stomach would seize up, and she'd have to crawl back into her bed to escape. Sleep became her only freedom.

She lost track of the weeks. She knew there were things happening because sometimes she could hear them. Shouts of joy or moans of sadness. Sometimes, she heard Gabriel's voice. One day, she felt him enter her room and walk over to her bedside. She had pretended to be asleep, squeezing her arms and limbs tight into a ball under the covers. He had stood there, and his smell, like watery sweat and a smoking pipe, filtered into her, and she fought not to move or make a sound. She didn't want to see him. She didn't want to talk to him. She didn't want to find out what had happened, what had gone wrong, or how many more had died. She almost didn't care how the vote had gone either.

Gabriel had stood there for a few seconds more, and then his voice came to her, muffled through all the layers over her head: "There are ten states left to vote." He spoke slowly. "The tally is tied, three to three. I know you might wish that we had halted the vote, to give you time to...come back to yourself and recover. But the states had already scheduled their votes, and they made the decision to move forward with putting the legislation to a consideration of their full Councils with or without your presence. Though they have expressed some regret at you not being present, the keepers of the vote have found the final votes to be going much more smoothly in your absence."

He stopped. She still didn't move. Her eyes were squeezed closed, and she kept her breathing slow and even—in slowly, hold, out slowly, hold. She grew transfixed by the rhythm of her own breathing. She didn't even hear Gabriel leave the room. His smell lingered in the days after that visit, but he did not return.

And Essien couldn't make herself get up and get back to normal.

By that time, she wanted to. She knew she had to. Gabriel's words had sunk in, and she lay awake into the night, watching the shadows of orange orbs bounce over the ceiling and the walls. The campaign was proceeding without her. She wasn't there to hear the people's demands and use their pleas as leverage to turn the vote in her favor. She'd had no chance to persuade them. But what happened in Hausa State had shattered all her strategies and laid bare that she had no idea what she was doing. Outside of the magic flames that flowered in her veins aching to get out, she hadn't the first clue what it would mean to be Queen, to actually lead. This, lying in bed for weeks now, unable to rouse herself beyond what had happened to someone else, was not leading. She had to find it in herself to get back onto the zebra. No one was coming to save her from herself. Not even Gabriel could save her, and she knew he wanted to.

ESSIEN WAS SITTING ON THE CHAISE, STARING OUT AT THE SKY outside the patio windows, when the door to her bedroom opened, and Gabriel stepped through. He paused at seeing her sitting up, dressed in a peach-colored silk dress, her eyes clear and looking back at him. He came into the room slowly and let the door close behind him. He stayed near the door, slipping his hands into his pockets as they stared at each other.

"I don't know why it's affected me like this," she said, her voice softer than he remembered.

Gabriel walked over, his steps reluctant to come closer. He stopped a few feet away from the chaise. He looked her over, searching for some sign of what might have improved to finally get her out of bed. He knew it would take more work to get her back to herself, but this was a start. When he'd come up to this room, he'd expected her to still be lying prone and unreachable.

"Losing a guard is always hard," he said. "They sign up to give their lives for us, but...you never want them to actually have to do it. You hope they'll go their entire term never having to shield your life with theirs. But it's the job they sign up for. Saving our lives. He did his job."

Essien shook her head, looking away to hide the wetness that welled up in her eyes immediately. She went back to concentrating on her breathing. Gabriel moved closer. When he sat down next to her, his side bumping into her knees where they were curled up in the seat next to her, she whipped her head around to look over him. He was wearing a loose white tunic and stiff indigo slacks, the material looking brand new. His feet were bare and starkly dark against the white, white carpet on the floor. She uncurled her legs and moved down the chaise to put space between them. Even as part of her wanted to move closer.

"Who was the woman?" She asked him while looking out the window.

She felt his eyes on her face, studying her side profile. Her voice dipped low. "The one I saw in your bed."

Gabriel sighed and sat back. They both sat in silence. She refused to turn her head the few degrees it would take her to look at him.

"She is nothing to me," he said at last. "If she becomes more, you will be the first to know."

A sound came out of her that might have been a laugh, but there was too much pain in it to sound like true laughter. "And if I'd said the same about Koi?" Now she did look at him. Her eyes were red and puffy, and he knew that no matter how much time had passed, that night in Hausa State was still fresh in her mind. Like it was happening to her over and over again. He didn't know how to help her with something like this. Magic, he understood magic. This level of smoldering, unquenchable emotions was outside his realm of expertise. She said, "You remain free to do whatever you wish, with whomever you desire, while I am tied down by invisible chains."

Looking down at his hands, he said in a low voice, "Not with whomever I desire."

She ignored that comment and said, "You have separated me from everyone and everything. Lying here until I die is the only freedom you have left me."

He asked her softly, "Is there anyone from your childhood you might wish to see or have visit you here? Your Nne or Nna? I can arrange their travel here, if you would like, if it would help you to...feel better."

She whipped her eyes back to his face. "*No*, I don't want them in your compound! I don't want them to see me like this. I don't want them to know what you've reduced me to."

Gabriel sighed. Essien knew she was being unfair to him, and that what happened in Hausa State that night wasn't any more his fault than it was hers. But she had found a target for the angst and torment she'd been mired in for weeks now, and she would force him to experience even a fraction of what she was feeling. Seeing that guard fall, again and again, his arms still bound behind his back so that he couldn't even catch himself.

"What was his name?"

Gabriel covered his face, rubbing his forehead and the bridge of his nose, pressing his fingers into his eyes. When he looked back at Essien, there was a wildness in his face that scared her. "His name was Ifeoluwa Folorunsho of Yoruba State. Will knowing their names make their deaths any less painful? I wished to spare you this."

"No, you wished to isolate me and force me to deal only with you, doing whatever you wanted. Well, I did Gabriel, and look where it has gotten me."

"You are almost there, Essien. The tally of the vote is not tied anymore. It is now five to four. There are seven more states to go. The way the votes have gone, we will lose. My advisors predict it will be ten to six in the end. Not having you on the campaign has been a disaster."

She was so tired and weak, but still, she smirked.

Gabriel went on, "Are you ready to hear what happened?" She shook her head, the side-to-side motion a little frantic. "Very well. The Guard will still be adamant that you are not to be left alone. They will still ensure that your schedule is followed exactly with no deviations of any kind. And there will be no distractions either. Your remaining schedule has been condensed into a day of meetings at the Council Houses right before the vote. Instead of three days of meetings, you'll have just one day of meetings in each state. The remaining days can be spent doing any activities of your preferred leisure."

She eyed his face. "That's what you and your Guard decided?"

"Once we knew where we had gone wrong, we knew what changes to make to reduce the likelihood of something like that happening again. It happened because—"

Essien raised her hand up. "Please, don't. If it was my fault, I've already blamed myself, so I don't need the double lashing. If it was your fault...I don't want to know. Your fault, my fault, nobody's fault, everybody's fault. I don't want to know. It won't get me back on the campaign. Don't bother telling me. Let them vote how they will."

Gabriel leaned closer to her, his hand coming up like he meant to take her arm. But then he let his hand fall back onto his knee. "Did you hear me say that you are going to lose? That the legislation is going to fail?"

"I don't care."

Gabriel was still leaning toward her, peering into her face from inches away. They both knew that was a lie and not what she truly felt.

"I know you are still grieving. Grieving everything that has happened to you since joining my military. I know it has almost broken you. That you feel broken now. But you do not have to be, Essien. There is still strength in you. And if you feel weak? I will be your strength." Then he lifted his hand from his own knee and placed it onto hers, squeezing the bones, pressing her skin. Her first instinct was to jostle his hand away. The reaction was so strong, she had to grit her teeth to keep herself from doing it. Because right on the heels of that first feeling, she felt a radiating calm coming from where he touched her, and the instincts went away. Suddenly, all she wanted him to do was touch her. To put that hand everywhere he could reach and never break the contact by taking it away. She wanted to cuddle into that touch and let the feeling of peace and calm wash everything away.

When she turned her face up to him, two tear drops slipped off the end of her chin. He reached out with a finger crooked to wipe the wetness. She leaned away as he came closer even though all she wanted more than anything else in the world was to feel him touching her. Gabriel retracted his hand slowly. The calm remained. She took a deep, shaking breath, her shoulders rising and settling.

"I know that you are not to blame for that night," she said slowly. "I know you did everything you could to keep me safe. I don't want to know what happened.... Just tell me...if I don't continue this campaign...will the legislation truly fail?"

It was Gabriel's turn to look out the window. "There will still be a group of guards posted outside your rooms at all hours, and we are doubling the number of guards surrounding every step you take. Now, even more precautions will be taken. There will always be a group on standby, waiting for check-ins to assure all is fine. If those check-ins don't happen as scheduled, the group stationed nearby will arrive on scene for rescue or emergency efforts within thirty minutes or less."

Essien shook her head thinking about what all could and had happened to her in just thirty minutes. She wanted to say no, to curl up on that chaise and never move. But the calm that Gabriel had infused into her had settled and replaced what she had been feeling for all these weeks now. She studied his face while he looked away from her. On the heels of that realization was the ever-present anger, still there and ready to spring out at him. Such was the space he took up in her head now, teetering on the edge hovering between intense hatred and obsessive fascination. She hated both sides that she kept flipping between. She'd rather be indifferent toward him.

Staring into his eyes where they had risen to meet hers, she asked, "If you can touch me and make me feel better, then why haven't you done it before today?"

He shrugged, his face continuing to display his seriousness. "We weren't about to lose the legislation yet."

CHAPTER THIRTY-THREE

◆

AFTER ALL THE TRAVELING FROM STATE TO STATE, FROM ORnate Council House to less ornate Council House, Essien didn't have to fight to get time alone to do what she'd like to do anymore. She had arrived in Berber State, gotten through her meetings with mindless determination and one thing on her mind. Tucked into the front of the portfolio where she still carted around her copy of the QUEEN Act was a map of the Muséon, one of the museums at the world-famous libraries in Berber State. The collection had topped one billion texts over a decade ago when they first published their tally of the collection. Essien's interest was piqued, and suddenly, sitting beside her bed and never leaving her floor had seemed like the cop-out of all her years fighting toward this goal. So, that's how Gabriel was able to get her back onto the campaign trail with just a few states left to go. She could do a few more states, she resolved to herself as she packed her canvas bag on her own, including only uniforms and boots she preferred.

Sitting through the hours of demands had left a cringey, exhausted feeling over her mood. How had she done it so patiently before, she wondered. How had she endured the endless streams of speeches? What was it about watching a guard die that had made her unable to stomach sitting through another boring session of other people's wants and needs? Essien couldn't think of a single answer. She still cared about her people, and she still saw them as her people. But now, it was through a triple layer of guards surrounding her in an impenetrable bubble wherever she went.

As she prepared herself to set out for the Muséon, she remembered how expansive the museums were, how she'd only gotten to explore a tenth of the treasures they held from all over the country. When she'd come as a teen on her Levels outdoor field trip, they had spent three days following a guide through the tomes, only getting to view what was on their preplanned trek. Now, as an adult, she wouldn't let anyone stop her from seeing everything she wanted to see.

The Guard silently fell in around her when she'd exited her rooms at the military compound wearing casual clothes—a thin tunic and pants that hit at her ankles. She wore casual sandals and carried her picto capturer on a strap around her neck, her new communicator on a strap around her wrist. It had been a gift from Gabriel one of the last times she'd seen him right before departing for this final leg of the campaign. In case she needed to reach him when he was unreachable, he had said as he handed the small, silver device to her. His words had been delivered with a grin that let her know he was making fun of her.

Essien waved away the opened doors of the engine. The Guard looked at each other and then trotted to catch up and surround her. They headed through the city on foot straight to the Muséon, that ancient ulo akwukwo, a library dedicated to the goddesses and powerful women of Alkebulan. A statue of Ifri greeted visitors to the tan stone complex standing fiercely with a golden shield on one arm, a golden spear in her other hand, and a curved dagger with ivory hilt at her waist. The gold and browned ivory statue towered blindingly over the entrance that had curved arches and pillars holding up the front tiers of each floor. The head librarian, a quiet and small woman wearing light pink head coverings and robes with everything except her eyes covered, bustled over as soon as Essien entered and introduced herself as Talia Sufian. Her voice was husky and matched the sea-green eyes and golden tan skin that Essien could see.

"Would you like a personal tour of our facilities? I am free now and might accompany you." Essien smiled and wanted to accept. She thought of Talia entering the bubble of guards around her, walking alongside her as they both preceded and followed them. The only other person who had experienced the guards' sphere of protection was Gabriel. And the people she had met on this campaign so far, like Koi. Thinking of Koi made the smile slide slowly away.

"I'd like to spend hours getting lost in the passageways and alcoves of this library. Just going where my whims take me. Could you provide me with a personalized map? I'd love a list of specific artifacts and installations you'd suggest I might look for."

"Of course, please give me a moment." Talia disappeared around a corner behind the circulation desk. Essien peered around the foyer of the building. The black marble floors rose up to the ceiling in pillars. The ceiling was high, at least four or five stories, and she craned her neck trying to make out the design painted all the way up there.

Talia came back with a smile and a stack of pamphlets. She spent a few minutes explaining how to use the maps and showing Essien where she'd marked spots for her to explore. Essien took the pamphlets in her hands and felt bad that she had rejected Talia's offer to join her. It would have been lovely to have her husky voice explaining the significance of what she saw without having to interact with the small square screen projectors next to each artwork.

"If I need help with anything, where can I find you?"

The smile Talia flashed at her showed only in her eyes as they crinkled at the corners and sparkled across her cheeks. "I will be here at the circulation desk. I will make sure I stay until I see you leave." Essien returned her bright-eyed smile with one of her own and turned to enter between the two towering marble pillars leading into the rest of the library museum.

For the rest of the morning and afternoon, Essien stared and stared in breathless wonder at the exhibits organized throughout the library. The paper-thin pages of the first religious books ever written telling the origin stories of all Alkebulan's many tribes, the hand-painted murals depicting life in east Alkebulan thousands of years ago as the birthplace of human-kind, the glass-domed antiquities and relics that were too delicate to be exposed to the elements or even breathed upon. There were other statues, entire halls for each goddess, and busts of metals and stones and woods and hybrid materials for the Alkebulanian women who had helped to shape the nation. There were paintings framed behind glass and drawings in old, deteriorating sketch pads that had once belonged to some ancient artist from long, long ago.

Before she knew it, the guards were standing in her way, barring further movement, signaling that it was time to go; the final meeting for the vote was looming. She hadn't even explored half of what the quiet librarian had written down for her to see. Essien vowed that she would return as soon as she could to continue her trek deeper into the halls. Perhaps she might accept Talia's offer of a tour the next time she came. She could see from the map that there were catacombs beneath the library, other floors below and also above. She felt enlivened and invigorated, looking at the art and culture of her people, seeing what had been done before her, realizing that all was not hopeless. All was not lost. There was a chance for a life, even within this cage. She'd find a way to escape, she'd find her freedom again. She was not meant to be chained. Seeing the work of her ancestors made that surety thrill through her fingertips as sure as her flames could spark up there, too.

260   WIELDERS OF FLOODS & FLAMES

While they were on their way to the Council House, the guards received a message on their communicators that sounded like an emergency. They glanced at each other first before looking quickly back at her.

"The vote is completed. We don't have to be at the Council House anymore."

Essien put a hand against her chest. "What was the result?"

The second guard said, "You're seven to six now. The vote totals were close, too close, but you secured the Tribal Council's approval."

Essien let loose the breath she'd been holding. Everything that had been stripped from her by what happened in Hausa State seemed to flow back to her. She could feel the eagerness return. Just three more states, and she'd be free.

One of the guards took a transmission on his communicator, speaking low into the receiver. When he finished the call, he turned back to look at her.

"Your trip in Berber has been cut short. You don't have two more days here. We'll be heading to the transportation center now. The next vote is scheduled for tomorrow."

Her voice instantly went higher in volume. "Gabriel said I was to have two days to myself, to spend however I'd like."

The guards pretended they didn't hear her. She considered pulling out her own communicator to contact Gabriel. But what would she say? That she wanted to spend another two days at the Muséon playing with dead letters while the Councils continued their vote? He wouldn't understand that at all. Quietly and sullenly, Essien slipped the list of artifacts to explore in the Muséon between the sheets of the portfolio behind the schedule. She would come back one day. One day soon.

From Berber State, they took her all the way south, down to Bantu State. Essien wondered at the logistics of passing up all those other states to return her to the place where she had done the most damage with the rebels. As the engine took her to her first stop, the Bantu Council House, Essien was shown exactly why the state had been chosen next: The people loved her.

The skycraft landed on the familiar paved landing strip. The fervency of the welcome song Essien could hear as soon as the skycraft powered down shook the windowpanes on the skycraft. She climbed down, her eyes on the faces of the people. The crowd was like one big mass of singing, clapping, dancing people. Essien was immediately swept up in the excitement and joy of the occasion. The singing voices rose up to the sky like an offering, and quickly learning the song's simple melody, Essien's voice joined them. She began to sway her hips to the sounds, imitating the women's moves as they danced. As the songs began to sound like chanted prayers, Essien let the exuberant energy flow through her, dispelling the last of the grief and sorrow. It wasn't gone, it never would be, but for now, she had other focuses that would keep her in the present and not reliving every terrible event she'd ever experienced.

Despite what she had done in their state as a rebel, the public reception was the warmest she had received so far. From the way they cheered and ran alongside the engine as she drove away, Essien could clearly see that despite the people backing the rebels, that had not altered their opinion of her.

The Bantu Council House looked unlike the buildings of any other state. The building was a large circle with two stories. Running along the outside of the building was a covered patio with gated entry at specific intervals. Inside, high-vaulted ceilings divided the building into wedges with the very center room reserved for the full Council Chambers. Essien was led in by the guards and settled in the seat in the very front, despite her subtle attempts to be seated elsewhere.

The speakers lined up, and this was familiar to Essien. She knew they would make their requests known, and from the looks of the line, Essien predicted this meeting would stretch on for hours yet. As the people began to speak, Essien realized that their demands would come with a greater price than any of the others had demanded.

One activist speaking on the voice projector shouted, "We want a full investigation into every property sold over the last twenty-five years. We want charges laid to bring the corrupt Councilmen to punishment for enabling theft."

A farmer came up to speak next: "We are even more eager to have our lands returned to their rightful owners. My family has had over one thousand stadia of land stolen from us. We want our land back, Eze Nwaanyi."

After that, there was a commotion in the line that made the guards step over to sort the situation out. A Bantu elder, a stooped man wearing a black and white tunic and a dark brown cap, greeted her with warm smiles and offers of a tight embrace.

He eyed the guards standing between her and him. Essien wanted that hug from the nna nna, this grandfather, but she knew the Guard wouldn't allow it. She smiled sadly.

"I appreciate the gesture. I accept it fully in spirit."

The elder stooped even further to reach into the canvas bags at his feet. The bags were stuffed full to bursting. When he lifted his hands, he held handfuls of gold bracelets and precious gemstone bracelets and chiseled diamond necklaces. Essien gasped as the jewelry sent a shatter of sparkles around the Council House, the bright light reflecting off the ceilings, the walls, the floor, their faces.

"I could never accept such treasures," Essien replied graciously.

The elder frowned. "Do not send me away with full hands. I was sent by my village with these offerings, and you must take them. It would be rude not to. It would be downright insulting."

"Then I accept them. I wouldn't think of offending or insulting anyone in Bantu State." The guards stepped forward to gather up the bags. She could tell from the way their arm muscles bulged and they gritted their teeth that the bags were indeed as heavy and full as they looked.

After the meeting ended, she was glad that she had not come empty-handed. The people who had come to speak to her had brought gifts, so many gifts: a dangerous looking ngulu, the execution sword taller than her; yards of fabric in bright colors with rich patterns; designer dresses that would need to be fitted to her size; a set of four curved daggers with diamond hilts; a pair of leather boots with a matching leather overcoat thickly padded on all sides like armor; several carved wooden masks and statues; plus the bags and bags of jewelry, including thick bangles, dangling earrings, and beaded necklaces on thin, invisible chains. The guards hauled the gifts out to one of the waiting engines, one of them remarking that the items would surely weigh down the skycraft for the return trip.

Seated in the engine, she admired the stack of gold bangles she had slipped over her wrist. The bangles felt cool and heavy against her skin. The jingle they made every time she moved made her lift and drop her arm a few times every second.

Before the engine pulled away, one of the guards turned to her. "The schedule has one more stop planned. Another trip to a school."

Essien groaned. She had hoped she'd head to a military compound, so she could rest before she had to hop on the skycraft to the next destination. She could see the last four states waiting just ahead. One meeting in each state, Gabriel had said. But then he'd already gone back on his word to give her a few days to herself. She rolled her eyes, but said, "Is it another presentation?" The thought of listening to anyone else speak to her felt like more than she could bear.

"You're just here to deliver a shipment of new screen projectors and other electronics to a school that you burned down."

Essien stilled with one of her arms still propped up on her thigh. "What do you mean a school I burned down? I never burned a school!"

The guard said, "You did. This school was burned down by one of the fires that you likely started, although we don't have proof. It was during your time with the rebels in Bantu, and it's in the area near the underground camp we found. The odds are that you set the fire, but without proof, you have deniability."

The bangles clanged again as she dropped her arm. "I deny it. I do deny it! I had a line with the rebels, and I didn't cross it. There were things I wouldn't do, things I refused to do. No buildings with people in them, no buildings near people. I always made sure people weren't injured by my fires."

"Well, nobody was injured. But the village wasn't wealthy enough to pay for the repairs needed, the extensive renovations to fix everything, so the shell of the school building has sat burned out and unusable since."

"So this is my fault, too, then."

"No need to talk about blame. I wouldn't mention it if I were you."

"Then why tell me at all? I'm obviously going to feel guilty. This might send me back into a spiral."

The guards looked at each other again. The one who'd been trying to console her said, "You're here to make it better. That should keep you from feeling too much guilt. Once you see the extent of the damage, you'll know better what's needed to repair. This is an opportunity to win them over, Essien. Just see it like that."

Despite the chaos she felt waiting to erupt all over her, she nodded and focused on her breathing. The engine rolled up, and she had to face her failure head on. The burned-out hulk of the school building loomed as they stopped, and she climbed out.

Beside the burned building, a set of lean-to sheds had been erected. Just three wooden walls with a palm leaf roof and a packed dirt floor for each of the three buildings. Inside each lean-to, children sat on the ground working on various activities with teachers walking or sitting among them. Small groups of children shared a screen projector between four or five of them. There was a textbook, singed along the edges, being shared among eight children with papyrus pads and pens.

Seeing the desolate hope in the faces of the children and their teachers made tears fall to mark her own shame. She didn't confess or admit any wrongdoing. She turned her eyes to scan the devastation. She didn't remember this site being one she'd come to burn. The surrounding area didn't look familiar either. But she'd often traveled with the rebels at night, when it was dark. She wouldn't have been able to see any noticeable landmarks anyway.

Now, staring at the destruction she had caused, she knew she had to act now. Not waiting until the legislation was passed. She took a deep breath and simply reached inside to that mental door with one knock. Gabriel answered right away, the door opening wide with no delay.

"Essien, you look better." His voice sounded relieved.

Without words, she shared with him what she wanted, what was needed. Gabriel was nodding before she'd said a word.

"I can have a convoy of engines sent your way within the next hour. Sojas and materials to rebuild. We can have the other supplies for the school ordered and delivered in days."

"Thank you," she said and meant it.

"Anything, Essien. Anything you need."

She didn't want to ask, but she had to know. *"Were you aware that I'd burned the school?"*

Gabriel made a sound and then was silent.

"You did know," she said.

"It was in the reports I received while you were with the rebels. I didn't put it together that it was you until after. If you hadn't asked me to help just now, I wouldn't have known which state specifically."

"I never knew you could be this responsive," she said. *"I have to give you credit. Even though I know you're doing all this ultimately to serve yourself...I appreciate the steps you've taken to help me get over this hurdle."*

"Just five more states, Essien. Five more, then the legislation will be approved, and you can come home." She didn't even want to correct him that his compound was not her home. He had done all of this to help rebuild her reputation and her image. She decided that in exchange she could endure the displays of his power to control. Even if deep inside, she still hated it, but hated him less and less each day.

CHAPTER THIRTY-FOUR

◆

EVEN MORE SURPRISINGLY, ESSIEN REALIZED THAT THE COUNcil of Bantu State was run much differently than all the others. For one, there were way more women in the ranks than she'd seen in any other state; a little more than half the Tribal Council members were women. As soon as her engine pulled up to their Council House for the end of the final vote, she was greeted by women at the front wearing the traditional tribal wear of the Bantu: brown robes with embroidered gold at the neck and feathers. She was escorted inside to the Council Chambers.

Before the vote commenced, a sharp and formal-looking group of teens gathered at the front with percussion and string instrument players standing off to the side. The music began, and the teens danced a traditional dance of welcome. Essien found herself clapping and swaying to the beat as they moved with athletic grace. There were so many amazing dancers all over Alkebulan, she thought. Essien wondered what it might take to create a national dance troupe, one that combined the dancers from all over the country, perhaps to travel all over the world.

After all the dances were performed and the clapping had subsided, Essien grew silent as the vote began to approve the legislation. She couldn't bear to look around the room at anyone. She decided she wouldn't blame them if they rejected her. They had every right, more than anyone else. The majority of her damage had been in this State. Even if they saw her as their savior, there was still a debt that wouldn't be repaid until the school was repaired, and she'd found and routed out the corrupt Councilmen responsible for all the land theft.

Finally, the vote keepers went up to witness the final tallying. The whoop that cascaded through the room like a volleying ball, back and forth from voice to voice, rising with the exultance of victory, made her sit up on the edge of her seat. It was announced; she had won. The room erupted into stomps and cheers that drowned out her own thoughts that still berated her despite the sweetness of this Council's approval.

The smiles around the room sent her on to her next stop with optimism brightening even the darkest, most defeated parts of her soul. If this is what the countryside looked like, after everything she had done, after everything Gabriel had done, then perhaps...perhaps the country was destined for greatness and not ruin. Perhaps her joining with Gabriel wouldn't bring about the end of everything she loved and held dear. Watching the sun set through the small, round skycraft window next to her seat, she couldn't help wishing that he were beside her to share in what she had achieved so far. With his help especially. This was a side of Alkebulan she had never seen, definitely not while working as a soja or his Guard. She was happier than she had words to express because she got to experience it now, at a time when she needed it the most.

EVEN COMPARED TO BANTU STATE, ZULU STATE WAS THE EASIEST to persuade, the people even friendlier and more easygoing, wanting only promises of safety and jobs in order to be won over.

At the transportation center in Zulu State, she had watched their dances, transfixed by the hypnotizing chants the women sang out in rhythm to the dance moves they performed in unison. Their toned, golden-brown legs went up together and then the reverberating smack of their feet hitting the ground together added to the swirling cadence. When the dance was over, one of the dancers waved Essien over to join a line of other excited women who were eager to teach her their moves. Essien found that she could kick her leg up almost as high as the Zulu women did. It made her feel proud when they all clapped for her. Essien kept hearing their melodic chants even after she was gone.

At the Council House, nobody argued or dismissed her after her first few assurances that she had come to help. Nobody retaliated or tried to attack when she allowed the rumors to be spoken in front of her, other voices giving space to the veiled threats that she would never utter. Then, she would calmly explain every accusation, the flames only a small flicker deep down in the depths of her eyes. After hearing how she spoke with such passion and yet restrained, they simply stopped arguing and signed their names to the voting roll.

She had promised them a new technology center to train teens in the latest electronic devices and innovations, as it was their greatest request.

She even floated the idea of universities and universal schooling. The Zulu Council Members were so in awe, there was nothing else to be said. When she called Gabriel, he had murmured that he would need time. The engines arrived to begin managing the technology center's building before her last day, so she knew he had kept his word to back up her promises on this, too, despite whatever reluctance he had shown.

Khoi San State flew by like the blowing of hunting horns over long distances. She thought of the woman who had pressed a diamond almost bigger than her head into her hands, how she'd cradled its weight while she shook her head and told the woman she couldn't possibly accept such a treasure. The woman had insisted, speaking in a San language that Essien did not understand. She felt bad that she couldn't figure out what the woman was saying, and none of the guards understood her either. One of the other Council Members translated for her, and the fervency of the woman's speech made her yellow-gold skin glow shinier than the diamond tucked against Essien's stomach. She held tight to the woman's hand, giving her the full force of her attention, and vowed that she would learn whatever language this was when she returned to the President's compound and had time to herself again. The list of Alkebulanian languages she had to learn would take the rest of her life to master. The diamond was packed into a padded container and carried by one of the guards who escorted her around that day.

Xhosa State seemed more volatile than any of the other states, except for Hausa State. There was a protest at the transportation center, blocking her engines for hours on the day she arrived. As the procession moved, they quickly noticed how many people were out in the streets, stopping the flow of traffic, forcing the guards to get out and move people with the threat of the end of their rapid fires. The Council House was surrounded by sojas already ten deep. Essien remembered that day, so many years ago, when she had disrupted a protest to protect the President. Standing in that Council House watching the streets fill up, she didn't want to make the same mistake. She turned to one of the guards and said, "Find out who is in charge. Bring me their leader."

It was a demanding gathering of young people who were led in wearing their tribal attire, their faces covered by dark paint and tall, feathered and beaded head coverings. Essien could hear their liberating chants before the doors of the Council Chambers were even opened.

Her Guard were on high alert, visibly worried for her safety, not trusting her decision to let the protest leaders inside. Essien thought of the men and women, the teens, who had come out to protest the President's legislation that would turn his term into a lifetime position. That felt like decades ago. She didn't want to break up the protest now. She wanted to listen to them and hear what they had to say. Even if they spoke against her own lifetime position.

The man they led up to the dais where she was seated was young, barely out of his teens by a year or two, if that. Essien studied him at first, the face hidden under layers of bright paint, the broad shoulders and bare chest, the strong legs.

"What's your name?" she asked. This was a boy who would live and die on behalf of his country. She could see it and sense it on him; the way his jaw clenched, that familiar line reminding her of Gabriel.

"I was given the name Umntwana KaThixo. As a man, I have taken the name Iwe Chineka."

Essien's head tilted, recognizing the name. "You took an Igbo name?"

The boy smiled for the first time. He nodded and said, "It was the only name that truly showed who I had become, who I wanted to be. To save my people, to save these lands, to serve my Queen, I would become God's wrath on earth."

Essien shook her head at the preposterousness, but as ridiculous as he sounded, she believed him. This was a boy who had what it took, who would stand on the principles of protection and service, not the filmy-eyed indolence and corruption of Mansa Musa, however righteous he might have started out. Was this the silent rebellion that her fire had inspired?

So, she spoke honestly to the boy, issuing warnings and reminding him of the expectations, and she could tell he listened. Then she let him be heard, and he had so much to say. But she listened. His voice commanded everyone's attention. The others who had come behind him watched the way he spoke with the open-mouthed awe of devoted followers. He convinced her of his passion with his arm swinging around seeming to encompass all of Alkebulan beyond the room, too. After he was done speaking, Essien promised him everything he wanted, denying him nothing. The fierce pride that crossed his face, the jaw growing even harder as he bared his teeth in a smile of triumph. Without fanfare, the boy bowed, all the way at the waist, his eyes on the ground, and when he rose, Essien realized he had transformed that quickly into a man.

It was Iwe Chineka's agreement that spread the word of her Queendom to the last remaining states the fastest.

The newsreels were rolling, but it didn't matter. She had won over the Tribal Councils in each of the last states and its members would handle spreading the word of their acceptance throughout the villages. Essien knew it would not be easy to gain those final few votes, but from the outside, it was a simple enough process. Meet the people, let them see her and hear her, listen to them, and if that failed, use the magic that Gabriel had poured into her, but only as a last resort. Essien had wanted to avoid using magic, and she'd been successful up until Hausa State.

With a deep sigh, she stepped off the skycraft in Asante State. She was wheels up again in six hours, the vote handled swiftly and painlessly by all the news that preceded her. She didn't have to win people over with her smile or her ears or her promises that she would try her entire life to keep. No, the Council Members of Asante State were won over by what she had already done more than what they hoped she might do for them. Their list of demands was short and aligned with things other states had already requested. The six hours hadn't even been necessary, but Essien had insisted on at least hearing what they wanted.

In Igbo State, there was no one at the transportation center to greet her, not even an attendant. The silence and the lack of a greeting did not bode well for this next to last state. Upon arriving at the Council House, the one she had already seen many times before, the Tribal Council members sneered at her and shouted over her speech at the Council House. Essien had sat up on the dais and listened in horror as they berated her. And she couldn't deny any of it.

"It is you who caused the death of our most esteemed Council Member in all of Igbo history. You who have turned against your people to worship Ekwensu."

Essien tried to keep her face blank, but being accused of evildoing made her recoil within. *It's Gabriel, not me!* she wanted to shout, even knowing that she had no right to defend herself. Or to keep blaming him.

The dinner they held for her after they finished berating her was a disaster. Despite having attendants bring her into the dining room, everyone else arrived much later, and after a stony silent meal, they all left early. She sent messages requesting private meetings with each of them, as a final tactic, the following day, but everyone refused. Essien thought hard about why this state was so difficult, when it should have been the easiest, as both her and Gabriel's hometowns, and also the birthplace of her Nne. It wasn't until the sting of ashes burned her nose and the jagged particles of partially burnt organic matter gouged into her palms as she gripped her hands into fists that she realized why this state might be least favorable to her of all.

Essien sat alone in her room on Capital Island. At first, the Guard had wanted her to stay in the military compound in Igbo State. It wasn't the compound where she had spent her early years as a soja, but the layout and feel were identical. She had questioned that decision, pulled rank, and ultimately had them redirect her to the President's compound. He hadn't been present when she arrived, and she ruminated for longer than she cared to admit over whether he was with that woman she had seen and heard previously or with another one.

For the first time since her complete breakdown, she let it register in her mind how tired she was. There was just one more state after Igbo. She could get through this. She *would* get through this. She had to. Suddenly, as if it only dawned on her then what state she was campaigning in, she thought of visiting her family. Her mother and father still lived in the family compound, as far as she knew. It was just over the bridge to the northeast. She could reach her family's compound in less than three hours of travel if she got a fast driver for the engine. She wondered if at least Nifemi might still live in the state. He had attended university in Igbo State, and she had hoped he would remain close to home when everyone else had traveled so far and wide, their careers taking them away, and their families now keeping them from returning. She wasn't sure about any of the other elder brothers as she had not heard news or word from them in years. Even Femi might have moved on. Essien didn't even know if he had been married or had children. She did not know how many nieces and nephews she had, or if they had started to have children of their own.

Essien looked longingly out the patio window, but she wasn't seeing anything on the other side of the glass. There was so much she had missed. So much life just on the other side of that bridge connecting Capital Island to the mainland. Her family had been just hours away, and she hadn't been allowed to see them. It was too much for her to sit with alone in that moment. Despite the late hour, she contacted Gabriel by mind, and before he had even cracked open that locked door between them, she was asking to see her family.

"*No,*" he said, before she'd even finished asking. The instant wave of sadness and dejection that swept out of her speared right into him. She felt it when it hit him, making his shoulders slump, and his chest cave inward. Feeling her pain hurt him more than just hearing it in her voice had. She felt him sigh and then say, "*You are allowed to visit your family compound only. Go on your way back to the Council House tomorrow. You still need to convince the Tribal Council, and I heard it didn't go well.*"

CHAPTER THIRTY-FIVE

◆

DESPITE GABRIEL'S INITIAL DENIAL, ESSIEN'S RIDE OVER TO the mainland was quick and took less than the three hours she had predicted. From the moment she arrived, she had known the visit with her parents would be sweet and heal whatever had been broken in her. She had walked in through the back gate where she'd instructed the engine to let her off. Two guards had posted up at the back entrance while several others trekked inside the unlocked back gate after her.

The garden was completely gone, turned into flower beds with bright splashes of color and organized patterns that drew her eye in. She followed the granite stone steps up to the back door, now sitting open with a piece of wood. She stepped inside the door, which opened onto a back hallway that led into the kitchen and the front room, passing her old bedroom along the way. She walked through the kitchen and into the front room, and there was her mother sitting next to a beautiful woman with a close-shaved head and the most elegant facial structure Essien had ever seen. She must have stood there gaping for a few seconds because when her Nne finally saw her, she gave out a yell that was both young and old, excited and full of sorrow. Then her mother was up and running toward her with outstretched arms, and she was wrapping Essien up in the tightest hug she'd ever received. Essien let herself be held, and then she was crying, the tears squeezing out of her tightly closed eyes. And then she felt light, warm hands touching her back, her arm, her head where her hair had finally grown out of that harsh copper color and reached past her shoulders in twists, usually held back in a bun. Essien didn't know who that woman was, but the touch of her light hands on her back made Essien cry harder. And her mother held her and rocked her and murmured words in Igbo that Essien could barely translate. It was like a dam was flooded, and she couldn't stop the sobs if she'd tried. She was home, and safe, so she didn't try.

Eventually, Essien heard the slow shuffle of steps up the long hallway leading from her parents' room. She looked up in time to see her Nna's face appear around the corner. He looked so much older, his skin an almost ashen gray. But his eyes, still dark and wide and intense. The woman who had been rubbing her back rushed over to help her nna walk closer. She helped him sit in one of the plush armchairs that circled the rug in the front room. Essien sat next to her father and leaned her head on his shoulder. She closed her eyes, and still, the tears fell. None asked her why she cried. They just patted her hand, her head, her knee, while she cried and didn't even try to hide it.

When she was dry and empty as a bone, Essien finally looked over at the woman who had her hand resting on Essien's knee. Looking full at her, Essien was hit again by how beautiful she was. Her eyes were a dark honey brown, her hair almost bald, but it was her face that really drew. Something about the shape of her mouth combined with those bright eyes, and she was just beautiful. Her mother noticed her staring and finally introduced them.

"Essien, this is Nifemi's wife, Obechi. She arrived with his two daughters just this week to keep me company while Femi is away on business. Her daughters are at the early learning center. Oh, is it too late to go and bring them here?"

So Femi had gotten married and become a father while she had been away. It was almost too much for Essien to process. She asked after the girls, and Obechi promised her that she would bring them to see her the next time she came. They lived just an hour away, still in Igbo State. Essien wondered then about her other brothers and asked for updates. All were fine, and it was she whom they all worried about.

At that moment, a guard rapped on the back door. Essien rushed to open it. She knew they would tell her she had to go, and that the Council House meeting still awaited her. Femi's wife followed her to the back door, away from her Nne and Nna's ears.

"The President came to visit your brother and me," she started calmly.

Essien was instantly angry. "He did what? When?"

She shook her head and grabbed onto both of Essien's hands with her own. "He wanted us to help lure you back to him. He was adamant that he might be able to use us to fox you out of hiding. It didn't work, but he tried."

"I didn't know." Essien rifled through every conversation she'd had with Gabriel since he'd recaptured her. She skipped over the night he'd given her some of his power and traced their interactions all the way up to the last time she'd seen him. "He's never let on to me about it. I didn't even know my brother had gotten married."

274 WIELDERS OF FLOODS & FLAMES

Obechi squeezed her hands. "I love your brother. And through that love, I also love you, and all of his family. I will do anything I can to help you. Anything. Just ask."

Essien was so tempted. How connected was this woman? She was taller than Essien, but not by much. Femi likely dwarfed her, too. She couldn't put Femi's family in danger. Not when he had two daughters, little girls she might never get to meet, who would always wonder about the mysterious nwanne nne, the only aunt whom they would never get to see. Essien took in a deep breath and nodded, accepting what this woman now was to her, but knowing that she could never draw on that help. She wouldn't for Femi's sake, for her parents' sake. They deserved a nwunye nwa, a son's wife who would become like their daughter. To replace her. Because the rap of the guards' knuckles against the door again reminded her that she couldn't stay.

Obechi opened her mouth to say more, but Essien squeezed her fingers where they were still holding hands.

"Thank you for loving my brother and my family. I hope I can repay your kindnesses to them one day." She felt a sting in her nose, and she knew it was more tears threatening to fall. She entered the front room one last time, to bid her parents goodbye. Her father was stoic, but her mother's face crumpled, and she held on to Essien for a long time, even as the guard rapped on the door loudly.

ESSIEN KEPT THINKING ABOUT OBECHI'S WORDS AND THE knowledge she'd shared about Gabriel attempting to take them as hostages to bribe her with. She kept turning those thoughts over and over in her mind as the engine rumbled through the streets north to Lagos. Essien would have liked to stay the night in her old bedroom and perhaps venture to the forest that night, to commune with akukoifo who had not yet returned to her the way they had as a child. It would have been even better if she could have gone into the waters to see the Mothers again, but she wasn't ready to see anymore visions of her future, not just yet.

When Essien met with the Igbo Military and Tribal Councils again, the hostilities had only grown. And it was her own fault. She knew it before they hurled even more accusations at her. Shouted in accents that reminded her of her own family, they called her names that burned because they were true. Staring down, Essien still could not offer a single denial of any of the statements made against her. Yes, she had burned and looted across Alkebulan with the rebels. Yes, she had assassinated an Igbo Council Member without trial or sentencing. Yes, she had magic that was ultimately untamed, threatening to erupt at any moment she was angry. Besides the loud voices of the Military Council members, the Tribal Council members levied their own attacks. And she had to sit there and take it. She was almost ready to accept that the legislation wouldn't be approved in this state either, when she smelled Gabriel.

Her head whipped around, looking for him. Everybody else was still intently focused on the man who stood at the voice projector, shouting what others had already said many times before: She was evil made into female flesh; she was Ekwensu, the source of all evil, and she would never sit on a throne in Alkebulan. Their voices were drowned out by the fact that her skin suddenly flushed with sweat, and she knew that her magic had creaked open and was about to erupt all over them.

Essien didn't know how she knew Gabriel was about to use her power for his own, maybe it was that he'd heard every word she'd said and listened to, but he'd also heard her thoughts. And he could feel what she was feeling, too. She felt defeated because if this state didn't approve the legislation, all of her work, all of her sacrifice, would have been with no results. She felt resigned, like she had no right to challenge what her own statesmen were saying. Like their accusations were as good as the trial that had not been a trial to pronounce her guilty of all the crimes she had racked up. She wasn't even sure she wanted to fight back. But Gabriel did. Oh, how he did, as he reached into her, not with hands but with that part of him that was always wanting to merge with that part inside of her.

With Gabriel steering the magic, she was forced to use her power not to burn or bleed, but to possess and overpower. One moment, the room was outright hostile, the people only moments from carrying her out bodily. The next, she was lashing them all on leashes like the one Gabriel had so resolvedly snapped on her. She poured a thin stream of that power that was a conduit of Gabriel's power into all of them, feeling it coiling like a hook into the deepest parts of their psyches. She could feel them all, knew them all by name, could call them at any time now, whenever she wanted to.

When she was done, when Gabriel was finished with them, one by one, they each signed the voting rolls, every Military and Tribal Council member, their eyes a shining blackness full of nothing but her face and the sound of her name. She left Igbo State that same day, more powerful than she had

276 WIELDERS OF FLOODS & FLAMES

been when she arrived. The power thrummed in her body making her feel like she might never sleep again. Like she'd never lose another battle again. She felt invincible, and she knew it was Gabriel's power talking. The weight of all he was settled more fully into her, and it made her feel heady and unstable around the edges of her vision. It would take some getting used to. Being able to tame the untamable. Essien worried for a moment if enjoying how it felt for him to use her made her just as bad as the Council Members had said she was.

After Igbo State, she was down to the last state. Even though she'd been out of it for weeks at a time, she knew from its reputation that Gabriel had saved Amhara State for absolute last. She remembered the state from being a child, but the reports she had been getting so far were not good. Amhara State was expected to be the most hostile of all. And Igbo State was a close contender.

There were rumors from when Essien had been a soja that the north was an entry point for foreign weapons and foreign terrorists backing the homegrown rebels. They had never been able to prove which state might be colluding with outside interests beyond an abnormal number of shipments and parcels sent in and out from international companies, all of which might be legit, and a mysterious cache of illegal weapons found in an abandoned rebel hideout years ago. No more of those weapons had been found since, but Essien recalled that oddly designed weapon she'd seen in the rebel camp in Bantu State. It hadn't looked like any weapon she'd seen manufactured here, and she knew them all. She'd have to get to the bottom of that illegal weapon now, or at least be sure Gabriel had someone on it. A Queen might not be tasked with such menial work anymore, but it still needed doing.

Essien remembered finding that cache of weapons again, when she was still a brand-new soja, and wondered whatever became of it. She'd been promoted to the Guard soon after and had not been given any updates on the incident. She had heard nothing else about foreign terrorists lately. She couldn't remember ever seeing any foreigners during her own stint with the rebels she had been rescued by. Then she stilled. That night in Hausa State. The language the holy men had been yelling. She hadn't recognized it because it wasn't a language native to Alkebulan. That meant it was a foreign language. Gabriel hadn't told her anything more about what had happened that night because she had asked him not to, had prevented him even broaching the subject with her. She knew she'd have to ask him for that information now, to see if this was a clue that tied to a lot of other strings. For now, she hoped her visit to Amhara State would not be mired by anything as terrible as what happened in Hausa.

Her welcome at the transformation center in Amhara was chaotic but peaceful. The people clamored to meet her, pouring out and stopping up the streets, even following in her procession whenever she rode in her engine toward the cities and villages. It was from there that she beheld for the first time in her life the Al-Qarawiyyin Library. The tan sandstone buildings surrounded by stone gates sprawled out over several stadia worth of land. She'd held her breath as she walked through the entrance held up on both sides by tall pillars with brown metal spikes driven through them. The librarian here was a tall, thin man with reddish-brown skin wearing dusky dark blue robes that covered everything but his eyes. Essien had never seen a man so fully covered, only ever women in the northern states. He stared at her with eyes like chips of the sky right before it rains. Like all librarians she had met on this trip, he spoke quietly in a near whisper. Essien let him lead her through the hallways into rooms filled to the top of the ceiling with books, large leather-bound ones that you needed a podium to flip and read and small books handwritten in hasty, desperate scrawls. So many texts— and that wasn't all. The librarian, Haile, showed her ancient texts written in scripts that less than a hundred people could still translate. Essien was in awe as he allowed her to touch one fingertip to a page of the oldest scrolls in the world, the pages feeling like precious silk against her fingers.

After leaving the library, she made her way down to the riverbank. As all riverbanks usually were, it was bustling and crawling with people from all over the city and the state; Essien even spotted other foreigners. At the edge of the river, a black stone building with lapis lazuli embedded into a mosaic pattern around the door and on the tiled floor leading inside loomed up over Lalibela, the holy city, it was once called. The temple acolytes beckoned to her from inside. The women wore shimmering pale shift dresses that might have been white or silver. Their feet were bare, and their heads were shaved smooth.

Essien walked closer. She glanced back at the Guard.

"We cannot enter the temple with you," one said. Essien stepped inside the cool, dark interior of the temple, and all sound was washed away. The clear blue tiles continued along the floor and walls leading up to a stone pool filled with ice-blue water. More of those blue tiles lined the bottom of the pool. There was a trail of the tiles leading around the edge of the pool and into a hallway that led deeper into the building. The acolytes again beckoned to her as they backed slowly into the pool of water. She stared down at her staple tunic top and pants, the sandals open and showing her toes.

"Come in and be washed by the Mothers," one, or all of them, whispered. She stepped into the water fully clothed. One of the acolytes came to her with a gold chalice. They dipped it into the water and offered it to her. Essien held the glass underneath their hands as she took a sip and swallowed. The water tasted clean and fresh. The acolyte then poured the water over Essien's head. They did it two more times. After the third time, the acolyte made a symbol in the air with a finger emblazoned with flames. It looked like an infinity loop and almost seemed to stain the air.

Essien was so calm; she had been since she'd walked into this temple. She hadn't known there were worshippers of the Mother this far north. It was a pleasant surprise, and even more reason for Essien to one day return when she'd finally gained her freedom. A small prick of despair tried to rear its head, but the light and joy she'd felt, especially after receiving a water and fire blessing from the guardians of the Temple of the Mothers...there was no way she would submit to that hopeless state. There was much she could do before she'd succumb ever again.

At the Council House, a white stone building built into the base of a mountain, the Council Members fell all over themselves to invite her to have dinner with their families and attend their local meetings. She knew she had just one day in the state, so she'd smiled and thanked them for the generous invites, promising to return once she was crowned. They offered her young men as her attendants, and despite the muscles inflating their limbs, she turned down the offer with a silent head shake.

The rest of the Tribal Council and Military Council of Amhara State heard what she had done in the states before. Then they heard about the blessing she had received at the Temple of the Mothers, about how two twin pillars of fire and water had intertwined over her head after the blessing was said. Each and every one of them cast their votes without incident. For the third time, every single one of the Council Members voted to approve the QUEEN Act.

Out in the streets after the vote, Essien decided that she wanted to visit the pyramids before they forced her to leave. The Guard did not deter her as she instructed the engine where to take her. She arrived to find tourists swarming everywhere, families with children from all over the continent. She made her way to the foot of the pyramids, doing her best to ignore how crowded it was around her. People jostled the Guard, not on purpose; there were just so many of them. She wore her ordinary clothes, hoping it would not draw attention. The guards standing around her were obvious, but she ignored them, too.

She was standing at the foot of one of the largest pyramids, staring up at the massive structure, when she felt the earth beneath her feet shift. She looked down, and then up and around. The guards she could see were several paces away and not facing toward her. Suddenly, without sound or warning, figures seemed to materialize from the very sand around her, bursting up from hidden tunnels that collapsed as they broke the surface. Startled into a terrified panic, Essien didn't think twice or look back at her Guard for protection. Within seconds, the flames had blazed up almost taller than the pyramid behind her, the tongues licking around the peak of the great hulking creation.

Someone called her name, but it only made her burn hotter, faster, consuming more. The pyramid couldn't burn, but her flames tried, scaling up the sides all the way to that pointed summit. Then Essien remembered where she was, that there were tourists everywhere, that they couldn't withstand her fire because they were only human.

Slowly, she pulled the flames back, the heat and burning thirst receded, and she was alone, everything singed to black around her, the bodies of small children disintegrating in the ashes. There were not even guards left to escort her safely out of the area. Essien fell to her knees, her brain refusing to catch up to her reflex reaction, while her eyes had already begun to leak. She looked around her at the destruction she had caused because she had been startled, because she still did not have proper training, because there was a growing threat that they still needed to eliminate. She wept, her sobs echoing out into an empty stretch of land where the crowds had before teemed.

News of the second failed assassination spread, and because she had been so public and far away from Gabriel, there was no way to hide what she'd done. The families of the murdered came on the news not to denounce her or demand retribution but to berate the assassins and their family members, too. They asked for her forgiveness and to spare them of her wrath.

She was unharmed. The guards who arrived to reinforce her now non-existent protection were solemn but not deterred. If it bothered them that her wanton power was responsible for killing her last squad, it did not show in how they responded. She thought it was unusual that she was not taken directly to the transportation center and flown back to Igbo State. The next morning after the incident, she received a message from a guard that she would be featured on a news report, without Gabriel, to broadcast the passing of the QUEEN Act and the announcement of a formal crowning ceremony in half a year's time. Essien was told that night that she would be flying back to Capital Island.

Her campaigning was over. She had won. As she stared at the terrain rushing by underneath the flying skycraft, Essien felt an immense loss of something just outside the grasp of her exhausted understanding. She slept the rest of the flight.

PART III

RISE

CHAPTER THIRTY-SIX

◆

"I FINISHED WHAT YOU WANTED DONE, GABRIEL, AND NOW I have something I want to do. Put me to work as Queen. I already know where I want to go. I have a list of states...and even countries. Assign me a squad, and I will be gone tomorrow. Doing what my position as Queen provides."

"No, Essien, that will not be necessary. Your time to work will come soon, but it is not yet."

"When then? How much longer will I be cooped up here?"

"As you well know, your ascension ceremony needs to be planned. It will be the event of the millennia. It will take several months of the year to plan it all. I'd think that would be more of an interest for you at this time."

"You do know that you've kidnapped me, and I'm being held hostage, right? That I am being kept here against my will despite holding the highest position in all this land? Let's not forget that rather significant detail." She rolled her eyes and pushed food onto her fork knowing she wouldn't take another bite.

Gabriel eyed her over his wine glass, and then he sipped for a long draught. She had been home from her tour for just five days and already she remembered that he was an alcoholic. He drank palm wine with every meal, even breakfast, and he ended the night with two short glasses of amber elixir, a special blend he had the chefs prepare exclusively for him, or imported rum. It made her wonder about him in ways she never had as a soja. Sojas didn't care if their President drank too much.

"I want you here, Essien. The other option was a prison cell. Is that where you would prefer to be? Surely not before you've been crowned." He smiled and went back to sipping his drink.

"At least in prison I'd know I was rotting in misery. Here, you expect me to thank you for the privilege of being imprisoned."

"You will not rot, Essien. Neither here nor there nor anywhere else."

"I meant that metaphorically."

"And I meant it literally. You will never rot, suffer illness, or die."

She knew that his words were serious and of grave importance to her, but she was bored and lonely in the massive compound she wasn't allowed to roam, and she needed something to do. She had hoped that it would be actually reigning and implementing all those promises she had made, realizing her own dreams for the country, too. Whatever she'd given up to him to be here, there was truly nothing she could do about it. She might not rot, but her mind would surely feel like it.

"As a soja, you had me in a demanding job, working seventy hours or more every week, and now you want me to sit around and do nothing?"

"I didn't think of that."

"Of course you didn't. You just wanted me here, at any cost, and now that I'm here, your wishes have been met, so now you think it's done; your desire is fulfilled, I did what you asked, and there's nothing left to do. Wrong. I'm going to work Gabriel. I am going to actually be Queen."

"You will. But not until your official ceremony. In the meantime, you can rejoin my Guard. It's no longer one of your official job definitions, but if you insist..."

"I told you that I didn't want that job anymore."

"Part of my international security team? I always need more sets of eyes when I travel overseas. You'd make the perfect distraction."

"No. I don't want to do anything that involves you or your body."

Gabriel smirked. "You can go back to being a soja then.... Would you enjoy such a demotion? All those new compounds you've got being built, I bet they could add in a floor just for you, if you ask nicely."

Essien sighed, all the air in her lungs running out in a near defeated slump.

He went on, "What about my maid? There are parts of this compound that never get cleaned even with all those well-paid attendants around."

Essien's eyebrows met in the middle of her forehead, the frown deepening even as she stared at him silently. "Gabriel."

"Perhaps...my wife then? I can make it a more formal engagement if you'd prefer?"

"NO!"

Gabriel stared at her face for a second, letting her know that there were words he wanted to give her that she would not like, and neither would he. He set down his napkin and pushed his plate away. "Then you will do nothing."

"I am going to find something to do on my own, that doesn't include your presidency or you." She stood up and left the room, heading up the first of many corridors that would lead her to her own floor and her own set of rooms, the same set of rooms she'd occupied when she was part of his Guard. He followed her to her space without moving. He could see her and feel her undressing from a simple sheer dress into cotton drawstring slacks and a light tunic. The running shoes she put on were old and worn and fit her perfectly. She knew he was in her head as she walked out the front door of the compound, and there was nothing she could do about it. The crunch of rocks behind her let her know the guards were following her. She didn't look back to see how many.

She set off on a jog through the gates that surrounded the compound. The gravel path led down to a larger dirt trail running alongside the paved road and straight into a tall stand of thick-trunked trees. She thought Gabriel might cut himself off from her when she started to run, but he didn't. He stayed right there in her head, thrumming in her body, and she found she could run faster. She wanted to see how far she could run. She didn't care if she made it out the other end. She let him hear that thought loud in her head and then pushed herself to eat up more ground with every stride.

She was running down the path and didn't know that it would take her around the back of the compound, down to a long, sloping lane. The country dirt road descended down and down, and she ran at a faster than normal pace. At the end of that road, she saw nothing but green and more green, darker green forest trees far off. She ran toward those trees.

The green umbrella of tree branches and shiny leaves covered a well-worn track that ran along stretches of open air and brisk wind. There was an orchard on one side of the path. The mingled smells of mangoes, peaches, coconuts, and lemons breezed out to her as she ran past. She came to the cool oasis of a beautiful garden filled with white blossoms and light green vines with tiny red blossoms covering trees that grew taller than nearby bushes that had bright orange and hot pink blooms. Here, she slowed down only enough to scent the air deeply, enjoying the sweet smell of living flowers and sunbaked earth.

The trail ran suddenly out of the lush greenery into the bright harsh sun and scorched grass. She passed a creek with just a trickle of water running alongside what had become a wider lane covered with smooth gray rock. She ran faster. There were more orchards and a small village of small compounds with hens roaming freely through the tall grasses and some goats drinking from a pond. She didn't know she would start to feel so quaint and majestic, running through that village and seeing into the windows and knowing there were other people living this close. Gabriel couldn't be what she thought he was if he chose to live near such simple peace and purity.

Her run took her all the way through the farming village, out to the edge where the compounds started to grow larger and were spaced further apart in between more trees and dense forests, and occasionally, a gurgle of creek water. She could have gone further, all the way out to the coast, but at some point, she turned around and took the path back to where she started. She saw faces peeking out at her, little dark brown children hiding behind fence posts and trees.

When she returned to the path that led uphill to the front of the compound, she stopped. The compound stood up on the mountaintop like a chunk of stone, secure and settled deep. She turned around and ran back down the mountainside again. In some places, the descent was so gradual, she didn't even feel like she was running downhill.

Exhausted after several laps back and forth, she stopped in the oasis of green and sat in a patch of grass at the base of a tree. Golden light washed down like the taste of honey made into slow, thick brightness. Her breathing evened out, her skin cooled, and her anger calmed. The situation she was in felt awful and limiting, but she'd find a way. She would not let it consume her completely. She could find good moments in it all. She could figure out a way to keep parts of herself for herself. Gabriel did not have the last say, not in her head nor in her heart. Essien felt that ultimately, she would win against him; she would be free of him. She just had to be patient and bide her time.

The sky was already a dark purple with streaks of silvery pink when she returned after her final lap. There had been squares of light off in the distance of the trees, so she knew there were other compounds out there and even more people than she'd seen.

She began her climb back uphill to the compound's gates. She pushed against her own exertion and that feeling of needing to vomit in the grass. She sucked in air, and made it to the top of the mountain. The ground leveled out, and she kept jogging, going around in circles until she could slow down and take deep breaths. At last, Essien realized Gabriel had gone from her head, and the power inside her was floating, still, and placid.

GABRIEL'S ATTENTION WAS ON HER THE MINUTE SHE WALKED into the dining hall. He was alone, as usual. Essien had not stopped to think about the Guard that she knew was in the compound but always also eerily absent. They were almost as invisible as the attendants when they wanted to be. Posted outside whatever room the President occupied, even here inside the compound. She had grown accustomed to these private meals with the President years ago, and now that he had returned to the compound, so had they. She wondered if she'd be allowed to take her evening meals alone now that they were both in the compound again.

Before she could ask, Gabriel was saying carefully, "We received a regretful message for you while you were out."

Essien's head reared up at the sound of his voice. It felt like he was holding back, keeping himself in check. There was something he didn't want to tell her, but he was obligated to anyway. She looked at his face, and he was closed off, not looking directly at her. There were words underneath his words, and she could just barely hear them without his stopping her. She took a deep breath and knew already what the message contained.

"Which one of them?"

"Your Nna."

Essien squeezed her eyes closed in an attempt to stop the instant spring of tears. The sadness she should feel about a parent's death welled up in her suddenly, as if she'd been pushing it away, holding it off, and the first wave of it had burst through anyway. She put her head down on the table, and the tears pooled in between her fingers. It was Nna. She had saved him once; perhaps if she hadn't been here, she could have saved him again. A high keening sound came out with her silent wails, and she knew she had to stop crying. It felt wrong somehow for her to cry in front of the President. She was so quick to cry now, and she wondered if it had something to do with Gabriel binding her to him. She didn't remember crying this often during her years in the military or even as a teenager. Maybe she'd been an emotional child, but weren't they all? Of course, she was allowed these tears for her father. She would cry these and more.

She spoke with her eyes closed and covered. "Will I be allowed to visit my village during the mourning period?"

Gabriel didn't say anything at first. With the binding had come some interesting side effects that she could learn to exploit if she was smart. And capable of being as manipulative as she knew he was. Knowing what he was thinking or feeling, the tone underneath his words saying more than he meant to reveal, even remembering what he had experienced before she'd even known he existed. The closeness worked both ways, and she wondered what he might be picking up from her in that moment.

A hand dropped down onto her shoulder. A big hand that felt gritty and smooth at the same time. Gabriel squeezed her shoulder once, twice, three times, and then he rubbed a circle across her back. The tears instantly dried up, and she tried to stretch for them by wondering how her father had died. No more wetness would fall. Disturbed but relieved, Essien sat up, and Gabriel's hand dropped away.

"Even though I know I should be feeling sad after such devastating news, I still...thank you." She hoped he knew what she was thanking him for. There was still so much she wanted from him, so much she knew he wouldn't want to give. But this small comfort, taking away some of her sadness, made up for some of their past together. She filled her lungs with air and pushed through her hesitance.

"Will you give me permission to attend my father's mourning?" she asked again.

That insight into his head let her see that he wanted to say no. Every part of him wanted so badly to deny her the right of attendance, which all military personnel had regardless of rank.

He stared into her tear-streaked face, her eyes red and watery, her lip trembling with the strength she was trying to maintain. He made himself step back from his emotions, a task that had become harder and harder where Essien was concerned. He was determined to get what he wanted, and it only occurred to him at times like these that she was a separate person, and he must treat her as such.

She was seeing this clearly and this far into his head, so there was no barrier to keep him from seeing into hers. She would try to escape. Even if she knew it would be fruitless, she had to still at least try. He stared at her face, the hope peeking through despite the grief eating at her.

"You may go," he finally said, "but I shall go with you."

She figured as much. There was no space in her to be worried about how her brothers would receive him or how her mother might react. She cared only that she would get to see her family, maybe for the last time.

"When can we depart?"

Gabriel stared down at his plate and considered her question. He could clear his schedule with ease. There were only a few meetings coming up over the next week. He had another month before his own countryside tour began and the next round of local appointment selections. His time was his to spare or save. He looked up at her and still felt a callousness where she was concerned. She would try to escape him again, and she would be unsuccessful, that part he also knew. Still, it bothered him greatly that escape was her first thought.

"I'll have a skycraft prepared for our departure tonight. How long are the mourning customs in your family's village?"

Essien had never attended a mourning before. Her grandparents had died before she was born. Her mother's sisters were all young, healthy, and vibrant. Her father was an only child. People in the village had died, and she had seen their family members wearing the customary white silk to show their grief. She had been considerate when it was closer neighbors, not shouting too loudly outside and dropping her eyes when they passed on the streets. But she had not kept track of how time had passed. One of the elderly women in her village had lost her only son and wore her white silks for years afterward.

Essien stood. "Some people mourn for the rest of their lives..." she answered. "I'll need mourning attire." The tears came again, overwhelming that artificial peace he'd given her, and she turned away, so that Gabriel wouldn't see them falling, even though he could feel the sorrow spilling into and out of her without seeing her face. It was a sticky, grasping emotion that covered everything in sight with pulsing points of pain and hopelessness.

Essien thought perhaps he would close their link, but it remained open wide. As she packed, she began to feel lighter, optimistic even. With a thought, she knew that Gabriel was siphoning off her sadness, like sipping hot tea. She tried to feel around for it, but the pressing weight of grief wasn't there. She found this was the first benefit of their bonding that helped her rather than him. If he hadn't bonded her without her consent, she'd have felt more gratitude.

CHAPTER THIRTY-SEVEN

◆

HER MOTHER LOOKED BEAUTIFUL. HER DARK SKIN WAS SHINY and smooth. Her hair, a black cloud around her high-cheek-boned face. She looked radiant.

"Your father is free of suffering," she whispered to Essien as they hugged for a long time. "He suffered so much in his final weeks. But he's done now. He finished. He is with the Mothers now."

Essien nodded with her face pressed into her Nne's soft, sweet-smelling neck. She never wanted to let go. She forgot about Gabriel standing so closely behind her. She cared only for the woman in her arms. The woman who had birthed her, swaddled her, fed her, taught her to walk, helped her learn to read and write, walked her through her development into womanhood. The woman who had healed her countless hurts even more often than she was the cause of them. Essien regretted ever joining the military and going away from her. She'd have given every ounce of her blood to return to her parents' farm and live out her days as a farmer's daughter. It would be paradise compared to what she had fallen into.

Her mother released her, and she drew back slowly, reluctantly. Then there were her brothers, crowding around and wanting to hug her, too. Idara was slight compared to his younger brothers, and his smile showed pink gums and wide teeth. Malachum was big and burly with his hair in thin locks. Manai kissed her gently on the forehead and both cheeks. Chukwu was the shortest and chubbiest, but still taller than Essien by two heads. Nifemi, always Femi to Essien, was serious and stern, not even the hint of a smile on his face.

Gabriel shook hands with each of the brothers. Essien noticed that there was a reluctance in Femi to take the President's hand, but when he noticed her eyes on him, he eventually did. Then Gabriel took the hands of Essien's mother and kissed them. Her mother had small tear droplets hovering in the corners of her eyes.

"Ara Ezinulo. I am sorry that you have suffered a loss. Is there anything you need for your comforts?'

Nne shook her head but tightened her grip on Gabriel's hands. "Ser, might you release my daughter from her service? I am to be moved from this home to Iroquois Nation to live in a home that my sons have prepared for me there. If my daughter were with me, I would be able to stay here with her care."

Gabriel kneeled on both knees, taking her hands more firmly in his own. He lowered his voice and whispered to her. Essien didn't hear what he said, though she was standing the closest to him. She could have linked with him easily, but something in her didn't want to do something so intimate and foreign in front of her family. She watched Gabriel's back and the side of her mother's face. She saw a look spread over her mother's face that was a mixture of happiness and relief.

Her mother was weeping and shouting and throwing her arms around the President's neck. As Essien watched the momentous eruption of her mother's happiness in the midst of her sadness, Essien only had to look at the back of Gabriel's head to know what he had told her.

He had told her of his pending marriage to her only daughter. And that he would be paying dowry to marry Essien; more than the amount normally required for a man of his stature and a woman from her village. With that marriage would come health attendants to help her remain in her home. The ones her Nna had needed, but which her mother had never let enter their home. She had cared for her husband and now she would be taken care of by others. All of this in spite of the fact that her daughter was to be elevated to a marriage that she had not agreed to.

Essien's hands clenched into fists, but she did her best to keep herself quiet and still. It wouldn't be good to have anyone in that room see her melt down even the slightest.

Her mother was rocking back and forth in the chair where she had been positioned amid cushions and colorful throws. She was holding Gabriel's hands in hers. She didn't smile, but there were no teardrops in her eyes anymore. She stared at the President's face as he spelled out his lies and convinced her mother that he meant well, that Essien would be safe with him, and Essien could see him asking whether he had her permission. Her mother gave it—easily, willingly, feeling blessed that he had asked her first and not the brothers.

Essien glanced at all five of her brothers spread out around the room. Femi was the closest to her. He didn't know yet for certain; he hadn't heard what the President said to their mother, but Essien felt that Femi might have a good idea as to the gist of the conversation. She had been avoiding looking at him because of what those eyes held. Femi knew what Gabriel was, in his own way, without knowing all or the why of it. His stare was a warning, and Essien had already moved beyond being warned.

Gabriel stood up and finally faced her brothers.

"Well, would it be alright if I excused us for the evening? I know the last rites will be performed tomorrow evening. There is a lot to plan for the future. That's if Essien would like to announce?" Gabriel still held the grin on his face, and it looked oily and slimy as eel skin. She looked at each of her brothers in turn and then back at Gabriel—her mother still holding on to one of his hands with both of hers.

And so Essien announced, "The Military and the Tribal Councils of Alkebulan have called me to another role. A higher one. One that I didn't expect, honestly wouldn't have asked for, but...perhaps I should have known it. They want me to ascend to the position of reigning, not just serving. I started off as a soja, but that is not all I will remain. Gabriel will still be in the role of President, but I...I have been promoted to Queen."

Gabriel's own face was even more shocked than any of her brothers. He eyed her face, the hidden message in her words clear only to him. He had thought he would use her mother and the offer of a dowry to manipulate her into saying yes to his proposal when he already knew how she felt. Oh, Essien had other plans than that, and they didn't include allowing him to take any of her family as hostages. Not if she could stop him. And if that look on his face was any guess, she had a lot more power than she'd realized before going on her campaign. He might control her more completely than one person had the right to control another person, but there was room to wiggle. And Essien was determined to make even more room for herself. She managed to smile at Gabriel while her brothers gaped and her mother beamed, the glance she gave him across the room secretive and clearly hiding something.

CHAPTER THIRTY-EIGHT

◆

"YOU LOOK MAGNIFICENT, ESSIEN," THE PRESIDENT GREETED her from the far end of the table. "Sit down please." Her eyes had found him as soon as she entered the dining hall. He always sat in the same spot on the same end.

She took her seat, the one he'd pointed out for her, catty-corner to his own, within touching distance, if he felt so inclined. "Well, I'm glad I don't look how I feel because I feel lower than low."

"Even on your worst day, you look beautiful, Essien."

"Then today is one day beyond worst."

"We'll have dinner. Surely, you'll feel better after eating."

She made a fuss about putting the napkin in her lap because the frosted gray uwe she wore happened to be silk and looked the least expensive of all the uwes in the closet of her room.

She'd woken the day after returning from her mother's house to all of her uniforms and boots replaced with flimsy dresses that she hated—all of them hitting her just above the knee—a few thicker tunics that hit her just below the knee, and sandals in a rainbow of colors. Her running shoes were still there with a new pair next to them. She'd been dismayed to see the dresses and heartbroken that her uniforms were gone, but she'd slipped into the least offensive uwe and vowed to say nothing about them. She'd have preferred the uniform still.

She sipped from the water that was already placed at her seat and sucked on the ice that floated into her mouth. She leaned over to touch the white flower petals in the center arrangement, and yes, they were in fact real, satiny and delicate against her fingertips. She finally looked at the President, allowed herself to meet his eyes because she knew that they would be on her even if she never met them once this night.

"How do you feel now?" He smiled at her, and she wanted to smile back. She frowned instead and shook her head. "Not better? What would make you feel better?"

She looked at him, and the thoughts inside her head played across the blankness of her face before she said, "I would be asking for something that you are not eager nor ready to give."

"Try me."

"I want to leave. Leaving here, leaving you, would make me feel better. Barring that, I want you to let me start my work as Queen, before the crowning."

"I cannot do that."

"I said that you wouldn't."

"You won't even try to let yourself—"

"Be overtaken by whatever hold you have on me? No, Gabriel, I will not be okay with you doing that to me! It's like you've taken possession of me or something else equally bad that I have not agreed to!" She disintegrated from rational words into sob-choked statements that hit her out of nowhere. She tried to wipe her face with the other hand but missed most of the tears. This is exactly what she hadn't wanted to do, break down in front of him, loud enough for anyone passing by to hear. She used the napkin in her lap to cover her face until she could control herself better than this.

"But you did agree, Essien," his tone was placating. "We keep rehashing this, but you have to accept that this is what you were signing up for."

She wiped harshly at her cheeks, angry at the tears and herself, too. "I didn't realize. Nobody told me that I'd have to decide between having a life and being a soja. And when you offered me the chance to join the Uzo Nchedo, I didn't have a choice at all."

Gabriel's eyes narrowed. "You had a choice."

"When? When I was standing trial for murder? You never asked me. You told me. It was never an option. You don't give options, Gabriel."

He had his required short glass of dark honey-colored liquid with chunks of ice floating at the surface. He sipped and said nothing.

She wasn't done. It was like the tears had opened the floodgates once again, and she was letting it out. "You never keep your promises. You always go back on your word. Your word means nothing to me. I can't trust anything you say. I don't trust you." When she stopped, she was out of breath and fuming. She thought about getting up and storming off, but then she might not have anyone deliver the evening meal.

Gabriel stared at her while she dried the remaining tears on her napkin. She went back to avoiding looking at him.

"I see," was all he said. The food came in after she'd gotten it all out. Her tears were wet streaks on the cream-colored napkins.

She ate a few bites of what was placed before her through tears on the tips of her eyelashes and dripping over her lips. The salt of her tears mixed with the stew, and she felt miserable enough to not be able to finish, the spoon dropping loudly into her full bowl. Gabriel looked up at her, but she didn't look at him. She felt his eyes touching all over her, but she refused to meet them.

She waited until he was done eating and had put his own napkin on top of his empty bowl. She stood up, turned her back on him, and walked out of the dining room, back down the hallway and up to her room. Surprisingly, he let her go. She did not reappear until dinner the next day.

SEVERAL DAYS PASSED IN THE SAME WAY. TIME FELT LIKE IT HAD paused and was waiting for them to decide whether it would proceed as planned. Or if one of them was about to twist a kink into the tubes. Essien watched Gabriel's face as he sat next to her and felt nothing but contentment coming from him. He was content, with himself, with her, with everything that was happening. And she? She was too busy hiding what she truly felt to actually feel it. She knew she wanted to ruin that contentment she saw all over him. He didn't get to feel good about himself while she felt trapped. All those promises she'd made were urgent, and they needed to be started right away. Especially providing schools for all of Alkebulan's children. Once she told him, there was no way he would deny or make her go back on her promises. Once she told him, he might take up the cause and champion it himself. That is, if he wasn't so distracted by his scheming for empire. She just had to figure out the best way to tell him—and the best time. Timing was everything with Gabriel. If she caught him on a day when he wanted to be supportive and sympathetic, he'd of course be eager to help her. But, if it was a day that he wanted to be cruel, then no amount of begging would make him agree to anything she requested. As she sat across from him on the covered patio off the back of the compound, she eyed his face, his body, the way his arms hung down casually and relaxed, the way his thighs flexed as he pushed himself on the swinging chair with one foot. His eyes trained on her face with a slight gleam.

As she caught him staring back at her, he said, "I am set to meet political acquaintances in Obum-Otu for meetings, dinner and cocktails, other things you probably don't care about anymore. You may accompany me for the day trip into the city, though, if you'd like. After my meetings, I can accompany you anywhere in the city that you wish, even at a distance if that would suit you more. It is up to you."

"Is it?" That was her reply, staring down at her own toe where she slowly pushed herself back and forth in the swinging chair on the other side of the patio closer to the wood railing that wrapped around the patio on three sides. The chairs sat two each, but she had sat across instead of beside him. Gabriel had ordered her to come and sit with him outside after dinner instead of retreating to her floor where she stayed permanently when she wasn't down in the mgbati, out for a run, or having the evening meal. So, she had no illusions about whether she'd get to choose not to go into Obum-Otu, a city over the bridge in Igbo State. The wooden swinging chair creaked and groaned as she pushed herself lazily with one toe and didn't look at him.

"I only thought that you might want to get out of this mansion, as you called it. The city is quaint, just across the bridge, east of Lagos, and it won't be so busy on a weekday. Less tourists, you know?"

"Obum-Otu is always busy, sunup to sundown, and then even after the sun goes down, it is still busy. It's almost worse than Lagos." She kept scanning her eyes up and down the grooves and curves of the pillars that held up the ceiling of the patio above them.

"I had this compound built for myself, you know. I am its first owner. No other President has lived here except me. The Presidential Palace in Lagos was too outdated. And small. It wouldn't have fit a fourth of my Guard."

She had known that about the first Presidential Palace, or rather, she had learned it since arriving here, but she said nothing, moving her eyes to glance out over the view of the miniature village nestled in the sides of the mountains below and the trees layered on top of each other in shades of verdant greens. She listened to the wind singing through the leaves and wished she could feel the sun pressing onto her skin. It was a cloudy day, and she thought for sure that it would rain.

Gabriel sighed, "It's magnificent, isn't it? Living on Capital Island? Beautiful up here. I could never live in the city. I like to see it and visit occasionally, but I prefer wide-open spaces, high-up places, towers."

Essien stopped looking out at the horizon that as far out as she could see was land and water mixed together in the gravity-sucking hold of the dropping sun.

"Will you accompany me tonight, Essien?"

"No. I'd rather not."

"Pity, I thought you might have said yes. We shall go to the city anyway, and you shall be with me wherever I go while I am there. We'll have guards, of course. You'll meet my political allies, and then we'll make rounds through the city with my arm around your waist."

She stared at him now, too outdone and yet resigned that she didn't even protest. She stared at his face and thought very hard about not thinking what she really wanted to think, which was that he was retribution sent to torment her for killing all those people and only being sorry about some of them.

She tried not to think then the thought that wanted to taint her mind while she knew he was listening. If he kept the door between their minds open, he would hear her every thought. There was urging from him, gentle yet seen, but she did not think the thought. There was no part of her mind that was safe; even her memories were his for the taking. Maybe she was only safe in her dreams. She fought not to think the thoughts that she wanted to think, and then he said to her:

"I know that you could kill me, Essien. I've known that since before I hired you. If I hadn't bound you to me the way I did, when I did, you would never have submitted to me. You would have gone on fighting me. Even now, you still do not love me as you should—bound to me the way you are."

She gave an irreverent shrug, like what he'd said didn't matter or concern her at all. Then she said, looking right at him, "It's good you know all that about me. It makes it easier for me if I don't have to explain what I could do to you if you ever let me free of this bond."

She let herself think of it then: her snatching his throat with her hand and his blood gurgling out between his lips; her hacking his head off in one smooth, forceful blow; her letting off her rapid fire and watching him split in half with the top part of his still blinking body sliding off to the side. He was in her head when she thought those words and even made images for herself, so she could really enjoy it.

"Is that what you want to do to me, Essien? A shame, so gory. Where there are much better things I can think of to do with you." And he was flooding her mind with his smell, the feeling of him kissing her, his hand holding her where her skin always ran hot, and she shot up out of the chair, watching his face as he sat across from her on the other side of the patio.

"Don't, Gabriel, don't!" She wanted to cover herself, but she knew that it would only accent what he'd done to her with just his mind and his will and that awful power he shouldn't have had and that she was just barely learning to figure out.

"Say you will go with me to the city and let me have one kiss as the sun goes down, and I won't ever do that again."

"You're a liar. You'll do it anyway, even if I promised it all to you."

So, he did, and she didn't scream this time, but she bit her lip and squinted her eyes closed, trying not to sigh or relax into that invisible pressure. She thought then that he had never kissed her, had barely touched her, and had never touched her naked skin at all with his hands. He had never before done with his hands what he was doing with his power, cupping her and squeezing and making her so uncomfortable because she knew it wasn't discomfort that she truly felt.

"I'll go to the city with you!"

"And the kiss?"

She frowned at him, her entire face telling him what she really thought of him. She tore out, "Okay!"

He stopped immediately, that invisible hand drawing slowly away and trying to keep touching up to the very last moment. Her body gave a visible jerk, and she seemed to settle. She wouldn't look at him.

"Don't ever do that again. What you were just doing. You said you wouldn't ever do that again. It's wrong, Gabriel." She felt nearer to that edge of vulnerability, which she thought she had guarded herself from ever having to face. What she felt for him was tangled up in every emotion she felt, from positive to negative—mostly negative.

"Of course, you are right, Essien. My apologies if it upset you."

Her anger struck back up again because she didn't have a choice whether he did what he did or not, whether he used his power to make her feel him without actually touching her. She wondered again how he was able to do that, why he did it, why he'd chosen her to make his particular battery of sorts, to charge up on and get buzzed or high or whatever it did for him when he could reach across to her with invisible electricity and make her feel things that weren't possible. She shifted and looked at the doors that led into the house.

"How much time do I have?"

"Be ready in an hour."

CHAPTER THIRTY-NINE

◆

Essien had been to Obum-Otu many times as a teen, usually for some reason Ntoochi had conjured, like seeing if a boy she liked lived at the address he'd given her. The city was smaller than Lagos and Biafra, but much bigger than Delta River village where Essien grew up. The streets were paved with tan stone, and Essien noticed the glint of gold everywhere.

"This is where I was born," Gabriel told her from the seat beside her.

Essien's interest piqued. This was new information that she hadn't learned in any of the history books she'd read over the years. The books she'd read, some even snatched from his own library, did not give a deep dive into the President's background or his childhood. It was as though he had materialized for the first time into existence as a soja in the military, and his life didn't begin until that moment.

"Is your family still here?"

Gabriel shook his head. "My parents died when I was very young. My Nne nna raised me. She died soon after I was elected. She never got to come to the Presidential compound on Capital Island; I hadn't finished building it yet."

Essien watched the side of his face as he stared down at his hands in his lap. "Would she be proud of you? Your Nne nna?" Gabriel's head whipped up, and he looked at her with his eyebrows raised. She went on, "Would she be proud of the man you have become? Would she approve of what you are doing to me?"

Gabriel kept looking at her, his hands still between his thighs. The engine was passing underneath a tunnel and suddenly the car was plunged into darkness. Gabriel's eyes flashed silver-blue in that darkness. Essien closed her eyes then looked out the front of the engine to see how much longer they'd be traveling underground.

"My Nne nna saw you before I did, by the side of that lake," Gabriel responded, not answering her questions. "She saw you when I was nowhere near. She said, 'A new goddess comes to Alkebulan, to protect her people and defend them against all threats.'"

Essien started to tremble at his words, the power and the truth in them sending vibrations up and down her limbs. She pressed herself up against the side of the engine door. She looked back at Gabriel, and his eyes were glowing blue orbs. Something reached out of that glow, and Essien slammed her own eyes shut. Then Gabriel's energy was all over her again, like she'd been plunged into an electric bath that sizzled and zapped every inch of her skin. She opened her eyes, and she was still sitting beside him in an engine, his eyes glowing neon blue and casting bright reflections around them in the darkness.

"My Nne nna's dream was for Alkebulan to always remain the most powerful nation on Ala-ani. She took me to that lake time and time again for that one express purpose. My Nne nna was old...she never told me just how old, but her memories stretched back for eons, back to the beginning of man it seemed. She could remember the time before human language, before the first civilizations, before the great kingdoms rose and fell.... She told me I would be the leader of Alkebulan when I was barely four years old. She told me later that you would come to me when Alkebulan needed you. She said, 'the Queen of Alkebulan will arrive when the nation is ready for her. The Goddess of Alkebulan will come when you are.'"

Sunlight burst into the windows all at once as the engine traveled out of the tunnel, and Essien felt like she could finally take a deep breath. Gabriel stared at her with eyes that were his normal jeweled brown. She looked out the windows at the landscape that had changed to a residential neighborhood with gated compounds. Some of the gates were made of stones or wood; others were made of iron with spikes. Essien thought about the little cottage she had left behind in the woods of Bantu State with its long, curving lane you had to travel to reach it nestled snugly between trees as green as these. Essien tried to calm her breathing and failed. She could still feel Gabriel's power spilling over her skin like an uncomfortable fabric. She turned to look at him again, and he was peering at her closely.

"You dream of going back to a life of such simplicity. Why do you want one room when you can have an entire floor of lavish rooms to yourself? Rooting around in the mud when here you never have to lift a finger if you don't want to? It is not a choice I would make, not if I had your power...your prowess. When you could have so much more? It's right here for the taking. Right in front of you. You pretend you're afraid of me, and maybe you really are, but I know what's under that fear, I can feel it. A sorrow so great and wide you'd rather climb into it than be here in reality where we are facing a battle that neither of us can win without the other."

Essien again looked out the windows, so she did not have to see the earnestness in his face, hear it in his voice. Something dislodged from her memory, faint as a half-remembered dream that haunts throughout the waking hours. "I was so curious...and rebellious as a teen. I would not have joined the military if I weren't.... I disobeyed everyone...I hid, I schemed, I plotted, but I never lied...and now here I am, still curious and rebellious, too, but you've subdued me. I have nothing left to want except what my people want...and my freedom from you."

"You are as free as you were ever going to be, Essien. The minute you walked into that lake."

Essien cut him off. "So you're saying this—you—are my fault? That by going to the lake all those times, I led myself to be tied in these chains?" She was so angry she had to stop talking. Then the words she had to say erupted out anyway: "We'll never know now, but having the choice could have made the difference. I chose one thing, being a soja. All the rest? You never asked me. And it's too late now. I'm here. I'm here, and according to you, I'll never leave, nor should I even want to." One minute she was grinding her teeth from how angry she was. The next, she just felt tired. She shook her head.

The silence stretched between them, allowing her to realize that the engine was slowing and stopping.

GABRIEL INTRODUCED HER TO HIS FRIEND, IKENNA NWADIKE. His was a medium brown with dark brown eyes and hair in short locs that were just starting, so they looked like curly squiggles all over his head. He looked so familiar, Essien thought, as she touched palms, and he laced his fingers around hers instead of the customary touching and moving away. He pulled her hand toward his face as he leaned over and placed a kiss against her knuckles. His lips stayed there, pressed against her skin, and Essien felt the tiniest flicker of wetness touch her. She frowned and tried to tug her hand away.

Gabriel made a small movement toward them, and Ikenna brought her hand down as he rose, but he didn't let go. As he rose, his mouth spread

302   WIELDERS OF FLOODS & FLAMES

with a smile that dazzled in its wideness. There was a deep dimple on the right cheek that made him seem young and friendly.

"Let me show you where the other guests are gathered," he said, addressing Gabriel with a hand sweep showing the way forward. Essien followed behind them. The Guard went before and behind, silent and formidable.

Ikenna introduced her to all of his guests with an arm around her waist, the one Gabriel had taunted her would be his when he'd ordered her presence beside him tonight. Ikenna poured her drink himself, a frothy purple liquid with a trio of white and blue flowers floating on its foamy surface. The first sip Essien took was cool and sweet; there was no hint of the taste of poison she'd once experienced at a bar in southern Alkebulan.

She smacked her lips and complimented the mixologist. Ikenna wore a pleased grin on his face as he swept her from room to room. He took the liberty of also pointing out the extravagant pieces in his art collection, floor-length portraits of his ancestors on the walls in the halls, masks hanging in artful displays, gold statues and regal busts on shelves that looked as if they belonged in the Muséon. Gabriel tagged along behind at first, his presence looming over both of them. Then, between one room and the next he was being pulled away to chat with an excited group of his political associates and allies, a reluctant glance back over his shoulder at her still with Ikenna.

The man of the house let go of her waist for a second, to shake the hand of someone who stopped them on the outdoor patio. The two men became engrossed in a conversation, so much that Ikenna momentarily forgot about her, turned his back to her, and put his arm around the man's shoulders. Essien took that moment to step away from his side. Glancing around for Gabriel, and not seeing him, she disappeared through the glass doors leading back into the compound.

Inside, the guests were gathered in merry conversations. Essien could not even tell which were the politicians among them. There were no Council Members that she recognized. Some of the guests smiled at her and offered her lines of conversation to see if she might stop to chat. She stopped long enough to be polite but not for too long.

She spotted another mixologist shaking metal tumblers full of ice and stepped up to his bar. She set her empty glass on the counter and asked in her sweetest voice if they could recreate the delicious drink she'd just had with its fruity purple color. The man behind the counter smiled and proceeded to dash several different elixirs into a tumbler before shaking it up with ice and pouring it into her glass. He topped the lavender drink off with more of those small flowers. Essien downed the drink in a few sips.

The sweetness was deceiving because she was already starting to feel a looseness spreading into her limbs. She politely requested another one, and the mixologist was more than happy to mix it up, pouring it into a bigger glass this time. Essien took the drink and moved away from the counter. She found a couch against a far wall, hidden behind a potted plant stretching its leaves up to the ceiling. She finished almost the entire glass, sipping it while she watched the people moving to and fro, completely unaware that she was sitting just behind the plant. As she swallowed the last few sips, she knew that she couldn't stand on her own if she tried. She felt so relaxed and friendly. If someone came over to talk to her now, she'd welcome the interaction. She might even be feeling social enough to smile and crack a joke with them.

A person suddenly sank down into the seat beside her, shifting her relaxed body into their side with such force, she had to use a hand against their hard thigh to regain her balance. Glancing blearily up into their face, she realized that it was Gabriel who had finally come to find her. She recoiled, trying to remove her shoulder from leaning into his chest and her hand from resting on him, but her body wouldn't cooperate. She couldn't move away, and her movements only made her sink deeper against him until her head was leaning against him and her eyes were closed. Her mind was telling her to stop touching him, to get up, to put distance between the heat of his body and hers, but all she could do was sink further into him, snuggling harder against his side so that one of her arms wormed around his waist while the other one was still in his lap, on his thigh, dangerously close to other parts of him.

Essien knew she'd had too much to drink. And around him of all people. Her mind was screaming at her, but her body wouldn't listen. She rolled her head back against his shoulder to see his face, to try and tell him that she wasn't herself, that she wasn't feeling well, and he should take her back to the Island, so she could sleep the drinks off. But in tilting her head up, at the exact same time that Gabriel tilted his head down, their lips met, the softness like the harshest shock to her system she'd ever received. She was so out of her mind with the purple drink that she felt her own mouth moving against his, her lips opening to better taste his, and her tongue, oh Mothers, her tongue was tentatively flicking against his, and—

Gabriel's hand came up to her cheek, and she felt a zap that cleared her head instantly. She could control her body again as she pulled her mouth away and then her hands, and she stood up so quickly from the seat that she tripped over her own feet. She was breathing hard, her chest heaving as he stared down at her. He didn't hide the look in his eyes, a look that told her what his mouth against hers had already conveyed.

Gabriel stood and strode past her. "Come on," he said over his shoulder. She had no choice but to follow him, that connection between them suddenly thick and hard as a diamond stone.

WHILE SHE WAS STARING INTO THE GLOWING BLUE WATER AND watching the silver fog roll toward her like a stampede, Gabriel was slipping into the water naked, the warm caress making him float onto his back in utter relaxation.

Essien heard the splash and glanced first at the pile of his clothes discarded in a heap far back from the edge of the water, before turning to him. His eyes sparkled like a nighttime sky filled with stars. His shoulders were broad and dark, rising up out of the water to show his chest, the muscles tight and firm under skin the same dark color as his eyes. He continued to rise, walking closer toward her back on the shore.

Lines of water curved down his arms and his stomach, the flat smoothness showing no signs of hair anywhere. He was still coming closer, and just as she would have seen what he obviously wanted her to see, she turned her head away, glancing back at the engine idling even further back from the shore.

"What are you doing, Gabriel?" Her voice was lighter than a whisper.

He stopped walking closer, a smile in his voice. "Going for a swim."

"In the nude?"

"I forgot my swimming suit."

"I doubt you own one."

"Oh, I do. Several, actually, in different colors."

His voice was as light as hers, but she could feel him getting closer. He was being so calm, but it was a facade. She could feel his energy swirling around her like a storm, a hurricane come to blast and twist her to pieces.

"You keep surprising me." He was so close now the heat of his body licked and tickled the line of hers closest to him. Then she had to turn and look up to see his face. She didn't want to look at his eyes, but she did. The silver glow of the water seemed to make his dark eyes look lighter than she'd ever seen them.

His eyes looked shiny and full, like he was on the verge of tears, but she knew that wasn't it. She could feel what he was feeling. He wanted to touch her and pull her to his naked chest. He wanted her pressed against him, skin to skin, with nothing in the way. He wanted to swim in the water with her pressed against him, and she got a confusing image of them entwined in the water, her arms and legs wrapped tight around his waist, and his...

Essien stepped back, away, closing her eyes, so she couldn't see him anymore.

"I never seem to have a choice with you," she said, her voice louder than before. "Shouldn't it be my choice? Showing me that? When I haven't told you I would, or that I even want to!"

Gabriel was still looking at her, but he'd turned his body away, so that she couldn't see anything except his shoulder, the sides of his ribs, his thigh and calf. She stared at his feet rather than meet his eyes again.

"I won't take your choice away. I want it to be your choice, too."

Anger was a hot prick in her temple, and she almost looked back at him. "You've made that damn near impossible for me now. You're in my head... you're in my dreams...you're in my...how can it be my choice now when you took away my choice back then?"

Gabriel sighed and started walking back toward the edge of the water.

"You can come into the lake fully clothed if you wish. But come in."

Gabriel swam out to the middle of the lake with strong, sure, swift strokes. He was farther out than Essien had ever been the times she'd come to this lake alone. As he swam farther and farther, Essien saw what he was swimming toward. A figure that had risen out of the surface of the water when she wasn't paying attention. The same figure she'd seen almost every visit to this very spot.

The silver-blue translucence of the figure let her know that the figure was tall and had the definite shape of a man. A similar shape to the man that was heading straight toward it. Essien wasn't sure what she expected to happen when Gabriel reached the figure, but she had moved closer to the edge of the water. She heard the small splashes of her shoes hitting the lapping water. She moved back a step and when she'd glanced back to where the figure had been, there was nothing. The surface was still, and Gabriel was gone.

Essien took a deep breath and then made herself take a step back up to the edge, and then another so that her foot was almost in the water. She remembered at the last minute she was still wearing her shoes and reached down to take off one flat and then the other.

She glanced back at the engine behind her. The guards were facing outward toward the dirt road they'd taken to get here. None of them were looking at her. Quickly, she slipped the tunic dress over her head, wanting to have something dry to put on when she came out, and let it drop onto her shoes. She stepped back up to the water, took a deep breath, and stepped her foot all the way in. The water was so warm, warmer than she'd felt through Gabriel's skin. She sank down into it, taking in a deep breath, and going under the surface.

Suddenly, there were hands—Gabriel's hands—reaching for her, and pulling her down. She closed her eyes and let herself be dragged deeper. When she opened her eyes, she was kneeling in the same throne room that she always came to when she entered the lake. Before her were three stone thrones, the age of the carved rocks showing in their smoothness in all the places where bodies had rubbed over ages.

The Mothers were sitting in the thrones, their faces solemn and stern. Essien's eyes went first to the one in the middle. Her skin was the darkness of midnight, an obsidian so dark and shiny it became a mirror reflecting everything she saw. The one to the right of her was brown like the sweetness of cacao spreading thick and syrupy over your tongue and dripping down your skin. The one on the left was so pale she seemed to glow and emit light in an orb of rainbow colors at the tail end of a storm. Each of their heads and bodies were covered in cloth of different colors that shimmered and pulsed as they breathed and moved.

Gabriel was smiling like an accomplished child before their proud parents. Essien was starting to tremble. She was thinking of the prophecy, of Enyemaka's warning, of the Councilmen's accusations, of the promise she had made. She was afraid, kneeling there before the Mothers with Gabriel next to her.

"I come to ask your permission," Gabriel said, and his voice was so loud that it seemed to echo into the caverns inside her chest.

A voice like the murmur of crowds coming from all of them at the same time: "Permission for?"

Gabriel stayed kneeling, but he seemed to grow taller there on his knees. "I wish to bring the prophecy to its Godhead."

Their eyes were like golden liquid swirling in the sockets of their heads. Essien looked down at the floor, and the trembling turned to shaking.

DIDI ANOFIENEM 307

Their voices quaked like the earth rumbling deep within its core: "Which prophecy?"

Gabriel's height shrank a tiny fraction. "The one that promises a God and a Goddess to walk on Ala-ani among Your people."

Their voices were terrible to hear, the hiss of snakes and the roar of lions all rising at once: "Is it Our permission you need?"

Gabriel dropped his head, too. "My gravest apology if I have offended You, Mothers. I want only what You want, what will bring about Your wills."

Echoes of thunder without end: "Do you think it is We who are offended?"

Gabriel shook his head and then looked up. "I don't understand. The prophecy affirmed that a Queen would be born to reign over Alkebulan, and the fate of the country as one nation wouldn't be sealed until she was enthroned. I am here to ask Your permission because it is Your blessing I need. If You wish it, Mothers, the prophecy will be dead in the water, so to speak. And if You declare it, the prophecy will flow as smoothly as the Nahla."

The shaking was getting worse, and the pressure on Essien's knees started to sting. The eyes of the Mothers all turned to her at once.

"You may rise," They said together. Essien went to put her hand on the floor to help her stand, but Gabriel was already standing and offering her a hand. She thought about not taking it because she didn't want him touching her right then or at any time. The look on his face went from cool to arrogant with a flexing of his nostrils and a thinning of his lips. The look said that she was being silly to refuse such a small gesture.

Essien put her hand into his, and his palm was wet. But more than that, as her hand slipped in the liquid on his skin, she felt like she slipped into him, her skin no longer providing a barrier against anything. She was back in his head, his vision, and the weight and simplicity of it made tears sting her eyes.

He was holding her around the waist with one arm, and in the other, he was holding a baby—Essien knew he was their son. It wasn't just the child or his arm around her as though it belonged there; it was the happiness and the peace he felt, and she felt it, too. The feeling that everything was right and good and would always be that way. She knew in the front of her head that it was a terrible lie because bad things happened all the time, and they had happened to her. But in the back of her head, that primitive, prehistoric part, the happiness felt more sacred, holier than any religious experience Essien had ever dreamed of having. She wanted to take her hand back, but she knew that this feeling wouldn't go away just because she stopped touching him.

She was on her feet, and he was still holding her hand. She forgot about the warnings and the fear. She forgot about not touching him and not letting him touch her. She was reaching her arms around his waist and letting her body fall against his, so that he had to catch her. She pressed her cheek against his chest, and all the rest of her pressed against him, too, as her arms held his sides and his back. She was squeezing him, her fingers starting to dig into his skin. She'd never felt happiness like this; one that wanted to ooze out of her pores and scatter her body into a million pieces to share it with everyone everywhere. That's when she realized they were both still naked. She started to move away, but he tightened his arms around her, bending his face down to kiss the top of her head.

If his vision had shown her that he was thirsting for power, taking over foreign lands, or murdering people, she'd have turned from him. He'd shown her his idea of happiness. Was it hers? She didn't think so, but the tears still seeping slowly from her eyes let her know that maybe it had hit on something she'd never acknowledged.

He wanted a family, a family with her. Essien had said she wouldn't let him use her to war against the whole world. Perhaps he had known that, too, and had chosen carefully what he showed her. Her suspicion was back, and she tensed in his arms. The tension made her bare breasts pressed up against him no longer feel comforting and secure. She fought not to look down at what she was pressed up against as she stepped back to get away.

He had to let her go or tighten his grip. She dropped her arms from around him. She didn't look up at his face to see what emotions went with the tension in his body, but his arms started to loosen, and she stepped away from him to face the Mothers.

The gold in their eyes was pulsing like boiling gold, sending sparks and glints of bright light to sparkle in front of them. Essien wanted to cover herself, but the Mothers were inside her head already. There was nothing she could hide from them.

"There are more prophecies than just the one," Essien said, speaking for the first time.

"We know of the ones you speak." She waited for Them to say more, but They remained silent.

Essien went on, "If what the President wants will not bring about the complete end or the destruction of the world, then..." Essien stopped. She wasn't ready to commit to anything, not with something that serious and potentially devastating hanging over her head. The happiness was still buoying up inside her like a shaken fermented tea, and the fizz was waiting to explode all over everyone. She wanted so badly to sink into that feeling, but she was terrified. It felt unreal, too good to be true. She couldn't suddenly switch on or off what she had been thinking and feeling for the last few years. He had thought she hated him, and perhaps he was right. Now, she had no idea what she felt, but she knew this happiness wasn't hers. It was his feelings and emotions projected all over her, and though it felt good, it was still a lie. Essien looked back at Gabriel who was standing where she'd left him. She looked at his face but didn't meet his eyes.

She spoke, still staring at him while avoiding looking directly at him, "...then I will not oppose his efforts to earn me as his own true Queen."

Gabriel's mouth moved, and she realized he wanted to smile but was holding himself in check. It was the laughter from the Mothers that startled Essien. The sound was like sunlight made into octaves to rise and fall into the room, brightening and energizing where it touched.

"You are still a human woman, Essien, though that is not all you will be. Take special care that the next time we meet, you have good news to share with us and not bad."

"The child?" She tried to keep the anxiety out of her voice. She had never wanted to have children, not since joining the military at least. It had not been an option for her, so she had ignored it. Now, with the President's vision lingering, she wondered if that is what the Mothers meant by good news.

There was laughter again. "You are still young. And there are many wars yet to be fought and won, or lost. We know of the timeline, but we trust you to make your way through it at your own speed."

Essien nodded. It wasn't so much that they wanted her to bring that small boy to life, it was that they were so certain of her that eventually, she would know all on her own if she wanted it or not.

CHAPTER FORTY

◆

It was a week later when Essien spoke as though she would burst if she didn't.

"You said that I cannot work as Queen until the ascension ceremony. Okay, I accepted that. Never mind all the Alkebulanians waiting for me to do what I said I would do. So now that I have found something else to do to occupy my time until I can get to work, while you jet off anywhere you please, I am suddenly being followed by guards around the Island and blocked from freedom of movement again? I thought we'd moved past your Guard following me around, Gabriel."

The President didn't even look at her. His eyes kept their side-to-side slide over the lines of a thick stack of papers. She knew the papers were reports on military strategies, economic projects, and new legislation concerning international trade agreements for him to consider. She had chosen this time to speak with him in his office because it was one of the few times he was alone in the afternoons. His advisors were like a parasitic cluster attached to him whenever he was on the Island. She knew she didn't have to schedule an appointment to speak with him, but he didn't always provide her with a rapt audience.

"You are not allowed to work outside of your clearly defined role as Queen, Essien. This has been repeated to you again and again. Now that the legislation is passed, I told you—"

"And I told you that I have pages and pages of agenda items, deeds I promised the people who voted for me I would do. Do you want to hear my best ideas?" He didn't look up to show any interest, but she plowed on. "I want to start a universal school system. Making sure every child in Alkebulan can attend schooling for free from the age of six up until they complete their Upper Levels. Then, I want to expand the disciplines offered by our Universities, so that people who don't want to study religions or the military have options for their education, too. I also want to create at least one new university in each state. Medicine is the first new discipline I want to add to our current universities, especially the military universities. I think if we lead by example, the religious universities will be more willing to follow our lead. Gabriel, don't you see how urgent it is that I start working as Queen? Now—not in less than a year's time. And if not, then at least when I try to find something else on my own, do not blockade me!"

"I don't want you working for anyone if it is not for me, or for this country. Your ideas sound ambitious, but I know as Queen, you will turn them into reality. But for now, focus on resting...and planning. I am handling everything else involving this country's rule, so you needn't worry at this time."

The way he spoke made her feel condescended to, like he considered her less than him, less important, less powerful, just lesser. "Why are you so arrogant?" She didn't expect an answer and was actually surprised to get one from him.

"I was bred to be a King, and I have had to settle for being President. As the President's permanent house guest, you will not work until your role as Queen is finalized."

"Gabriel—"

"Essien."

"I am not a toy you can put on a shelf when you're done with me. I am not a thing that you can do with what you want. I can make decisions for myself."

"No, Essien."

Hearing that no, so final and abrupt, she felt a viciousness rise up in her that made all of her reservations and fears of him burn away. The anger was intense enough to make her grab the nearest book sitting on a low table between two chairs and throw it at him. It was a copy of the previous year's approved legislation, and she had to chuck it at him with two hands. The book hit him on the shoulder and fell to the floor behind him. He lifted just his eyes to look at her. She grabbed the next book on the stack and threw it, too. He batted it away with one hand and stood up.

"If it's a fight you want..." He didn't finish the words as he unleashed that fierce strike of lightning against her, into her. She didn't fall to the floor or squirm or tremble anymore, but it made her wince. The minute he let up, she reached for another book and barely missed his head. He was already pummeling her again from behind his desk so that she had to let herself down to the ground or risk hurting herself by falling. She tried to roll up into a ball, but he was around the desk and grabbing her up with one hand.

When he touched her, the sizzle of electric energy jabbed sharply from the point of contact into all of her, and she finally screamed. The sound made him startle and pull back. He set her down into the nearest chair.

He was out of breath. "Essien, I do not wish to harm you."

She had to breathe deep a few times before responding, "Liar. You like doing this to me."

"No. You make it impossible for me not to have to use—"

"You do what you want, when you want, even when I don't do anything. I'm done letting you dictate what I can and cannot do. Shock me, kill me if you've got enough magic for it, but I am going to control this part of my life, Gabriel. Mothers help me!"

"Do not call up the Mothers in front of me, Essien. I am forbidding you from working. You cannot fight me on this."

"Watch me!" She moved to try and get up, but he pushed her to sit back down, his power turning on at the same time, and she stared up at the ceiling through a watery sheen. Not getting the response he wanted, Gabriel slid that searching, seeking heat down to parts of her that she had sworn him away from. She finally let out a sound when he did that, and it didn't sound like pain.

"Mothers damn you!"

He hated it when she used vulgar language like that. It made him remember the part of him that was still a gentleman. He knew that he had made it impossible for her to respond in any other way. He turned that current off again.

Essien used that opportunity to bring her hand up in a harsh smack to his cheek. His face felt half stubbly and sharp, half smooth and soft underneath her palm. She threw at him, "Bastard!" She waited for him to lash into her again, but he didn't. He stared down at her from his tall height and said nothing. The fast breeze of their harsh breathing was the only sound between them.

"We cannot go on like this," he said after a while.

"I refuse to sit around here watching you work while I do nothing." Her voice was tired, resigned. She did not want to fight him, that much he knew. With that same foresight into her being that he had crafted for himself, he knew she would keep fighting. She would not give up on this issue. In her mind, to let him control her fully and completely would reduce her into less than nothing. She was still trying not to be what he wanted, what she was.

"The woman only offered you the job because she feels sorry for you."

"And I took the job from her, Gabriel. I told her yes. I told her I would help her every day of the week on her little pocket farm on this Island because it would be something you could not control me through."

"You keep fooling yourself. I control everything on this Island, in this nation."

"Did you tell her to give me the job, then?"

He didn't respond, but he kept staring at her. The familiar clench of muscle in his jaw let her know she had him, whether he would accept it or not. There was only so much he could control, no matter how boisterous he talked.

"I am going to work for her on her farm, Gabriel. It's right below this mansion, so I don't even have to leave the Island to get there. Are you going to keep assaulting me with your demonic presence to stop me?"

A quirk in his jawline, and his eyes sparkled darkly. "Leave."

She slid out of the chair and had gone from the room in a dash of quick feet. She shot a quick look back at him, and he was watching her leave. She was outside in the wide expanse of clean, blue air and trekking down the mountain into the valley below. She had been down this track many times after that first run. She'd seen the farms then, the stadia upon stadia owned by Gabriel and the nation, with the old woman's small farm set at the edge of all the land that everybody and nobody owned.

She did not look back to see the twelve guards following her with new orders to let her roam but follow her at a distance. She was intent on one thing and one thing only: getting down to the farm and food stand in the valley below them to accept the job she had already made for herself; lugging, hauling, filling, chopping, preparing, moving, organizing, anything. Anything to give herself the illusion she had some autonomy remaining. She had felt herself on the edge of a madness that would end her; she had to do something or lose herself completely.

CHAPTER FORTY-ONE

◆

EVERY MORNING, ESSIEN AWOKE JUST BEFORE THE RISING OF the sun and hated it. She felt as though she were living in an impossible nightmare, worse than her scariest dream. She saw Gabriel in almost every one of her dreams like a tokoloshe dogging her every night.

As she regained consciousness each morning, she thought back to the first time she had seen him up close. She'd been heading to a hearing about her enlistment in the military spurned by her parents' own complaint. They hadn't wanted her to join the military, and if she hadn't been so ambitious and rebellious, she'd have heeded them. She remembered how Gabriel had thundered down the hallway toward her, and she had been both certain and unsure that it was him. He looked so familiar and so not, so inviting and still so unwelcoming. Her steps had stuttered as they passed, and it felt like the air became staticky around her limbs.

Now she dreamed about him floating around her bedroom and crawling lightly onto her bed. She dreamed about him holding her hands, their fingertips fusing together as he swung her around. She dreamed about him splashing her with blood like a deluge out of the sky and then setting her loose onto a waging battle. There were other dreams, ones that made her sweat and twist herself in her bed covers. She avoided remembering those dreams in the daylight because she knew Gabriel could experience them with her if she thought too hard. With a heaving sigh, Essien rolled herself out of bed.

Gabriel had started having her followed everywhere around the Island, even before she'd managed to convince the farmer to let her help around the farm. She had accidentally let slip in her mind that she was keeping track of the arrivals of watercrafts and engines coming and going from the detached island and cross-checking them with times when she was alone. He'd read these thoughts and followed their eventual conclusion.

The next day, two guards were put on her detail. She'd slipped their chase easily just to see if she could. The next day, there were ten guards. For the sport of it, Essien eluded their detection and made it out to the edge of the Island before Gabriel had thought to check on her whereabouts. He had used his power rushing beneath her skin to keep her still until they could catch up with her. She had spit at them in anger and frustration, angrier at him, the one who had given their orders.

But she had won the right to work on the farm, even if it was temporary, just until her crowning. Gabriel would know where she was at all times; the older woman lived less than ten stadia away. It took her the better part of an hour to walk there. It would have taken her thirty minutes if she had run. It would have taken her less than ten minutes if she drove, but an engine was not available for her use—Gabriel's terms.

Thinking again about how much he had conscribed her life to him, his mansion, and this Island they inhabited with the continent he controlled and his Presidency, she started to get angry again, and no amount of blaming herself and feeling guilty would get rid of that seething ache grinding into her every time she thought about being here.

This is why I tried to leave, she realized with a jolt. Because too much of my life was being controlled and dictated. She had allowed too much of the military mentality to overtake her own self-interest, and she thought it was just the military, but...it was him. He was controlling her through her service to him. He was trying to control her through magic. She quit, and she disappeared, and he found her, and now she was back. She had to ask him just to work, to leave, to move...to breathe! Was this really her life? Was this all she was to be until the end of her days?

ESSIEN WOKE TO THE FEELING OF HANDS SLIDING UP HER STOMach and the scent of warm musk wafting over her face. She snapped her eyes around the room fully expecting to see Gabriel; she was alone.

She rolled over, buried her face into the pillow and waited for the general feeling of guilt and shame to subside. Hot water and clothes cool enough to keep her comfortable took all of ten minutes before she was out of the President's compound and marching down the hill to the farm in the valley below.

The woman who owned the farm wasn't old, just older than Essien. Essien called her Nwaanyi for weeks upon first meeting her. When she'd asked for her formal or surname, the woman had laughed and said such concepts didn't exist for her people, but that Essien could call her Onu.

Onu had weather-tanned brown skin that had not yet begun to wrinkle, and her dark brown hair had streaks of gold—her version of going gray, she said. Essien had met the woman on one of her runs, stopping to chat with her after they nearly collided on one of the dirt paths leading down from the compound at the top of the mountain all the way to the port on the northeastern coast of the Island. The woman had wanted to introduce Essien to her parentless grandchildren, two teenage boys and two little girls who also lived on the farm.

When she'd finally talked the woman into giving her a job to help around the farm, Essien saw the teen boys and little girls every day. Both the teens and the younger ones learned how to make dough for meat pies and chop herbs and vegetables for green stews and bean salads right alongside her. The teenaged boys worked with her outside as she harvested and collected the purest, freshest ingredients straight from the sun-warmed earth.

The boys liked to ask her questions that embarrassed her. Once, when they were standing on the top rungs of tall ladders leaning against coconut trees, one of the grandsons, Nwata, was joking that the President's balls were hairier than the coconuts. His brother, Obiuto, laughed so loud and long that he started to lean back, forgetting he was on a ladder against a tree. The yelp he let out as he caught himself with an arm gripping the trunk echoed several times. Essien had glared at them with embarrassment across the space separating their trees and said nothing.

Over time, going down to the farm became an aspect of the things Essien was permitted to do on any given day. Determined to make whatever time she had until she could start working as Queen endurable, she promised herself at least that she would enjoy the time she could spend alone and away from the compound, even as she waited to know what would come after for her and Gabriel.

IN THE MOSTLY UNBOTHERED ACRES OF GARDENS AND ORCHARDS and yards and yards of open fields, she remembered how to eat mangoes fresh off a tree without washing them or peeling off the skin. She waded into a cold river to collect fish out of cast nets, the ends of her pants slipped to dangle in the flowing water.

Chickens clucked softly around her feet as she sprinkled leftover green cuttings on the ground for them to peck at. Yam peels twirled as she slid the edge of a sharp knife under the thick brown spotted skin to reveal milky white flesh underneath.

The muscles on her arms continued to define as she hauled barrels and boxes down to the street vendor stand set up near the entrance to the farm on the road that curved up the side of the mountain all the way to the top. Local islanders stopped by to get their produce, none taking much notice of Essien as she sliced fruit for fruit bowls and fresh fruit juices or put freshly plucked and cut-up chickens on slabs of ice. The first day she manned the food stand by herself, Essien watched as the cook for the compound up at the top of the mountain bought all the fish filets they had for sale with plans to serve them to her and Gabriel and the rest of the guard that very night.

As the sky darkened each day, Essien brushed crumbling dirt off her hands and looked toward the edge of the farmland. A row of barely visible dark figures was posted near the base of the trees in the distance, all their attention focused on her. She blew out a burst of air and turned back to the woodpile in front of her.

The Guard had complained to the President that staying beyond night-fall was cumbersome and requested a curfew be established. Not looking at her at all, Gabriel had ordered that she return to the compound by sun-down at the latest. Essien had exited his office with an elegant hand gesture that fully encapsulated all that she felt for everyone in the compound. After that, Essien began setting out for the farm in the morning before the sun began to lighten the sky for the day.

When Essien wasn't needed on the farm, the old woman had to threaten her not to show up anyway, which she would have if not for the woman's insistence that she take the day off. So, she stole writing tablets and books to read from Gabriel's library. She walked right in as he sat behind his desk discussing legal matters with Antonious and his other advisors. Gabriel looked up as she entered and kept staring at her as she walked around the circular-shaped room, peering at books, taking some down to read a few pages and then put them back up. She completely ignored him, while he could not help watching her. The stack in her arms grew to three books. She turned to go and noticed that Gabriel's eyes were on her.

"Found what you were looking for?" he asked her.

"It's nice to see you, Antonious," Essien called. She hadn't known when the President's right hand moved out of the compound, but she knew he arrived by engine every morning now.

Antonious had inclined his head toward her, his face set in the deeper lines of his older age. She would have liked to walk over and ask the man how now, pat him on the shoulder, verbalize how much she'd appreciated his help when she'd first joined the soja. He'd likely saved her life, given her something to fight for.

Essien ducked out of the office before Gabriel could ask her another question.

She carried the books in a canvas bag with her down to a spot she had found hidden among tightly spaced trees on the western side of the compound. She had stumbled upon the clearing during one of her treks eluding Gabriel's Guard.

In the middle of the trees, there was a fallen tree that someone had rubbed smooth into a chair. It had a curved back and curved arms, the surface smooth enough to run her fingers along the wood without risking splinters. She was allowed to come to this spot without the need of a group of armed men following her because it was within sight of the compound. Gabriel could probably turn and look out of his office window to see her walking into the cove. The clearing couldn't actually allow him to see her, though, unless he walked under the canopy the leaves made and squeezed between the tree trunks.

The tree chair looked like it had weathered centuries of storms and been shaped by the climate into a grooved space with supports for arms and back. The tree was warm against her bare calves. She pulled out the books she had grabbed. It was a volume set of history books. The first book was titled: *From Evolution to the Great War of Unification: Pre-Unification History*. The second book she'd grabbed from Gabriel's library: *An Accurate History of Alkebulan: The War of Unification to Present*. The third book was titled: *Land of Warriors: Alkebulanian Presidents*. She flipped open the second book and scanned through the pages until she came to a section titled: Presidents. She read through the first few lines and then stopped after flipping the page to a diagram chart. She ran her finger over the chart, taking note of the names, historical and notable figures throughout Alkebulan's history. Men, and women, who had helped defend the nation from invaders, who had pioneered international travel, who had shaped the social and cultural growth of the country. There had been twenty-three presidents in the country's five-hundred-year history. All of them had served for longer than fifteen years with some serving as many as fifty years. So far, Gabriel had been serving for almost ten years. A shadow fell over the book as it lay in her lap.

She looked up, and there was Gabriel standing over her looking sterner and darker than the photo in the history book. She closed the book, so its front cover faced down.

"Learn anything new?"

"You're the twenty-third President."

Gabriel smiled. "Doing research on me, ehn?"

"Just trying to find out as much as I can about what you are."

That stopped his smile in its widening tracks. He cocked his head looking down at her. "What I am?"

"You're obviously not like the other leaders before you."

The smile was back, this time more arrogant and self-satisfied around the edges. "A compliment if ever there was one."

"The things you can do...It's not normal. You're not normal."

"Keep talking like that, and I won't be able to resist."

"Some call it amoosu, but I know that is not what you do, Gabriel."

Amoosu was Igbo for white magic, witchcraft. It was the closest Essien had come to naming and understanding Gabriel's ability to turn the air and the very cells of her body into vibrating vessels in his service.

What he could do to her was unnatural and unheard of; there was no one she could ask; she didn't even know how to explain what it was that he did, not really. If she tried to explain it, she would be embarrassed at the sexual overtones. How could he touch her without touching her? Why did she wake with the sensation of his body all over her? What was it that sent painful arrows of pleasure through her with him as the bowstring? She thought if she could learn to understand his power, she could protect herself or...something, anything...

"You should spend more time with people, Essien, not consorting with dead letters."

"If you would give me access to an engine, I could drive across the bridge into Lagos every day. I always wanted to be a city girl."

"You will do no such thing."

"And that's what I mean. What right do you have to be this powerful?"

"My power has been earned."

"It's akukoifo then?" That magic she knew. She had studied it intimately. Though she had been unable to lock her shields since returning, the akukoifo had not magically begun flooding her. They didn't come to her, but she hadn't tried to call them either. She still only caught glimpses of them. It was almost as if they were avoiding her, or Gabriel, or that well inside her that Gabriel had dug so deep. Surprisingly, she had yet to find any books on the subject of akukoifo in Gabriel's library. She had finally ventured into the room on her floor to search her own library, but there had been only fiction texts—poetry anthologies, plays and book-length dramas, thick novels. Those texts wouldn't help her figure Gabriel out.

Gabriel smiled wider, staring down at her.

"You're getting hotter, with akukoifo. Soon enough, you'll answer your own question. Ask me what I am, and then ask me what you are, too."

She grew uncomfortable and gathered up the books to leave her reading spot.

He called a parting shot after her: "Come to me, Essien, when you're ready to learn more than any of those books can teach you."

ONE NIGHT AS SHE SAT AT HIS DINNER TABLE TRYING TO IGNORE him, Gabriel told her, "A military convoy was attacked at the exact same time that nine other military compounds were attacked."

Essien's head came up swiftly as the reality of Gabriel's words made sense.

"How many does that make?"

Gabriel sipped from his short glass of rum. "Thirty."

"What's being done?" she asked. She put her fork down and her napkin on top of her plate. She turned in her seat so that she faced him more fully.

"Investigations have turned up nineteen villages actively housing foreign and tribalist militants. Five of the attacks are traced directly to these mixed groups via traffic in and around the areas. The others I believe are splinter groups, some of them made up of foreigners; we're still working to locate their sources and exact locations. The early reports have the attacks scattered through the states, even hitting some of our secret compounds that no one without inside knowledge would know about—the military compound in Lagos, the one in Benin, the one in Timbuktu...we are still waiting to find out more of the others. We're not sure yet how many individual locations we'll need to track."

"It's both a rebellion and an invasion, then."

Gabriel nodded. "They've switched up their tactics since you were among them. They're making themselves known in public now. We have agents trying to gain access undercover, but three of them have already been killed and a fourth turned reverse informant. We do not want to risk a fifth out in the field. We're collecting our own information using less than legal channels, but eventually we have to strike back."

"You need an aggressive and deadly response; and you need it fast." Essien felt once again that feeling that had prompted her to join the military in the first place. The desire to protect, to wage war only in service of the innocent and defenseless.

"We're planning a multipronged strike back. Information is being gathered as we sit here. I suspect the source will lead overseas, but I will wait to see what the investigations reveal. I thought I would let the military handle it, but a few guards are also needed. I can spare at least twenty-five."

Essien had sworn that whatever happened to the President's military was no longer her concern. Sitting there beside him, crown or no crown, she realized that it wasn't exactly true anyway. A deep and abiding feeling of responsibility and obligation made her respond, "You need somebody out there who can use magic, but it can't be you."

Gabriel's lip twitched; he did not want to smile just yet. "We can't burn them, Essien. We want them tried before the Councils and executed, not wiped out of existence. We need to send an international message. One that frightens whatever foreign entity is funding these rebels."

She bit her lip. If she told him that there were other things they could do, then she would be admitting to him that she was everything he had claimed her to be. She did not want to be a goddess. Just being a member of the Guard and now soon-to-be Queen had put enough responsibility onto her shoulders already.

"Not going to make them shoot themselves in the head? Or explode into bloody paint? Or leash them as surely as you've leashed me?"

Gabriel didn't flinch or take his eyes off her. "I remember how afraid you were the first time I showed you this power. You could do all that and more, if not for fear. What are you so afraid of?"

"Losing what makes me human. Forgetting that I come from a family and a community of people who value human life. I don't want that kind of power, not if I don't need it. The bodies I've piled up already, they haunt me, Gabriel—through me being stuck here with you." Essien's fingertips moved imperceptibly against each other. She stilled when she realized what she was doing.

Gabriel lifted his chin toward her. "How many times have people tried to kill you? How many times have you survived unimaginable threats? How many times have you saved your own life and the lives of innocent people?"

Essien looked out the window behind Gabriel's head. Even though she wasn't looking at him, she could feel his heart beating faster, thumping hard against ribs, his blood winding through elastic veins. Her own heartbeat began to speed up until it pumped in her chest at the same pace that his heart beat in her head. She shifted her eyes to stare at his chest as she asked him, almost absentmindedly, her voice a whisper so as not to drown out the beating in her head and in her body, "Do you want my help or not?"

CHAPTER FORTY-TWO

◆

IN THE DARKNESS JUST AFTER TWILIGHT DESCENDED, ESSIEN heard nothing in the silent void except the thick beating of her own heart in her ears. She breathed out through her nose, squatting with her back against a concrete wall.

The radio in her ear was muted, so the staticky crackles didn't distract from the pounding inside her. There were two hours remaining until they could strike the second largest rebel camp they had yet found, rumored to be where the group had moved their headquarters after Gabriel had captured the largest group in Bantu State. They were in the middle of a suburban town in Hausa State, and though she still hadn't gotten details of what happened the last time, Essien suspected that the investigation into the attack that night had led them here. That gave them two hours to hunker down until a voice in her ear gave her the go signal. There were hundreds of men in the building; unconfirmed reports indicated there were women and children, too. She knew that was part of the rebels' strategy as well.

Essien tried not to remember the rebel camp she'd lived in underground. She tried not to remember the women who had cooked all the meals, lugging those heavy metal pots onto the burners, chopping endless mounds of vegetables, and stirring with ladles almost longer than their torsos. She tried not to remember that Enyemaka was dead, and it was her fault. This wasn't the time to remember every horrible thing that had ever happened to her, and yet her mind kept snaking back toward those thoughts that weighed her down.

Against other buildings nearby, on the rooftops and patios above, other special operatives waited for her signal. Essien didn't want to wait anymore. She wanted to charge forward, blindly if need be, and shoot whatever moved. The night seemed darker and darker still, the absence of light pressed down upon her with a tangible weight. She unbent her legs and sat flat on the ground, the blood slowly returning to her stiff extremities. She glanced to the left, barely making out the shape of a huddled mass next to her. There were many other such masses huddling in the dark, adrenaline waxing and waning as they all listened to the sounds of nature and the sound of blood rushing in their limbs.

Sharp pelts hit the ground where her feet stretched out, sending chunks of rock wall to shatter around her head. She was up and sitting on her haunches instantly.

"Radio X-M-O, we have fire."

"Hold your position. Do not return fire. Repeat. Do not return fire." Those words sank into all of their ears, suddenly on high alert, crouching and holding the barrels of their weapons. Essien eased her finger away from the trigger, breathing out a stream of air. She moved to the opposite end of the wall, peering around its corner in the direction the shots had come.

Closer in front of her, another round of shots sent a hail of stone shards pinging against her. A crunch of gravel underfoot, and then the entire night began to pop and sizzle with bullets. It was coming from every side at once in spatters of light. Essien felt a ramming force that slammed her back into the wall and then her side felt like it exploded with wetness. She reached down to touch the place, feeling wet warmth spreading across her uniform and squishiness underneath. She dropped herself flat to the ground. Over the radio, she shouted, "We are under attack. Repeat. We are under attack!"

She shuffled over the ground to the other side of the wall, the ache in her side increasing in its intensity as she moved, trying to stay low. More sharp whizzes into the wall and a blizzard of rock and wood splinters hitting her eye and the side of her face. Even amid the resounding shots all around her, she still managed to lift her head to get a visual. The shots were coming from everywhere as metallic glints sped toward and away from her.

She spoke into the radio again, "Taking heavy fire from all sides! We have wounded!"

Essien lifted her head again, her barrel coming up with her. She tried to aim at something, anything, but there was nothing but the constant sparks popping everywhere she looked. She couldn't tell which fire was enemy fire. She lifted her head higher, trying to get some sense of direction in the chaotic scene.

Without thinking, Essien opened herself wide, freeing every particle of her being into a thinness that floated up like a breeze. Once again, the power she'd called wasn't fire or water this time, but the very essence of being human. She could feel everybody everywhere, the meat of them a choking thickness. If she'd had the time, she could have identified man, woman, or child and separated them all out. On instinct, she'd identified every single enemy within a hundred-stadia radius. She knew instantly that they were all in front of them, but their position on the upper floors made it seem as though they shot from everywhere. She saw a spark explode not even three yards in front of her and then another impact in her shoulder. Bones shattered, and she felt a piercing sting in her neck. Blood filled her mouth, choking her, going up and down her throat in a salty wave. She couldn't breathe or swallow around the blood pouring out of her neck.

Die, she thought. There was no time to fine-tune her focus enough to use that powerful magic against only her enemies. Every single body that she had been connected to felt the sharp sting of their own blood exploding all at once, their bodies dropping in a bloody wave at her nonverbal command. Everywhere there was the sound of wet bursts now, thick, meaty sounds that gurgled and splashed.

Essien struggled to breathe through the tsunami of blood pouring out of her own neck. She was drowning. She was drowning, and yet she knew she wouldn't drown, some recollection struggling to come to the front of her memory that now concerned her greatly.

She screamed a choking sob into the radio, "Mothers!"

She was vomiting bloody foam and strands of gelled blood. In the distance, muffled and far away, she could hear Gabriel's voice. She couldn't make out any words or see him hovering below her in vision the way she usually did. But she knew it was his cadence, his timbre, and that he was trying to soothe her. She could feel the wound in her neck pulsing and trails of drying wetness soaking down her chest. Every heave made her abs contract around the bullets in her side, and she could feel perforated intestines spilling slowly inside of her. Tears from the pain like spreading ice. Anger because she had wanted to strike hours ago and had been denied and now felt betrayed.

Gabriel's voice got louder then, but it was still like static in the background. Getting louder but never getting any clearer. There were sharp stings and radiating burns all over her body, and she couldn't concentrate on anything but the pain.

Underneath those immediate feelings that twisted her insides with agony, she felt a desperate fear that she should be dying, and she wasn't. The wounds she felt were killing wounds; she had seen and made neck shots and stomach shots with automatic rapid fires that kept spitting bullets into the target until her finger stopped clenching the trigger. Some of the bullets had gone straight through her, but the ones that remained felt like hot, jagged rocks. She sensed life mingling in her still expanding lungs and death spilling out of her onto the ground. Essien was certain that what she was experiencing—this dying life—would go on forever if she stayed here.

She tried and failed to hold back the waves of nausea, sending trickles of blood to spill onto the dark concrete where she had already spilled so much, rivulets still surging from the shredded meat that was her side. She put one bloodied hand on the nearest bullet-riddled wall. The weight she put on her feet spilled more blood and bile and thicker things up her throat, but she held on to the wall and closed her eyes tight against the retching made worse by the fact that she was standing and couldn't sit back down. She thought she was done and put her head against the jagged roughness of the wall. She shed more tears, and all of her wanted to slide down the stone and stay pressed up against it. But she wasn't going to die. She could feel that this torturous pain would be an endless loop of agonizing misery. She couldn't see clearly through the thick red caked on her eyelashes, so she used her hands to touch the next space of wall so close to this one and the tip of her toe to find an empty space on the ground.

Another tentative step and her hand brushing against another building close by. She kept stepping and touching, going slowly because if she fell, it would be a long time before she got back up. Steps further, and she stepped on the hard, pronounced metal of a rapid fire. It even had a strap. With shaky arms and slippery fingers, she hooked it around her shoulder and held it loosely aimed with one hand. She didn't know where any of her weapons were or the pack she'd been wearing or the helmet or the earpiece. She kept groping her way through the neighborhood and the silence, the blood now a bare gurgle coming from her neck and her mouth and her side. She stopped several times to dry heave, but the metallic sour taste of bloody vomit stayed at the back of her throat, or what was left of it.

Then there were no more walls to cling to. She edged her foot out gently and felt the loose, pebbly texture of gravel and the whooping of skycraft blades and the crackle of a loud radio flaring to life: "Eyes on the Target. Proceeding with rescue."

CHAPTER FORTY-THREE

◆

SHE SMELLED MARSHMALLOWS. STICKY AND SWEET. WATER surrounded her, flowing over her body. She lay back and felt supported by strong arms. She opened her eyes. Gabriel's face hovered over her. Above him, the sky was a pale gray with floating clouds that covered the sun. She started to resist the hands that held her at the waist and neck, but the energy escaped her. She wanted to ask Gabriel where they were, but she knew.

They were back at the lake in the middle of the jungle. The place where they had first met. The place where he seemed to bring her every time she was hurt. The waters were warm, and she wanted to sleep. Her eyes started to close again but quickly snapped open. She remembered vomiting blood and touching her neck to feel shredded meat. Gabriel's words came back to her then: "You will never die."

She hadn't died, and she should have. She had seen people dead from lesser injuries. She couldn't move her arms, but she wanted to touch herself to feel the damage that had occurred. She hadn't believed him then, or at least, she had brushed it aside when he'd told her. The water splashed against her as Gabriel shifted.

"Don't think about it now," he whispered. "It doesn't matter now."

She wanted to trust him. She wanted to believe that he wouldn't hurt her or let her be hurt intentionally. She wanted so badly to just let go, relax, and let him take care of her. She wanted to stop resisting him.

Staring up at his face, she could only think about all that she had endured and wonder whether this, too, was another attempt of his to manipulate her as he had been doing from the start. She didn't trust the feelings smoothing through her psyche. She knew all the things he could do, and this might very well be just another one of his powers over her.

She tried to wiggle out of his grasp, but his arms around her tightened.

"No, Essien," he whispered gently, his face suddenly looking older and sadder. "I am never letting you go again."

328   WIELDERS OF FLOODS & FLAMES

He took in a great draught of breath and then dunked them both underwater.

GABRIEL'S VOICE WAS THICK IN HER HEAD. SHE DIDN'T KNOW IF she was hearing him out loud or only in her mind. Either way, she could hear and understand every word he said. She kept her eyes closed as she lay on her back on a bed where she knew she had been for some time. She should have felt worse than she did, but there were no aches or pains anywhere on her body. She didn't want to move and do a more thorough examination because she could still hear Gabriel, and he was sitting very close to her. "She didn't go into it unaware, Antonious. I told her we were fighting rebels. We were—That's not the point; we always tell our sojas what they need to know when they need to know it.... She was never in danger.... No, she wasn't.... We knew where she was at all times.... I know she is mortally hurt...I knew it the minute she was... I'm taking care of—You don't have to—Okay, Antonious, a skycraft will be waiting for you. Yes, Antonious, she will heal.... No, Antonious, you cannot. We will talk about it when you get here."

The voice communicator beeped and hit something hard rather forcefully. "You can open your eyes now."

Essien peeled her eyelids apart and stared up at the ceiling. She was afraid to try and move even though she knew that she could. She lifted one arm and then the other and pushed the coverlet down to her hips. She was so scared that her hands started to tremble, and she fumbled with the tunic someone had put on her. She finally got the fabric up enough to bare all of her stomach. She used her hands to feel around the side that her fingertips still remembered as so much hamburger meat. Smooth skin, a slight raised pattern over her rib that spread down to her hip, a tender ache that was vanishing even as she touched herself.

Gabriel's face came into view above her, and Essien hadn't noticed him moving closer. She'd been about to put her hands up to her neck but hadn't built up enough courage yet. She stopped moving with her hands still pressed over the fading scar on her side.

"I should be dead." Her voice was a croaky whisper. She swallowed and tried again. "How did I survive that?"

Gabriel's knee came down on the bed right beside her hip. Then it was his hands touching her neck, moving her head side to side, massaging the muscles. None of it hurt; in fact, it felt good enough that she closed her eyes and relaxed into his hands. His breath breezed over her forehead a second before his lips touched the same spot. "I am more glad than you will ever know that you cannot die."

"How?" she repeated. Maybe the knowledge could wait, but she needed to know why she wasn't a body on a battlefield, why she was here, in his bed, in his bedroom, lying underneath him with his hands on her neck.

Gabriel focused on her face and measured the demand in her. A demand she didn't even know she was exuding. *Tell me what I want to know,* she was saying. *Touch me while you do it,* he heard. "Like this." And his hands against her neck spiked in temperature and radiated heat into her through the press of his rough, indented skin against hers. She felt the warmth spreading down her shoulders like seeking fingers of heat, over her chest, over her ribs, collecting near the almost invisible bullet wounds that had traced fiery tracks through her body. She could feel the heat spreading down below her waist.

"I get it," she said. "Stop now."

Gabriel slowly pulled his hands away. She felt electrical surges filtering down and down. She raised her head slowly, so she could sit up and not be staring up at him like this.

"Don't rise," he said. "I like looking down at you."

That made her try harder to sit up.

"Really, Essien. You have nothing to prove. Please, just lie a little longer. You've been asleep for three days."

"Three days?" She stopped trying to sit up and searched her mind for some memory of what that might have been like; three days of lying here unconscious, unaware, unprotected.

"Yes. You were very hurt. You needed my power and energy to help heal you. And the surgeon, who took out the bullets. But the rest has been my life force supporting yours."

Essien stared at his face, trying to come to terms with this gentler President who sat close to her and put his hands on her and worked to make sure she survived. Had she missed some sense of this feeling, this emotion she felt staring up at him, in the years when she'd first known him? She found that she liked knowing that he had been tending to her, and she wanted him to take care of her, so that she didn't have to fight against him anymore. She had been fighting against him for so long, and as hurt as she had been, as close as she had come to dying, she didn't want to spend the rest of her days in the same state of conflict. She still needed to ask him why the mission had failed, what had gone wrong, and what they planned to do next. But for that moment, lying underneath him with his hand on her shoulder and his knee pressing against her hip, she would let the truth lie a little longer.

THE NEXT DAY, SHE GINGERLY ROSE FROM THE BED, TESTING HER muscles and strength. What she felt was more a fear of pain than any actual pain. She kept flashing back on heaving uncontrollably and the damp stickiness soaking her clothes. She walked slowly around the President's bedroom a few times. She had never been on this floor before, let alone in his room, and she hadn't let herself process what it meant that she had been sleeping in his bed. She wondered where he had been sleeping, and when it was expected for her to be well enough to go back to her own rooms. The state of limbo truly left her feeling more unhinged than when she had been hiding in the southern part of this country. At least there, she'd known what awaited her, capture or forever in hiding. But here, now, staring absentmindedly at the bed where the President slept, where she had been sleeping for four days, what she felt was a dreaded sense of free falling over the side of a cliff.

Whatever might be happening, she still needed to take care of the basics of living that death had reawakened to her awareness. An attendant appeared grateful to take her morning meal order and quickly brought her rooibos tea, imported to the island just for her, and hot porridge with cocoa spices. She ate eagerly, filling her empty stomach and feeling warmed by the sweet red drink. She felt energized and showered in the wide, tiled expanse of falling water with a rock bench in Gabriel's bathroom. She did have to sit down on that bench halfway through bathing, her energy suddenly bottoming.

There were clothes for her to wear folded neatly on a counter. She stood inside the paneled walls of the alcove next to the bathing room. She touched the face of a watch, the arm of a tunic sleeve, the shiny toe of a pair of loafers. She took down a ceremonial jacket in the dark green and black and gold of the country's flag done in an intricate pattern that drew the eye in. It smelled like Gabriel, sharp and smoky. She was sitting in his armchair underneath a floor-to-ceiling window when he walked through the doors, which she had opened only a few moments before.

"You look better," he said upon sitting down on the corner of his bed nearest her.

"I want to talk about what happened."

Gabriel studied her from the side, giving her his profile and only the full glance of one eye. She stared back at him, her hands limp in her lap, one leg tucked underneath her, the other dangling her flat from one toe. She paid attention to it now, that well of tenderness and cruelty mixed up inside him that made him harsher toward her than toward anyone else. That part of him that beat inside of her that would surely kill her if he were to die. She could sense that weak spot inside him more now than she ever had before.

When he'd found her in Southern Alkebulan, hiding out, he had been callous, removed, unyielding, and absolute. She had thought he hated her. She thought he meant to torture her forever. She had been a prisoner, then. She had been kept against her will and unable to go anywhere without an escort. She had almost hated him when she was undying out in the street, but now...she felt indebted to him, as though a balance was owed that she could never repay. She could thank him for saving her life, but what use was gratitude when it had been his own selfish interests that had kept her alive, had pushed him to send a rescue squad for her, and made him use his own energy to heal her.

In the space of just a few days, which could be considered a wider space than any of the time she had spent on Ala-ani, a widening chasm of emotions had opened within her, and she knew the same was true for him. She didn't want to meet his eyes or let him see how much just being alive had finally weakened her and made her pliant to his presence. The difference was astounding in more ways than one; she kept thinking about him above her.

"I feel like I should thank you," she finally said to the floor instead of to him.

"Not necessary."

"But I might regret it soon after." Now she did look at him. He gave off a feeling of boredom, as though he already knew what she was going to say and didn't even need to hear her say it. She went back to looking around the room, which was his, and not looking at him. She noticed that the walls were a cream-colored wallpaper with a light brown floral pattern. The carpet at her feet was the same cream color. So were the covers on the bed Gabriel now sat on.

"I've been trying to figure out how you did it...and I think it has something to do with...whatever you did in Bantu State...at my compound."

"I bonded myself with you that night for the first time, true."

"Will I ever die?"

Gabriel nodded, "Only if I do. Mortal wounds won't kill you."

Essien let that knowledge fill her, and she realized she had already known this. She remembered the feeling of bloody bile scratching up her throat and put a hand against her neck.

"Why were we attacked? Was it a setup? Did you have me set up again, Gabriel? I keep trying to trust you, and you keep putting me in harm's way. Is it on purpose? Are you trying to kill your Queen before I can ever sit on a throne?" It was hard to come off as brave and composed when she felt herself beginning to tremble.

"Is that what you think of me?"

"You don't care what I think of you."

"That's not true at all."

"Was it a setup? Yes or no?"

"I care what you think about me, Essien. I want you to understand me, to see my side of this whole situation."

"Did you betray me? Did you sell me out? Did you let me get attacked on our own soil, so you could maneuver me into a tighter bond with you?"

The laugh that exploded out of Gabriel made her jump and skirt her eyes over his face. She could see into the back of his throat and his tongue undulated with the sound of his amusement. He fell back against his bed and kept laughing, while Essien fidgeted and thought about leaving the room.

"You have me all figured out, Essien. What clue let you on to me?"

"I don't understand why we were left like chained goats when any second-rate celestial web could have picked up the movement toward us."

Gabriel stood up. "You accuse me of setting you up to be killed, knowing you wouldn't die, but could feel the pain of a bullet wound, after I just spent the last four days helping to heal you...I'll take the gratitude now..." He was going for the door. Essien didn't want him to leave her. She had liked him sitting across from her, almost as much as she'd liked him on the bed above her with his knee in her side. She always felt so uncomfortable with how much she liked being near him. His absence before had almost been painful. Still, he hadn't explained to her what went wrong with the mission and why almost all of their men had been killed. He was leaving without having given her any substantial answers.

"When am I being sent back out?" she asked his receding figure.

That stopped him. "Back out?"

"Out into the field. We failed; I failed. I want to get back out there and make sure we accomplish what we set out to do. If there are foreigners backing the rebels, we'll need a nationwide response. Perhaps an international one...now may be the time to draw on those foreign allies you've been courting all these years." She didn't really want to go back in the field or care what Gabriel did when he left the country without her. She wanted to turn her face into a wall and become stone, but that would never happen as she was being told, and so fighting against two-faced enemies with weapons was her next best option. It's not like she could die. She was the perfect military tool, much more useful helping rout out the infiltrators than sitting in this compound where she truly would never rot.

Gabriel had turned all the way around to face her. "You want to go back out into the field?"

Essien nodded, staring level at him, her hands folded tightly in her lap. *Please let this work,* she thought. *Please don't let him reconfine me.*

He tilted his head to the side, his eyes trailing down to what might have been construed as her chest, but in actuality was the place where he had just a day ago touched the raised angry welts of scars that crossed over her neck and which he knew weren't even visible to the eye anymore.

Gabriel shook his head once, twice, stopped, and then shook it again. "You got them all the first time. I asked them to stop reporting the numbers to me when they hit over two hundred. You're sad that all of your people died, but all of theirs are dead, too. That mission is done, but I'll let you know when we need your...style of expertise again. Maybe after you've practiced a bit more." And he left her alone in his bedroom.

CHAPTER FORTY-FOUR

◆

THAT NIGHT, SOMETHING IN HER CALLED OUT LIKE A SIREN screaming into the oceanic void. She felt an answering tug that hooked into the meat of her lower belly and yanked. She went searching for where that lure led, just to see where it was that Gabriel had gone, which left her still in his bed and feeling as though she couldn't return to her own.

The gold floors were so shiny, she could see herself in them. The metal felt cool and solid against her bare feet. A tug in her lower abdomen led her right to Gabriel in the bedroom next door to another office at the end of the hallway. She peered in at him around the corner of the opened door expecting him to be asleep. His head turned to look at her, but he didn't say anything to her sudden appearance at his doorstep. He kept staring at her in the doorway. She thought about going back to her room and locking the door. Then, she would wake up and do the same the next day and the day after that. Instead, she stepped into the room and gently pushed the door closed behind her.

Looking at him, she couldn't tell if he wanted her to stay or to go. She pushed the thick coverlets back and climbed beneath the sheets. She instantly felt warmer and safer. She covered herself all the way up to her nose and stared at him next to her. She breathed out a sigh of relief, relief that he hadn't prevented her from getting this close, relief that it didn't feel bad or awkward to lie next to him, relief that she didn't instantly revolt against herself and flee the room. She settled her head more comfortably against the head supports. She could feel him vibrating and humming with the energy that had drawn her here. He wasn't using it on her, not that she could tell at least, but she felt it, and parts of her wanted to be up close and personal with the source of that electricity. Parts of her that made her cringe with embarrassment. Yet here she was.

"Why are you here?" he asked, his voice loud so close to her ear.

She whispered, facing him, only a couple inches separating their personal spaces, "Read my mind."

A second later, she felt the release of his power over her with a violent shiver that made her draw closer and inch away. She moved to the very edge of the bed and used the coverlets to create space between them. This was new to her; this wanting to be near him, needing it, and his allowing it. She was afraid, but not enough to get up again.

Where it had first hurt her to feel this writhing energy against her skin, now she craved it in ways that made her ashamed to her core. She had called him a sorcerer then; now she felt fully bewitched and enthralled. Perhaps that had been his plan all along.

"Is it okay if I sleep with you? Just for tonight? I can return to my rooms tomorrow." The strong emotion she had been guiled into feeling for him was still fresh and untried. This was still foreign to her, not hating Gabriel, and the feeling itself left her grasping and getting nothing except vague and empty compartments. Like she was still missing some piece of herself, some miniscule but essential part left in those heaps of bodies where she should've stayed. This emptiness left her feeling as though it could be easy to settle into a fresh perspective...by becoming a completely different person.

Gabriel didn't say anything at first. She turned her back so that the thrum of his energy radiated along her spine, and she closed her eyes to sleep. She felt him rustling around behind her, and then the bed rose so suddenly that she sat up. Gabriel stood beside the bed, staring at her, and then he sat down in the chair next to the bed.

"What's wrong?" she asked. She suspected she knew.

"You can sleep. I won't...turn it off."

"I don't want to kick you out of another one of your beds again."

"I don't need as much sleep as you do if that's what you're worried about."

"You don't have to sit up all night either."

She knew he was still looking in her general direction, but it was too dark in the room for her to connect with the pupils of his eyes and read what he might be thinking. He could read her mind, and she could read his, if she wanted to, but she was afraid of what she might read there. Knowing what he was thinking unnerved her; being able to see it and feel it with him made her downright overwhelmed. She contemplated saying something else but decided against it.

She lay back down, still facing him. She was still staring at the dark presence that she knew was him sitting in the chair when she eventually fell asleep.

"Marry me," he finally asked her, and she had been both dreading and expecting it. His eyes were stained red around the flickering dark pupil from the fountains of wine he had drunk with their evening meal. His tie was undone and hanging from one side. He had been gone on the mainland all day, and this was the first time she had seen him since the night before.

She sat in her same seat as always, diagonal to him, at his dinner table, their meal completed, only her own two feet left to carry her up to her suites.

She hadn't quite gotten over the fact that this was her life now, that over and done was her time in the military, her time as his bodyguard, her brief stint as escaped fugitive, her return to his abode in shackles, her life as an adjunct to his military power, her recent injury that had revealed to her the plaintiveness of life. This was it, until she could be crowned. But even then, she knew that he would still attempt to limit her as much as he could. Though she hoped, she knew Gabriel well enough to know the new role wouldn't suddenly release her from his shackles.

Sitting next to him, still sensitive and spiritually scarred by that meeting with death, which only he had saved her from, she heard his words like a capitulating command that both she and he were supposed to fully understand.

She had not expected the feeling she felt now to be one of relief and acquiescence. The relief because if he wanted her in that way, then he probably wouldn't kill her or have her killed. Acquiescence because she had spent so much energy fighting against him, and it had drained her to stillness. The stillness of life forever entwined with death. For a second, just a second, she wanted to just say yes.

Almost immediately, she steeled herself against him, hardening the tenderest part of her against any emotion beyond distrust and rage. She rubbed an idle hand against the side of her neck where a faint tremble reminded her of a scar that no longer existed.

She could not submit to him so easily on anything; she wouldn't. She remembered the promise the Councilman had wanted her to make.... Deng was his name, and she shifted uneasily in her chair with the memory. She hadn't promised him, but she'd told him she would do her best not to marry Gabriel. That she'd make sure another woman took up space in that part of his life. She thought of Rashidah, the warning echoing again, a third time. And the person who had warned her first of all? He was dead.

Now, sitting in his empty dining room, she didn't have to wonder how she was to keep that particular promise. Thinking of Enyemaka, it was easy to rail against herself and what a small part of her wanted. She knew she could not let Gabriel win on the subject of their marriage as he won everything else.

Marry me; he was ordering it rather than asking.

"Does a man often order a woman to marry him after asking her in front of her family? Is that not what we all learned growing up? Isn't marriage something a man asks of a woman, not orders? What marriage might this be where I am being given a summons as surely as all the ones I received in the military, as a bodyguard, as an operative in the country's fields? This isn't at all how a proper proposal is to be done after asking for the family's blessing."

She had only gotten to see one of her older brothers propose to his wife, Chukwu, the fourth born. She wasn't yet born when Idara and Malachum got married. She was a toddler when Manai brought his wife. She was ten when Chukwu's wife appeared, and she was in the Soja when Nifemi finally got engaged. In her parents' living room, her older brothers brought women home to meet the family. Women with strange accents that stretched out their words or sped up their tongues. Women who had all been short dwarves next to her brothers. Each of her brothers had brought a woman home to show off and propose to. Marriage had been something she learned early that all men asked. It was a woman's prerogative to accept.

The man brings the woman to his family. He shows them the beautiful woman he would like as a wife and to become a part of the family. The woman smiles. The woman nods. Everybody hugs. The man and woman go away. That's how the engagements had gone as she had watched from the periphery of her large family. She had thought once when she was much younger that she did not ever want to be taken away to some foreign land and married for the joy of a family she didn't know.

"I can arrange a more formal proposal; I told you that I could. Would you like it televised?"

"No." Just that one word, but it held everything that she felt about being asked—no, ordered—by Gabriel, after fighting so hard to hate him as she did, to not view him as anything beyond the callous, barbaric tyrant she knew him to be. Did he expect her to accept and agree? Had she ever accepted anything that had occurred since being brought here to the Island he had built, an isolated sphere of his influence within the wider sphere of his current reign? Was she now going to stop the months of protest she had put up simply because he was offering, or seeming to offer, what she thought all men did?

"I won't marry you, Gabriel. I can't."

He shrugged, and she knew that careless movement was as practiced as all the other lies he had used to manipulate her. "If not you, then I must marry someone. Nobody smacks their lips at the thought of a President without a wife, even a divorced President like me; nobody says a word. But a King? A King cannot be without a wife."

"Queens do just fine without husbands," Essien said. She stared directly at him, her eyes poring over his face. There had to be someone in there she could reason with. He had to accept her word, or how could she go on with him? He might as well kill her there sitting beside him at his dinner table than to spend another day bound to him with no hope of getting away.

Gabriel's lip quirked. "I am never without admirers, Essien. I have kept you away from that part of my life, but there are other women who would be happy to say yes. There are women who have asked me, although...they are not my first choice...or even my second."

Essien looked down then. She had said that she would make him want someone else, but it would be a lie. She couldn't push another woman into his arms, his life...his bed. Not when she knew what he was, what she was to him. Essien thought of her face reflecting back to her from the surface of a gold floor.

"You should pick someone else," she said despite the fountain of emotions bubbling inside her, not looking at him. Her breath sounded like a gasp, like she was shocked by her own lie and deflection. "I've told you before, and I can only tell you again. It would be...better for us both, for me especially...if we didn't..."

"There is no precedent for what I am trying to do in this country. Other nations have tried it before, and failed or succeeded, but never on this continent, not to this scale...I do not fear the unknown. I fear not being enough for my people when they need me. I fear not doing what I know is needed. I will ask one more time, and then I won't ask ever again."

Essien couldn't look at him yet. She was afraid he would see how conflicted she was. There was a softness in her now, and in him, that was hard for her to ignore or deny, even though she wanted to. Whether this was another manipulation on his part, Essien had made an agreement, and whatever else she felt, there was a sense of duty always holding her up to a different standard, especially in her own mind.

"I have to say no, Gabriel. I have to."

"Then, I must ask someone else. Know that I gave you priority, but I do not have to go where I am not wanted. I have a woman who is an alternative, but you will not like how alike you are. She will not like what we are to each other. You will both be pleasant, but it will be the silent animosity that I thought was beneath you."

"You don't have to do this, Gabriel. You could let me go, and you'd be free to have your Queen be whoever you wanted."

"There is no other woman as powerful as you, Essien. What would be the use of enthroning someone else when they couldn't be used as a weapon in my arsenal? No, I value the spirit of war you bring to my heart. I thought I knew battle until you showed me another way. If I am to pick another wife, no, I have just the woman in mind. You have never met her face-to-face, but you have seen her before. She will be easy enough to get along with...and marrying her will solidify international alliances I have been trying to improve for at least a decade now. This woman, she will not understand what we are to each other, for she knows nothing of akukoifo, but as long as we make it clear that you and I will not threaten her, she will make a lovely wife for us."

Essien's first thought was to think back to when she had seen the President with another woman. She thought back over all the times she had guarded him...back to that day at the Council Houses, but she couldn't remember Gabriel spending any extra time with any of the other women, not locals, not Council Members. She thought back to every time she had been with him in public, every meeting, every traipse through the streets....

She thought about the time when he had gone to the International Conference of Nations that took him to Nihon, Cyrene, Iroquois, and she didn't know where else. When she had tried to contact him, she had gotten a glimpse of him with a woman who was not Alkebulanian. That much Essien knew from the shiny flatness of her hair strands that had hung down around her shoulders like silky strings, and the color of her skin, a milk white color that didn't have the vitalic pale of the palbinos or the golden yellow of the lighter-skinned tribes. Then, the night in Hausa, she'd seen another woman in his bed. Was that the woman?

Essien opened her mouth to say something she would regret and then swallowed what she wanted to say to him. She stared out the window across from her and then tried again.

Gabriel spoke before she could. "I had hoped it would be you, taking my name, bearing my children, but I will settle for the options you have left me with instead. The plans will stay the same, though, since I had already started the cheetah running. We'll have the wedding on the beach at Tear Drop Falls. I know you told me once that you had never been, so I had figured I would make the occasion as special for you as possible, considering..."

"Considering?" Essien mimicked him.

"A marriage of politics, Essien. This will be merely a marriage of politics. As it would have been even if it were you."

"Even if I had said yes, I don't have any land you can possess. I don't have any wealth outside of the money you have given me as first a soja in your military and then as a member of your Guard. I don't even have any heirs or estates for you to claim as the sixth born of my parents. What about it would have been politics? What will make your remixed plans any more political?"

"The people want a Queen...I intend to give them one. I had hoped to make them even more confident with a marriage between their future King and Queen, but I think I would have another kind of battle on my hands, if I forced the issue. Perhaps this is better anyway. There will be no fights to rip apart the country on our behalf. I may have led you to believe otherwise because I'm not used to it, but I know how to be a nwa amadi and take a gentleman's loss."

"I'm glad we're in agreement then," Essien said, and the feelings she felt beneath the surface bubbled over. "How do you expect a marriage to help me become Queen? Isn't the legislation passed? I saw to it that every vote you needed you got. Why would a marriage make that anymore real? All that's left to do is get through the ceremony in a few months' time. I've yet to be fitted for the ogodo to be wrapped into a beautiful uwe from akwette fabric, straight from Igboland."

The light in Gabriel's eyes was already shining and casting shadows over his face. "You. All that's left to do is you."

She was already frowning. "What does that mean?"

"The legislation was passed; you're right about that. The woman to achieve the highest military status would be established as the Eze Nwaanyi, with special rites, responsibilities, and privileges afforded to her and all her female heirs after her."

"Now you're quoting," Essien cut him off. She had read the legislation herself, every word of it. She had known the Military Council would approve of it without question; it gave them inordinate power and a clear incentive for enlisting and promoting women.

Maybe one day it would change the minds of Alkebulanians in the hearts of the villages across the country. Though she had used magic to solicit the agreement of some of the Tribal Councils, she knew they were not subdued. If Gabriel wasn't willing to use her out in the field, they may yet rise up with even greater strength. She had no idea how strong her hold was on those whom she had bonded. She did not bring it up because it was not something she had discussed with Gabriel since he'd unwittingly shown her how to do it.

Gabriel went on, "Thank you for your role in guaranteeing every signature. You only had to promise them the future of your life to achieve it, but you forgot that's something you no longer own."

Essien bristled, hating that he was reminding her of the freedom he had taken from her only after she had already given it up voluntarily. "Marrying me will not make you King. Having me as your wife would not suddenly catapult you onto the throne. The legislation you helped write made sure of it. You'll have to get the KING Act passed."

The grin Gabriel gave her was downright devilish. "Oh, I'm so glad you caught that part. I was worried you wouldn't." Gabriel wiped his mouth and stood. "Our joining in matrimony would have been the final step to implementing the monarchy. The people would never reject a Queen as virtuous and capable as you've been." He was mocking her. Nothing about Essien's career or public persona could be described as virtuous unless taking lives and piling up slaughtered bodies was an accomplishment.

"The people will crown me," Gabriel was saying, "only after I have crowned you."

"You're still using me for a power play? Even after you asked the permission of the Mothers? And my Nne? Even after you showed me what you wanted...really wanted? Even after you made me feel..." Essien stood up, angry finally. The justified heat felt good, but staring at the look on his face, she wasn't sure she truly wanted to tussle with him if it got as bad as he could make it.

Gabriel smiled, turning his bloody eyes into slits. "One thing you should realize now, since you haven't already, is that I am always making a power play. I will use anything and anyone to achieve my aims. You of all people should have realized that by now. I haven't hidden much from you."

"That I disbelieve."

"I will have to disprove your disbelief then."

Essien shook her head, but she turned to leave the dining room. She could feel Gabriel behind her watching her walk away, his own curiosity about her making him open that door into her mind that he had made for himself.

A blink and a misstep, and he was in front of her, blocking her way out of the dining room. She collided with him and the abruptness of his appearance where he wasn't just a moment ago made both her arms clasp around his waist to catch herself. The surprise of feeling her hands holding on to him was so much of a shock that Essien gave out a girlish squeal that she had never heard come out of her own mouth.

Staring up at his face from this close, she knew right away what he wanted from her, but not how he'd gotten in front of her. She was quick to pull away, already her hands remembering the feel of his strongly muscled sides and widely spread back against her palms. The President laughed loud, and Essien jumped because the laugh felt like it erupted out of her own chest, or burrowed deep into her chest, she wasn't sure. She backed up, rubbing her hands down her legs to try and erase their memory.

"Same time, same place. See you tomorrow, Essien." He moved out of her way and used his arm to sweep her toward the door. She left the dining room feeling both lower and higher than when she'd entered it.

CHAPTER FORTY-FIVE

◆

ESSIEN WAS TO BE PAMPERED BEFORE HER CROWNING CERE-mony with the rites and rituals that befitted a Queen of Alkebulan. Since there had never before been a Queen of Alkebulan, Essien got to make them up as she went. Even with the wicked little grin adorning her face as she handed him her list of demands, Gabriel thought she was the prettiest she'd ever looked.

The first item on her list had been to have a custom dress made for her by an obscure dressmaker from Bantu State. It was an entire ordeal getting the snappy elderly dressmaker to remember who she was and then to agree to being flown to Igbo State to fit Essien for her new attire. She'd been sold when she'd seen the layers of fabric Essien wanted used. Gabriel had set her up with accommodations on a floor of the compound, so she'd be close enough to complete the dress. This was the first task Essien wanted done.

Once the dressmaker understood her assignment, she offered to make Gabriel a matching suit and a second matching outfit for them both to wear at the reception after the ceremony. Essien had held her laugh at the look on Gabriel's face when he declined. Her fingers smoothed over the fabrics in different colors, all made in Igboland. It took several more sessions for the fabrics to be pinned on Essien in different arrangements, the thin bite of a prick meeting her skin several times.

The result, a beautiful uwe the color of cream with a gold lace embroidery over all of its length, the extra lace hanging down her back like a cloak that could be pulled over her head like a shawl, with silk panels at her arms, chest, and waist in an almost invisible white and cream pattern. When she tried the dress on in the shoes the dressmaker thought looked good, the hem whispered over the floor when she twirled, the sparkly gold stacks catching her eye at the bottom. Essien had to practice walking in the stacks to be sure she wouldn't embarrass herself as Queen as her first major act in front of everyone.

THE DAY OF THE ASCENSION CEREMONY, ATTENDANTS WOKE ESsien up with light knocks on her door. She didn't recognize any of their faces and felt alarmed at the trio of young women who bustled into her room, the washing room beyond, and began moving things around and setting out bags and boxes and glass bottles and brushes. One of the attendants, a girl with pale yellow skin and even paler golden hair in braids, took her hand and led her into the bathroom.

"You'll have to tell me your name before we get more acquainted than this," Essien said, grabbing hold of the bottom of her night shirt before it could be lifted over her head.

The girl pressed her lips together and then said, "I am Abena." She put a hand on her chest and then flicked her fingers toward the other two. "She is Zuri," she said pointing at the one with deep, bark-brown skin and hair in a cloud around her face and shoulders. "She is Nnenna," pointing to the other attendant with skin a clay brown and her head shaved clean. Essien nodded.

"Great. Now, I don't need as much assistance as you've been told I'll need."

Abena waved her hand out again, signaling Essien to proceed. None of them turned their back as she undressed herself.

The deep tub was filled with foamy white bubbles covering a creamy red lake of bath water, the red from all the concoctions they'd spilled into the water. The steam wafted up to her as she slipped one foot and then the other into the hot, swirling water. The fruity, milky smells of hibiscus and coconut milk enveloped her, and she sank down into the cloudy water. She looked around for a scrubbing brush but found none. The attendant she thought might be Nnenna kneeled beside the bathing pool, her hand coming toward Essien with a white net in it.

"I'll do it," Essien said softly, her voice firm but gentle. The woman ignored her, eyes on the flowing faucet as she dipped the net into the water and rung it out. She then grabbed Essien's arm and began scrubbing before Essien could do more than squeal. She'd never had anyone bathe her before. The maturation rites she should have gone through at eighteen were not performed, and it was her own fault then. Her Nne had been so upset about her enlistment in the military that she had not even marked her date of birth that year with anything more than the usual porridge for morning meal and pounded yam and stew for evening meal. The feeling of the net exfoliating down her back now was a harsh reminder of the present, where her actions had led her, and how ultimately, it was up to her to find some peace and live with those decisions.

After her body was thoroughly scrubbed with the net, the woman had her stand up, so she could heap pearlescent black globs onto her skin.

"What is that?" Essien asked, looking down as the lumpy black mixture shimmered on her skin.

"Exfoliator made from volcanic rock and pearls," Abena said before continuing to rub and scrub briskly with her hands. Essien had to lean her palms against the stone walls around the tub as the woman raised first one leg and then the next, so she could reach everything. Essien shivered, giggling, as she was scrubbed in her most sensitive areas. A water hose connected to the faucet sprayed her down, and she closed her eyes as the woman's hands guided her to the end of the tub to a built-in bench.

Sitting on the bench, she had her hair washed with coconut-ginger soap, the spicy scent tingling her scalp as the woman's fingers deftly massaged. Another rinse with the hose and then her hair that had grown down to her mid-back was styled with shea butter and okra gel into tight ringlets that lay almost flat to her head, draping over her shoulders in shiny, springy coils.

While her hair lay drying in a style that she had never worn before, the trio of attendants buffed and polished her hands and feet, using sharp metal tools on her nails that she had never seen before either. When Essien had requested to be pampered in the manner of a Queen, she'd had no idea that it would be this thorough. A fourth attendant entered the bathroom carrying a case that looked ominous. When she opened it to reveal small pots and glass jars, Essien just shut her eyes and let them work on her. She reminded herself again that she had asked for this and clearly Gabriel had obliged.

She wasn't allowed to look at herself again until after she stepped into the cream and gold dress. She briefly contemplated how the night might end. Perhaps, the President would come to her here in her bedroom, the floor where he never came, and perhaps he might make his own demands of her, quietly and confidently making his requests known, irresistibly, her door closing behind him with a kiss of locks. Essien snorted at the fantasy and shoved it away with every ounce of strength in her mind.

When she was done, she stood in front of the wall of mirrors in the bathing room. Her eyelids, the tip of her nose, and the curves of her cheeks sparkled with silvery-gold powder. Her lips were painted in a dramatic golden-brown color that made them look bigger and the first thing anyone would notice. The dress reminded her that she had the figure of a short, curvy woman. She almost never wore anything too fitted. Even her fitted trousers were only close to her ankles. Essien stared at herself for a long time, the attendants cleaning up their products and mess behind her. They were all smiling when they left her standing in front of the mirror.

ESSIEN SAT ON THE EDGE OF HER THRONE, THE MONSTROSITY OF a chair that had been built just for her, at her request. She had not imagined that the chair would take up an entire wall, the obsidian stone face of a fierce lion snarling overhead. The seat was a cushioned bench with a fabric of reds and golds and browns that molded to her sides and back. It presided over the largest Council Chamber at the Igbo State Council House, redesigned entirely to fit her throne set against the far wall, diagonal to the dais in the center where the President would sit.

With her arms pressed against the padded smoothness of the throne arms and her thighs clamped tightly together, she tried her best to listen to what the President was announcing. He had been speaking for quite some time, over there on the dais that felt like an ocean away, and the slim, pale-skinned woman who had come into the gathering hall with him and sat at his side now stood just behind him at the foot of the dais, her dark eyes cast around the room, the edges of her straight black hair obscuring her profile from Essien. She held her hands clasped together behind her back; her fingers interlaced. She was wearing a simple white tunic dress and white sandals. Her black hair gleamed in a wave down her back.

The President spoke to the people in the room that stretched almost from one end of the Council House to the other. The pale wood floors were shiny, and the walls were covered in gold and white textured wallpaper that begged to be touched.

As Essien glanced around the room before her, the faces of the people were turned up to Gabriel, most with acceptance and adoration of all their President meant to them, only a few eyeballs flicking over to peer at her, still seated. There was her Nne in the protective circle of her brothers, all six of them, with their wives, and their children. Essien hadn't known they would be arriving, their presence not something she'd included on her list of special requests. She'd been more surprised to see them than they were to see her, but the formality of the occasion prevented her from going to them. The Guard stood in a silent, threatening line that separated the dais and throne from the rest of the room.

The new Tribal Councilman for Igbo State stared at her openly, his eyes holding a look of tender hostility, as though he hated her and wished desperately that he didn't. There was the Onye Isi Ndi Agha, the Ori of the Sojas, his face reminding her so much of her father's, with its harsh planes like obsidian stone. She smiled at him because she suddenly remembered the visit he had made to the military academy in her second year. It had been just a speck of her time enlisted, what seemed like so many years ago. He had been present for their morning assembly, his voice serving to rouse them out of the mundane and setting her soul on fire again with that passion that had fueled her through some of the worst times in her life.

There was Koi, as close to the throne as he could get with the guards in the way. He had to sneak his stares at her, only able to catch her line of sight out of the corner of his eye. He was dressed in a smart-looking black suit jacket and slacks with a blood red tunic shirt underneath. He smiled at someone standing next to him, and her heart longed to speak to him. Essien found herself staring at him, too.

There was Antonious, at the edge of all those people, closer to the dais. He was watching her, too, and she wondered why she hadn't noticed him sooner. He no longer served the President as much as he had seemed to when she had first entered this world, and she wondered if there had been some rift between them while she had been gone. She met Antonious's eyes and held them, wanting to smile and not expecting him to give her anything back in return. He had helped to train her well.

Breathe, she told herself. Keep breathing. Her chest inflated and deflated rhythmically, the only movement from her. She suddenly wanted to run from the gathering hall in a flash of skirts and kicked-off stacks. She wanted to yell at Gabriel to be done already, his voice still going on and on, the tone melodious and hypnotizing. She wanted to show them, his admirers, what monstrousness lay hidden behind the careful clink of straight teeth and spread wide lips. She tried again to listen to his words, but when she looked at him, standing just at the front of the dais across the room from where her throne sat, he was staring back at her.

She looked out over the room, and the people were clapping and smiling and shouting out words that felt like a loudspeaker in her chest. Gabriel made a gesture to someone off to the side of the room, and an attendant, one of the new group of women she had seen scampering throughout the compound all day, came forward holding something shiny and heavy with black gloved hands.

As she walked closer, Essien realized what the woman carried and sucked in a breath of air that froze in her lungs. She started to tremble all over, her legs quaking, even her lower lip trembled. She wasn't going to cry, not now, not when everyone was in that audience watching. She remembered to breathe and tried to concentrate on just that.

The attendant—Essien recalled that she was Nnenna—handed the golden gem-encrusted crown to Gabriel. His hands were now covered with a pair of gloves that matched his ornately embroidered agbada, the flashy suit an opposite of Essien's in a dark brown color with gold embroidery that seemed to sparkle just like the gold crown as he took it between his hands.

He wasn't smiling when he turned to Essien. His face was serious but not calm. There was so much beneath the surface of that blankness, a whisper she could hear if she opened herself to him. He smiled and nodded his head, signaling her to rise.

She walked to the edge of the dais on legs that felt stiff and wobbly at the same time. She hadn't prepared for this nervousness to hit her like this. She kept breathing and breathing, and then her toes were at the edge of the dais. Even with the three steps up from the ground, she still came up just barely to his neck. But she didn't have to tilt her head back to look up at him.

His next words were directed right into her eyes: "Do you, Essien Ezinulo, daughter of Igboland, promise to serve Alkebulan, the people of this country, and to lead the Uzo Nchedo as Queen, for as long as you shall live, and even beyond?"

Essien couldn't help the smile that tugged at her lip, though it wasn't one of merriment. "Yes," she said and nodded.

"Then I anoint you, Eze Nwaanyi, the first Queen of Alkebulan, the greatest nation on Ala-ani, ready and willing to serve until your dying days. Bow your head to receive the crown."

She didn't mean to let the water that sprang to her eyes drip down, but when she bowed her head, gravity did the rest for her. The crown that Gabriel placed onto her head was heavy, its weight sinking down over her hair like a solid press against her skull and resting against her temples. She inhaled a deep chest-rising breath and lifted her head.

CHAPTER FORTY-SIX

◆

DURING THE RECEPTION THAT FOLLOWED THE CEREMONY—held in the dining hall on Capital Island—Gabriel stood up from his seat at the head of the table, intending to speak. He didn't have a microphone to amplify his voice, but when he waved his hand, the room fell silent. Essien sat in her usual seat, but across from her, the woman who had stood behind him sat on his other side. She still hadn't been introduced, Gabriel taking extra pains to keep them apart until just before they each sat down. The bustle of people around them, moving from the Council House back to the Capital, had prevented a natural introduction.

Gabriel smiled down first at Essien and then at the mystery woman, and that smile was full of something younger and happier than Essien had ever seen on his face. The woman rose to stand beside him. Instead of clutching her own hands, her fingers interlaced tightly with Gabriel's left hand. Seeing that, Essien's heart beat twice where one beat should have been, and she sat at the edge of her seat.

She could hear Gabriel's words as each one lanced into her with the painful stab of jealous rage and hypocrisy. This is what she had told him to do, she realized with a sickening regret that she could never take back. This is what she had promised she would allow. Still, she wanted to scream at them to stop smiling, stop clapping, stop congratulating him.

Don't you see that he has done this to hurt me? So what if I cannot let myself go to him ever? So what if I promised that I would never marry him? So what if I will never give him sons or daughters to continue our lineage together? It dawned on her that he had finally crowned her as Queen, and now, here he was announcing his plans to take another woman as his wife.

As Gabriel spoke about the woman, staring into her face without looking away, Essien learned that she was not a native of Alkebulan, but one who had resided for many years in Ebe Osimiri Na-ezute, the City Where Rivers Meet, northeast of Lagos. Even among the beauty in that room, she was beautiful, and that hand wrapped around Gabriel's precluded a warm

350   WIELDERS OF FLOODS & FLAMES

companion in comparison to her. She had never willingly held his hand, and that before she even knew what they were to each other. It was not the woman's fault, Essien tried to reason, but the seething emotion she felt spilling into her fingertips included this soon-to-be wife, too.

As one collective, all the eyes were looking directly at her, the President's, too. She was expected to speak. This ceremony and event meant exclusively for her, that she had gotten to plan for herself, was no longer a celebration. Why did this farce need to include words from her to let them all know that this declaration was made with her ultimate complicity? They were all being duped, her the greatest dupe of all.

Her lace embroidered skirt swished as she stood and swayed as she walked over to where Gabriel stood with his new kwere nwka, his betrothed. He eyed her warily, hesitant of her response, curious to see how she would take this unexpected announcement at a ceremony that was supposed to be all about her.

Keep up the act, he seemed to be saying. Do not spoil this for the country. Essien wished she could respond with the violence she felt humming in her palms. A strike to his cheek, a snatching of the woman's fluted throat, blood upon the dishes.

"Welcome to Alkebulan, Akai." The Queen tipped her chin down just slightly. "May the nation be as forthcoming and generous to you as it has been to me." She took a step up closer to Akai, her stacks between her sandals, and stretched upward. Gabriel, suddenly skittish, leaned subconsciously away from them both. Akai did not know yet to fear her, and so she smiled, showing a deep dent in her left cheek. She blinked slanted chestnut brown eyes and did not move away from the Queen.

With the utmost trepidation, the Queen placed a single press of lips against her cheek, a child needing her protection from the perils of nightmares. Akai made a humming noise through her nose and touched the back of the Queen's hand with elegant, pointed fingertips.

"I look forward to our making acquaintances." Her voice was as quiet as the wind.

The Queen stepped back, not smiling, her eyes all for Gabriel. There was nothing she could say to him now. So, she bowed to him, at the waist, going low, staring at the gold buckle on his dark brown loafers. Then with the swiftness of gray clouds passing behind lightning strikes, she stepped up close to him with her toes between his, her chest and stomach pressing up against his, and she kissed him on the lips. She knew it would be the only time she would ever get to do so again. His mouth tasted like the faintest twirl of cigar smoke and the amber elixir he loved to drink. He sighed as she pulled herself away. She did not look at him again as she stepped back to her seat at his dining table and settled lightly upon it.

The President determined instantly that this easier, smoother, nonconfrontational reaction had been much worse than the one he had imagined with his heart, bloody and still beating, clenched in her hand.

CHAPTER FORTY-SEVEN

◆

GABRIEL HAD BEEN SERIOUS ABOUT THE WEDDING ALREADY being planned. It almost made Essien feel insulted that he had merely wished to put her into the spot he'd reserved for a wife, and that it had been so easy for him to find someone else to replace her.

Watching the busyness of the compound suddenly with shipments and vendors arriving and going constantly, Essien regretted her choice again. She had yet to really get to know the woman Gabriel would be marrying instead of her. Truthfully, she did not want to become too familiar with the woman. It was petty and based on her irrational jealousy. She never wanted to see Akai or speak to her again. But Essien found out very quickly that she was to be included whether she wanted to or not.

Within the weeks following her ascension ceremony, she was shipped bodily off to a house on a beach that they told her was Tear Drop Falls, but which she could not confirm for herself. The island looked new and unfamiliar, the trees and roping vines seeming different from the jungles on the mainland. She knew it was somewhere she had never been before, but she felt no excitement or intense desire to go exploring or to even try feeling content. She pouted, she scoffed, she spoke seldom, and she made sure everyone knew how obstinate she truly felt.

Essien was given the freedom to explore the island on her own with guards following her as they had done in the past, a row of twelve men trailing behind her through city streets and shaded gardens. She knew that Gabriel was busy with the wedding preparations and his soon-to-be wife.

On one such walk through the gardens surrounding the beach compound, Essien spied Gabriel's shiny-waved head bobbing around hedges. She stilled and made to step back around the bush she had just come around. Gabriel sensed her, and his eyes met hers. He smiled and called out, "My Queen! Come closer!"

And there was Akai, and Essien was staring at her full on in the face for the first time since their marriage had been announced. She touched palms with the woman who knew the custom of not holding on or for too long. Gabriel led their conversation, steering them with questions he wanted answered and information he wanted revealed. Like the fact that Essien was the first woman to join his Guard, the customary tales he always told.

She discovered very quickly from his line of presenting that Akai was an interesting ethnic mix that spanned half the globe. From the tidbits the woman shared at Gabriel's urging, Essien learned Akai was half Nihon-jin, a country in Yaxiya, from her father, the Shogun of Nihon, and she was part Kanien'kehá:ka and part Kānaka Maoli from the Hawai'i Islands of Iroquois Nation. But that wasn't all.

Akai seemed almost embarrassed as she said, "Mayapan and Taino from the southern part of Turtle Island, and Palawa from Lutruwita, the southernmost island on Ala-ani, from my late mother." The woman dropped her head, her hair cascaded down to cover the side of her face, and Essien hoped the woman wouldn't start crying. She had to admit that she was fascinated by her unique features, more than politely interested in her ancestry. She was enamored with her great dexterity with Igbo, going back and forth from colloquial to more formal terms in the same sentence, and her shift into Nihongo when Essien asked to hear it, even though she didn't understand a word. Essien wanted to hate her, but she couldn't. Gabriel stood near them with a small smile threatening to overtake his lips. He could hear everything she was thinking.

"We should take a tour of your home countries, Akai. Have you visited them all?" Akai was so surprised and flustered that it made her pale cheeks turn a cherry red that flamed her face even after they'd moved on.

"You'll be pleased to know I haven't," she said. "Parts of Iroquois, yes, but none of the places my mother's people were from. Not yet. I would be honored to escort you to my homelands."

Essien turned to Gabriel with a mischievous grin. "When can we start planning our international campaign?"

THE ACTUAL WEDDING HAPPENED A FEW DAYS LATER NEXT TO AN arch of twisted and woven branches painted silver and gold. An orator declared their lineage to showcase their heritage and their accomplishments to showcase their talents, both apart and together, and then took their oaths of commitment, which was a custom of Igbo State that the President had decided to observe to satisfy his tribal elders. They each drank a sip of palm wine held in a golden chalice to symbolize their union.

Then they took part in the rituals for Akai's cultures, melding them in a beautiful representation of all that they were joining together with their marriage. Essien could barely look at Gabriel because she could feel what he was feeling. It wasn't happiness or joy. It was anger and sadness. He was so angry at her that it colored everything she looked at on what should have been an enjoyable day for him.

The beautiful shades of flowers in pink and yellow were tinged with a red that made her want to crumble those delicate petals into wet smears. She wanted to disappear from the wedding as soon as the new bride and her groom had traveled down the aisle to the reception, but two guards standing subtly behind her disrupted that line of thinking. Essien was directed to follow the rest of the wedding attendants to the reception hall.

Gabriel held Akai's hand against his thigh the entire time they sat next to each other at the long banquet table through the obligatory reception and dance celebration afterward. They danced, a chaste, gentle, subtle movement on the dance floor that made Essien feel embarrassed watching more than any other emotions. Gabriel was a good dancer. He kept holding Akai's waist very tightly and lining his torso up against hers to rock side to side or back and forth to a beat that was loud but still low. A few guests merrily tried to get Essien to dance, but she turned them down with a bashful smile.

Akai wore a mischievous grin on her face staring up at Gabriel, holding his hands while they swayed and rocked back and forth. When he was so sweaty that wetness seeped through the layers of his ceremonial attire, the dancing was over. Breathless, Akai drank enough wine to start a small winery of her own, the bottles piling up before her as the night grew late. The guests, both people from their hometowns who had grown up with them and political acquaintances, flowed past the banquet table in a near steady stream. Most wanted to take pictures, and a few of them leaned in close to either one or both of them to whisper something that was met with smiles and laughs or blank stares.

It wasn't until Gabriel stood with Akai that the party was signaled to end. He spoke some words that Essien tried not to hear because they did not match what he was feeling. They sounded boisterous and celebratory, but the emotions wafting off him into her were ones of weariness and something that felt like regret. Essien watched them disappear through the doors back into the beach compound where the wedding party was staying, along with Essien. The guards standing over her finally signaled to her that she could leave the hall. They followed her to her room, which was through the same doors where Gabriel and his new nwunye, his bride, had gone. Essien stumbled at the dual images that were suddenly flooding her mind like an overlay.

Gabriel held Akai's shoulders and steered her through the dark hallways. His Guard was posted at every door they passed. He led her through the dark halls with his hands on her waist. She walked as if in a dream, going where he directed her. They entered a different room, not the one Essien knew he was staying in. She didn't notice anything in the room because she was forced to feel his fingers as they helped Akai to free herself of the tight skirt around her waist along with everything else that kept her bound. Then he was above her on the bed, rising like a wave that kept receding and rushing forward, holding her down, even though she wasn't fighting back. She held his sides, and Essien could feel how soft and cold her hands were against Gabriel's ribs. She knew that this was not their first time. He moved, so strong and sure, so swift and sudden. She pressed all of her body against all of his and muffled her mouth against his neck. She was holding his face close and using her mouth to tell him just how willing and cooperative she was, how much she wanted him.

Essien had already closed her eyes to try and block out the images and sensations, but they flowed into her regardless. She pressed her fingers against her eyes, making red, white, yellow, and blue fireworks spread over the dark insides of her lids. She didn't know how she could stop this, how she could stop him in a room several hallways down. He had taken control of her mind in a way that she had never felt him before, not willingly. This was worse than anything he'd done before.

It felt better even than when he touched her without touching her because he was touching Akai, and she could feel it on her own body. She could feel his hands and his mouth everywhere with the urgent sweetness of eager exploration. It was like she was getting sensations from both of them, when that shouldn't have been possible at all. Gabriel kept going like that all night, and Essien marveled at how much energy he had. She tried to sleep, burrowing underneath blankets that were warm and suffocating, but there was no space in her own mind for her own tiredness.

THE PALE LIGHT OF MORNING SET ITS FOOT DOWN AND STRETCHED. Essien lifted her head from the cushion of a head support. She could feel the brain-numbing effects of all the wine she'd drunk, that vacuousness just beginning to fade as everything around her spilled into focus. She was in her own body, but with a thought, she realized that she was still in his, too. The white skirt and blouse on the floor, Gabriel's overcoat lying on top of his overturned shoes, the circle of cool metal around the weakest finger on his left hand. She put her head back down as she began feeling the effects of the wine draining, and her stomach flipped over. She watched out the window above the bed as she thought about where she was and why, what had happened the night before, what she had seen and felt just hours before, and what all of it now meant. She closed her eyes to the brightening day.

CHAPTER FORTY-EIGHT

◆

SOON AFTER, ESSIEN WAS SENT ALONE TO THE LAKE WITH ONLY the orders that the Mothers had a message for her. That was unusual, but Essien relented seeing as she didn't have a choice. Escorts took her through a wooded area with trees so close to the dirt road that branches scraped against the engine's sides. She couldn't see anything past the dimness of tree trunks. The trip reminded her suddenly of the trip she had taken here with Gabriel. A trip deep into a forest as dark and uninhabited as this one. She had been on foot the first time she'd come and just as alone. The two guards in the front of the engine hadn't said a word to her.

When she stepped out of the engine, the edge of a cool blue lake lapped at her feet. The lake spread out to an end she couldn't see. She looked back, but the guards were quietly smoking herbs and did not look at her. There were no structures or buildings anywhere.

There was only one place where she might find them. She took a deep breath and blew it out hard. She stepped up to the edge of the lake, the toes of her boots getting wet. Better to do it fast. Before she could hesitate or change her mind, she jumped into the lake, sending waves of water splashing everywhere.

Immediately, she was pulled down and down, to the bottom. She didn't resist the tight tugging that brought her down to the very bottom. She opened her eyes, and she was in a white room. Seated in a circle of black stone chairs were some of the most beautiful women she had ever seen. Women with long, kinky hair that reached the floor at their feet and skin that was smooth and glossy. She walked forward into the center of their half-circle. There were eight women total, all wearing loose tunics. A relaxing smell of spearmint and eucalyptus wafted off them. The Mother in the center spread her arms wide.

"Welcome Essien, Sixth Born Son but not."

Feeling it appropriate, Essien did a deep bow, dropping to her knees and putting her forehead to the ground.

"Rise, young one. You shall not always bow to Us. One day soon, We shall bow to you."

Another of the Mothers said, "We are sure you have questions. You may ask them now."

Essien observed each of them, wondering if any had actually given birth to Gabriel, or if they had merely adopted him as their own because he had come to the lake. The last time she had come, there had only been three of them. Besides Gabriel and the man made of water, she had not seen anyone else.

"Did I make the right decision?"

The women looked at each other before one of them answered, "Which one?"

She had been talking about rejecting Gabriel's offer of marriage, but they were right. So many decisions she had made, back to that very first one that brought her here.

"He thinks he's fulfilled the first part of the prophecy, to make me a Queen, but it is only so he can be King, and I tried to resist him, I did...even now, but... Did I do the right thing?"

The Mothers murmured among themselves.

Finally, one of them spoke up, "That is the reason We invited you here. You know that We gave you Our blessings, and you still have them. We had hoped that it would not be so, that you would be enough, the love he feels for you, but it won't be...as We had feared, your rejection of the marriage offer has set off a linked chain of events that will now turn into an impossible journey for you. He is exactly what he seems and will become worse than you could imagine. The marriage would not have tamed him, but now? You must ensure you do what is right for the people, at all times. You must be his voice of reason. He will not listen every time, but you must try."

"Can I trust him?" Essien stared at each of the Mothers' faces as they now looked at each other instead of her.

Finally, one answered, "No, young one. He is not trustworthy. Never for a second forget what he can do."

"Will I... Will I have to fight him?"

The Mothers nodded, all together, looking at her sadly.

"Is it too late to undo?"

Again, they looked at each other first before they all nodded.

"Is it too late to change it?"

The Mothers looked at each other again before answering. "As his powers grow, so will yours. You are afraid of yourself. You only use your powers when you need them, which is wise. Do not let him see you at full power. If you do, he will attempt to limit you long before you reach your greatest height. Despite needing to hide, you must explore your power, to ensure that you become as powerful as you were meant to be. You must be the voice of the people, even when he will not listen, especially when he will not listen."

Essien felt that she was hearing what she had already known. She stared at each of the Mothers, seeing the face of her own mother in each of them.

"How can I keep him from knowing everything in my soul? How can I keep him from seeing so far into me and making me see so far into him?"

The Mother in the middle smiled and held out her hand. All the other Mothers held out their hands, too. A gold medallion materialized in her palm and floated toward Essien. She snatched the coin out of the air as soon as it was close enough. She looked down at the palm-sized coin attached to a chain, and what she saw made her heart punch her throat. A roaring flame conflagrated over the golden surface at the same time that the roar of flames burned into her senses. Essien flipped the coin over, and a cascading wave fell over onto itself again and again as she watched. Mesmerized, she tore her gaze away as her fingers clenched over the coin. She smiled her gratitude and opened her mouth to give her sincerest thanks.

"One final thing, young one. Whatever you do, give him no reason to turn to you. You have pushed him into the heart of another woman; now you must make sure he stays there. If you and he were to have offspring and bring that boy child to life? He would be more powerful than both of you combined. And the power that you can feel growing unchecked inside you is powerful enough on its own. There is no need to ever combine your powers with his again. His bonding with you helped draw off some of his energy, which is what We had hoped. Take care that nothing you do returns that power to him."

Essien didn't understand the final warning, not after what she had seen last time, but she nodded. She had told herself already that she would never be Gabriel's wife and that she would be his Queen in name only. The Mothers had confirmed for her what she had already known and not wanted to accept. Now, she would always be on her guard against the President. She had to, for the life of the country and its people; perhaps even for the future of the entire world.

ACKNOWLEDGEMENTS

◆

An eternal thank you to my agent, Felice Laverne, for seeing the potential and the magic in Essien of Alkebulan, and making it possible for this work to exist in the literary world.

Thank you to everyone on my team at Turner Publishing: Amanda Chiu Krohn, Ashlyn Inman, Kendal Cliburn, Makala Marsee, and all the editors and production team. Thank you!

Thank you to my early reviewers who provided valuable feedback: Britney Glover and Amy Oates.

Thank you to everyone who purchased a copy and read Essien's story with an open mind and appreciation for innovation in literary arts.

Thank you to my family both in the US and abroad for always having my back and supporting all my endeavors.

A special shout out to my sisters, Ginger Gayden and Jaclyn Clark, for holding me down at my first book fair in New Orleans and capturing all my good sides.

Thank you to my seventh grade English students and the faculty at Westmark School who asked me dozens of questions about the book, challenged my own perspectives, and made me feel in awe of my own writing and author self. Thanks, folks!

A final thank you to the readers who will have this book in their hands. Whether you're just jumping in or continuing on this journey with Essien, you are the reason I write and keep writing. THANK YOU!

GLOSSARY OF IGBO TERMS AND PRONUNCIATION GUIDE

ABAGHI URU
(uh-bag-ee oo-roo)
Worthless

AKUKOIFO
(ah-coo-co-ee-foh)
Spirit guides

AKWETTE
(ah-kweh-teh)
Hand-woven cloth

AKWUNA
(ah-qwu-nuh)
Prostitute, slut

ALA-ANI
(ah-la-nee)
Earth

AMOOSU
(ah-moo-sue)
White magic

ARA
(ah-rah)
Madam, ma'am

AZOBE
(Ah-zo-b)
Alkebulanian ironwood

BOONA
(boo-nuh)
Internet café

DAMBE
(dam-bay)
Traditional style of fighting

ELUIGWE
(el-oo-ee-guey)
Heaven

ENGOLO
(en-go-low)
Traditional style of fighting

EZE NWAANYI
(Eh-zee nn-wan-yee)
Queen

GELE
(jeh-leh)
Traditional Igbo headwear worn by women

IHEBUBE
(ee-hey-boo-bay)
Blessing

ILDOROBO
(eel-door-oh-bo)
Hunter

ILMEEK
(eel-meek)
Farmer

INDOMIE
(in-doh-mee)
Noodle dish with eggs and peppers

KENYEMAKA
(Ken-yeh-ma-ka)
Friend

KWERE NKWA
(Kweh-ray nn-kwah)
Promised one

MGBATI AHU
(em-bah-tee ah-hoo)
Gym

MMANYA
(man-yah)
Bar

NNA
(Nn-nah)
Father, dad

NNE
(Nn-neh)
Mother, mom

NNE NNA
(Nn-neh-nah)
Grandmother, father's mother

NNE NNE
(Nn-neh-neh)
Grandmother, mother's mother

NWA AMADI
(Nn-wah uh-ma-dee)
A gentleman

NWA M NWAAYNI
(Nn-wah mm nn-wah-nn-yee)
My daughter

NWANNE NNE
(Nn-wah-neh neh)
Aunt

NWA NWANNE
(Nn-wah nn-wah-nn-neh)
Nephew

NWAANYI
(Nn-waah-nn-yee)
Woman

NWANNE NWOKE
(Nn-wah-nn-neh nn-woah-kay)
Brother

NWANNE
(Nn-wah-nn-neh)
Sister

NWATAKIRI
(Nn-wah-tah-keer-ee)
Child, little girl/boy

NWAYI NKE NÊLE IME
(Nn-wah-yee nn-kay nay-le ee-meh)
Midwife

NWUNYE
(Nn-wun-yeh)
Bride, wife

NWUNYE NWA
(Nn-wun-yeh nn-wah)
Son's wife, daughter-in-law

ODACHI
(oh-dah-chi)
Pain/suffering

ODIBO
(oh-dee-boh)
Servant

OGODO
(oh-go-doh)
Formal gown

ONYE NDU
(Ohn-yeh-nn-doo)
An eternal spiritual bond

PALBINO
(pal-bye-no)
Albino

SOJAS
(so-jus)
Soldiers

ULO AKWUKWO
(Oo-low ah-kwoo-kwoh)
Library

UMU NWOKE
(oo-moo nn-woah-kay)
Sons

UWE
(oo-way)
Traditional Igbo dress

UZO NCHEDO
(oo-zoh nn-che-doh)
President's personal bodyguards

GLOSSARY OF CHARACTERS

◆

ESSIEN EZINULO
(Eh-see-ehn Eh-zee-new-low)
Woman who led the Guard

ENYEMAKA
(En-yay-mah-cuh)
Essien's rescuer

GABRIEL IJIKOTA
(Ee-gee-ko-ta)
President of Alkebulan

MANSA MUSA
the twenty-first Descendant of
Mansa Musa

SUNDIATA OSIRIS
(Soon-dee-ah-tuh Oh-sigh-russ)
Holy man

ANTONIOUS
Gabriel's right-hand man

NIFEMI
(Ni-fem-ee)
Essien's fifth elder brother

OBECHI
(Oh-bay-chi)
Nifemi's wife

NNAMDI
(Nam-dee)
Nifemi and Obechi's daughter

CHINASA
(Chi-nah-suh)
Nifemi and Obechi's daughter

PROFESSOR MULEKATETE
(Moo-leh-ka-teh-teh)
Professor at Soja's Inn University

PROFESSOR HAKIZIMANA
(Ha-kee-zee-man-uh)
Professor at Soja's Inn University

PROFESSOR RUSANGANWA
(Roo-san-gahn-wah)
Professor at Soja's Inn University

UCHE NWABUEZE
(Oo-che Nn-wah-bwee-zeh)
Interviewer

COUNCILMAN DENG
Councilman of Dinka, Mbuti State

AMINA NANA ASMA'U
(Ah-meen-uh Nah-nah Ahs-moo-uh)
Tribal Council member of Fulani
State

HAMMADI DIALLO
Director at Timbuktu University

KOINET NYAGA
Tribal Councilman from Maasai
State

IDARA EZINULO
(Ee-dar-uh Eh-zee-new-low)
Essien's eldest brother

MALACHUM EZINULO
(Mal-uh-coom Eh-zee-new-low)
Essien's second elder brother

MANAI EZINULO
(Muh-nai Eh-zee-new-low)
Essien's third elder brother

CHUKWU EZINULO
(Choo-kwoo Eh-zee-new-low)
Essien's fourth elder brother

ABOUT THE AUTHOR

◆

ORIGINALLY FROM HOUSTON, TX, THE HOMETOWN OF BEYONCÉ and Megan Thee Stallion, **Didi Anofienem** is a novelist and educator residing in Los Angeles, CA. She earned her MFA from University of San Francisco in 2017, a BS from UT-Austin in 2010, and a BA from University of Houston in 2014. Passionate about words, Didi wrote her first story at the age of eight. She grew up reading Toni Morrison, Alice Walker, and Ntozake Shange. As an adult, her favorite authors are Octavia Butler and Laurell K. Hamilton. In the past, Didi has written romance novels, a poetry collection, several short stories, plays, and personal essays. She just recently completed a Master of Education in Private School Leadership from Teacher's College at Columbia University. When she's not teaching English and creative writing, Didi spends her time traveling back and forth to Houston, rereading her favorite books, dancing to Beyoncé, and playing The Sims 4.

www.ingramcontent.com/pod-product-compliance
Lightning Source LLC
Jackson TN
JSHW022222180425
82910JS00001B/1